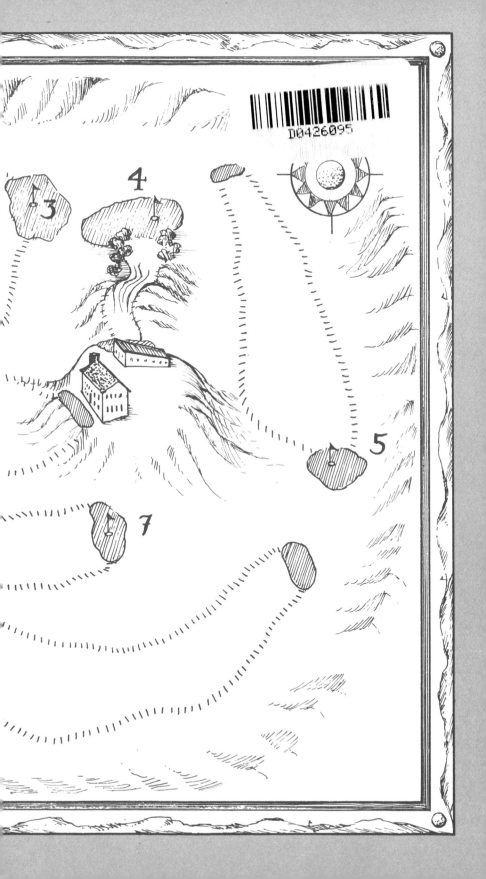

THE

KINGDOM

OF

SHIVAS

IRONS

Scotland

Orkney Islands

North Sea

Outer Hebrides

Inner Hebrides

Dornach

Loch Ness • Inverness

Aberdeen•

Island of Mull

Scarba

Jura

Dundee
Firth of Tay
St. Andrews• Crail
Kingdom of Fife
• Glasgow
Firth of Forth
Edinburgh

Firth of Clyde

NORTHERN IRELAND

North Channel

Belfast•

Solway Firth

ENGLAND

Detail showing important routes

Ben Cruachan
Ben Lui

Loch Awe
A819
Inveraray

Dundee

St. Andrews•

A816
B840
A83
Scarba
A83
Jura
Beinn Bhreac
A82
Loch Lomand

Kingdom of Fife

Loch Fyne

Glasgow
M8
Edinburgh

Martie Holmer 97

THE KINGDOM OF SHIVAS IRONS

MICHAEL MURPHY

BROADWAY BOOKS

NEW YORK

BROADWAY

Broadway Books titles may be purchased for business or promotional use or for special sales.
For information, please write to: Special Markets Department, Bantam Doubleday
Dell Publishing Group, Inc., 1540 Broadway, New York, NY 10036.

BROADWAY BOOKS and its logo, a letter B bisected on the diagonal, are trademarks
of Broadway Books, a division of Bantam Doubleday Dell Publishing Group, Inc.

Grateful acknowledgment is made for permission to reprint the following:
Excerpt from *The Kabir Book,* versions by Robert Bly. Copyright © 1971, 1977 by Robert Bly.
Reprinted with the permission of Beacon Press.

Adaptation of *Poems of Kabir* by Rabindranath Tagore. Copyright © 1986 by Rabindranath
Tagore. Reprinted with the permission of Macmillan General Books.

Library of Congress Cataloging-in-Publication Data
Murphy, Michael, 1930 Sept. 3–
The kingdom of Shivas Irons / Michael Murphy. — 1st ed.
p.   cm.
Includes bibliographical references.
ISBN 0-7679-0018-9 (hc)
1. Golf—Psychological aspects—Fiction.   2. Occultism—Fiction.
I. Title.
PS3563.U746K56   1997
813'. 54—dc21   97-19937
CIP

FIRST EDITION

Designed by Brian Mulligan

Illustrations & Maps by Martie Holmer

97 98 99 00 10 9 8 7 6 5 4 3 2 1

For George Leonard

Comrade for the ages

Between the conscious and the unconscious, the
    mind has put up a swing:
all creatures, even the supernovas, sway
    between these two trees,
and it never winds down.

Angels, animals, humans . . . also
    the wheeling sun and moon;
ages go by, and it goes on.

Everything is swinging: heaven, earth, water, fire,
and the secret one slowly growing a body.
Kabir saw that for fifteen seconds, and it made him a
    servant for life.

– Kabir
Version by Robert Bly

THE

KINGDOM

OF

SHIVAS

IRONS

SHIVAS, Shives, Chivas. Of territorial origin from the old barony of the name in the parish of Tarves, Aberdeenshire. John Sheves, "scholar in Scotland," had a safe conduct to study in Oxford, 1393. Thomas apud Scyves is recorded as a tannator (tanner) in 1402, Andrew Schewas appears in Aberdeen, 1408, and a payment was made to John Seues for wine in 1453. William Scheues, "an accomplished physician and astrologer," ignorant of theology, coadjutor bishop of St. Andrews, became archbishop in 1477. John Scheues de Kilquhouss was juror on an inquest made at Edinburgh, 1506, and William Scheuez witnessed a bond of manrent in Fife, 1519. John Scheves, a follower of the earl of Cassilis, was respited for murder in 1526. Bessie Schives, spouse of Robert Blinschell, 1596. John Scives, trade burgess of Aberdeen, 1647. Mr. James Shives, professor of philosophy, 1648, and James Chivas, shipmaster, Fraserburgh, 1759. Cheivies 1685, Chewis 1690, Chivish 1652, Scheauis 1640, Scheeves 1685, Schevies 1672, Schevys 1477, Schewas 1512, Schewess 1476, Schivis 1689, Schiviz 1685, Sevas 1473, Shawes 1521, Shevas 1768; Chevis, Chives, Civis, Schevaes, Scheviz, Shevas, Sheves, Shivis, Seves, Sivis.

In *The Surnames of Scotland, Their Origin, Meaning & History*, by George F. Black, Ph.D. (1866–1948), The New York Public Library, Second reprinting 1965.

INTRODUCTION

O N T H E R O A D Hole at St. Andrew's Old Course, Costan-
tino Rocca's ball rested on pavement near the green. Lying
two, Rocca needed a four and then a birdie on the eighteenth hole
to tie John Daly in the final round of the 1995 British Open. He
chose a putter for his shot. Watching on television from my home
in California, I sensed the first tremors of the uncanny. In ways I
couldn't predict, the Old Course was about to make itself known
as a theater of the occult.

In my office on the floor below, the fax machine was ringing.
Rocca putted, and his ball bounced off the pavement and rolled
over a path and grass-covered rise to within four feet of the hole.
With wonder in his voice, Jack Nicklaus asked the television audience if Rocca could do it again in ten or a hundred tries. A telephone sounded in the kitchen. As commentators noted the long
odds against his tying Daly, Rocca sank his putt.

During a commercial, I went downstairs, found two messages
in my fax machine's receptor tray, and carried them back to the
television. Rocca had driven, and excitement was building at the
Old Course. I looked at one of the messages. It was from a friend
in Vancouver, British Columbia. "Are you watching the Open?" it

read. "Something's going to happen!" Rocca had reached his ball now and was appraising his shot calmly. From his slightly bemused expression and jaunty carriage, it was hard to tell what demons raced through him. As he took his practice swings, I looked at the second fax. It was from Buck Hannigan in Edinburgh. "Watch the Open. We have a visitation. There's been another Shivas sighting."

Startled, I looked at the screen again. Since 1987, Hannigan and I had studied moments like this when hints of the uncanny appear in sport, but the word "visitation" had a meaning for him beyond suggestions of telepathy or mind over matter. I knew he would send me another message. There was a hush in the gallery. Would Rocca play a bump and run, or pitch onto the putting surface? Reading Hannigan's fax, I hadn't heard the commentators say what club he was using. The silence deepened. Millions watched. How would the energies of their attention affect him?

A shadow slowly crossed the green, or was it my imagination? An image arose of the Masters that year. On the last few holes at Augusta there had been something like this, some presence I couldn't quite see, and in the days that followed, there had been stories that some of the players had felt the ghost of their mentor, Harvey Penick. As I pictured Crenshaw's emotional victory, Rocca stubbed his shot.

His ball rolled into the Valley of Sin, a treacherous swale in front of the green, and a groan passed through the crowd. With uninhibited anguish, Rocca looked skyward as if asking for help. My kitchen phone was ringing, but I didn't answer it. The camera was panning across St. Andrew's famous eighteenth green, and I thought of my own visitation on the last hole at Burningbush. Did Hannigan have reason to think that something like that was happening now?

Rocca regathered himself. He could still tie Daly to force a playoff, but faced an uphill shot that would have to roll out of the swale and across some seventy feet of slick and undulating putting surface. One commentator said that the best players sometimes flubbed their shots, and another reminded the audience that Rocca had missed a short putt to cost Europe the Ryder Cup. The Old Course was charged with silent expectancy. Like a supersaturated solution, the atmosphere around the eighteenth green might crystallize into something extraordinary.

The Italian player stroked his ball, and it rolled swiftly from the Valley of Sin over a rise and across the huge green into the cup. The crowd exploded, and Rocca went down on his face, pounding the ground with both fists. Like his shot on the previous hole, this one had defied enormous odds. The game's best players would have trouble duplicating it in a hundred or a thousand tries. It would be talked about for years. It would live in golf's history books. Italy's best player had won a place in our hearts.

But had there been a visitation? Some barely tangible presence, like a shadow, had crossed the green, but I hadn't sensed more than that. For the third time during the last fifteen minutes, the phone in the kitchen rang. Not wanting to get trapped in conversation, I waited until it stopped then picked up my voice mail. Three friends had left messages urging me to watch the tournament. The last was from Steve Cohen, founder of the Shivas Irons Society, reminding me that the eighteenth letter of the Hebrew alphabet represented holiness and the goodness of life. Remember, his recorded voice said with soft insistence, golf courses had 18 holes because the Old Course had 18 when the Royal and Ancient set the game's standards. And this eighteenth hole was built on a grave. Rocca had died and been reborn.

Resolving to disregard further calls, I watched Daly win the playoff. But nothing either of the players did gave evidence of the occult, and no one reported inexplicable sightings. Yet I couldn't stop thinking about Hannigan's fax. In the last few months, several people in the Kingdom of Fife had experienced visitations related to Shivas Irons, and now Buck was reporting another. Was this strange phenomenon going public? Was it pressing to be recognized in the world at large? At that moment, holding Buck Hannigan's enigmatic message, I decided to write this book. Our findings were too important to keep to ourselves. Since 1972, the year that *Golf in the Kingdom* was published, more and more people had told me about their mystical experiences in golf. Their reports had convinced me that the game was more than it appeared to be, and provided reason enough to write a second account of Shivas Irons, the mysterious golf professional I'd met in 1956.

But there was more reason than that for a second book. For eight years, Hannigan and I had collected data in several countries from religious scholars, research librarians, anthropologists, and other people that, when assembled like the pieces of a jigsaw puzzle, suggested that Shivas Irons and his teacher, Seamus MacDuff, were involved in a momentous transformation. Our language is poor in describing this. Taken as a whole, our findings indicated that the two men might be realizing a new condition of body and soul, an unexpected power and beatitude that points the way to a greater life for those of us willing to follow. It was time to tell the world about our discoveries.

PART ONE

SUMMER, 1987

CHAPTER ONE

"*WHERE IS SHIVAS IRONS?*" The familiar question echoed off the cliffs above me. "Is he down there?" Looking up, I saw a man some thirty feet above me on the fairway that borders the beach. "Do you want a line to the flag?" he shouted.

"It's okay!" I yelled back. "I can see it!"

"Good luck!" he yelled, disappearing beyond the cliff edge.

The incident was a little odd, but not as strange as some of my meetings with people who wanted to know the whereabouts of Shivas Irons. It was 1987 now, and they'd been asking for fifteen years.

Where is Shivas Irons? It was hard to imagine him here. Though he'd called Pebble Beach one of the world's greatest golf courses, it seemed too glamorous a place for his ascetic, solitude-loving nature. He belonged in Scotland, in a town like Burningbush that was swept by winds from the North Sea and wrapped in long winter nights. . . .

We'd met there in 1956, played a mind-altering round of golf, enjoyed a memorable supper with some of his friends, searched at midnight for his mysterious teacher, and spent the next day in conversation before I left abruptly. Later I would realize that my sudden departure was driven in part by fear of the things he had revealed to me, but at the time I told myself that a longer stay would be a diversion. I was headed for India to study philosophy and practice meditation. Though Shivas Irons was giving me the very things I sought, I was conditioned to think they couldn't come from a golf professional. That belief was strengthened at my ashram retreat where golf was held to be a frivolous activity. I remember telling a friend that my trip to Scotland had an illusory quality induced perhaps by the large quantity of whiskey I'd drunk. Today, I can see that this shift of attitude permitted a deep relaxation. My adventures in Burningbush had produced a shock I wasn't prepared for, whereas the slow pace of India provided relief and comfort. Ironically, the protection from threatening change I found in my contemplative community provided a largely unconscious defense against the transformative consequences of a relationship with Shivas Irons. I was no longer challenged by memories of the man. Questions about his teacher faded. A firebreak against recollections of Burningbush was established in my subconscious mind.

Then in 1962, on a piece of family land on California's Big Sur coast, I started an institute with my college classmate Richard Price. This enterprise, which joined laypeople and experts in many fields to explore the human potential, was sometimes contradictory to the transformations I'd looked for in India. In the late 1960s, Big Sur was a gathering place of the counterculture, much of it serving as a campground for uniquely American experiments with Buddhism, yoga, and shamanism heavily flavored with sex and drugs.

In these, the most tumultuous days of our institute, I began to think about the remarkable golf professional I'd met in Scotland. His glowing presence suggested a balance between the austerity I'd experienced in India and the drunken mysticism now prevalent in Big Sur. The fire that began in 1956 hadn't been fully extinguished. It had gone underground, and it flamed up again when I revisited Burningbush in 1970. Shivas Irons was gone, but I was flooded by memories of our day together. Recalling our magical golf round and spirited conversations, I marveled at my failure to recognize the extraordinary gifts he had offered me. It was depressing to think what my life might have been if I'd accepted his invitation to study with him. I left Burningbush with a sadness that did not lift until I decided to write about my Scottish mentor. A book, perhaps, would summon his presence and bring me closer to the joyous freedom he embodied.

In 1972, following the publication of *Golf in the Kingdom,* readers started to tell me about their own extraordinary golf experiences. To my astonishment, some of their reports called up further memories of Burningbush. When, for example, a New York lawyer wrote to tell me that from the tee of a four-par hole he'd seen a ball marker the size of a dime on the green some four hundred yards away, I recalled my frightening visual acuity after glimpsing a figure I later took to be Shivas's teacher, Seamus MacDuff. Recalling the incident, I saw that I had suppressed my new perceptual ability because it threatened to reveal the terrifying nature of the thing I'd seen. And when a woman correspondent described a round in which her surroundings became transparent, as if they were "God's silken robe," I remembered my similar perception. Everything had become diaphanous as I played the eighteenth hole at Burningbush, to such an extent that it seemed I could pass through solid objects. I'd repressed the memory all these years: For fifteen minutes or more, everything around me—the fairways, my body, each blade of grass—had seemed to be nothing more than a radiant pattern.

These restorations of memory were both exhilarating and disturbing. That I had suppressed, overlooked, or simply forgotten so much made me wonder what else I was blind to. For several years,

I'd been writing a book that involved research into areas of human functioning that were as strange as my experiences in 1956, but this hadn't revealed failures of memory comparable to those I'd experienced in relation to Shivas Irons. Why had my adventure with him triggered so many of my psychological defenses? To answer this question, as well as to overcome my lapses of consciousness, I started to record certain striking discoveries related to my day in Burningbush. By 1987, these had cohered into a pattern which suggested that Shivas Irons was engaged in an experiment with implications far beyond golf. And like the man on the cliff, more and more people were asking: *"Where is Shivas Irons?"* It was time, I decided, to begin a systematic search for him. In June of that year, I went back to Scotland looking for leads to his whereabouts, and there met the spirited, skeptical, and adventurous Buck Hannigan.

I t was one of those long June days that lovers of Scotland treasure, when Burningbush alternates between sunlight and fog-shrouded mystery. Though I had been there only twice before, the town seemed deeply familiar. With its winding streets, cathedral ruins, and stone houses built in centuries past, it cast an immediate spell upon me, and I enjoyed a leisurely walk from the train station reminiscing about my previous visits. On my way to the inn where I would stay, I stopped at a store recommended by a friend to look for golf memorabilia. The owner, a lively, sweet-faced lady in her seventies, was disappointed that she didn't have a photograph I wanted of Bernard Darwin as a member of the 1922 Walker Cup team, the first to visit America. He was her favorite golf writer. Did I know that he was the grandson of Charles Darwin?

"Yes," I replied. "Have you read his *Links of Eiderdown*?"

"Isn't it beautiful!" she said, looking over her horn-rimmed glasses. "More people should read it. And do you know *The Mystery of Golf* by Arnold Haultain?" When I said that I did, she seemed impressed. "Do you enjoy philosophy?" she asked. I said I'd written a book about golf that had some philosophy in it.

"Oh!" she said brightly. "What's it called?"

"Golf in the Kingdom. But it was published fifteen years ago. You wouldn't have heard about it."

"Now Mr. Murphy!" she scolded. "It's set here in Burningbush. Of course I've heard about it." I was flattered, but afraid to ask if she had any copies for sale. "Have you read it?" I asked. She said that she had, and I asked if she'd known Shivas Irons.

"No," she sighed. "I moved here after he left. What an extraordinary man he must have been. Was he everything you said he was?"

"As the years go by, he seems even more amazing. I'm looking for clues to his whereabouts."

"So you think he's still alive?" she asked.

"I'm not sure. When I was here last, in 1970, no one knew where he was. He'd be in his late sixties or early seventies now."

"Well," she said, "I might have a lead for you. A gentleman from Edinburgh, a Mr. Hannigan, comes here for books from Mr. Irons's collection. I have his address."

Startled, I asked how such books came into the store's possession.

"People have them. Every now and then we get one. Each has that special mark."

"What mark?"

"Didn't you see it? That insignia? Didn't you describe it in your book?"

"No. I didn't know his books were marked." I was amazed at my good luck. "Can you draw it for me?"

She led me to the back of the bookstore, sat behind a little desk, and wrote Hannigan's name and address on a slip of paper. Then she drew this mark above Hannigan's name:

"Is it a caduceus?" I asked.

"I think it's his initials, with two S's mirroring each other."

"He was left-handed and could do mirror-writing," I said. "Maybe he made the mark with both hands. But what does the second S stand for?"

"I don't know. It's too bad we don't have one of his books to show you. Leave us your address in case we find one." She stood abruptly, with an energy that belied her years. "Ah, but I have something else you might like! Here, let me find it for you." She crossed the store and took a book from a shelf of rare editions. It was a handsomely bound but well-worn tome, published in 1893, entitled *Golf: Its Roots in God and Nature.* Turning its yellowed pages with care, I saw that its author was one Mortimer Crail, a professor of Greek philosophy at the University of Edinburgh. These chapter titles caught my attention:

"In Praise of Slowness in Love and Golf"

"The Mutual Entailment of Virtues in Aristotle, the Stoics, and Golfers"

"The Unmasking of Atheists in Golf"

"The Platonic Ideas as Exemplified in the Circularity and Other Archetypes of Golf"

"On the Reconciliation of Dreams with Actual Shots"

"Ectoplasmic Phantasms on Golf Courses"
"Ochema: The Subtle Body in Golf"

Ochema is a word used by ancient Greeks to represent the spirit-body. I turned to the chapter with that title, and found a catalog of terms used by Neoplatonists to describe the vehicle of subtle matter in which the soul travels in ecstasy, dreams, and the afterlife. Crail related each of these terms to golf. *Astroeides,* for example, a word for the spirit-body in its "star-like" aspect, was equated with the "shining face, physique, and emanation of Angus Pattersone, the golf champion of Fife." *Simulacrum,* which refers among other things to the soul's mirror-imaging of the flesh, should be used by golf instructors to emphasize the fact that "mind and body have an immortal marriage, in brain and muscles now and the *ochema* hereafter." Crail seemed to have brought considerable erudition to his subject. The book was an astonishing encyclopedia of connections between golf, human nature, God, and the life to come. There was even a chapter on the fairy faith, with reports of brownies observed on Scottish links, and a discussion of apparent demonic possession during a tournament for pairs at Muirfield. The madness of the game had surfaced again in this Scottish professor. Though I'd ventured into such territory in my own book, Crail had gone beyond me. Turning to the chapter titled "The Unmasking of Atheists in Golf," I read:

> The game irresistibly leads to prayer. You have only to think of your most recent outing. Perhaps you felt a prayer of gratitude after a beautiful shot, or of supplication, or of spontaneous conversation with God. Every golfer on occasion blames Deity for golfing misfortune. No golfer escapes the urge to pray. The impulse is involuntary, constant, and irreversible.
>
> A portrait of Dr. James Sterling, celebrated by The Honourable Company for his successful litigation for the rights of golfers on the

Musselburgh Links, depicts the gentleman, who was famous for his militant atheism, kneeling in front of a bush. It is much debated whether Dr. Sterling was kneeling in prayer or looking for his ball. Like the rest of us, atheists are driven to prayer by the game. Golf's peculiar stress induces the Platonic *anamnesis,* as the soul remembers its origins. The game unmasks our deepest nature, which is rooted in God.

I turned to a passage on the Platonic Ideas. "More than any other sport," Crail wrote, "golf dramatizes the noetic archetypes. Its circularity expresses Perfection. Its rules reflect the True. Its etiquette embodies Goodness. Its fairways reveal eternal Beauty."

"Isn't it a wonderful book!" said the lady. "Would you like to buy it?"

"It's unusual," I said with hesitation. "Have you read it?"

A dimpled smile appeared on her round and lively face. "Every chapter!" she said. "Even the ones with Latin and Greek."

"He must have been a dedicated golfer. I didn't know you could find so much Platonic philosophy in the game. I mean . . . well, it's a long way from Plato to golf."

"Not in Scotland!" she exclaimed. "If he lived here, Plato would play."

Her remark made me think of Immanuel Kant. It was inconceivable that he would play, whether he lived in Scotland or not. And what about Hegel or Schopenhauer? I couldn't picture them on the links. "Well, Plato was an athlete," I murmured. "But it's hard to see him teeing it up."

Turning to Crail's essay on slowness, I found a long comparison of golf with erotic love written in an elevated style punctuated by vivid anatomical details and sentences in Latin and Greek. Playing golf with calm recollection, the professor wrote, produces bedroom ecstasies as yet unsuspected by the human race. But to receive such grace, one needs to make a deliberate stand—in both golf and sexual concourse—against "the momentum of habitual rapidity." According to Crail, each of us is "fixated upon a limited version of the life to come" and for that reason cannot experience "the full splendor of golf or the wedding bed." Indeed, we are a collection of cells that behaves like a "thundering buffalo herd." Because "our chief exemplar is always the person we were just a moment before," most of us cannot slow down sufficiently to hit a golf shot or caress a lover properly. With stately cadence, Crail described the right way to stroke an iron, a drive, a putt, a cheek, a breast, a stomach, a thigh.

Reading these elevated but explicit instructions, I was suddenly aware that the lady was watching me. She stood nearer than she had before, her eyes magnified by her horn-rimmed glasses. Could she tell what I was looking at? Deciding that she couldn't, I continued to peruse Crail's golf erotica. Because certain holes are female, he wrote, they have to be approached with special care. Their undulations, like the curves of a lady's physique, "should be caressed with the eye before play begins, lovingly embraced in the mind before any blows are administered to them." This principle was especially evident on the final hole of a links then famous in East Lothian, which ran between long, gentle rises that converged at the green. "It is a difficult hole to penetrate," he wrote. "The terror it causes male golfers can only be understood if one recognizes its female soul, which threatens annihilation."

Without my noticing, the lady had moved closer and was reading the chapter with me. "Isn't it *romantic!*" she said with surprising boldness.

"Romantic?" I said, pretending innocence as I turned to another page. "It's certainly big. I wonder who published it."

"Let's see." She helped me find the title page. "The Crail Press. It must have been a family business." She finally moved away, and I continued to leaf through the yellowed pages. There were soaring passages on the ontology and ethics of golf, on the connections between the game and mesmerism, on certain relations between the number eighteen and the hierarchical triads of Neoplatonic philosophers. Did Crail actually play? I wondered. Had golf's frustrations driven him to these speculations? During a faculty golf tournament at Stanford University, a noted physics professor had suffered a manic episode in which he claimed to understand the secrets of string theory and multidimensional space. Perhaps Crail had experienced a similar inspiration.

Then I turned to his description of an apparent demonic possession that happened on the Muirfield Links in 1892, during a competition for man-woman pairs sponsored by the Edinburgh Company of Golfers. It involved a barrister from Edinburgh named Stewart Garrick and his wife, who were matched against a Major James MacDougall of the Coldstream Guards and his fiancée, Anne Forbes, a great-niece of Mrs. Garrick. The barrister's wife, Crail wrote,

> had a famous and vicious wit, which she frequently used against her husband in public. Mr. Garrick, a stern and exemplary figure, a model of probity in the courts and leading member of the Scottish Church, who is celebrated for his occasional lectures on Moral Theology at the University of Edinburgh, was well-known for playing with only three clubs. Miss Forbes, a great beauty who was much admired it seems by Mr. Garrick, with Major MacDougall made a formidable team in such competitions. In this match, the Major and Miss Forbes won every hole until the infamous incident on the tenth green.
>
> As their losses had mounted, Mrs. Garrick's remarks to her husband had grown increasingly venomous, causing either consternation or mirth among the approximately seventy onlookers. After their loss on the ninth hole, with their match in immediate jeopardy, Mrs. Garrick loudly declared that Mr. Garrick needed a new

set of balls, to which Mr. Garrick responded with quiet solemnity by asking if she would lend him hers. They did not speak again until the foursome reached the next green, where Garrick began swearing profusely.

The eminent gentleman, it is said, exhausted the entire Scottish lexicon of curses, uttering words in Gaelic as well as English while viciously beating the fairway with his putter. During his tirade, which would last for fifteen minutes, Mrs. Garrick forfeited the match, and with Miss Forbes and every female onlooker, as well as several men in attendance, returned to the Muirfield Club House. The men who remained attempted to pacify Garrick, without success, until three of them began to curse in the same wild manner. One of these gentlemen, a Mr. James Ramsay of Edinburgh, was a frequent partner of Garrick's at golf, and the remaining onlookers believed he was trying with misplaced good fellowship to give his friend's embarrassing behavior a semblance of normalcy. But he was then joined by two other men in a grievous display of rage and profanity. Those who watched said they had never witnessed such a frightening spectacle. Mr. Ramsay, like Garrick a person of impeccable reputation, later said he had felt possessed. Never before, and never since, had he felt such anger toward his wife, who with a group of their friends had watched the match until Garrick's seizure.

But the most arresting feature of the episode was not the cursing. In the midst of it, there appeared a phantom hovering directly above the unfortunate Garrick. Subsequently, about half of those present claimed to have seen it, though there were different accounts of its aspect and activity. Some thought it resembled Mrs. Garrick. Others took it to be a double of Garrick himself, and a few declared it to be a demon. It is beyond dispute that approximately half the onlookers saw this disembodied spirit. Some attributed the entire incident to group delusion, some to demonic possession, some to the cumulative effect of golf's frustrations upon the four men, while others thought it might have been caused by the mushrooms served that noon at the Clubhouse.

In my judgment, the incident gives further evidence of golf's power to elicit those supernormal events lately studied by the Society for Psychical Research and its leading theoretician Frederic Myers. Using Myers's felicitous language, the apparition might have been the result of *psychorrhagy,* that is, the spontaneous hemorrhaging of psychic contents, in this case so strong that it formed a phantom. Such an eruption might have come from Garrick himself or from his wife, each of whom appeared to harbor murderous impulses toward the other. According to Myers, all strong emotion can be directed subliminally to the production of supernormal functioning.

Reading this passage, I thought of my own experience while playing with Shivas Irons. I, too, had seen a phantom which, like the apparition at Muirfield, had produced different reactions among various onlookers. But I had repressed my memory of it and hadn't mentioned it in *Golf in the Kingdom.* And here again was Frederic Myers! For several years, I'd sensed that the way to Shivas went through him.

Suppressing my excitement, I asked the lady how much the book cost. Almost certainly, bargaining would be necessary. But she wasn't a business type. "Why, there's no price listed." She pointed to the back of its front cover. "Even though there's this dollar sign."

"Is that a dollar sign?" I asked. "Or is it Shivas's mark!"

"Well!" she exclaimed. "Is it? There's only one S. No, I think it's a dollar sign. Here, you can have it for thirty dollars."

With a sense I was robbing the store, I paid her and waited impatiently as she put the book in a paper bag. "It makes me happy to think you have this." She smiled sweetly and squeezed my arm. "Oh, and give me your address. Maybe we'll get another book from Mr. Irons's collection. And remember to look up Mr. Hannigan! He's looking for Mr. Irons, too."

Outside, fog was curling through the streets. I hurried my steps to The Druids' Inn, where I had made a reservation. Finding Crail's book was an omen, I thought, a sign that this trip might produce important discoveries. In my room, I read Crail's entire account of the Muirfield episode, which he related to other visitations on golf courses. According to the learned professor, the royal and ancient game—like long sea voyages and mountain climbing—had a remarkable history of phantom figures. But more than ninety years had passed since Crail had published his book, and no one else to my knowledge had explored this phenomenon. Was there an unconscious conspiracy of silence about it? Even though several sportspeople, including two well-known players in the National Football League, had told me about similar visions, I had never written or talked about the apparition I'd glimpsed at the end of my golf round with Shivas Irons. Recalling the dramatic stories people had told me about phantoms in sport, I was amazed at my selective memory. Maybe I could recapture the experience more fully when I revisited the eighteenth hole.

CHAPTER TWO

THE BURNINGBUSH CLUBHOUSE, a stately grey building constructed in the early nineteenth century, overlooks both the first tee and the eighteenth green. Viewing it on this foggy summer afternoon, I was flooded by memories of my visit in 1956. I could hear the resonant inflection of Shivas Irons, smell the fragrance of heather and surf as it wrapped me round that day, and feel the same uplifting mood. . . .

Our playing partner MacIver, dressed almost like a cleric in black and white, had set a compelling example for me. His unpretentious approach to the game, his simple devotion to the practices his mentor gave him, had helped me play with a relinquishment of hopes and regrets I'd never experienced on a golf course. On the thirteenth hole the state had deepened, and now, as I walked down the eighteenth fairway, it suddenly intensified. All at once, a veil dropped from my consciousness. Addressing my ball, I knew that everything—the club, the grass, this human flesh—was fundamentally light and awareness. What held it all in place? I wondered. What kept us from falling through the ground? As the ball rose toward the pin, I felt the air it passed through. Light was holding light. The evening sky, my companions, the clubhouse cohered in a thrilling but tenuous embrace.

With the slightest shift of volition, it occurred to me, I could reach through the shaft of my club. By turning my mind subtly, I could alter my atomic patterning. I paused, sensing the terror that lurked in these perceptions, then picked up my golf bag and walked to the green. MacIver was approaching his ball, and Shivas held my gaze for an instant. It was clear that he knew what I felt. MacIver sank his putt, and Shivas nodded to indicate that it was my turn.

Some thirty or forty spectators stood on the embankment above the green, but the place was completely silent. It was as if this was an important match, even the climax of a tournament. A tremor of fear passed through me. Famous matches had been played here, and more would be played in years to come. One could sense the ghosts of champions. Old Tom Morris, young Tom, Harry Vardon, Bobby Jones. Were they somehow present? This green had been built on a graveyard and was now a theater of the occult. A second wave of fear passed through me, but I made our threesome's second birdie. As I lifted my ball from the hole, the commanding professional's resonant voice rose above the applause. "Ladies and gentlemen," he said. "A cheer for the American!"

As the clapping subsided, Shivas stood back from his ball, which lay about ten feet from the cup after his prodigious tee shot. There was only the sound of a distant car, and a few barely audible shouts from the golf links. A seabird's cry echoed off the grey stone buildings. Our onlookers now stood motionless as Shivas approached his ball, placed his putter blade behind it, and calmly putted. The sequence was evenly paced and efficient. Each movement was a thing in itself. The ball dropped for an eagle two, and cheers rose from our gallery. They were louder than they had been for my shot. "They're Scottish," he said so that everyone could hear him. "They're rootin' for the home team!" Standing beside the hole, a luminous figure in the shadows of early evening, he waved with a dramatic sweep of his arm to his cheering audience. And then, with a grave, disconcerting expression, he turned and walked toward me.

At that moment a declivity opened around him, like a hole in the air, revealing radiance with some sort of movement in it. This apparition—this shining space within ordinary space—opened and closed in the few seconds it took him to cross the green.

When he reached my side, we stood in silence. "Michael," he said softly. "Everybody feels a part of what we're feelin', each in their own way, that this flesh is the tenderest part of the soul. But only some can see it."

As if to confirm the fact that something extraordinary had just taken place, most who watched appeared to be transfixed. Mac-Iver, however, seemed oblivious to the apparition. "A 67." He nodded toward Shivas. "An 84 for me, and an 86 for the American side. And Murphy," he paused, "ye shot a 34 comin' in, the same as Mr. Irons."

Shivas placed a hand on my shoulder. "Ye deserve a drink," he said. "Come join me in the clubhouse."

During this brief exchange, most of our onlookers stood without moving; but a few seemed agitated. One who appeared to be especially disturbed grabbed my arm as I walked toward the pro shop. He was a short, nervous-looking man dressed in a yellowed suit and dirty necktie. "Ye a student o' Irons?" he asked, almost snarling.

"We met today," I said, quickening my steps to avoid him. "I'm not his student."

"What was he tryin' to show ye?" He held my arm. "Cut right through his putter, didn't he? *Cut it right in two.*" He passed his hand like a blade through an imaginary golf club. Startled, I turned to face him. "Ye know what I mean." He glanced around to see if anyone heard us. "His putter. He cut it in two! Ye saw it. Ye were right in front of him!" Dismayed, I started to move away. But as I did, I remembered my own sensation that it would be possible to reach through a golf club.

For a moment we stared at each other in silence. "So what did you see?" I asked. "He cut his putter in two?"

"Ye saw it," he whispered, pressing close like a fellow conspirator. "I've seen 'im do it before. He's not a normal man. Ye know, *ye played with 'im!*"

"But he *didn't* cut his putter in two!"

"Oh, but he did. I could tell ye saw it." When I protested again, he turned away in disgust.

Avoiding an elderly lady who was eager to ask me something, I walked briskly to the pro shop. It was closed, and I put down my golf bag. The exaltation I'd felt on the links was gone, and I needed to compose myself. The apparition, and my encounter with the man in the yellowed suit, had caused a mild state of shock.

A fragrant breeze was blowing, and surf was sending plumes of spray off rocks beyond the fairways. A man and woman were standing near me, gazing toward the sea. Had they watched us finish? Had they sensed what I'd seen around Shivas Irons? Something about them reassured me, and I moved closer to them. The man, who looked to be in his fifties, was absorbed in reverie, but turned as I approached. "Quite a finish we had there," I said. "You seen Irons play before?"

"Watched 'im practice," he said with a heavy Scots burr. "And seen 'im finish here. But ne'er followed 'im from hole to hole."

"You live in Burningbush?"

"We do. On a farm out there." Extending his hand, he introduced himself and his wife, and we talked for a moment about the beauties of his native Fife. Then he turned to face the sea. "Watchin' you and the professional there"—he nodded toward the eighteenth green—"started me thinkin' about an experience we had. I feel like tellin' ye about it." He was a muscular man with an open, friendly face. "Ye'll think it's crazy, though. Me and my wife here had some sort o' vision. A phantom figure, a ghost. I thought o' it watchin' ye finish the hole."

His wife, a sturdy woman with a broad ruddy face, looked embarrassed. "We both saw it," he said. "Watched it for five or ten minutes hoverin' over the farm as the sun went down. Like a shinin' light, movin' slowly up and down . . ."

"Oh, stop!" the woman exclaimed.

"Happened four years ago," he continued as if he hadn't heard her. "But I couldn't help rememberin' it watchin' you and yer playin' partners. The memory came up real strong."

His wife tugged his arm. "James!" she said with irritation. "The gentleman doesn't want to hear about yer vision."

"No," I protested. "I'm interested. I'd like to hear about it." But she walked away indignantly. "It's a sore point," the man said with resignation. "She won't admit it now. Says she never saw it, which is amazin' to me. Amazin'! Been talked out o' it by our sons and friends." Shaking his head apologetically, he turned and followed her.

At that moment, a tall, aristocratic-looking man approached. What revelation would he bring? "Good show," he said with an English accent. "You held your own with that mighty professional."

"You saw us finish?"

"Watched you play the last two holes."

I asked if he knew Shivas Irons. "I don't know the man," he answered. "But what a *mighty* drive! Are you an American?"

I said that I was, and we talked for a moment about the pleasures of golf in Scotland. But no revelations were forthcoming, and he gave no indication that he'd noticed something strange during our play on the eighteenth green. His main purpose in approaching me seemed to be a genuine desire to express his admiration for Shivas's golfing prowess.

The golf links now were shrouded in mist, but the apparition I'd seen thirty-one years before was brightly present to me. Like the visitation at Muirfield that Crail had described, it had elicited different responses from different onlookers; and through most of the intervening years, I had either repressed my memory of it or taken it to be an illusion. Now, however, it seemed utterly real. A living thing, something conscious, had appeared for a moment near Shivas Irons. This would be a good time to revisit the thirteenth hole. Perhaps my glimpse of Seamus MacDuff would return with similar clarity.

The thirteenth hole at Burningbush runs for two hundred yards up a steep gorse-covered incline to a small green situated between two twisted cypress trees. Many have called it the product of a demented imagination, and to most who see it for the first time it seems an impossible challenge. There are steep ravines to its left and beyond it, so that the only places for the ball to land are the green and its narrow fringe of fairway grass, the gorse, and the rocks below. The field of brambly bushes between tee and green, called Lucifer's Rug, is an arena of untold suffering. Several people have been injured on their second shot, either by falling onto rocks or skewering themselves on gorse thorns, and it is said that at least one corpse has been found "under the Rug." Some people think it is the world's most difficult golf hole.

I remembered looking at the distant flag, which was whipping in a strong left to right wind, while holding my ball to the blade of my two-iron. Merely imagining their union, as Shivas had advised, seemed a deficient means of concentration. Now I needed to commune with their physical joining.

MacIver, too, made special preparations. Without expression, he stared toward the green which, given his lack of distance, seemed out of reach, then pointed bravely up the hill to mark the path his ball would follow. But our mentor had adopted the strangest ritual. Standing one-legged, he yodeled a cry that echoed off the cliffs below. It made me jump, but didn't faze MacIver. Seemingly unperturbed, the ever-disciplined student stood motionless facing the field of gorse that appeared to stretch into the heavens. Was he paralyzed? Legend had it that some people froze on this tee. But when at last he swung, his ball traveled high and straight—and fell short, into the brambly receptacle of Lucifer's Rug. With a grimace, he marched to his golf bag and waited for me to play.

But as I addressed my ball, there was another terrible cry from Shivas. Louder and more eerie than his first, it caused my mind to empty. There were no thoughts of rocks or gorse, no thoughts of the Rug or desirable shots, and I swung without mental imagery. The ball rose on a low trajectory—white against yellow and then white against blue—until it hovered more than two hundred yards away, held high in the wind before dropping onto the putting surface.

Stepping back from the tee blocks, I felt both gratitude and excitement. Deliberately calming myself, I picked up my golf bag and turned toward Shivas. But as I turned, my perception faltered. He seemed distorted, as if the space around him were somehow warped; and when he swung, I couldn't follow his ball. As I climbed the hill, I sensed that MacIver had experienced something strange, but we didn't talk about it. Instead I felt the land with new closeness, and let the stillness carry me. The quiet buoyancy I felt swept away questions about Shivas's performance and the figure in a tattered black suit moving along the ravine.

S tanding again on the thirteenth green, I remembered the exaltation of that moment thirty-one years before. It had made me oblivious to the man in black who was gesturing urgently toward us. The memory of the enchantment I felt still lingered in my cells—the sound of surf, the taste of salt, the fragrance of summer grass and heather. All this green and purple land, the towering clouds and sky above, were suspended in a timeless stillness that made it hard to think about the strange-looking figure.

But where had he stood? The opposite side of the ravine, upon which I'd presumed he had been walking, wasn't visible from the path up the hill or from the green itself, yet he had seemed to be on a level with me. Had I spontaneously produced an apparition by the process Frederic Myers called psychorrhagy? Had the gesturing figure been a product of my hemorrhaging psyche, a projection of my subliminal mind? Or had Seamus MacDuff projected himself in some sort of spirit-body? An entry from one of Shivas's journals implied that he could do that. Reaching into a jacket pocket, I found the slip of paper with Buck Hannigan's address. If the man collected books from the library of Shivas Irons, he might help me answer these questions.

CHAPTER THREE

ON THE EVENING following my visit to Burningbush, with Crail's book in hand, I found Buck Hannigan's studio apartment near Edinburgh's Princes Street. "State yer business," a man yelled when I knocked. "Yer name and yer business."

"I'm a writer," I shouted back. "I'm looking for Shivas Irons."

There was silence, then a distant thumping. "Yer lookin' for who?" the man shouted again. His voice had a hard, slightly nasal quality. "Who is it ye're lookin' for?"

"Shivas Irons! The golf pro from Burningbush."

"Are ye carryin' a weapon?" the voice responded. "If ye're not, come in."

Cautiously, I entered a small foyer, and closed the door behind me. The thumping continued in another room, along with heavy breathing. "Keep comin'." The voice was accompanied by grunts. "Through the door to your left." I stepped into a large, dimly lit studio to find a man doing sit-ups with weights held to his chest. "Have a seat," he gasped. "I'm Hannigan."

The room had just a single window, which faced onto buildings across the street, and a ceiling some thirteen or fourteen feet high. As the sit-ups continued, I sat by a large wooden desk. Hannigan wore brown slacks, a white shirt, and a narrow red tie. With each rise from the floor, he grunted, then exhaled loudly as he lowered himself to a supine position. When he was finished, he remained motionless for several seconds, then put his weights down, sat up abruptly, and jumped to his feet athletically without touching the floor with hands or elbows. After wiping his face with a handkerchief, he put on a pair of glasses and, without apology, sat at the desk across from me. He had a thin face and closely cropped hair, and appeared to be about forty years old. With his round wire-rimmed glasses, he bore an uncanny resemblance to James Joyce. "So ye're lookin' for Shivas Irons," he said with a jaunty and slightly sardonic Scottish lilt. "What kind o' trouble has he caused ye?"

I told him about the lady in the bookstore and handed him Crail's book. There was silence as he studied my face. "We've met," he said, his eyes narrowing. "Ye look familiar." In the soft light cast by a lamp on his desk, he seemed farther away than the five or six feet between us. "Well!" he exclaimed. "Ye're Murphy! From California. The man who saw the light of God and promptly fled." Startled, I didn't reply. "So ye're the man who told the world about Shivas Irons," he said with seeming disbelief. "This is a surprise. A surprise indeed!"

"So you've read *Golf in the Kingdom*?"

"Oh, I've studied it. Studied it well." He pulled a battered English edition from a drawer, slid it across the desk, and watched as I thumbed through it. There were notes on some of its pages. One was inscribed in a subchapter titled "As Luminous Body." It read: "Murphy on the 13th hole. What really happened?" Another chapter, titled "The Crooked Golden River," had seven or eight question marks in its margins.

"You've really read this," I said uneasily. "You seem to have questions about it."

"Have ye found any traces of Irons?" he asked, disregarding my remark.

"Just that." I nodded toward Crail's book. "But I take it that you have."

"No letters?" he asked. "No reports of his whereabouts? No word from his friends?"

"Not a trace."

It was hard to tell what he felt during this exchange, but I sensed that he was stunned by our meeting. "Murphy," he said, "I've been meanin' to write ye for several months, ever since I read yer book. I've got my own questions about Shivas Irons." He paused, as if to gather himself. "But let me ask ye first. How much of the story can ye vouch for? How much of it *really happened?*"

It was a question many readers asked, but I never felt comfortable answering it. "Most of it," I said with hesitation. "But there's more to the story than there is in the book. My memories are still developing."

"Still developing?" He looked surprised. "After, let's see— *thirty-one* years? Ye're still rememberin' things after a third of a century!"

His ascetic features had a stern, slightly pugnacious cast, but in the room's soft light they also had a strangely luminous quality. Had we met before? "You seem familiar," I said. "Have you been to San Francisco?"

"In '82. But I doubt we've met. I was holed up with colleagues in Berkeley."

"At the university?"

"At the Lawrence Lab. I'm a physicist."

"What kind of a physicist?" I was certain now that we had met.

"Ye look surprised." He gave me a sardonic but engaging

smile. "I don't work in a lab, if that's what ye mean. They pay me to *think*. I've a research post at the university here, to ponder things such as Bell's theorem and hyperspace. D'ye know the terms?"

"My institute has conferences on Bell's theorem. You must know John Clauser and Henry Stapp."

"Well, it's a little world. So ye're acquainted with the mysteries o' quantum theory. Yes, I know Clauser 'n Stapp. But I didn't see either of 'em in '82. Another group paid my way, to work on supergravity." He shook his head with amusement and just the slightest hint of regret. "But it didn't turn out as expected. I pretty well shot down their theories."

Hannigan, I thought, might be a world-class physicist. "What are you working on now?" I asked.

He hesitated, as if deciding what I would understand. "Officially, on string theory. Unofficially, on possible relations between hyperspace and living systems. Does that make sense? It should." He leaned across his desk, his blue eyes brightening behind his steel-rimmed glasses. "In case ye're wonderin' why I collect books from the library of Shivas Irons, I think there's a connection between my theories and him and Mr. Seamus MacDuff."

"Between hyperspace and Shivas Irons?"

"There are hints o' it in yer book."

"In my book!"

"Ye've never thought of that? Weren't ye hintin' at it with all the talk o' 'true gravity' and yer experience on the thirteenth hole?"

"I'm not sure what happened on the thirteenth hole. You might find this hard to believe, but my memory of it has evolved through the years. Not simply changed, but *developed*."

"Developed? Ye mean yer memory's *better* than it was before?"

"Yes."

"After thirty-one years?" He leaned toward me, his face filled with skepticism. "Better? I find that hard to believe."

It took me a moment to muster an answer. "Memory's a funny thing," I said. "Often it depends on the state you're in, and sometimes it needs support from others. You can believe it or not, but I'm still uncertain about some of the things that happened in '56. People will tell me about an unusual experience they had on a golf course, and I remember something like it that I had with Irons. Did you ever meet him?"

"No. I never did." Leaning back, he cupped his hands in front of his face as if to mask his facial expression. "So people tell ye about their unusual experiences, and ye remember similar ones ye had in '56. You mean—what?—that ye see the contours of a green more clearly? Or the splendor of a sunset? Murphy, can I ask ye this? What do ye do for a livin'?"

"I have a trust fund," I said with a hint of embarrassment. "But mainly I'm writing a book."

"Another golf book?"

"No. A study of supernormal experience, part anthropology and psychology, part religious studies, part psychical research. It would take a while to explain."

"Like Frederic Myers and William James?"

"Yes!" I was startled that he understood so quickly. "In a way they're mentors."

"A modest enterprise." He smiled with irony and unexpected warmth. "Ye sound like *me* tryin' to explain what I do. At least ye've got words. All I've got is this!" He lifted an artist's sketchpad covered with mathematical equations written in a small and elegant hand. "Where d'ye get yer material?" he asked.

"Libraries. Interviews. Stuff people send me, some of it in response to *Golf in the Kingdom*. You might be interested in this." I took a letter from a jacket pocket. "It's from a lawyer in New

York who read the book, telling me he saw a ball marker the size of a dime on a green *four hundred yards* from the tee he stood on. His playing partners thought he was crazy, but when they reached the green, they found the thing! I believe this letter. You sense the guy's telling the truth."

Hannigan read it, then asked if I got many like it.

"One or two every month. Since '72, the year the book was published, I've gotten several hundred. They've made me think that in the States, golf is a mystery school for Republicans!"

"Here it's no mystery school. It's a true religion. So, some of these reports help ye remember what happened with Shivas Irons. . . ."

"That one did." I nodded toward the letter. "When I read it, I remembered that something like that had happened to me on the thirteenth hole. You might find this hard to believe, but I could see curtains in the windows of the Burningbush clubhouse. How far is it from the green? A mile, or mile-and-a-half, maybe? I remember the experience clearly now, but until I got this letter I'd forgotten it."

"Completely!"

"Not completely. But a lot of it. Later that night, at dinner with Irons and his friends, part of it started coming back. They were talking about MacDuff, when suddenly—I remembered seeing him near the thirteenth hole. When I got this letter I remembered the visual acuity, and yesterday even more of the experience came back. . . ."

"Murphy, now wait." Hannigan held up a hand to stop me. "How do you know you saw MacDuff?"

"Because a man was walking along the ravine. He was gesturing to me, trying to communicate, trying to tell me something. That night at dinner, Irons implied it was MacDuff. When I was out there yesterday, the memory was crystal clear."

"Maybe it was an apparition."

"It might've been. I've thought of that. Or it could've been something I projected, some sort of illusion. But standing there yesterday I remembered how solid, how lively, how vivid it was. I can't believe it was just my projection, and if it was an apparition, it had some sort of consciousness."

Hannigan rose, stepped away from the desk, and stood about ten feet from me. "Murphy," he said, "there's something you need to know. Some of the things in yer book are wrong. Mac-Duff was dead in '56. He died in '53, three years before you got there. If the thing you saw was a living person, it wasn't Seamus MacDuff."

"He died in '53?"

"I've been studyin' this thing, studyin' it carefully. MacDuff didn't live in that ravine, as you suggested in your book. Irons didn't spend time in the Hebrides. And his mother wasn't a priestess from the Gold Coast. But it's all right." He waved a hand in front of his face. "Ye got enough right to make a good book. I'm glad ye wrote it."

"Where was Irons in the war?" I asked with dismay.

"North Africa, but it doesn't matter. He had a vision like the one you described."

"God, it's awful I got those things wrong. Christ, it's embarrassing."

"Murphy, it's all right. Irons and MacDuff were not yer normal gentlemen! No one knows what 'n the hell they were really doin'. But how about a drink? I've got a Scottish beer ye've never tasted. And a single-malt whiskey with a horse's kick. Which'll it be?"

"A whiskey."

He crossed the room, took a bottle from a cabinet, and poured us each a glass. After handing me mine, he lifted his in a toast. "Murphy, we might be on to something here. Here's to Shivas Irons!"

The single malt had an immediate warming effect, and a deeply penetrating aroma. But its warmth did not relieve the dismay I felt about the mistakes in my book.

But Hannigan had more surprises. "Ye might be interested to know that this whiskey was made on a piece o' land that was owned by a certain gentleman named Seamus MacDuff." I looked with astonishment at my glass, which had a remarkably prismatic amber glow. "While we drink, let me show you some pictures of it."

Whether from the first effects of the whiskey or the impact of these revelations, I felt slightly disoriented. Sitting by his desk, I watched him cross the room, open a cabinet, and produce a large portfolio. "Look at this." He opened it on the desk. "These are pictures of MacDuff's highly unusual stretch o' ground." The case contained a stack of black-and-white photographs. The one on top, which was yellowed with age, showed a two-story stone country house surrounded by trees and hedges. On its back was the date "June 1940."

"This was taken forty-seven years ago, during the Battle of Britain." Hannigan picked up a second photograph, which showed the same house in disrepair. "But this is what it looks like now. For twenty years it was a distillery, but for the last four it's been deserted. Now look at this." The next photograph, which like the first was yellowed with age, showed MacDuff's house from a distant vantage point surrounded by golf holes. "MacDuff had his own private course," said Hannigan. "Not long. Just seven holes. But very interesting. Here's a view of what must have been the first hole, taken from the front of his house."

The picture showed a fairway running between two gentle rises that converged at a distant green. Beyond the green there was a hill, and to the northwest a mountain bordered with extraordinary light. "When was this taken?" I asked. "At sunrise or sunset?"

Hannigan took a drink of whiskey, then turned the picture over. On its back was the inscription: "Sunrise at noon. August 6 again, but 1950."

I picked up the photograph and held it close to the lamp. "August sixth," I said. "It could mean Hiroshima. Irons told me the day was important to MacDuff. What's this a picture of?"

"Your guess is as good as mine. It was noon, all right. Look at the trees. They don't have any shadows."

"But with such bright light on the horizon, shouldn't there be some?"

"You'd think so. But Murphy, that mountain is northwest of the place. There can't be a sunrise or sunset beyond it."

"Could the picture be faked?"

"It's possible. But for what? Why would Irons or MacDuff have faked it, and then written this inscription?" Hannigan took another photograph from the portfolio. "Here's one I took last year from the same spot." It showed the same converging rises, but instead of a fairway and distant greens, there was only a field of wild grass. "The golf course is overgrown now," he said. "Here's what the rest of it looked like in the forties and early fifties."

By the look of the photographs, almost every hole had some eccentric feature. One, which appeared to be a three-par, required a tee shot to a green that was hidden in a glen far below it. "To play this one," I said, "you'd have to be clairvoyant. It looks harder than the thirteenth at Burningbush."

We were silent for a moment. "Maybe," Hannigan said quietly, "the course was designed to practice the powers ye're studying. Every hole required nearly impossible shots. Did Irons tell you he practiced on it?"

"No."

"He might have, if you'd stayed a little longer."

His remark brought a wave of regret. Yes, if I'd stayed longer in Burningbush in 1956, I might have learned something about this strange-looking course and the experiments conducted on it. I asked where it was located. "In the west," said Hannigan. "Near Loch Awe, on the way to Oban, about a three- to four-hour drive from Burningbush, I estimate, when Irons spent time there in the '40s and '50s. With the new motorways, though, ye can get there from here in a couple of hours."

"And MacDuff lived there how long?"

"From 1919 to 1953."

"How did you track all this down? You've done quite a detective job."

Hannigan sat at the desk across from me. "By nature and by habit, Murphy, I'm a debunker of claims for the paranormal. But because of my peculiar theories in physics I've developed a speciality in that field now commonly called 'the study of anomalous phenomena.' I came to know about this particular anomaly when one of the Scottish papers ran a story that the distillery was about to be closed. People wouldn't work there because they felt the place was haunted. Look at this."

From a desk drawer, he produced a page from *The Herald* dated "September 3, 1983." An article near the bottom was headlined: "Ramsay Distillery closed by hauntings and medical cases." An underlined passage read: "Several employees have reported mysterious marks on their bodies, and others have heard voices or music. Such reports have persisted for several years, baffling engineers, psychologists and physicians hired by the Ramsay family and their managers at the distillery."

Holding up a photograph that showed MacDuff's entire estate when its golf course was still intact, Hannigan traced an imaginary line. "On certain days after dark, everything in this perimeter, including MacDuff's old house, the distillery building, the golf holes, and the fields around them, goes through extraordinary changes. Something remarkable happens. Something the people who lived there didn't understand. Something I don't understand. Something no one understands. From time to time the whole place—how to say it?—is filled with a presence, a feeling, a force that was finally too much for the people who worked there."

"Is it threatening?"

"Not necessarily. Some people thought it was healing, even holy. Others thought it was menacing, like a big angry ghost. It scared almighty shit out of most of the distillery workers, and the caretakers the owners hired when the place was closed. No one lives there now."

"And it's been closed since '83?"

"Closed and deserted. In '56, a family named Ramsay bought the land from MacDuff's estate and eventually built the distillery, but none of the family ever lived there. I tracked down the senior Ramsay, and found he'd bought the place in auction through a law firm here. It seems MacDuff had no heirs, no family at all, and left the proceeds of the sale to a retainer who'd lived with him since the '20s. In '83, the year I got onto this, there wasn't much left in the law firm's files except these photographs." He paused. "But there was another lead. The senior Ramsay had met MacDuff in '45, here in Edinburgh, at a lecture on psychical research, and had gotten into a long conversation with him. Learned something about his ancestry, that his mother was African—you got that right in yer book—and that his father was big in the Africa trade. She was part Fulani, part Tuareg—Ramsay remembered that somehow—and according to MacDuff was a real beauty. Ramsay said MacDuff had extraordinary looks. Striking, he said. Unforgettable. Dark brown skin, curly white hair, and deep green eyes that looked right through you. But here's what I'm leading up to, Murphy. Ramsay also remembered the name of a golf professional whom MacDuff described, a young pro from Burningbush named Shivas somethin'. That was my first lead to Irons."

Hannigan took off his glasses, closed his eyes, and rubbed the bridge of his nose. "But I must tell ye, my friend, there are days when I think that Irons and MacDuff were trapped in the world's weirdest folie à deux. Driven to it by golf, perhaps. They wouldn't be the first to go bonkers from the game! But then— there's MacDuff's estate, the hauntings there, these photographs, some other leads I'll show ye, and the picture that starts to emerge from Irons's books." He paused. "And from your book. What ye wrote encouraged me to think that others were on to this. Readin' *Golf in the Kingdom,* I saw that I wasn't alone. For example, look at this." He took a book from a shelf, opened it, and pointed to a margin note. "Read it," he said. "Ye'll recognize the handwriting." The book was entitled *Phenomena of Materialization,* and the note was written by Shivas Irons. It read: "Like S. last night. Step by step. Lasted for five or six minutes." In the text beside the note, this sentence was underlined: "The special characteristic of Eva C.'s phenomena is that, not only does she produce complete materializations, but that she produces, step by step, the necessary teleplastic material, and forms it in successive stages."

I had seen the book and knew that its author had been a prominent figure in the development of dynamic psychiatry.*

---

* *Phenomena of Materialization* (Kegan Paul, London and New York, 1920; reprinted in 1975 by Arno Press, New York) is a collection of evidence for materialization. In 1896, its author, Albert von Schrenck Notzing, a Munich psychiatrist widely known for his studies of hypnotic suggestion, dual personality, and unconscious elements of personality, was General Secretary of the Third International Congress of Psychology, a historic event in the development of modern psychiatry. The lines cited above refer to "Eva C.," a medium who was observed by various scientists as she materialized "teleplastic" material. One of her observers was the well-known psychologist and physician

" 'Like S. last night,' " I said. "Does that mean Seamus? And step by step? When did Irons write this? Before MacDuff died?"

"There's no inscription to tell us. But we do have this." Hannigan crossed the room and came back with another book. *Evidence of Personal Survival from Cross Correspondences* had Irons's mark on the back of its front cover above the date "December 5, 1960." Below the date there was this inscription: "Step by step. More and more visible. Last night, this morning, again at noon."

"Nineteen-sixty," I mused. "What was the date on that picture of his first fairway? Nineteen-*fifty?*" With a sudden sense of recognition, I found the photograph with MacDuff's inscription. Between the tee, which stood in the immediate foreground, and the green at the end of the fairway, there was a barely discernible oval light. "What's this?" I handed the picture to Hannigan.

"What d'ye mean?"

"This!" I traced the shape I saw.

"Some o' these photos are faded," he said. "This one's damaged."

"But look at this! It's like something I saw around Irons."

"Something you saw? I don't see it!" He turned toward me, his jaw thrust forward aggressively. "Murphy," he said. "I have to tell ye this. In yer book, some of your so-called facts are wrong, and a few of your experiences are impossible for me to believe. So you'll have to forgive me if I question yer powers of perception." He looked again at the photograph. "For Christ's sake! I can't see what ye're pointin' at."

Dismayed, I studied the picture again. The luminous oval was

Gustave Geley, who in 1918 lectured in Paris at the Collège de France to members of the Psychological Institute on "Supranormal Physiology and the Phenomena of Ideoplastics." In this lecture, which is summarized in Von Schrenck Notzing's book (pages 327–36), Geley described different stages and kinds of materialization.

as apparent as it had been a moment before. "Well," I said with a shrug, "there it is. I see it clearly. I don't know what to tell you."

Hannigan took the photograph across the room, and held it up to a lamp that was brighter than the one on his desk. "Well, maybe there's a smudge there, but no shape," he said with irritation. "So what did ye see?"

I described the apparition on the eighteenth green. When I was done, he picked up the photograph. "I still don't see it. I can't tell what you're pointin' at. A little smudge, maybe, but nothing like an apparition."

But the luminous shape was apparent to me. I reread the inscription on the back of the photograph: " 'Sunrise at noon. August 6 again, but 1950.' "

For a while, we studied the picture in silence. "You hungry?" he finally asked. "It's past seven. There's a place around the corner."

Ten minutes later, we sat for supper at a pub nearby. Waiting for our meal, I felt both excitement about Hannigan's revelations and an elevation that was caused, I guessed, by the whiskey from MacDuff's estate. But Hannigan seemed deeply troubled. "So you actually thought you could cut your golf club in two?" he asked in disbelief.

"The whole thing came in stages," I said. "The round with Irons had put me in some sort of altered state. An exaltation, really. But on the eighteenth hole, it went to another level. Everything—the fairway, the clubs, the people around us—seemed to be penetrable, as if they were nothing but radiant patterns, as if they were made of light. In a way, the apparition I saw on the green, that shining space around him, was an extension of the state I'd been in for—I don't know, maybe an hour, an hour and a half."

"And ye actually thought ye could pass yer hand through yer golf club?"

"That was an illusion, of course. It came from the way everything looked. But it was strange—exceedingly strange—that the man who came up to me thought Irons had done it."

"And ye're absolutely sure o' that? After thirty-one years, ye're *really* sure? Ye don't worry that yer memory's playin' tricks? Ye know we can embellish. Does it worry ye that yer story's grown bigger through the years?"

"But people *suppress* unusual experiences as well as confabulate them. Have you heard of the San Francisco 49ers?"

"You mean the football team?"

"Yes, the football team. They had a well-known player, a quarterback there named Brodie, who read *Golf in the Kingdom* and invited me to their training camp in '72 with the thought we might do a book together. My first day there, we're drinking beer with some of his teammates. A big beefy guy, a defensive lineman, starts to tell us about a voice he heard during a game, a voice in his ear telling him what the opposing team's next play would be. The other players started to laugh when he told us this, but he got real excited. He'd guessed the plays correctly, he said, because when they looked at the game films, they could tell he was making inspired adjustments before the ball was snapped.

"Well, he went on and on about his experience, how real it was, how he would never forget it. But the next day, he tells us that we had gotten him drunk. He'd told the story to impress us. The minute he said it, I said to myself, 'He's going to be ambivalent about me. He's going to struggle with this as long as I'm here at the camp.' And sure enough, he kept coming up to me, saying that maybe there *was* something to it, maybe that voice *was* real, maybe he did have a special power. But then he'd change his mind again, and say he'd been full of crap. He did this three or four times. And why? Because the experience was threatening to him. It was too strange, too far out, too disturbing. It didn't fit his self-image.

"Then finally one day he came up to me and said he'd just heard about MacArthur Lane, the great running back, who claimed to see the field at times from a place above his head. Maybe his voice was like Lane's ability. Maybe he had a special power too. Hannigan, he didn't confabulate. Getting the experience out of him was like doing a C-section on his mind. All of us have trouble accepting capacities that our teachers, friends, or families disallow. Have you heard of the 'strangeness curve'?"

When he said that he hadn't, I traced this diagram on a paper napkin:

"Given these axes, what's the shape of the curve?" I asked.

After studying the diagram for a few seconds, Hannigan shrugged, took my pen and traced a bell curve. "Aha!" I said, "but there's more. Starting here, at the left end of the horizontal axis, which represents completely ordinary experiences, there are few—if any—reports. For example, I'm not likely to tell a golf partner that the fairway grass looks green. As my experience gets stranger, though, I'm more likely to talk about it. If the air is suddenly radiant, in a way I've never seen, I might tell my partner about its beauty or uncanny light.

"But if my experience seems too strange for my friend, I will probably keep my mouth shut. Say, for example, that the air around him opens into a space within ordinary space, with some sort of movement in it, I might feel it's a risk to tell him. Or I might dismiss it, as reflected sunlight maybe, or the result of eyestrain, or the effects of hypoglycemia. And if the experience is even stranger, I might not report it to *myself*." Taking my pen, I extended the right-hand tail of the curve so that it looked like this:

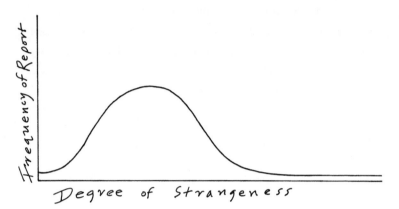

"Out here," I pointed to the tail I had added to Hannigan's curve, "there's neither reporting to others or to one's conscious self. This end of the strangeness curve represents experiences suppressed so completely that it takes drugs, hypnosis, or maybe someone's sympathetic ear to remember them. Say, for example, I see an apparition around my friend and realize subconsciously that it's interactional, that it's caused in part by *something in me!* That might be too much for my conscious mind. Too much to tell myself. Maybe that's what happened on the eighteenth hole in 1956."

For a moment, Hannigan studied my addition to the strangeness curve. I could tell he was partly persuaded. "In America," I said, "maybe ten million people play golf at least once a month. You know and I know that two or three out of ten want to tell you about some wonderful experience they've had on a golf course. That's two or three million people. Now, if just one out of every thousand of them experienced something mystical, something truly supernormal, that would be two or three thousand such experiences in the United States, and you can add to that for other countries. We all know these experiences happen. The question is 'How many?' and 'How many different kinds?' "

"Interesting," Hannigan murmured, signaling a waiter for our check. "But let's get out of here. I want to look at that picture again. It's bothering me more and more."

Five minutes later, we stood at his desk. "What the fuck!" he exclaimed, holding the photograph close to the light. "There *is* a shape. You're right! Has somebody fiddled with this?" He turned the picture over. "There must be something wrong. I've never noticed it. Is it a water stain?"

"It could be a developer's artifact."

"No. I've had it since '83. If it's an artifact, I would've seen it. But maybe it's a water stain. 'August 6 again, but 1950.' What did he mean? What did the old bugger mean? Is it the two-edged sword of God?" An angry expression crossed his face. "Murphy, let's drive out there. We'll have light until eleven and can get there in less than three hours. I want ye to see the place."

CHAPTER FOUR

WEARING A WINDBREAKER over his shirt and tie, Hannigan carried his photographs to my rented car. At his suggestion, we drove to my hotel where I picked up a jacket and running shoes, a toothbrush and razor, and my golf clubs and practice balls. I might want to hit shots on MacDuff's abandoned golf course, he said. By nine o' clock, with him at the wheel, we reached Glasgow and turned onto the A82, which would take us northwest past Loch Lomond.

It was a sun-filled evening, with a sky streaked by grey and lavender clouds, and I enjoyed the views as we drove in silence. To our right, long stretches of fir and pine covered the hills above the loch, which was silvery blue in the lingering light and framed by the rugged peaks of Ben Lomond. Rolling fields of green grass and barley, stone walls covered with rhododendrons, and villages of sturdy stone houses swept by as if on a rolling sea. Scotland was more beautiful than I'd ever seen it.

But the excitement of our search for Shivas Irons was stronger than my enjoyment of the countryside's beauty. As the Highlands unfolded before us, the possibilities of our adventure multiplied in my imagination. Between us, we probably had more leads to Shivas Irons and Seamus MacDuff than anyone else on the planet, and there was no telling where they would take us. As we turned onto the A83, which went west to Inveraray, I asked Hannigan to explain why he, a scientist, was so willing to sacrifice time and energy exploring such a bizarre and tenuous set of phenomena.

"Do I have to tell ye?" he answered. "Ye spent a day with Irons. Have ye met another like him? Ye know that he and MacDuff were tryin' for something big."

"But what was it?"

"That's the question, my friend. What was it? What were they really up to?"

For a moment, we didn't speak. "Whatever it was," he said at last, "might've started before they met. It could've started with the mother, in Africa. By all accounts, she wasn't yer ordinary lady."

According to the senior Ramsay, MacDuff claimed that his mother came from the Fulani, a largely nomadic people who are famous for their beauty and grace. She was born in the Sahel, not the Gold Coast as I'd remembered, at an oasis visited by Tuareg people and other North Africans influenced by Islam. Hannigan had found confirmation of this through margin notes in a book from Irons's library. To find her prospective mate, she had traveled across French West Africa, eventually meeting him in Nouakchott, the present-day capital of Mauritania, where he'd established a trading business. According to notes in Irons's books, she had seduced him into thinking they would produce a child who would "make a great discovery." Having seen this in a vision, she'd been led to the adventurous Scottish merchant through clairvoyant practices Hannigan guessed were derived from both Fulani and Sufi esoteric traditions.*

Surprised by his openness to these possibilities, I suggested that passionate imagery might affect one's genes. Through strongly held mental images, Catholic saints produced the wounds of Christ, and Muslim saints the battle wounds of Muhammad. Maybe through her religious practice she'd produced genetic stigmata that gave MacDuff extraordinary powers.

"It's possible," Hannigan conceded to my surprise. "He wasn't a normal fellow. Yes, he might've had altered genes. But they also gave him a great education. When I show you some of Irons's notes, I think ye'll agree she taught him Fulani and Tuareg shamanism and Sufi exercises. Then his father sent Scottish tutors to teach him French and English, and brought him to Oxford when he was seventeen or eighteen. Ye got some of that right in yer book. MacDuff was there from 1888 till 1893. His name's in the university records."

I asked if he'd discovered anything about the early life of Shivas Irons.

"Nothing," he said. "Checked the birth records for all of Scotland, but didn't find a trace. The names Shivas and Shives are rare, and hardly used at all as a first name. You say in your book that his mother was Irish. Named what—O'Faolin? Did Irons tell you where he was born?"

---

* One such margin note is written in the hand of Shivas Irons on a map of French West Africa. Its first sentence reads: "S.'s mother dowsing in Mbout, Kaedi, Aleg, St.-Louis, Dakar, Nouakchott." These cities and villages are located in present-day Mali, Senegal, and Mauritania, and were presumably the places in which MacDuff's mother searched clairvoyantly (or "dowsed") for the elder MacDuff.

The notation's second sentence reads: "Fulani-Sufi clairvoyance good for finding European bull. Fulani-MacDuff genes good for producing flesh of the gods." Hannigan guessed that "flesh of the gods" was a term from either Fulani shamanism or Sufi lore to signify the "luminous embodiment" that Seamus MacDuff and Shivas Irons were exploring.

"If he did, I don't remember."

"We'll have to check in Ireland, then. If he was born in England, it could be a long search."

"I'm surprised at your openness. Do any of your colleagues know what you're doing?"

"Just a few. Scientists are *supposed* to be open to the facts, but the Irons-MacDuff variety are not the kind most of 'em like. I'm an empiricist, I tell myself, but a *real* empiricist. A *radical* empiricist, if ye will. That's what yer William James called it. Ye want the facts? Well, here they are—*but all the facts.* Apparitions seen by more than one person. Telepathy. Altered states of mind. These are facts of human experience. Not theories or fantasies, Murphy, but *facts.* I'm open to all possibilities, my friend, though I don't believe anything on the face of it."

I asked what anomalous phenomena impressed him besides those related to Shivas Irons.

"There's a lot worth studyin' in Gurney, Myers, and the Sidgwicks." He recited a litany of those who founded the Society for Psychical Research. "And Mr. William James. All of his essays on the subject are good. There's a lot of material that's been looked at by smart people, a ton of it really if ye know where to look, and all sorts of leads to the things going on with Irons and MacDuff."

"Such as?"

"Such as that picture of MacDuff's first fairway, the one with the funny light. There's been a history of photographic anomalies. It goes way back, to the daguerreotype." He paused, as if troubled by the mysterious picture. "Tomorrow or the next day, when we've got some time, I'll show ye more things I've found."

"I've got to salute you. To most people, this thing would seem crazier than looking for the Loch Ness monster!"

"It's the pattern. The overall pattern, Murphy. And its persistence." He shook his head with both wonder and resignation.

"And the fact that it fits some of the crazier implications of my work. That's the strangest twist of all. It fits with some of my work in physics! Can ye beat it?"

After stopping for gas, we drove through Inveraray and turned onto the A819, which would take us to Cladich, the last village we would pass before reaching our destination. He drove more slowly now, and I felt myself nodding. The long day, and residues of drink, had overcome the excitement of our adventure.

As I started to doze, images appeared that seemed vaguely connected to Shivas Irons. Many of these were centered in sports—in the San Francisco Seals baseball team of the 1940s and their first baseman Ferris Fain, the first athlete who was numinous for me because an older cousin equated him reverently with Joe DiMaggio; and Joe Sprinz, the Seals' catcher, who'd lost his teeth trying to catch a ball dropped from a blimp during some sort of team promotion, an extrahuman figure because of that ball, invisible until it exploded from the sky through his catcher's mitt; and Frankie Albert, whom I watched with my parents and brother in 1940, passing to a sprinting Pete Kemetovic out of the T formation presented to the world that year by Clark Shaugnessy at Stanford University. Fain, Sprinz, Albert—why were their images so vivid now as we drove through the gathering dark?

And I saw a young boy—was it me?—catching a high fly ball, which at the apex of its flight was just a speck against the sky, evanescent, almost invisible before it fell . . . then accelerating and exploding like a bomb in his glove. These memories seemed part of a script. What were they pointing toward? What secrets did they hold?

Then I was walking down the eighteenth fairway at Burningbush with Shivas Irons. Was my adventure with him related to events of my early life? Suddenly I was cradled in my mother's arms, tossed in the air by my red-haired father, and lying on my back on the Big Sur coast staring at a twinkling North Star. How distant was the little light? Now it seemed inside me, a luminous speck on the curve of my eye, a shining presence in my brain. There were secrets in all this, a connection, something new and frightening. . . .

"God damn it ye bastard!" Hannigan woke me with a start. "Fly up yer own ass!" he shouted at a passing vehicle. "It won't be a pretty sight!"

Closing my eyes, I settled into the seat. An image of Shivas was forming, his rugged features softened by candlelight. We were sitting at a table side by side, as we had in 1956, at supper with his friends.

". . . paintin' a picture on the sky," he was saying in his resonant Scots inflection, "or shapin' space as our friend Adam Greene likes to put it, is not a trivial thing. If it's only imagination, it's imagination as the poet described it, not mere fantasy. It's imagination with *hands,* imagination that opens curtains between us and the life to come. All o' ye know it. Every man or woman who's played the game knows what I'm talkin' about. It's there in our memories, our talk, our old gowf literature. As some o' ye know, there's the story about that prodigious drive hit in the early nineteenth century. Hit with a featherie ball, across the icy fields o' winter, with a baffin' spoon on the eighteenth hole, right here, on the Links of Burnin'bush. 'Twas such a prodigious thing that a poet was hired to tell the world in the local paper.

"Accordin' to this printed account, which I have studied carefully, the ball stayed aloft long enough for many to see. An entire gallery o' the members, it seems, and a good part of the town was there to watch it. Seems the featherie was caught in some sort of upwind, hangin' aloft for several minutes. It was, said the poet, 'like a stately goose, black against the snow-white sky, movin' like it was migratin' to its original home.' The poet wrote that those who watched *knew* it would reach its ultimate destination. For ye see, my friends, that shot was a *double-eagle hole-in-one,* a one on our four-par eighteenth hole, and the memory of it still lives with us. Now, I would be willin' to bet that Angus Pattersone, the great champion who hit it, had a powerful mind to go with his mighty swing, a mind that could reach like a hand to place his featherie on that upwind.

"But we've all got stories to match it. All of us have painted on the golf sky, as Adam here will tell us. Curvin' the ball to the left or curvin' it right, shapin' it low or high before we hit it. In all this, our mind shapes space itself. And after we shape it, nature colors it, if not black against white, as it did for Pattersone, then white against blue on a summer day, or black against grey in the morning mist, or gold in the setting sun. Ye'll all admit it, will ye not?"

There was silence when he finished. His eloquence had quieted the group. But I was subdued for another reason. During his speech, a light had appeared around him, and had grown more dense until it formed a rosy, fleshlike envelope. Was it produced by hypnotic suggestion? Was he secretly shaping my perception? I squinted into a candle flame, making a golden halo around it, then looked again at him. If I could alter the aura's appearance deliberately, it had to be an illusion. At that very moment, with that very thought, the light around him disappeared. . . .

"Murphy, wake up," Hannigan said loudly, pulling off the road. "There it is. The wizard's laboratory in all its unholy splendor." Below us, half a mile away, MacDuff's stone house stood on a hill enclosed by a little valley. It was clearly discernible in the evening light, though the fields around it, upon which the golf course once stood, were covered with shadows. I got out of the car. To the north, a vast amphitheater stretched for miles toward distant peaks; while to the west, we could see Loch Awe, a long silver ribbon running through dark wooded ridges. The land rose steeply behind us toward an indigo sky. It was windless and warm for eleven o'clock. A dog's distant barking accentuated the deep evening stillness.

"Ye can see the whole place from here," said Hannigan. "The first fairway ran from his house through that field to its left. That's where the apparition would've been."

For a while, we watched the land grow dark. The stillness now was more pronounced. There was only a rustling of grass, and a presence in which the darkening landscape seemed suspended.

Hannigan got back in the car. "It's going to change!" he said with quiet excitement. "Let's go."

He drove down the hill, turned onto a narrow dirt road, and parked on a flat stretch of grass. "We're on the property now." He got out of the car. "It's about half a mile to the house."

"What about the clubs?" I asked. "Do you want me to hit some shots?"

"Are you crazy?"

"But you told me to bring them."

"For tomorrow. After the sun comes up."

"But this is a good time to hit some."

"Oh, Christ!" he swore. "Then bring one."

"Which one?"

"For Christ's sake! I don't care. Bring your sand wedge."

"No, I think I'll bring my driver." I reached over the seat to pull the club from my bag. "And balls? Won't we need balls?"

"Oh, fuck! If ye're going to hit some shots, ye've *got* to bring yer balls. So bring 'em!" Without waiting for me, he headed into the dark.

With my jacket, driver, and practice balls, I hurried to catch up. The house was a ghostly silhouette about a hundred yards away and twenty or thirty feet above us. I put on my jacket. The temperature had dropped, I guessed, from about seventy to fifty degrees Fahrenheit. "What's made it so cold?" I yelled.

But Hannigan seemed not to hear me. "Look!" He pointed up the hill. "Look!"

"Where?" I called back. "What are you looking at?"

"There." He gestured emphatically. "Right there, around the house!"

Enveloping the entire building like a second sky, there was a barely visible luminescence. But as I reached him, it faded and then vanished.

"Look!" he whispered. "Ye can't see any stars through it." To my astonishment, the aura reappeared, blocking starlight above and to both sides of the old stone house.

Hannigan started up the hill, and I followed slowly. Again the aura disappeared. Was it static electricity? Suddenly I was struck by the absurdity of my balls and driver. "Let me hit a shot from here," I said to break the tension. "Hannigan, you were right—I should have brought the sand wedge."

The aura was pulsing now. Was it an impression caused by my rapid heartbeat? When I stopped, the oscillations subsided. But the aura remained, clearly visible against the sky, a faint but definite envelope that extended some eight or ten feet beyond the sides and top of the old stone house.

A moment later, we stood at the top of the hill. Towering in the dark some twenty-five feet above us, the building was taller than I'd expected.

"It's stronger than I've ever seen it." Hannigan waved me on. "Hurry! Something's going to happen." I jogged after him, past an oak tree and a shed, to find the vista depicted in the photograph with MacDuff's mysterious inscription. The abandoned first fairway stretched through the deepening shadows between rises that converged at a two-tiered elevation some three hundred yards away.

"Look!" I pointed at the house. "The aura's gone!"

"Quiet down," Hannigan said sternly. "Something's going to happen."

Though the temperature had dropped, there was little wind. In the distance, a dog was barking. Suddenly I remembered Shivas Irons, sitting as he had after our rousing night, eyes half-closed, lost in ecstasy. I tried to picture him more clearly. . . .

"Murphy!" Hannigan whispered. "Look! See what's happening!"

The building's luminescence was expanding outward, reaching down the stretch of land that once had served as MacDuff's first fairway. In the illumination it provided, I could see the distant rise upon which the first green had stood.

"Christ!" said Hannigan. "It's alive. The goddamned thing's alive!" The aura was condensing to a pearly light, and he walked toward it, swearing and shaking his fist defiantly. But I was immobilized. As if it had arms, the light was reaching toward me and seemed about to lift me up. Transfixed, I felt myself tightening.

Then it was gone. Suddenly the land, the air, the buildings were dark. "Murphy!" cried Hannigan, who stood about twenty yards from me. "Come here! It left marks on the ground." I sat on the ground. "Come here!" he yelled insistently. "You've got to see this!"

Cold sweat had risen on my forehead. My arms felt weak. My knees were shaking. Lying supine in the grass, I felt the tenuous pleasure that comes after you've come close to fainting. The stars seemed brighter, more numerous, and closer now.

"Murphy!" Hannigan shouted. "Come here! There's another mark." But I couldn't summon the strength to stand. A profound silence filled the land. Everything was effervescent. The afterglow of shock was turning to a deep and sensuous pleasure.

"Did you hear it?" Hannigan came jogging toward me. "Did you hear the sound it made?"

"What sound?" I asked weakly. "I didn't hear a thing."

"That rushing sound. You must've heard it. Are you all right?" He stood above me, his jacket unbuttoned, his glasses reflecting the starlight. Again I was struck by his uncanny resemblance to James Joyce. "I'm okay," I whispered. "I'm okay. But let me rest. I don't have your energy."

"When you get up, look at the marks over there by the door. I'm going to see what else it did." He disappeared, and I lay for a moment in silence. Though the hairs on my hands stood erect from the cold, heat was spreading through me. Impulsively, I stood and took off my windbreaker.

The air and the land seemed to sparkle. Everything was freer now, more elastic, and filled with new life. Again I thought of Shivas Irons. . . .

H e'd been sitting erect in his armchair, eyes half-closed, with an expression that suggested both serenity and ecstatic arousal. His cataleptic body seemed to provide a stabilizing frame for a potentially shattering flight of his soul. This impression was reinforced by the energy flowing through him, which was also flowing into me. The presence I'd felt in our golf round was spreading now throughout the room, like fuel for an inward journey. His exquisitely balanced physique, the energetic structure suffusing it, and his consciousness were aligned for ecstatic release.

Then a subtle presence wrapped around me. It stretched the

muscles of my spine, prompting me to sit erect. It gently brought my shoulders back so that my chest expanded. Step by step, an invisible force had reached from him to me, opening a vista, preparing me for a voyage . . .

T he state I'd experienced three decades before was close to what I was feeling now. There were uncanny similarities between the two moments.

And at the heart of the stillness I felt, there was a commanding impulse. A subtle presence—a force—was impelling me to swing my arms. To turn my shoulders. To pivot. As if guided by invisible arms, I swung an imaginary golf club. The pattern and rhythm of the swing came from somewhere or something beyond my normal volition.

"What are you doing?" cried Hannigan, striding toward me from the house. "Damn it, I feel energetic!" He lowered himself to the ground and started doing one-armed push-ups. "I've never done more than five. But look—seven, eight, nine, ten." He collapsed in mid-sentence and lay gasping for breath. Turning away from him, I picked up my driver and swung it. My muscles and joints had new elasticity, which allowed me to swing with extraordinary arc. The driver felt weightless. The swing was happening by itself.

Stretching away into the night, MacDuff's first fairway beckoned. I teed a ball, aimed toward the rise, and swung with a power that amazed me. The ball sailed high against the starlit sky, then vanished in the darkness. "Hannigan!" I cried. "It went about three hundred yards!"

But he didn't hear me. To my astonishment, he was again doing one-armed push-ups.

The distant rise still beckoned. I hit a second ball, and watched it sail beyond the first. For a long moment, it hung in the sky like a planet or satellite. "Holy Jesus, it'll never come down!" said Hannigan, who lay some ten feet from me. "If I hadn't seen it, I wouldn't believe it. Hit another!"

I hit a third ball—and a rock that caused sparks to fly in all directions.

"Try it tomorrow," said Hannigan. "We'll have all day." A wind had arisen, and clouds had appeared above us. "Let's go!" He jumped to his feet, and gestured for me to follow. "Maybe a storm's coming up."

I put on my windbreaker and followed him. Near the house he stopped, searched the ground for a moment, then pointed to a stretch of scorched grass.

"But it could've been there already," I said. "How do you know it just happened?"

"You're right." He nodded. "It could've been there before we got here." The burnt grass formed an oval about five feet long and three feet wide. Conceivably, it could have been caused by someone who'd dropped a cigarette.

We started toward the car. "Some people would think a UFO just landed," I said.

"Tonight they would've," he answered quietly. "People who worked here thought they saw just about everything. UFOs, brownies, fairies, ghosts, even demonic possessions. Everyone had such different stories, there's never been agreement. But let's go! There's a place down the road to spend the night."

CHAPTER FIVE

T HE WINDOW SHADES of the little room were drawn
so that I could sleep past first light, which on a June day
in the Western Highlands comes between three and three-thirty.
But sleep did not come easily. At ten- or fifteen-minute intervals, I woke to images of the presence that enveloped Mac-
Duff's estate. Twice I sat up, sensing that it was entering the
room and reaching to embrace me. But this tension was not entirely uncomfortable. Eventually it produced a state that some
call lucid dreaming. As if in a theater of the mind, viewing images that were vividly three-dimensional, I relived my day with
Shivas Irons. . . .

W e were walking down a narrow street after our golf
round. "Standing by the eighteenth green," I asked,
"what did you mean when you said that the body is the tenderest part of the soul?"

"That this flesh is our most fragile part," said Shivas softly.
"That it's passing every moment. How did the Greek philosophers say it? That the body is the densest part of the soul? It's

also the tenderest part, the part of us soonest to go. *'Tis the part of our soul that's closest to death."*

. . . and then by a fire in the dark ravine that borders the thirteenth hole. "Swing with the inner body." He helped me make an arc with my arms to hit an imaginary golf ball. "Swing from the part that's full o' new life, the part of ye nearest the light of yer soul. That part's smarter than this flesh. Has more power, rhythm, music." He leaned closer, and I could see my wavering reflection in each of his large blue eyes. "It'll serve ye longer than these arms," he whispered. "It's played this game a long, long time. It was there before ye were born."

S itting up with a start, I saw that it was eight o'clock, the hour we'd agreed to have breakfast. A few minutes later, I found Hannigan reading a paper in the inn's little dining room. Bacon, eggs, scones, and jam were generously spread in front of him. "We said seven," he said brusquely.

"I thought we said eight."

"Seven," he said from behind his paper. "The lady's bringin' coffee. Or do ye want tea? She'll give ye haggis if ye'd like." A merry-looking woman who appeared to be in her fifties poured us both coffee, and asked in a broad Scots burr what I wanted to eat. "The same as I," said Hannigan. "Not the haggis, or spotted dick."

"Not the haggis!" she said. "What a shame." With a slightly sinister laugh, she went back to the kitchen.

Through latticed windows, I could see a thick stand of silver birch and the silver blue water of the loch. We were the only people in the room. Hannigan asked how I'd slept, his Scottish burr more pronounced than it had been the day before. Did it grow stronger as he got farther from Edinburgh? I told him I'd dreamt about Shivas Irons.

Before he could answer, the lady returned with a plate of scones. "Where ye headed?" she asked. "Comin' in so late, were ye lost?" Without thinking, I said we were looking for a nearby distillery. Did she know its whereabouts? "D'ye mean the Ramsay place?" she asked.

Lowering his paper, Hannigan shot me a look warning me to be careful. "That's the one!" I pretended ignorance. "Is it still operating?"

"Been shut for years," she said. "There's nothin' left but some sheds and a deserted house." A look of suspicion came into her face. "But ye must have some very old bottles. Are ye members o' the Ramsay clan?"

After glancing at Hannigan, I said that we weren't Ramsays. It was just the whiskey we wanted. "Well, there's no distillery left," she said. "And I don't think ye'd want to go there. Some people 'round heer think the place's haunted."

"Haunted?" I pretended surprise. "What makes them think so?"

Holding a coffeepot in one hand and an empty plate in the other, she looked around the room to make sure it was empty. "There's no consistent story," she whispered. "Some say banshees, some say ghosts, some don't know wha' to call it. There's a Mr. Haig who lives down the road. Says his body was changed by the place. Used to run sheep there after the distillery was closed, and says he's not been the same since."

"His body changed?" I glanced again at Hannigan, who pretended to be absorbed in his paper. "How was it changed?"

"Ye'd have to ask him." She leaned closer to me. "He told me once that none of his parts work the same anymore. None of 'em! Says he was taken apart by the place, and reassembled badly."

"Is he in pain?"

"I don't know about that. Said he felt *strange* in his body.

That he was 'out o' joint,' that one part wasna' connected the same to this part, or that part to the other part. But I really don't know. Ye'd have to ask 'im."

"Some coffee, please," Hannigan interrupted, glancing sternly at me. "Murphy, do ye want another?" It was clear that he wanted me to end the conversation.

Motioning the lady to refill my cup, I said that we wouldn't go looking for ghosts. When she left, I asked why he'd wanted me to stop. "We want the place to ourselves," he whispered. "It's a village out here. Everyone talks to everyone else. Let's not get them thinkin' we're up to something."

"But what about the man she was talking about? Shouldn't we talk to him?"

"I have. Three years ago. He couldn't tell me anything more than she just did."

"But I've been talking to people for years about this sort of thing. If you ask the right questions, it's amazing what they remember. I know what to ask."

"Murphy, I talked to 'im. Ye're not goin' to learn a thing if ye do. Remember"—he tapped his chest, "I've been following this for more than five years. Believe me, I know what I'm doin'!"

We ate in silence for a moment, until the lady came bursting into the room with a plate of eggs and bacon. "I just talked to Mr. Lauder, the owner," she said exuberantly. "He has some bottles o' Ramsay's whiskey, can ye believe it, and is willin' to sell ye one!"

"Well, thank you," I said. "What a favor!"

"Damn it!" Hannigan whispered when she'd left. "Now we're in for it. In a minute, they'll want to go out there with us."

A broad-shouldered man came into the room and proudly

placed a bottle between us. "So yer lookin' for Ramsay's whis-key," he boomed. "Have a look at this!"

"But you shouldn't," I said. "That bottle's too precious to sell."

"It's *different,* not precious." He winked. "It'll kick ye to the moon, and there's no guarantee ye'll get back. Lauder's ma nemme, what's yers?"

"Murphy." I shook his hand. "That's Hannigan."

"Ye're an American," he said. "Where's he from?"

"Edinburgh," Hannigan said coolly.

"But ye look familiar. Have I seen ye heer before?"

Hannigan said that he'd stopped for dinner once.

"Well, good to have ye back," said Lauder. "But heer, I want ye to have this bottle. Consider it a gift o' the house!"

"No," I protested. "Let me pay."

"Not on yer life. I've got more, and ye can't drink much at once. It's not the best whiskey, mind ye. Too much o' it does funny things to the brain. 'Tis the source o' the rumors about Ramsay's distillery, I think. But take it to remember us. I'm glad to let ye have it."

Hannigan disappeared again behind his paper, but Lauder didn't seem to mind. "Well, thank you," I said. "When I drink it, I'll think of this wonderful place."

"If ye don't drink too much." Lauder winced. Then a smile appeared on his broad ruddy face. "I suppose ye know this, havin' drunk it before; but with more than two shots, ye'll forget yer name, and the difference 'tween up and down. Once, after three shots, I drove to Oban and took the ferry to Mull—for no reason at all—and thought I'd gone to heaven." He was a robust presence, with an energy that seemed younger than his weathered features. I could see that he wouldn't leave easily.

But I couldn't resist another question. "What gives it such a kick?" I asked. "What did they put in it?"

"Old man Ramsay never knew. Some thought it was barley fungus; others, the water they used. There's an old lady down the road thinks it's mushrooms! But ye want to know my theory?" He glanced around the room. "I think it was the place, the land out there, the air itself. It's not a normal piece o' ground."

"Oh, my God!" Hannigan put down his paper. "I'm sorry, Lauder, but I just remembered. We need to make an important call. Is there a phone we can use?"

"Indeed there is," said Lauder proudly. "In tha' cubicle by the door." Hannigan stood, gesturing for me to follow. Dismayed, I went with him and waited while he called his own number in Edinburgh and feigned a brief conversation.

"What's going on?" I asked.

"Murphy, I warned ye. What d'ye want to do now? Take Lauder with us to MacDuff's? And the waitress, too? And Mr. Haig? Why, let's round up the entire neighborhood. Maybe we can have a picnic. Or a séance. Or a seminar on the teachings of Shivas Irons." Shaking his head disgustedly, he went back to the table, and we finished our breakfast in silence.

A half hour later, we drove toward the abandoned distillery. It was evident that Hannigan was bracing himself for whatever would happen next, and I felt myself tightening as well, with both excitement and a slight foreboding. But before we reached the entrance to the property, Hannigan pulled off the road. "Take a look," he said. "Last night you couldn't see it." We got out of the car and looked in all directions. I wasn't prepared for the vista that confronted us.

To our west, the sunlit waters of Loch Awe snaked through

densely wooded hills, and to the north and northeast a vast amphitheater stretched for twenty miles or more to the Grampian
Mountains. From Ben Cruachan on our left, which rose nearly
four thousand feet against a cloudless sky, to Ben Lui on our
right, we could see down Glen Orchy and Glen Lochy for dis-
tances that were impossible to calculate. It is one of the world's
most commanding views, marked by green and golden fields,
grey-lavender walls of mountain rock, and mist-filled valleys
that trail off between distant peaks.

"Ye can see why MacDuff came to live in these hills," Hannigan said with irony and wonder. "The views must've helped
his morale when his experiments faltered." I pictured the old
man standing here. This enormous vista was an appropriate
backdrop for his work. It suggested the immensity, beauty, and
loneliness of his aspiration.

Ten minutes later, we parked as we had the night before in
a field below the old house. The little valley in which the abandoned golf course sat had a secluded feeling. Its hills and fields
were punctuated by oaks and sycamores, and mostly covered
with high yellow grass. Two hawks circled overhead. Except for
the distant bleating of sheep, the place was deeply silent.

But within the land's soft and sunny embrace, there was a
brooding presence. Would it congeal into the luminescence of
the night before, or make itself known in some other way?
"Take your clubs." Hannigan lifted a lunch box and his portfolio from the car. "Let's haul everything up there."

Slowly we hiked toward the house. In the morning sunlight,
signs of its decrepitude were more pronounced than they'd been
in the dark. Its shutters sagged. Grass covered its walks. Its
grey- and sandstone-colored walls were scarred by the elements.
Some forty feet from it, we found the stretch of bare ground
from which I'd hit drives that night. Hannigan put his lunch
box and photographs on the ground. "This whole stretch was

planted with fescue," he said quietly, as if someone might be listening. "Irons must've practiced his drives here. The field out there is the longest flat stretch on the course." Standing on the approximate location of MacDuff's first tee, we could see the distant rise upon which the first green had stood. It occurred to me that I could reach it with a single shot.

I pulled my driver from the bag, removed my sweater and, with abbreviated take-aways, took some practice swings. There was a fluidity in my turn, a sensitivity in my hands, and a stretch in my arms I'd rarely felt before. The club seemed to move by itself.

Yes, I could reach the distant rise. Though it seemed about 350 yards away, there was bare ground in front of it that would give my ball extra roll. I teed up, waited for my energy to gather, then swung with a force that seemed to come from beyond me. The ball sailed high toward the morning sun. For a moment, it seemed suspended. "Hannigan!" I cried. "It doesn't want to come down!"

Was it held aloft by a wind from which we were shielded? Was I suffering an optical illusion? The ball seemed caught in some sort of updraft as it grew smaller and smaller. Then it fell to the ground with an enormous bounce, and a second, and rolled to the rise. Had it really gone 350 yards? Perhaps I'd mistaken the distance. "Hannigan," I said. "It reached the green. I'm going to pace it off."

"Yer gonna' do what?" He turned to look in my direction.

"Measure the length of the hole."

"Why?"

"Because I just reached MacDuff's old green. It must be 350 yards from here. I can't believe I did it."

"Ye only think ye reached it." He shielded his eyes to look down the field. "That elevation yer talkin' about is 400 yards from here."

"Then I'm going to pace it off."

"Ye don't need to. I've done it. I tell ye, it's 400 yards."

"But I can't hit a ball 400 yards!"

"I know that. That's why I'm sayin' ye didn't reach it!"

"But I did!"

"But ye didn't!"

"But I saw it!"

"Well, go ahead." With a dismissive wave, he turned to look at his photographs, now spread on a blanket around him.

But as I started down the hill, he shouted, "Murphy! Why don't ye hit some more? Ye're not going to learn what's goin' on here flappin' up and down these fields like a wild goose. Let the place into yer swing."

"It *was* in my swing," I shouted back. "I want to see how well it worked."

Careful to keep my stride constant, I waded into waist-high grass. By the time I reached bare ground, pieces of straw had gotten under my pants and into my underwear. My excitement was growing, however. The field was longer than I'd thought. It stretched for about 250 yards to the edge of the grass, and for another 150 across bare ground to the rise.

But my ball was nowhere in sight. After searching for several minutes, I saw that Hannigan was watching me with binoculars. His scrutiny was irritating, compounding the discomfort of straw in my pants and sweat running down my shoulders. Cursing loudly, I looked for declivities in which the ball might be hidden. Had it gone down a rabbit hole? Then I heard Hannigan shouting. He was headed toward me with his portfolio, waving as he came through the grass.

"No luck?" he asked as he approached. "Why don't ye look on the upper rise? Maybe ye hit it there." Looking away from him, I tried to gather myself. More than anything else, I wanted to remove the straw from my pants. It was getting warmer, and there were no trees nearby to provide relief from the sun. Why hadn't I brought a hat?

Hannigan held up a photograph. "Murphy, look at this. From here ye can get another fix on what the boys were doin'. Have ye felt it yet? The place is full of fuckin' illusions."

But I didn't respond.

"Murphy, are ye upset about losin' that ball?"

"I'm going back to my bag. I left my golf cap there."

"But ye seem upset. Was it a brand-new ball?"

"No," I said. "It's getting too hot. I'm going to get a hat." A few minutes later, itching from head to foot, I reached the hill. Taking off my pants and underwear, I looked toward Hannigan. To my astonishment, he was watching me again with binoculars. I shook out my clothes angrily, redressed, and sat in a shady place beside the house.

Hot air rising from the ground made the fields waver. Suddenly I felt light-headed. Wiping sweat from my face, I leaned against the building. Shivas Irons and Seamus MacDuff seemed part of a distant mirage, as evanescent as the wavering horizon. . . .

Then I heard a distant shout. Hannigan was pointing in my direction. When I didn't respond, his gestures grew more emphatic. Putting on my cap, I walked to the edge of the hill. He was pointing frantically now, and I turned to look around me. But the place was serene and deeply silent. Nothing was out of order. "What's wrong?" I shouted.

What caused his urgency? Was there something invisible to me that he could see from where he was standing? Alarmed, I circled the buildings—but found nothing to warrant such excitement. When I got back to the front of the house, he was jogging up the hill. "Did ye see him?" he gasped.

"I didn't see anything."

"Ye didn't? For Christ's sake, someone was there by your bag! Movin' all around it."

"I tell you, I didn't see anything."

"This fuckin' place!" he exclaimed. "Someone was standin' there! Came up to yer bag while ye were sittin'. He disappeared when I got yer attention."

"What did he look like?"

"I couldn't tell exactly. The air was waverin', or maybe my glasses misted up." He put down his portfolio. "And here's yer ball. Ye hit it 450 yards."

"Where was it?" I was astonished.

"On the upper rise, where I told ye to look. It must've taken one hell of a bounce." He shook his head in dismay. "So ye didn't see anyone? I yelled 'cause I thought ye didn't see 'im."

"Look at the horizon," I said. "See how the hills waver in the heat? It was a mirage."

"A mirage? Don't tell me that! It was a real thing. With arms and legs and a head. It looked at me. It looked at you. It was standin' there by yer golf bag. For Christ's sake! It picked up one o' yer clubs!"

"You had to be seeing things," I protested. But then a chill passed through me. Maybe he'd seen an apparition which had been invisible to me.

His hands shaking, he wiped his lips and forehead. "Here," he said weakly, sitting down by the house. "Let's stay in the shade. I feel a little woozy."

A breeze was blowing now, and a few clouds had appeared above us. "It's a bitch," he whispered. "Ye've got to stay calm out here; otherwise, the place'll drive ye out. That's what happened to the poor bastards who worked here."

I thought of Shivas Irons. What would he do now? Focusing on the ground in front of me, I let the quiet deepen. Something began to straighten my spine, relax my jaw, pull my shoulders back. A superior intelligence knew how to sit, how to stand, how to relate to this mysterious place. It was guiding me now toward a deeper silence.

An immense presence held the land, and as if from small concealed springs, there was a subtle streaming. It rose in my muscles that pressed on the ground. It was there in the space beneath my sternum, where my heart was beating. It coursed like tiny bubbles through my arms and legs. Were new elements forming in me?

And then there was a subtle but clear command. Something wanted me to bring this condition into physical movement. Not quite a voice, nor an image, nor a thought, its intention was unmistakable. It wanted me to feel this new effervescence as I moved to the front of the hill.

I walked to my golf bag, took my seven-iron from it, and emptied my practice balls onto the ground. Eyeing a clump of grass about thirty feet from me, I practiced my chipping stroke. It was pleasurable to swing the iron blade, satisfying to feel it graze the ground and kick up tiny swirls of grass. I kept swinging for sheer enjoyment.

But the presence that was guiding me had a plan that required a further surrender. Following its lead, I chipped toward the target I'd chosen and sensed that the ball was moving inside me. The ground's grainy texture, its dryness, its subtle contours were immediately present. When the ball came to rest, it seemed as close as it had when it lay at my feet. It was nicked and needed washing, and I remembered using it a year before at the Oceanside course of the Olympic Club in San Francisco.

Looking toward Hannigan, who leaned with his eyes closed against the house, I realized that I would have to make a decision. To continue in this state, to enjoy this mysterious guidance, I would have to make a quiet stand against the thoughts that were rising in me. An image had appeared of my topping the ball, another of my chipping short.

Aligning myself with the clump of grass, I took more practice strokes. "Wait 'em out." I heard the voice of Shivas Irons. "Be the one behind yer thoughts; then the worst'll pass." He had said it in Burningbush, as my mind filled with subversive images. The two moments, thirty-one years apart, mirrored one another. Then—as now—there had been a self-renewing presence in which thoughts of failure could dissolve. Through all the intervening years, that regenerative clarity was waiting to be rediscovered.

Addressing another ball, I hit it toward the clump of grass, then watched it bounce across the ground as if it were inside me. The stubble-covered dirt, its break to the left, a rabbit hole were vividly present. "Aye one fiedle 'afore ye swung," I could hear Shivas Irons whispering. One field before the game was invented. One abiding presence, before and during and after each shot. In this unbroken awareness, distant objects were as close as my skin.

Pausing to regather myself, I chose another target. Each time I let an image go, I felt a wave of pleasure. There was joy in this simple repetition, and a new stability. Come back to the one beyond your thoughts, Shivas had described the way he practiced. There's more and more pleasure in it. The ever-present awareness he wanted to show me held a secret delight. To move with its guidance made something as trivial as chipping golf balls a wondrous, self-renewing activity.

"So Murphy," said Hannigan as I hit my last ball. "Ye got nothin' better to do?"

He was standing behind me, holding a hand in front of one eye. "I've banished the ghost," he said proudly. "Back there on

the rise, my eyes went out of focus. I'm turnin' ye into two figures now, holdin' my hand like this."

His hands still trembled. Perspiration covered his face.
"How're you feeling?" I asked.

"Couldn't be better." He folded his arms across his chest and
assumed a manly stance. "But what're ye doin' there? Waitin'
for the rabbits to swallow yer balls?"

"Practicing true gravity," I answered. "It works with chip
shots as well as drives."

"And ye don't get bored?"

"No," I said. "There's an extraordinary pleasure in it. Why
don't you hit a few?"

"Never have, never want to, never will." A small sardonic
smile pulled at the corners of his mouth. "Come have a beer
when ye're finished."

He carried his lunch box and photographs to a shady place
near the house. Though he was forty feet from me now, I
could feel his anger brewing. It was evident that he was still
upset at his vulnerability.

"I'm wonderin', just wonderin' if this trip's a mistake," he
said as I joined him. "Will ye tell me what ye were doin' hittin'
balls into rabbit holes. And this picture. Look! This phantom o'
yers is nothin' but discoloration. Ye can barely see it now." He
held up the photograph with MacDuff's mysterious inscription.
The apparitional figure was barely discernible.

Crossing the tee, I compared the photograph to the vista it
depicted. About two-thirds of the way down the abandoned
fairway, a patch of bare ground reflected sunlight more brightly
than the field around it. In the picture, the faint oval shape was
located in about the same place. I read the inscription on its
back: "Sunrise at noon. August 6 again, but 1950." Almost certainly, the picture had been taken near midday. Though the

field had been covered with fairway grass, it might have reflected sunlight as it did now.

"Ye see what I mean?" Hannigan said loudly. "It was an artifact!"

"It could be. But not this place. Something's happening here. *For Christ's sake, I just hit a drive 450 yards.*"

"Ye bounced it," he said dismissively. "It's cement out there beyond the grass, and that's where yer fuckin' ball landed. Yer drive doesn't prove a thing."

"What about last night?" I handed him the photograph. "Don't tell me we didn't see that light."

"It might've been static electricity. I've got a physicist friend who studies this stuff. I'm going to bring 'im here." He opened the lunch box. "But let's eat. And have some beer. It'll bring us back to our senses." He opened two bottles and handed one to me.

The beer had a sharp, refreshing bite, and without thinking I drank half a bottle. He took two sandwiches from the box. "Self-hypnosis, Murphy," he said. "Ye ever tried it?"

"Several times."

"Well, that's what we're doin' now. Have ye had that thought?" The tremor in his hands had disappeared, and I noticed that he wasn't sweating. "What d'ye think?" he insisted. "Could we be doin' some sort of self-hypnosis? Maybe we've formed a little cult. A cult with just two members in it!"

The beer, and the pleasure left over from hitting balls, had put me in an expansive mood. "We've got to sort it out," I said. "Some of it's real. Some of it might be our imagining. It's probably a little of both."

"Well that's a sensible answer. My university colleagues would certainly approve. But Jesus! How I worked myself up, thinkin' someone took a club from yer golf bag. Can ye believe I did that?"

For a while, we ate in silence. The afterglow of my experience stroking chip shots, the sunshine, the beer, and the view were producing a marvelous dilation. Hannigan could wrestle with his doubts without my interference. "Murphy," he said, "there's another beer on ice in the bucket. I hope ye don't mind if I nap." Removing his glasses, he lay on his back, and a moment later appeared to doze.

Putting my empty beer bottle and what remained of a sandwich into the box, I sat looking at the rolling hills and the distant peaks that rose beyond them. The brown-and-yellow vista reminded me of California's Salinas Valley, where I'd grown up, and I remembered a day forty years before, watching a golf exhibition at our local course. Jimmy Demaret, dressed in a white tam-o'-shanter, red shirt, and bright yellow pants, was hitting irons with magical precision—one with a draw around a tree, another low with a gentle fade into our narrow sixth green. I could smell the newly mown grass, hear the bantering of friends, feel the excitement of watching Demaret shoot a 66. This hill was like our club's first tee. These fields, dotted with oak trees and dried by the summer sun, could be the ones I'd known as a boy. Everything now was familiar. The yellow grass, the house, the few cumulus clouds were just as they should be. Why argue with Hannigan? He could be right. The light we'd seen the night before could well have been caused by static electricity. My state of mind hitting chip shots was available to everyone, anywhere, any time of the day or night. There was nothing special about it.

Suddenly Shivas Irons seemed an impossibly distant figure. I'd searched for him in 1970, and might search for the rest of my life. Yes, Hannigan could be right. It was conceivable that we were making up evidence to support our little cult. Clouds were moving across the sky. One had a scowling face, another a nose growing longer. Was our search for Irons filled with lies?

The thought was liberating. The pleasures of beer and this lovely view provided relief from invisible presences that threatened to make overwhelming demands upon me.

Hannigan was breathing heavily now. Evidently he had fallen asleep. Not wanting to disturb him, I walked to the northern edge of the hill and sat on a little ledge that was protected from the sun. Below me, the land sloped steeply for about a hundred yards, to a crevasse surrounded by bushes. This was the striking three-par hole in Hannigan's photographs. I was sitting on what remained of the tee, and remnants of the green were hidden in the declivity far below me. Shivas Irons must have hit balls from here toward the invisible target, practicing clairvoyance in the service of golf.

Impelled by sudden curiosity, I descended the grassy incline and climbed into the crevasse. It was about fifteen feet deep and some thirty feet from front to back. To clear the foliage in front of it, a ball would have to be hit with an extremely high trajectory. Could I do it? I climbed the hill, went to my golf bag, and took out my seven- and eight-irons. Hannigan didn't stir. He lay on his side facing the house and didn't move as I walked past him.

Part of the ledge was covered with stubble from which I could get good loft on my shots. Pushing back the visor of my golf cap, I chose a ball, and looked again toward the crevasse. A shadow was moving across it, but the field beyond was brilliant gold. Standing back to admire this contrast of light and dark, I felt a breeze blowing gently toward me. It would add lift to my shot, and spin if I wanted a draw. I hit the ball cleanly from the springy turf and watched it hover for several seconds against a passing cloud. Like a bird of prey, it seemed to hesitate, then dropped what seemed an enormous distance into the steep declivity.

After teeing another ball, I checked myself. The shot I'd

just hit demanded time for enjoyment. Mindlessly hitting again so soon almost seemed an act of violence. Standing back, I savored the feeling of it. Something in me had stretched with the ball and fallen precipitously into the glen. Was it merely my imagination, or some part of that subtle flesh Shivas Irons had talked about? At Burningbush, he'd said to feel each shot in its entirety. Such empathy furthered learning, and to a slight but sometimes important degree won the ball's allegiance.

The next shot sailed even higher than the first, a little right of my line to the target—then, to my astonishment, seemed to stop. After hovering at the lower edge of a huge, slow-moving cloud, it moved to the left, stopped again, then fell as if aimed like a guided missile into the narrow crevasse. Though it had been hit with a draw, and the wind had increased its movement, it appeared to have broken the laws of physics.

The wind was blowing harder now, and the bottom edge of the cloud was turning gold. Something uncanny had steered the ball. Was it my own mental power, the "imagination with hands" that Shivas had described, painting on the golf sky? Or was it the power of this place, the presence I'd felt hitting chip shots and drives on the abandoned first tee?

Addressing another ball, I waited for inspiration. But a wave of excitement passed through me, and the shot sailed over the glen. It was time for patience now. My honeymoon with higher powers would have to give way to faithful practice and a discriminating surrender to whatever guidance was given me. Taking time to register flaws in my swing mechanics, I hit another twenty balls toward the invisible green. Some fell short, a few went past, and three fell into the little canyon. During this exercise, which lasted for nearly fifteen minutes, I felt a growing calm and pleasure. Mental activity seemed more distant as a larger, more stable awareness dissolved my attachment to passing thoughts. The state reminded me of lucid dreaming. There was a satisfaction in it that didn't depend upon the results of particular shots.

But this wasn't a passive enjoyment. Hitting shots from this little ledge without concern for immediate results, I was becoming more intimate with the planes, contours, and eccentric features of the land between me and the target. They were working their way to my subconscious mind, causing me to make tacit adjustments of my stance and swing. Gradually I moved my alignment left, as my impulse to hit a draw gave way to a sense that a fade increased my chance of success. My first two shots had been inspired, but they hadn't come from knowledge or mastery.

For despite its seeming simplicity, the hole presented a deadly illusion. Because the slope below me tilted down to the right, it invited a counterbalancing draw rather than a fade that might sail wide of the target. But the crevasse was angled in such a way that it afforded more room for error to a shot coming in from the left. Golf architects create such problems to add interest and challenge to the game.* Conceivably, MacDuff had designed his course to reveal the fallibility of untrained awareness. Shivas Irons might have practiced here in part to overcome misperceptions of greens and fairways. What other tests did this strange little course provide?

Inspired by these thoughts, I counted the remaining balls. There were twenty-three left, enough with which to get a good feel for fading shots to the target. With rising anticipation, I imagined a line to the crevasse that gently curved right to its very center. But the ball came off the heel of the club, sending a shock from my hands to my shoulders. Such a mishap is

---

* See Robert Trent Jones, Jr., *Golf by Design,* especially Chapter 8, "Illusions and Wind."

called a "shank." It is the worst way to miss a shot, one of the ugliest things in sport, and the hardest miscue to forget. A shank stays rooted for hours or days in the cellars of a golfer's memory.

But the feeling would dissolve in my newfound detachment. Regathering myself, I teed another ball, took careful aim, and paused for inspiration. After taking two deep breaths, I swung with a slower tempo—but shanked it. "Damn it!" I yelled. "This fucking game!"

"God, that must hurt!" said Hannigan. "Ye look like ye sat on a spike!"

Looking steadily at the horizon, I tried to compose myself. "There's nothing more serious than a child at play," I said without turning.

"That's good," he said. "Did ye make it up?"

"Yes." I teed another ball.

"No ye didn't. Nietzsche did."

Several options presented themselves. I could disregard him, then calmly hit a magnificent shot. I could give him the exact Nietzsche quote. Or I could decapitate him with my seven-iron. Choosing the first alternative, I teed another ball, imagined its path to the target—and shanked it.

Hannigan started laughing. "Ye look to be in pain," he said with unconcealed glee. "Why don't ye take a break."

"Do you want to hit one?" I managed a show of good humor. "Here, come and try."

"Hyperspace theory's simpler," he said. "You do the research. I'll do the theorizin'."

Deciding a break was needed, I picked up the ball bag and walked down the hill to retrieve my balls. The little glen was refreshingly damp, a good place to assimilate lessons learned in the wind and sun above. Finding a seat on a fallen tree, I pictured Shivas Irons. Conceivably, he'd practiced on every part of this course, absorbing its features one by one, making its various planes and contours part of his inner body. "In golf, ye can see yer way through more illusions and embrace more archetypes than anyone knows," he'd joked. "More than philosophy, more than war, almost as many as makin' love." He could have sat in this very place, opening himself to the changes that come from the disciplined meeting of body, mind, and earth. The thought gave me new resolution. I would hit shots on other holes. The place held secrets beyond the mysteries of golf. There were lessons to be learned all over this haunted ground.

T he rise upon which the second green had stood appeared to be no more than fifty yards from us. Taking a pitching wedge from my bag, I teed a ball on bare ground, then hit it high and straight. But it landed just partway up the hill. "Hannigan?" I asked. "How far is it to the top of the rise?"

"Fifty or sixty yards I'd say."

"That's what I thought. But it must be a hundred at least. I'm going to pace it off."

About thirty yards up the hill, I came to a swale that was invisible from where we'd been standing. The undulation was more than thirty yards across and accounted for part of the illusion, but the top of the rise was at least one hundred twenty yards from the tee. Something more than the swale had caused my misperception.

Rejoining Hannigan, I surveyed the entire hole. Though I knew that my perception was faulty, the top of the rise still seemed to be no more than fifty yards distant. "It's a hundred and twenty yards," I said. "There's a swale hidden up there that's thirty yards across, but you've still got sixty more to account for."

"It's the proportions." He shielded his eyes from the sun.

"The relations between the angle of slope, the horizon, and the shape of the hill. MacDuff studied this. He thought that contours of the land affect our feelings and perceptions, and what he called the 'inner body.' Ye know he got the term from his mother, who got it from Sufis and African shamans."

"The inner body? That's a phrase Irons used."

"He got it from MacDuff."

"So what was *this* hole designed for? To develop a sense of distance that doesn't depend upon sensory cues?"

"It was more than that. They were practicin' more than powers o' perception. MacDuff learned some sort o' mystic geometry in the Sahel. He worked on it here, I swear."

"But *how?*"

"That's the problem. That's the fuckin' problem. *How?*" We stared at the illusory target in silence, sharing our puzzlement and frustration.

"Hannigan," I said at last. "I'm going to hit some shots. Something is trying to give us a clue."

As I teed a ball on a patch of stubble, he sat on the ground behind me. "Murphy," he said, "I've got someone for ye to meet who knows about this stuff. Didn't ye meet some Russians who're studyin' altered states?"

Surprised, I turned to face him. "Yes. So what?"

"She's a friend of mine. Russian expatriate who communicates with the spirit world. Knows some things about mystic geometry. Ye want to meet her?"

There was a hint of pride in his voice, and a sweetness that surprised me. I sensed that he and the lady were lovers. "Sounds interesting," I said. "Where does she live?"

"Edinburgh. We can see her tomorrow night. She's got somethin' that'll interest you. A room she built to summon the dead."

"What's her name? Maybe I met her in Moscow."

"I doubt it. Her name's Nadia Kirova. Related to Sergei Kirov, the Bolshevik Stalin had killed. But go ahead." He gestured toward the hill. "Hit some balls. Test the old bugger's secret geometry."

For the next fifteen minutes, I hit eight-irons up the deceptive rise, gradually realizing that my position below the target caused me to lunge at the ball. Most golfers experience such effects caused by alterations of golf-course topography. This hole, like all holes, offered me a chance to overcome unnoticed constraints of body image.

As my impulse to lunge became more evident, my shots carried farther and farther. The guiding presence I'd felt through much of the day seemed to be teaching me now about my largely unconscious relations with the land around me. As if to confirm this, Hannigan asked what was happening. "Ye're swingin' better," he said. "You look stronger."

"They were working with illusions," I said. "Irons used this place to train his self-perception."

"But he used it for more than that. Ye know, Murphy, it's a funny thing. I could swear ye're lighter on yer feet. Are ye doing somethin' different?"

Hannigan was right. The power I felt was caused by more than insight into my relations with the hole's topography. My body felt lighter now, as if something were lifting every cell at once. I hit a second shot, then a third. A few readers of *Golf in the Kingdom* had told me about this condition. Like them, I felt strangely elevated.

Sensing that conversation would dispel the state, I decided to walk up the hill. But Hannigan ran to catch me. "Why so fast?" he insisted. "Ye look like ye've been goosed by a ghost."

Quickening my pace, I asked him to search for balls in the swale while I looked at the top of the hill. "I'd swear ye've got wind in yer pants," he said. "Enough to launch a blimp!" I started to laugh, and my apparent freedom from gravity vanished.

But not the clarity that was its companion. The blades of grass beneath my feet, a stretch of dark brown dirt, and the distant peak of Ben Cruachan all seemed closer now. The quieter the mind, the clearer the senses, I remembered Shivas Irons saying. The clearer your eyes and ears, the closer the world comes. Whether from the hours of practice, or the special presence of this place, the world was more present to me. This simplicity, this emptiness, made volition more efficient, movement easier, pleasure more immediate. "Hannigan, let's head back to Edinburgh," I said when we'd picked up the balls. "If we go now, we'll make it by seven o'clock."

But I vowed to return. There were things I could learn more fully here without human company. To surrender adequately to this extraordinary place, I would have to come here alone.

CHAPTER SIX

NADEZHDA—OR NADIA—Sergeevna Kirova lived in an apartment atop an empty warehouse on the edge of Edinburgh. Following Hannigan's instructions, I went up an outside staircase to her place, quietly opened its unlocked door, and tiptoed down a narrow corridor to the room in which she summoned the dead. Nadia called it her necromanteion, after similar chambers that existed in ancient Greece.* When no one responded to my knocking, I stepped into the darkened room and closed the door behind me. Hannigan had said they wouldn't respond if Nadia's ritual was under way.

Because the room had no windows and was painted black, I couldn't see a thing. There was only the sound of a woman murmuring, or moaning, or chanting, in what I took to be her summons to departed spirits. Sitting on the carpeted floor, I

---

* Pools of still liquid, polished caldrons and urns, crystals, and other devices were used among the ancient Greeks for mirror gazing, sometimes in darkened chambers constructed for that purpose. By focusing on reflective surfaces of this kind, supplicants could summon souls of the dead and other spirits. In *The Odyssey,* for example, Odysseus contacts his departed mother after gazing into a pit filled with the blood of a sacrificed animals.

waited for my eyesight to adapt. The mournful chant continued—at a distance, it seemed—but nothing was visible except the dim reflection of a mirror on the wall to my right. The barely perceptible glass was about six feet tall and three feet wide, large enough to accommodate ghostly forms with human proportions. Hannigan had told me that the light it reflected came from a carefully hidden source in the ceiling above it. If I watched it long enough, something would appear in its wavering surface.

Now the chanting was punctuated by sighs and heavy breathing, the results I guessed of Nadia's religious passion. Focusing my attention on the mirror, I waited for a sign from worlds beyond. But there was only a dim grey light in the tall rectangle. No face or figure appeared. No supernatural vista. No sign of lurking presences. The glassy surface looked like smoke in the pitch-black room.

Suddenly the chanting made me uncomfortable. But where was it coming from? Nothing was visible except the mirror—no silhouettes, no furniture, no shapes that resembled Nadia or Hannigan. I felt disoriented. If one sat here very long, it might be hard to tell the difference between the floor, the walls, and the ceiling. I looked again at the wavering glass, which seemed to have receded into the darkness around it. Like crystal gazing, this exercise required a patient surrender. Instinctive resistances had to relax. Perceptual rigidities had to soften in the light that would come from the other side.

Then a ghostly figure appeared.

A barely visible V-shaped form was coming into focus, as if from smoke or vapor. For a moment it was perfectly still, like a Roman numeral five; then its two arms came together, making a slightly narrower V. There could be no doubt about it. Something solid had appeared in the glass, something almost human.

For a moment it was perfectly still, its silvery arms pointed toward the ceiling in what seemed an ecstatic suspension. Then its upper tips began to rotate, conveying a deep seductive pleasure. I closed my eyes, as if this was something I shouldn't see, but looked again quickly. Now the entire form was undulating, its left arm stretching farther upward, the other dropping to form a right angle with it. The thing sent a shiver through me. It was deeply, calmly, wildly alive.

The chanting had stopped. The apparition must have silenced Nadia. Looking away from the glass, I tried to quiet my complex emotions. The ghostly form had deeply stirred me. My fear and astonishment were tinged inexplicably with both guilt and sexual arousal.

The place was silent. Should I make my presence known? Closing my eyes, I tried to gather myself. Hannigan had warned me that Nadia could have a seizure if awakened prematurely from trance. But I couldn't let go of the sensuous form stretching its parts before me deliciously. With embarrassment I looked again at the mirror. The two arms had formed a V and were stretching farther, farther upward as if toward some perfection. . . .

And then it hit me.

Its arms were legs. Its tips were toes. It was a reflection of Nadia. And superimposed upon it was the silhouette of a male torso.

Looking away with a seizure of guilt, I crawled to the door, stood, and stepped outside. A moment later I reached the street, filled with anger and amazement. Had Hannigan done this to challenge or taunt me? Or was this Nadia Kirova's idea of spiritual initiation? Then I had another shock, my second stunning recognition. It was only eight o'clock! Somehow I'd arrived an hour before Nadia would start her séance. Looking back to see whether Hannigan was watching from the apartment entrance, I hurried with embarrassment to my car.

F ifteen minutes later I sat in a pub near my hotel, drinking a glass of beer. It was impossible to erase the image of Nadia. Every part of her body, it seemed, had wanted to luxuriate in the sensations of love. It was as if she'd reached into corners of herself no one had touched before. Her thighs, her calves, her feet and toes all ached with delicious pleasure. No wonder Hannigan did those sit-ups! Before her defection from the USSR, she'd been the ice-skating champion of Novosibirsk. No one, he'd said, could match her combination of discipline, soul, and athleticism. A Nadia Kirova could emerge only in Russia. The night before, driving back from MacDuff's estate, I'd found it hard to believe his description of her, but now it made more sense. Forget the necromanteion. Forget her meetings with the spirits. A woman who joined so much athletic skill and erotic abandon was indeed a treasure. Conceivably, only Russia could produce such a combination of talents.

But what was her claim about love? That the body was "an erotic harp" in which there existed meridians of pleasure unknown to most of us? She had learned that from Sufi schools in Moscow and Samarkand. According to Hannigan, she also believed that our bodies were made for sex with angels. There were spirits, she said, who feasted on the aura of love in the flesh, enjoying human sex telepathically without suffering the dreary parts of personal relationship. The night before I'd been amazed at Hannigan's lyricism, but now I understood. Perhaps he'd made music this night with her secret strings of pleasure.

Philosophers talk about "unpacking" great ideas which, because they contain hidden complexities, yield understandings long after their conception. Nadia's image was like that. Despite my efforts to suppress it, her reflection continued to unfold in the mirror of my mind. Her flesh yearned to be touched. What ecstasies her thighs and calves suggested. What stomach muscles she possessed to maintain those graceful, leisurely postures! With their slow stretches and undulations, her legs had moved in apparent defiance of gravity. Had she learned levitation, too, in her mystery schools? If it could happen in golf, it could happen in the act of love.

But why couple with Hannigan at the gate of the dead? Was her necromanteion designed for sex as well as conversation with spirits? Maybe she was summoning angels now for a dance, an orgy, a slow pandemonium of love. I ordered another glass of beer. It was disturbing to think they might be doing it still. Suddenly I was jealous of Hannigan. Had he sensed I would come to the apartment early? It was conceivable that he'd done this to torture me. It took a moment for my anger to pass.

But my thoughts kept returning to Nadia—born in Tomsk, student of ballet, ice-skating champion, member of a Sufi school headquartered in Samarkand, and student of Djuna Davitashvilli, the darkly beautiful healer reputed to have eased the sufferings of Brezhnev. That was coincidence! I'd met Djuna in Moscow, working on Soviet-American exchanges, and four years before, my wife, Dulce, and I had taken Norman Mailer to meet her. Memories of that evening were vivid still—the line of supplicants in the street; the mingling of Russians, Georgians, and Americans; the East German ambassador relieved from gout; the dozens of icons on her walls, nearly all of them payments for her physical and spiritual ministrations.

In a corner, several men and women had gathered to watch a pornographic tape—provided, they said, by the Georgian, or Uzbek, or Sicilian mafia. But the film looked Danish to me, especially a rousing episode with a buxom blonde and large Samoyed. Later that night, I'd argued with Mailer about the tiles in Djuna's bathroom. The figures they depicted were Hittites, said Mailer, but I was sure they were Assyrians. Our discussion ended with a thumb-wrestling match observed by Djuna and some of her friends who encouraged us with Bulgarian brandy. It was amazing that Nadia knew Djuna. Had she studied with the well-connected healer? In the Kremlin the year before, Djuna had demonstrated her powers to a group of Soviet officials (one of our friends had attended), and was rumored to have held more than one séance for members of Brezhnev's family. Had Nadia learned about spirit-sex from Djuna Davitashvilli? We had several interesting things to discuss.

But it was nine o'clock. Quickly paying my bill, I headed back to the outskirts of Edinburgh.

With an anxiety that surprised me, I knocked at the outside entrance to Nadia's apartment. Did either of them suspect I'd been there already? When no one answered, I knocked again. Perhaps they had started the séance. Carefully opening the door, I stepped inside. Were they still making love? "Hannigan," I whispered. "Are you there?"

The apartment was completely silent. "Hannigan," I said in a loud voice. "It's Murphy. Should I come in?"

As if in response, Nadia's chanting arose from the necromanteion. It had the same aching insistence as the sound she'd made before, but with a slightly higher and more constant pitch. I tiptoed down the corridor. The sound reminded me of the call to prayer I'd heard in Muslim countries. Had she learned it in her Sufi school in the deserts of Samarkand? Summoning courage, I opened the chamber door. By the light of the corridor, I could see two figures, sitting cross-legged side by side, looking up into the glass. Slipping into the room, I sat some ten feet from them.

The chanting stopped. "Mackel?" Nadia whispered. "Is it you?"

"It's me," I said with surprise and embarrassment. "Don't stop what you're doing."

There was silence. Only the mirror was visible now, hovering in the silver light projected from the ceiling.

A moment passed. Then something moved. "Are you sitting?" she asked with a throaty Russian inflection. "You see saahmthing in our window?"

"No."

"Softly, Mackel," she said. "Look softly. It's a child's face. Someone you love. Someone you love *very much*. Look into its beautiful eyes with laahve."

My gaze relaxed, and the mirror started to undulate. Whether from the effects of beer or her hypnotic voice, I suddenly felt drowsy. Widening my eyes to stay alert, I stared into the glass. But my arms and feet grew heavy. My eyes began to close . . . and an image of her legs appeared, their naked calves and thighs stretching deliciously toward the ceiling, as if to spread the pleasure she felt through her entire body. Was it a memory or distorted reflection? As I straightened my back to stay alert, her legs dissolved into a stream lined with trees through which the sky was barely visible. A grey sky, like the dim silver light in the mirror, which I could see though my eyes were closed . . .

"Ma . . . ackel?" she called with a teasing inflection, stretching my name like she'd stretched her legs. "Maackel? Are you asleep? Keep your eyes open now." Her words jolted me. Had I snored? Perhaps she was tracking me telepathically. But the tall rectangle appeared to be empty. There was nothing there but dim grey light.

She started to chant, with a rhythmic, insistent pulse filled with joy and yearning. It seemed a call to God more than a summons of departed spirits. But again I had to fight off sleep, and couldn't hold a steady focus. My body slumped. My eyelids closed. . . .

And memories of infancy drifted past; my mother rocking me back and forth, my father singing by a fire and, from his strong arms, the view of a cloudless sky. Somewhere between my mind and the mirror, the image of a schoolyard appeared, with its swings and merry-go-round, its poplar trees, and me skipping to a teacher's embrace.

Then, as in a waking dream, I floated on a summer's day in the sea near a sandy beach—rocking gently, looking up, sensing I could fly. These images had continuity. They had a secret to tell. Straightening my back to drive away sleep, I stared into the glass. It was strangely familiar now, and I remembered the panic I'd felt as a child realizing that I wasn't my reflection. Who was I then? Who was I now? My boundaries had disappeared in the mirror.

"It's amazing how our thoughts, our bodies float in this emptiness." The voice of Shivas Irons seemed to come from the silver light. "From the day we're born, we have premonitions of the life to come. . . ."

Startled, I sat straight up. Nadia had stopped her chanting. Had she or Hannigan heard it? As with the images a moment before, it was hard to tell where the words had come from. "Premonitions of the life to come"—his voice was still vivid, though situated safely now inside my ordinary field of consciousness. Closing my eyes, I could hear him reminding me that "the life to come" had a double meaning. It signified more than the afterlife. "It can happen here," he'd said. "In this ever-aspiring Earth. From the day we're born, we have premonitions of it. As soon as we're out o' our mother's womb, through our childhood until we die, we have feelings of the life to come.

Did ye ever think ye were levitatin'? Did ye ever ask 'who am I?' and think yer mind might vanish. . . ."

"Mackel!" Nadia whispered. "Mackel, wake up!"

I awoke with a start. She had stationed herself behind me and was massaging my shoulders slowly. Embarrassed, I sat erect. "You were growling," she said softly. "Like a lion, a big poosycat."

"You mean I was snoring!"

"No, *growling.*" She rubbed my back with slow, firm strokes. "Like a lion!"

"Hannigan," I called. "Are you there?"

"He left," she whispered, rubbing my neck with one hand and the small of my back with the other. "He thinks you frightened the spirits."

"He left?" I asked with alarm.

"To the kitchen," she whispered in my ear. "To have a drink of vaahdka. Now we are alone. All alone. Just you and I."

"Thanks." I shook my shoulders to suggest that she stop. "I'm wide awake now."

"Now, Mackel, look." Holding my head with both hands, she aimed it toward the glass. In its silvery light, a dim silhouette had appeared. As if in a separate frame or spatial indentation, a male figure was forming. "Don't look away," she whispered. "It came and went when you were sleeping, and now it's coming back."

I watched it coalesce, then hover in the mirror. The figure of a man, shrouded in mist or smoke, from which there came a light like sunshine on a rippling pond. Nadia let go of my head and placed her hands on my shoulders. "It's trying to reach you, Mackel," she whispered. "What's it saying to you?"

Perhaps it was the power of her suggestion or some vagary of reflected light, but the mist-shrouded figure moved from an apparent indentation of space to a position closer to me. For a few seconds, it hovered between me and the glass, then returned to the recess from which it had come, dissolved, and disappeared completely.

"Can you see it now?" she whispered.

My heart was beating rapidly, and sweat had formed on my forehead. "No," I said. "Can you?"

"It's gone," she said softly. "Do you know what it was?" Her large almond-shaped eyes shone with a light stronger than the illumination reflected by the mirror. I said that the figure was unrecognizable.

"It was strange," she whispered. "The living are different from the dead. This was neither. This was both. I've never seen anything like it." She squeezed my arm firmly. "But Mackel, it said something to you. Did you hear it?"

"No."

"Or feel it?"

Wiping sweat from my forehead, I looked at the glass again. It seemed to be filled with smoke. "No, I didn't feel anything. Just amazement."

"Maybe something will reach you later." Her voice was barely audible. "It was trying so hard to reach out. Trying very hard. I think it likes you."

We sat in silence, then she tugged at my arm. "But let's see Bach," she said. "Before he's drunk!"

He was sitting at a table in her kitchen, with a loaf of brown bread, a bottle of vodka, and a dish of big pickles in front of him. "Christ, you snore!" he said as we entered. "It's a wonder you didn't crack the glass."

"Baah . . . ch," said Nadia reprovingly. "You are not nice to your friend."

The apparition had left me in mild shock. "Nadia?" I asked,

sitting at the table across from Hannigan. "Do you mind if I have some vodka?"

"Give him a glass, Baahch," she said. "Be a nice man." Then she turned to face us. Her bright almond-shaped eyes were either blue or violet. Thick blonde hair fell to her neck, framing her high, well-defined cheekbones. And she had a magnificent figure, which was accentuated by a white blouse that revealed part of her cleavage and close-fitting tan suede pants. She was part Russian, part Tatar, I guessed—and as beautiful as Hannigan had promised. I poured myself a glass of vodka. Its warmth, and her stunning looks, began to lift me past the shock of our visitation.

"It came back," she said, sitting down beside Hannigan. "It was strange. *Very strange*. It was reaching to Mackel." Poised at the edge of her chair with an erect but relaxed posture, she poured herself a vodka, tossed back her blonde hair, and looked at us both with smiling curiosity. "Murphy and Hannigan," she said with a lilt. "So Irish!"

"I'm Scots," said Hannigan. "Not Irish." His glasses reflected the overhead light, giving him a slightly menacing look. I wondered if he had any hint that I'd seen them making love.

"But you're a *little* Irish," she said. "Baahch, you're a little bit Irish."

Hannigan rocked back on his chair, looking into his vodka glass. Nadia winked at me to suggest she'd made peace with the thorny side of his nature. "So it came back," he said with a flat, hard inflection. "What the hell was it?"

"I don't know." She shrugged and her eyes grew wide. "It came close and was very far away. It was in two or three spaces at once. It was dead and it was alive. I never saw such a thing—here, in Moscow, or Samarkand."

"What did *you* see?" He looked at me. "Was it dead or alive?"

"I've never been in a necromanteion, or seen a ghost. I've never seen anything like it. Nadia, what do you mean, it was neither dead nor alive?"

She gave me a searching look. "You've never been in a séance?" she asked. "You've never seen a spirit-body?"

"Never."

"But Baahch," she said with disappointment. "You told me he had. You said he was a psychical researcher."

"I said he *studies* these things," Hannigan said with irritation. "He's only read about them."

I didn't know how to take his remark. Was he defending me or putting me down? "But Mackel," she said, "Baahch says you saw the ghost of your teacher's teacher. Didn't you write about it?"

"Well, that was a long time ago," I said with hesitation. "*Maybe* I saw a ghost. I'm not sure."

"But you wrote about it," she said. "Did you make the story up?"

"No," I said, embarrassed. "I didn't make it up. But I don't know what I saw. Actually, I saw two apparitions. Or three. I described only one—or two—in *Golf in the Kingdom.*"

"One or two? Two or three? It *is* complicated!" She leaned closer to me, her shapely breasts pressing against the table. "But what were they like? Did they say something to you?"

Suddenly I felt suspicious. Something about her reminded me of a woman in Moscow who'd professed to be an admirer. She had wanted to know about my interest in the paranormal, and I later discovered that she worked for the KGB. But that was in 1980. This was 1987. Glasnost had arrived. Nadia had defected. My suspicion was absurd. "Well?" she insisted. "What were the two apparitions like?"

"One looked like a man." I fumbled for words. "The other was, well, how to say it? Like a hole in space. A hole with fire in it. But it lasted for just a few seconds. I didn't mention it in my book because . . . well, I suppose it just faded from memory."

With her chin resting on her clasped hands, she looked into my eyes. It occurred to me that she was using my face as she did the mirror in her necromanteion. "Did you think these things were real?" she asked.

"Yes. Definitely. Though I've wondered about them since. I saw an old man—later I presumed it was my teacher's teacher— walking along a ravine. But Buck says he'd died by then. And later that night I thought I saw him again." I looked to Hannigan. "But what *was* Irons doing? He implied that MacDuff was alive. He suggested we might meet him. What was that about?"

"But Mackel," Nadia said insistently, "did Mr. Irons see his teacher that night?"

"No. He said I was imagining it."

"And the first time? Did he see his teacher then?"

"No. Or if he did, he didn't tell me. I didn't remember seeing MacDuff—that was his teacher's name—until later. Somehow I'd repressed the experience. But I tell you, it was real. I went back there two days ago, and remembered the whole thing clearly. But that brings up another problem! There's no place to stand where I thought I saw him. I didn't realize that until the day before yesterday. And now Buck says he was dead. It must've been an apparition."

As Nadia studied my face, she seemed to acquire a deeper focus. Had my face become a crystal ball? "And the other thing?" she whispered. "The thing you saw near Mr. Irons? That seemed real, too?"

"It seemed real to me. But not everyone saw it. Or if they did they thought it was something else." I briefly described my conversations with the man in the yellowed suit and the couple who owned a farm near Burningbush.

"So, Mackel? That thing you saw near Mr. Irons, that hole in space. You didn't think about it when you wrote your book?"

"No. It never came up. I didn't remember it until a lady who read my book described an experience that reminded me of it. She said that when she was playing golf one day, the world became transparent. The light of the setting sun, she said, 'was replaced by another light.' Her description brought back the whole thing, I don't know, maybe six or seven years ago. Playing with Irons on the last hole at Burningbush, everything seemed like that. The clubhouse, the fairways, the green. Everything seemed transparent. And then, that hole in space. I remember it clearly now."

"So now you remember." She leaned closer. "But you didn't until that letter. Have you thought that maybe there's more?"

With a mischievous and slightly seductive smile, she touched the bridge of my nose. "When you're falling asleep, or some other day in the necromanteion, you will remember more about that fire near Mr. Irons. Remember it here, in this little place between your eyes." She touched my chest. "And in your heart. Ask youself, 'What else happened? What was that hole in space?' Ask the memory to open. Ask it to unfold, to blossom like a wonderful flower!"

There are insights and suggestions which, though we reject, leave a deep and lasting imprint. Something in me knew she had triggered a process that would be hard to stop. Like a bed of embers, my vision thirty-one years before had been fanned to new life. "Damn it!" I poured myself another vodka. "I didn't ask for it then, and I don't know if I want it now."

She shook her head with an expression that combined disappointment and amusement. Then with a sigh she threw her hands up in a Russian gesture of resignation and relinquishment. "You are big boys," she said. "You know what you have to do. But saahmthing is chasing you, Mackel. It came through the glass tonight."

With a sigh, she rose and crossed the kitchen. As she moved pots and pans on the stove, Hannigan and I exchanged questioning glances.

"Nadia?" he asked. "What d'ye mean when ye say ye can't tell if that thing in the mirror was dead or alive? I don't understand. Murphy, do you?"

"Boys!" she exclaimed, turning to face us. "Didn't you see how solid it got to be? Dead people cannot do that, unless they are *very, very* strong. Unless they are great souls. Great saints. Or angels! But it lasted too long, and was too—how do you say it?—too *agile* to be the spirit of someone living on earth. It acted like something in between."

"Nadia," I said. "Buck tells me that you're friends with Djuna Davitashvilli. Did he tell you I know her?"

"Djuna!" she exclaimed. "When did you meet?"

"In 1980. Did you learn about the spirits from her?"

"Not from Djuna!" she said, as if the idea were preposterous. "She has energy. What energy! And connections. What connections! But the spirits, no. I learned about them from other friends." She stood beside a cupboard. "But Mackel—and Baahch—what do you want for supper? Something more than those pickles?" On tiptoe she looked into a shelf, stretching high with exquisite balance. She was about five foot eight, I guessed, and her carriage joined strength with remarkable grace. Watching her move around the kitchen, I thought of her reflection in the necromanteion—her legs stretching with pleasure toward the ceiling, rotating, undulating, asking for caresses. For the first time, I noticed that her pants had a silver zipper. "So Mackel?" she asked. "What do you want to eat?"

I glanced at Hannigan. Did he harbor a subconscious thought that I'd seen them making love? "Anything," I said. "I'll be happy with anything."

"Then soup!" She gave us each a dazzling smile. "My special

mushroom soup, *gribnaya pokhlyobka,* with mushrooms and herbs from Raahsha."

"What kind of mushrooms?" I asked.

"From Peredelkino. My friend Boris sends them to remind me what I left behind."

"Not Boris Mikhailkov?" I named a writer I'd met who had a dacha in Peredelkino.

"No." She wiggled her shoulders seductively. "Beeg Boris. Boris Ryzhkov, the Sufi man. He is my teacher."

It was amazing how easily she could turn from magus to coquette. Russian women of her generation, I thought, have a larger repertoire of behaviors than anyone else on the planet. "Did you learn about the spirits from Boris?" I asked.

"Yes." She turned to a pot on the stove. "From him and other friends."

She seemed reluctant to talk about her esoteric training, but drink had made me bolder. "And what did you learn from Boris?" I asked. "What did he teach you?"

"About laahve." She rolled her eyes playfully. "About the archetypes of laahve. The way spirits make laahve. You know why angels have harps and wings—and all those little pink bottoms?"

"No, I don't."

"Because angel bodies *are* harps. Erotic harps. With a million meridians of pleasure. And our bodies too. In love, they make music. In love, they can fly!"

"It's an early version of string theory," said Hannigan with a deadpan expression. "Wait till you hear her theory of superstrings and spirit music."

"You know acupuncture, Mackel. Did you know that our bodies are *filled* with meridians and pressure points? Filled with them! You press the right one, or caress it, or *bite* it, and wow! Our bodies light up. We go to heaven!"

Paintings of the Russian countryside decorated the wall behind her. A shelf was lined with lacquered boxes. A volume of Pushkin sat on the table near me. Our spirited conversation brought back memories of similar exchanges in small Russian kitchens. "The archetypes of love?" I asked. "What do you mean?"

She finished stirring the soup, and turned to face me. "Why are the positions of love so wanderful? Why do we like them so much? Because they reflect the archetypes of angel-love! Have you read Miltone?"

"John Milton?"

"Yes, John Miltone." Standing with her legs slightly spread, she placed a hand on each hip as if she were about to draw a gun. "John Mill Tone. Have you read *Paradise Lost*?"

"Some of it."

"Then you know he wrote about this, how angels merge when they make love. Merge all of their bodies with great blaahshing!"

"I don't remember that part."

Hannigan slapped the table. "What kind of education did you have?" he asked with mock disgust. "Where the fuck did you go to school?"

"In Raahsha, we read Mill Tone. Don't you Americans?"

"Less and less. But no professor of mine ever talked about Milton's archetypes like this."

"Ah, Mackel, that is too bad. More students would read him. But forget Mill Tone. There are other teachers. Did you know that angels make love like cosmonauts, *in zero gravity?* They can join any way they like. We can't do what they can. We are not as free, as flexible, as—how to say it?—not as alive!"

My mind was divided now between surprise at these conversational turns and images of her naked legs stretching high in the mirror. "Cosmonauts!" I exclaimed. "Are you telling me they make love in zero gravity?"

"Ah, you would like to know!" she said wickedly. "But I am sworn to be secret. The KGB would *keel* me if I told. But Mackel, listen. . . ." She crossed the room and whispered in my ear. "One of the cosmonauts is a friend of Borees. A great laahver, and a Sufi!" Her voice sent a shiver through me. "He made laahve like an angel in zero gravity!"

It was hard to tell if she were teasing. "Does he know?" I nodded toward Hannigan.

"He knows." She pretended sympathy. "And he's jealous! Aren't you, Baahch?"

"Have you seen the ladies the Soviets put up there?" Hannigan said caustically. "You call that love with angels?"

"There are others," she said proudly. "Women fliers you've never seen. Not everything's in your silly papers." She crossed the kitchen, turned off the flame beneath the pot, and ladled the soup into bowls. Hannigan watched her in silence, as if transfixed. But it was hard to tell what complex emotions he harbored. What was it like to have made love with this amazing creature? Was their intercourse in the necromanteion meant to summon angels? Perhaps I could find out indirectly.

"You know, Nadia," I ventured, "Shivas Irons thought that every physical movement reflects an archetype. He said that in golf there's an archetype for every shot. He was a golfing Platonist."

"You mean golf has angels?" She was astonished. "Golf!"

"Yes, golf."

"You mean that leetle game, where you do this?" Bending slightly from the waist, she stuck out her rear end and waggled an imaginary golf club. "Mr. Irons thought *this* reflected angels? *This!*"

"Not angels. *Archetypes.* Perfect forms for every shot."

"Oh! Oh!" She started to laugh. "Oh, that is funny!" It was a lilting but full-bodied laugh. The connection between golf and higher powers seemed hilarious to her. "Golf!" she exclaimed. "Golf and angels? That is wanderful! Unbeeleevable! Baahch, you should play this game."

"Not angels," I insisted. *"Archetypes."*

Her laughter subsided as she set the table, and for a while we ate in silence. The soup had dill and sour cream in it, as well as herbs I couldn't identify. An aromatic warmth spread through my chest. My hands began to tingle. Did the ingredients have psychedelic properties?

"You like it?" she asked.

"It's the best mushroom soup I've ever tasted! What's in it?"

"Herbs," she said with a knowing look. "Beeg herbs! And beeg mushrooms! I don't know their English names, except one—the 'Prince mushroom.' *Agaricus augustus.* They touch the soul. They touch the meridians of laahve and pleasure!"

It was true. The soup's afterglow was spreading from my chest and stomach into my arms and legs. In combination with the vodka, it was calming and lifting me high at once. "Nadia?" I asked. "With food like this, and Boris, and your other teachers, why did you leave the Soviet Union?"

She tasted her soup with a lingering sigh. The poise with which she held her spoon and moved it slowly to her lips seemed the product of aristocratic breeding. Her manners were as sensuous and elegant as the way she made love. Hannigan and I stopped eating, as if we were taking lessons from her.

But she didn't answer my question. As we ate, a deep silence came into the room. She continued to savor the soup. I took another sip of vodka. Hannigan's glasses reflected the light. "Why did I leave Raahsha?" she said at last. "I miss it, but love my freedom. Instead of my teachers, I have books and my necromanteion. Instead of Samarkand, I have the west of Ireland." She looked fondly at Hannigan. "And I have Baahch. So it is good here. But in many ways, it was wanderful there. It is a mystery. A mystery why I came here. Perhaps the spirits led me." She seemed completely sincere. "And you, Mackel? You know about Raahsha?"

"I've been there nine times."

"Nine times!" She looked surprised. "Baahch didn't tell me. Why do you go there?"

I told her that an institute I'd started conducted Soviet-American exchanges, that my wife was in Moscow now, and that we'd come to know many Soviets who studied paranormal phenomena and altered states of mind.

"You met Naumov, Nicolayev, Raikov." She named some of the Soviets we'd met. "The public ones. The ones your journalists write about. Ah, but Mackel, none of those call spirits from the glass, or reach the dead, or know the prayer of the heart."

"How did you know I met Naumov and Raikov?"

"Moscow is small town. A little place. A *village,* Mackel. They are the ones that Westerners meet. But you didn't meet my Boris, or his friends in Moscow and Samarkand. There is another Raahsha. The inner Raahsha. Soviet science and Communism can never kill it." She looked at me searchingly, sighed, then stood to refill our bowls.

Angels, archetypes, sex in zero gravity. From the start, our conversation had taken unexpected turns. "And there's another world of golf," I said with conviction. "The game has an inner world, too. Just like Russia. Western science and capitalism will never kill it."

"Golf!" She shook her head in exasperation. "Mackel, golf is not Raahsha. Baahch, it was a mistake to go to that haunted house. A *beeg* mistake. Now Mackel thinks golf is like Raahsha!"

"It can't be helped," said Hannigan. "He met Shivas Irons and wrote that book. Now he thinks everyone levitates on golf courses, or sees the wee people."

Whether from an excess of vodka, or the combination of Russian herbs and drink, or the cumulative effects of our lively meeting, my brain did not faithfully record the rest of our conversation. I can only recall my feelings as we argued about golf in its occult dimensions. I was jealous of Hannigan's concourse with Nadia. I felt a great attraction to her. And she seemed more and more complex. As she guided me down her steps to the taxi she'd called, I wondered whether she'd ever worked for the KGB, or if she might work for them now.

CHAPTER SEVEN

AROMATIC TRACES OF mushroom soup lingered in the air around me, the taste of vodka remained in my throat, and a vague sense of guilt mingled with the attraction I felt toward Nadia. But stronger than these was the image of our visitor in the necromanteion. Waking, I realized that it sat in my consciousness like a living thing.

The room's tall windows were covered with drapes, except for one through which there came a narrow shaft of sunlight. There was just enough light in the high-ceilinged room to see the clock by the fireplace. How long had I slept? It was nine o'clock now, but it was hard to remember when I'd gone to bed, or my conversation with the taxi driver who'd brought me to the hotel. My suspicions of Nadia the night before seemed ludicrous in the morning light. I'd have to examine the paranoia our meeting had triggered.

Turning onto my side, I felt a strange pleasure. Did it arise in part from Nadia's soup and the afterglow of her erotic presence? Or was it somehow connected to the thing we'd seen in the mirror? Through the partly uncovered window, I could see a stately stone building on the far side of Princes Street. One of its windows was like the glass in Nadia's necromanteion. The light it reflected reminded me of the illumination in which our visitor had taken shape.

Was something forming in it now? Squinting, I broke it into golden threads that danced above cars and passing pedestrians, between chairs and tables through the room. That photons were coming from the sun to a window across the street then into the cells of my nervous system was a delicious thought. Part of the pleasure I felt came from this river of light. Its shimmering reminded me of superstrings and Nadia's vision of fleshy harps. In its lingering caress, it was possible to think there were erotic connections between mathematics, angels, and the flesh. . . .

But the phone by the bed was ringing. "Murphy?" It was Hannigan. "Are ye in heaven, hell, or purgatory?"

"It's hard to tell." I let a wave of dizziness pass. "On my back, it was heaven. Sitting up, it's purgatory."

"Did ye get home all right?"

"I can't remember when I got here, what route we took, or how much I paid the driver. How was I doing when I left?"

"Adequately. Nadia says ye drink as well as her countrymen. Says yer liver must've adapted, what with all yer trips to Moscow."

"Was I well behaved?"

"As far as I know. Unless ye did somethin' behind my back."

Relieved that he sounded so warm and high-spirited, I asked why he had called.

"Because I want ye to come to my place. Something happened last night after ye left that might be related to Shivas Irons. How long'll it take ye to get a taxi? Nadia's brought yer car here."

"An hour or so. I've got to have breakfast. But for Christ's sake. What happened? Was there another visitation?"

He didn't respond at once. "Murphy," he said after a moment's pause, "did ye have any funny dreams?"

"No."

"Not a one?"

"Not that I can remember."

"All right," he said cheerfully. "I'll expect ye about ten o'clock."

Waiting for breakfast in the hotel's dining room, I wondered if Nadia's mushroom soup countered the damage of excessive drink, for instead of the hangover I might've suffered, I felt a growing clarity about the previous night's activities. Reconstructing my taxi ride to the hotel I started to toy with the objects in front of me, which included three forks, a knife, a tablespoon, two teaspoons, a butter knife, two glasses, a teacup and saucer, a basket of rolls, a dish of butter squares, a small tray of jams and jellies, and a basket of plums, figs, and peaches. Absorbed in reverie, I rearranged this entire setting, placing figs and plums at various places on the table. The waiter, a rugged-looking middle-aged Scots dressed in a formal white shirt and black bow tie, asked what I was doing. "That's a beautiful arrangement," he said. "Don't ye like the way we do it?"

Embarrassed, I started to move the things back. But then I hesitated. The arrangement of utensils, glasses, and cups resembled something that was vaguely familiar. Was it a garden in Burningbush? Or a golf links?

Suddenly I realized what it was. The basket of breakfast rolls was MacDuff's old house. The knife pointing from it to me was the first fairway of his seven-hole course, and the pieces of fruit I'd spread around the table represented the locations of his abandoned greens.

But there was something even more amazing. I saw that this

improbable map revealed ways in which Shivas Irons might have used the place to practice extraordinary golf shots. The dotted lines on the diagram below indicate routes which some of these might have followed. Apologizing to the waiter, I sketched the map on an envelope. This is what it looked like:

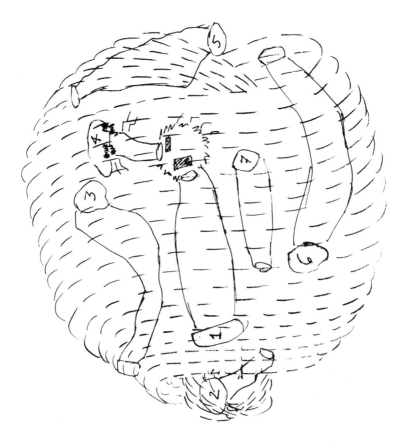

A half hour later, Hannigan greeted me at the door to his studio. He was unshaven and disheveled, but brimming with energy. "Ye seem all right." He looked me up and down, as if searching for marks of disrepair. "Have a seat, and I'll get ye a cup o' coffee."

His desk was covered with sheets from his artist's pad, each of them covered from top to bottom with equations written in his elegant hand. "You've been working," I said. "Boy, you've got stamina."

As he crossed the room with my coffee, I saw that his hands were shaking. For a moment he searched my face intently, then nodded toward the sheets of equations. "Look at these!" he exclaimed. "Been pourin' out of me since four o' clock. It's a breakthrough, maybe. One of the biggest I've had. One of the *very biggest.*"

Sitting down at the desk, he picked up a book from Irons's library that we'd examined during my previous visit. "When I got back here last night, something inspired me to look at this. It has these figures in it." He pointed to mathematical formulae inscribed on a flyleaf. "For the last two years, I've wondered what they were. Then last night it hit me. As soon as I looked at 'em. All at once. Like a bolt of lightning! The book was originally owned by MacDuff. Look at his initials here. But holy Jesus! He'd seen a world of mathematics that no one else has seen yet. Last night I realized it. Christ! Right now, I'd say he saw a way to solve some o' the greatest puzzles that appear when we try to use hyperspace to unify the physical forces." He shook his head in wonder. "But there's more, which is why I wanted ye to come here. This morning, Nadia calls in a wild state. Never heard her so excited. Says she's channelin' a *new kind o' music.* You heard her singing last night. Well, this morning she tells me she's gettin' *new* songs from the other side—and pictures, too. Pictures of something she calls 'spirit-matter.' " He held up a hand to forestall objections. "It sounds crazy. I know. I know. But Murphy, I've gotten to know her. She's not given to easy proclamations. And she's never come up with something like this. With the new music, she saw these. She brought them here this morning." From beneath his sketchpad, he produced a sheet of paper with these drawings:

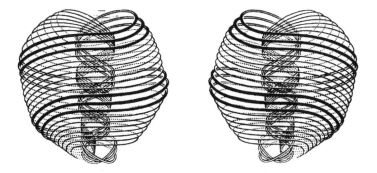

"What do they look like to you?" he asked.

"Two whirling spheres, each with a double helix or Möbius strip. Two spinning tops? Two hearts?"

"Ye've never seen it?"

"No, but let's see. . . ." Suddenly I felt uneasy. Maybe I *had* seen something like it. Without thinking, I reached into a jacket pocket and found the envelope on which I'd copied the chart I'd made with the table setting.

Hannigan laid the drawings on his desk. "So ye've never seen these," he said with disappointment. "Somehow I thought ye might've, with all yer studies of the esoteric. But Murphy, here's the strangest part. These drawings of hers are awfully close to models I use in my theories of hyperspace, models I've shown to physicists for years." He produced a sheet from his artist's pad on which he'd sketched a series of spheres that resembled the ones in Nadia's drawings. "Think of these, like the 'strings' in superstring theory. Ye can't model 'em in ordinary space, okay? Now let me ask ye. Does all of this remind ye of something?"

"No. I don't see what you mean."

"Just this." He laid her drawings next to his. "She doesn't know a thing about string theory. She's never seen my diagrams. I know that for a fact. Until she sees them comin' out of that goddamned mirror in her necromanteion! And she sees 'em about the same time I get the secret of MacDuff's equations! Naturally we thought about our visitor last night and wondered if somethin' hit *you*. A dream, an idea, a vision, a connection. Somethin' about Irons, maybe. But ye say there was nothing?"

"No. Nothing striking. Nothing like you're talking about."

"What ye got there?" He nodded toward the envelope.

"Oh, this?" I was surprised. "Just a sketch I made. A map of MacDuff's old golf course."

"When did ye draw it?"

"This morning, just before I came here."

He placed my drawing next to his and Nadia's. "For God's sake!" he whispered. "Don't ye think this is odd?"

"What?"

"Well, look. Isn't there a resemblance to my and Nadia's diagrams? What'n the hell led ye to draw it?"

"I don't know. It just happened. I was toying with things on the table, and, well, without knowing it, rearranged everything until I realized I'd diagrammed MacDuff's old course. I copied it on this envelope."

"So it just came to ye? Out o' the blue? Doesn't that seem a little strange? What are these crisscross lines?"

"Golf shots Irons might've tried. After I'd made the map, I saw how he could've used the course to practice unusual shots." Now the coincidence was starting to hit me. "But yes. It *is* strange. It *does* look a little like Nadia's drawings."

Hannigan stood. "It's a pretty strong coincidence," he said. "My equations, Nadia's diagrams, and this thing o' yers. All three of us inspired about the same time. Don't ye think that's interesting?"

"But they're so different," I protested. "You're always thinking about superstring theory. Nadia's fascinated with the body's occult secrets. I'm looking for Shivas Irons. So we have inspirations about our special obsessions. So what?"

"But Murphy, look!" He held up Nadia's drawings. "Are ye

proposin' that she read my mind—and yers!—before she came up with this?"

"Without knowing it, she could've fished those diagrams out of your subconscious. It happens to lovers every day. When you're intimate with someone, you can read their mind."

He looked at me suspiciously, then threw up his hands with exasperation. "I thought *I* was the skeptic here. Murphy, there's more goin' on than our readin' each other's minds. Look at these drawings! It has to be more than coincidence or simple telepathy. And wait! There's another thing. One more incredible thing. Look here. The old man's equations are written in this."

He picked up the book in which Irons had inscribed MacDuff's equations. Titled *Evidence of Personal Survival from Cross Corre-spondences,* it describes messages channeled through automatic writing and other means that make sense when pieced together. The recipients involved thought most of this material to have come from the discarnate spirit of Frederic Myers, the great pio-neer of psychical research.* Now I saw what Hannigan meant. He

---

* The book, *Evidence of Personal Survival from Cross Correspondences,* is by H. F. Saltmarsh, a British expert on psychical research. Published originally in Lon-don by G. Bell & Sons, it was published in the United States by Arno Press. Frederic Myers died on January 17, 1901, and the messages purported to come from him continued for many years afterward. Saltmarsh writes:

The very large bulk of those cases wherein evidence of a supernormal kind is put forward as proving personal survival, consists of communications of knowledge which is not in the possession of any living person concerned, but was, or could have been, possessed by the individual from whose surviving spirit the messages purport to come.

Now, it is clear that for such communications to be of any value as evidence, the information conveyed must be capable of verification, and this implies that some living person must know the facts or else that some record exists or some circumstances from which the facts may be inferred.

But if this be so, it is always possible to hold that the information was conveyed telepathically to the mind of the medium from the living person who knew the facts, or else that the medium clairvoyantly became aware of the record or circumstances in which it is embodied. We have to bear in mind that

was proposing that our visitor in the necromanteion had used the same method to communicate with us.

"You mean," I said, "that something's downloading into the three of us, using each of us to reveal different parts of a connecting pattern?"

"That's what I'm thinking. Our séance last night could've triggered it."

Has your flesh ever crawled as some unwanted recognition forced itself into consciousness? That's what I felt as the implications of Hannigan's proposal became apparent. He handed me the book with MacDuff's equations. "Frederic Myers," I said. "He was an extraordinary character. You know he invented the word 'telepathy.' "

But Hannigan didn't respond. He sat down at his desk, tore a sheet from his artist's pad, and started to write equations. For a moment I browsed through the book, reacquainting myself with the ingenious correspondences—some of which involved several languages, including Latin and ancient Greek—that emerged when transcripts from different mediums were juxtaposed.

"Ye ever heard of a mathematician named Ramanujan?" Hannigan gazed at the equations he'd written. "Little clerk in Madras. Poor. Sick. Self-educated. But one o' the greatest brains the field's seen. You should study him. Got some of his ideas in dreams, like

---

it is not only the ordinary supraliminal knowledge of living persons which is available, but also the subliminal; further that a telepathic impression may be received and lie dormant in the subliminal mind of the percipient, emerging into ordinary consciousness only after a lapse of time, sometimes of quite considerable length.

In these circumstances it is hard to imagine any possible evidence which could bring unequivocal proof of survival. Now Myers . . . was fully aware of all this, and what makes these experiments so peculiarly interesting is that, if we take the statements of the communicators at their face value, it looks as though his surviving spirit had invented a means of getting over the difficulty and had endeavored to carry it out.

Coleridge and Blake. It's amazing to see what he invented. And sometimes got it all at once, like Mozart got his symphonies. All of them were mediums. Everyone of 'em was channeling, from who knows where."

"Does this mean they're both dead?" I asked.

"What?" He looked up. *"Who's* dead?"

"Are you proposing that Irons is dead? Do you think *both* he and MacDuff are trying to communicate from the other side?"

"I didn't say that."

"It's plausible, isn't it? Why can't we find any traces of him?"

"Because we haven't looked hard enough." Hannigan put down his pen. "He could be living in Australia, or Spain, or the Outer Hebrides. Hell! Who knows? He might be living on Lake Baikal. He'd be in his late sixties now, or seventy at the most; and from what everyone says, he was strong as a bull. Maybe it was Mac-Duff in the mirror last night. Or maybe it was something we don't understand, somethin' we don't understand at all." He took off his glasses, leaned back in his chair, and rubbed the bridge of his nose. "Maybe it didn't come from the afterlife. Nadia says it was *neither* dead nor alive. Says she's never seen anything like it."

"Do you believe her? Do you really think she knows the difference? How can she possibly tell whether a thing like that is dead or alive?"

"Maybe she can't." He shrugged with what seemed to be genuine detachment. "But watchin' things appear in that glass, I've got to think she's learned a secret or two about whatever it is we call the spirits. In the circles she comes from in Mother Russia, they've kept this sort o' thing alive. If ye stick around, ye'll see what I mean. In any case, I'm not prepared to say that Irons is dead."

"But he could be."

"You think he is?"

"I'm just wondering."

"What does yer intuition tell ye?"

"I don't have a stable intuition. When I wrote *Golf in the Kingdom,* I thought he might contact me. But he hasn't, and that was fifteen years ago. Apparently, no one in Burningbush knows where he is. And there's been no word of him from anyone else. On the other hand, he wouldn't be more than seventy now, and he was tremendously vital. There's no doubt about that. So I don't know. He might be alive. He could've died."

"Yes, he could've died." Hannigan put on his glasses, stretched his arms above his head, and took a photograph from a desk drawer. "It's possible. But if he's dead, we have some problems. For example, what d'ye make o' this?"

It was a faded color picture of a male figure facing the camera. The man had striking aquiline features, reddish brown hair, blue eyes, and an athletic physique accentuated by a close-fitting open-collared shirt. It was a deeply unsettling photograph. The man resembled Shivas Irons.

"When was this taken?" I asked.

"Half a year ago," Hannigan said coolly. "It came in the mail last December."

"Who's it a picture of?"

"The man who took it doesn't know." He watched me calmly. "Does it remind ye of anyone?"

"It could be Shivas Irons, if that's what you're suggesting. It looks a little like him. But he seems to be in his late thirties, or early forties at the most—not someone pushing seventy. Where was it taken?"

"Dornoch. On the links there."

"Who took it?"

"Someone named Adams. Here's the note he sent. It was post-marked from Burningbush, but had no return address." He handed me this handwritten letter:

Dear Mr. Hannigan,

A Mrs. Webster at the Burningbush bookshop told me about your interest in curious events related to golf, and suggested I send this photograph to you. A few weeks ago, the man in the picture appeared—as if from nowhere—on the ninth green at Dornoch, walked for two holes with me, then inexplicably disappeared after I photographed him. He had an extraordinary presence, which I find hard to describe, that prompted me to take his picture.

He was greatly interested in why I was playing alone at Dornoch on a winter day, and we talked about the links there. He seemed constantly amused and was, as you can see, a well-built, attractive man. But I cannot account for his mysterious appearance and disappearance, which continue to trouble me. No one in Dornoch whom I talked to is acquainted with him. No one in the clubhouse had seen him that day.

It seems odd to be sending you this, but Mrs. Webster was insistent. I hope it is of interest to you.

Sincerely,
Martin Adams

I looked at the photograph. If it was Shivas Irons, he hadn't aged since 1956. "Hannigan," I asked, "what leads you to think this is Shivas Irons? You never met him."

"I'm not sayin' it's Irons. But it reminds me of the descriptions in yer book, and other things I've heard about him."

"Other things?"

"Murphy, we haven't had a chance to talk about everything I've learned about him and MacDuff. Ye're free today, I take it."

"It's why I'm here."

"All right. Let's start from the beginning." He crossed the room, took some folders and books from a shelf, and arranged them on a table. For the rest of the day and much of the evening, we talked about his findings, which included accounts of Mac-Duff's appearance, background, and habits; things he'd learned about the abandoned distillery; information about the two men's ideas and activities culled from margin notes and other material in books from Irons's library; and reports of apparent Shivas sightings during the 1980s. Here is a summary of what he told me:

F rom what the senior Ramsay had said, and from the notes of Shivas Irons, it was clear that Seamus MacDuff believed that his mother had been trained in Sufi and African shamanic disciplines, and that she had made a clairvoyant search for a mate with whom she could have a child who "would make a great discovery." This could have been mainly MacDuff family legend, but would—if true—help account for MacDuff's lifelong interest in human transformation and the further reaches of consciousness. But, it was not a legend that his father had brought him from West Africa to Oxford in 1888, or that he had made discoveries about flight dynamics that contributed to the development of rockets. This was established by Oxford University records.

It was also possible to picture with confidence what he looked like. Ramsay's description, a few notes in Irons's books, and accounts I'd heard at Burningbush in 1956 cohered to suggest that he was a striking, sometimes formidable figure, probably more than six feet tall, with dark skin, green eyes, and imposing carriage. Hannigan discounted stories I'd heard that the old man had lived in a cave near the thirteenth hole at Burningbush, though it was hard to say why people in the town believed that. According to a letter in the law firm's files from one of his trust's administrators, MacDuff rarely left his estate. He traveled to Edinburgh rarely and abroad just once, to Africa in August 1945.

In 1987, Hannigan was still collecting speculations and facts about the abandoned distillery. A story in the back pages of *The Herald* on August 16, 1984 described a couple who reported a "descending light" which they had seen on the property from their passing car. Their account coincided with UFO sightings by people who lived in the region. Another newspaper story, which appeared in *The Scotsman* of December 20, 1985, was a debunking account of beliefs that the place was haunted. Titled "The Wee Folk Are Growing," it quoted people who claimed to have seen brownies there, and noted that estimates of their size had grown since the distillery's closing. An elderly lady was quoted as saying that she'd seen the same brownie on several occasions, and that he had more than doubled in height, from about two to four feet tall. The story also included a brief description of the man named Haig, who claimed that his bodily functioning had been damaged by mysterious forces that haunted the place.

In the books that Hannigan had collected from the library of Shivas Irons, there were passages on flyleaves, underlinings, margin notes, and other inscriptions that agreed in various ways with things that Irons had told me and notes I'd copied from his journals. Partly because most of these were highly enigmatic, they fascinated Hannigan more than anything else he'd discovered about Irons and MacDuff. For example, he had several interpretations of this inscription from the book *Phenomena of Materialization:* "Like S. last night. Step by step. Lasted for five or six minutes." Since there was no date for the inscription, nor any explanation of what it meant, Hannigan thought it might refer to materializations by MacDuff of "energies or structures from hyperspace," or to an appearance by MacDuff himself as a phantom figure, either when he was alive or after he'd died. Most of the notes in Irons's books had a similar ambiguity, and for that reason challenged Hannigan's appetite for problem solving.

But a larger part of his fascination came from the fact that the activities of Irons and MacDuff seemed to resonate with his own theoretical work. Like many other physicists, Hannigan believed that all the physical forces, from gravity to the force that binds the atom, could best be unified by multidimensional—or "hyperspace"—models of the universe, such as those provided by superstring theories. If hyperspace was indeed a fact, which such theories suggested to him, human consciousness and the flesh could have relations with it that might be surmised by means of thought experiments and equations such as those he'd been developing. Though I couldn't follow his mathematics, I understood his reasoning, which resembled the thinking of my physicist friends. In 1987, hyperspace and string theory were the subjects of lively speculation, as they had been on and off since the early 1970s. It wasn't surprising that Hannigan was interested in them, but amazing to me that they'd been anticipated by Seamus MacDuff. His anticipation of them seemed to have been inspired, in part, by Pythagoras.

Shivas Irons had told me about the Greek philosopher. "Pith-uh-gor'-us had *the clue*," he had said with great conviction, which was "to ken the world from within." If we followed the ancient master's lead, we could find capacities within ourselves that technology would never give us. By listening to the "music of the spheres," for example, as Pythagoreans of antiquity had advised, we could extend our powers of mind over matter, uncover secrets of the flesh, and play golf with nothing more than an Irish shillelagh. Irons had been introduced to these ideas by MacDuff, who, like the Greek philosopher, believed that there were profound connections between geometry, consciousness, and the soul's adventures. Though some of this might have come from Sufi lore that MacDuff had learned from his mother, much of it had developed at Oxford, where he encountered conceptions of the "fourth dimension" then current among mathematicians and popular philosophers. In 1884, the clergyman Edwin Abbott had written *Flatland: A Romance of Many Dimensions by a Square,* which made fun of people who refused to admit the existence of other worlds; and H. G. Wells had proposed that it might be possible for humans to become invisible through a "formula (or) geometrical expression involving four dimensions." Shivas had owned Wells's book *The Invisible Man,* in which he'd inscribed this note: "S. says we can listen to hyperdimensional strings of the world-harp. Their music can't be modeled in three dimensions, but can be felt, heard, and embodied."

Showing me this, Hannigan was hugely excited. "D'ye realize, Murphy, that the old man probably came to this during his Oxford days *in the 1890s!* Now physicists from Berkeley to Princeton to Cambridge talk about ten-dimensional strings!"

"But they're not saying we should listen to them!" I protested. "When Irons said we could hear 'the music of the spheres,' he wasn't kidding. He and MacDuff thought we could do it, with the right kind of practice, and transform ourselves in the process. That's what they meant by practicing 'true gravity' and awakening the 'luminous body,' whatever the fuck that means. They were trying to join what they called 'outward' and 'inward' knowing, curvatures of space with bendings of the mind!"

In 1956, Irons had let me read his journals, in which there were constant references to the relations between "inward" and "outward" knowing, shamanic and scientific discipline, soul-making and world knowledge. He believed their marriage would set the stage for a momentous advance of humankind. But the nature of this transformation, and the specific methods that he and MacDuff were using to achieve it, remained a mystery. Several notes in Irons's books were opaque or indecipherable, a few were self-contradictory, and some were bizarre. And there was always the nagging question: "Why golf?" If Irons and MacDuff were trying to uncover the deepest secrets of human nature, why had they been so occupied with this time-consuming, often absurd, always frustrating game?

Hannigan also had reports from people who might have seen Shivas Irons during the 1980s. Besides the one from Martin Adams, there were two others. One came from a middle-aged couple who sometimes picnicked on MacDuff's estate. Hannigan had met them there in the summer of 1984, and had elicited a description from them of a man they'd encountered on the property a month before. He was six foot three or four, they estimated, with red hair, "soulful blue eyes," and a broad-shouldered athletic physique. The woman guessed he was about thirty years old because they had seen him running sprints—for sheer enjoyment, it seemed!—in the field below the house, and because he was filled with enormous vitality. But her husband thought he was more than sixty. There was, he said, "too much experience in his face" to be younger than that. And there were other discrepancies. She said that the man had a very slight Scottish inflection, but her husband swore he'd spoken with such a heavy burr that he could barely understand him.

And what had they talked about? "Murphy," said Hannigan, "ye know what he asked? Whether they felt somethin' strange in the place. Said he used to spend time there, but hadn't been back for several years and was surprised to see how different it looked. Then—if ye can believe this—he started swinging an imaginary golf club. That's right! Started swingin' a club and pointin' to places that would make good holes. They said he had a 'big wicked smile' when he said it, a smile that was hard to forget."

"It's *impossible* to forget," I said. "It's like the sun coming up."

"That's what *she* said! That's exactly how she put it. 'Like the sun coming up.' "

"What was he wearing?"

"A sweater, they thought, though they weren't completely sure, and corduroy pants. It occurred to them that he might be a golf professional."

"Jesus. It could be him! How long did they talk?"

"Just a few minutes. He was in great spirits, they said, and seemed to be enjoying himself. And the husband said another interesting thing. Said the man seemed to like *them*. Said he looked sad when he left, and apologized about having to leave so soon. Both of them were struck by his warmth. But there's a problem. They never saw a car, and wondered where he went or how he got there. Like the man in Dornoch. Just came and went, without any visible means of transport."

The third report of a possible sighting had come in this letter from an American physicist, which was postmarked from London on July 7, 1985:

Dear Buck,

I came away from the Edinburgh meeting more than ever convinced that string theory will succeed. After Schwartz and Green reopened the doors last year, I was excited. After hearing you, I'm ballistic! Keep going. You've got a chance for the brass ring.

But there's another reason for this letter. Remember our talk at the pub about your ventures into the paranormal? I was worried about you, right? Now I'm worried about us both. Near my hotel yesterday afternoon, I saw a man who might be your Chivas Regal. Red hair, athletic, Scots inflection, amazing blue eyes, and a presence that caught my attention. He was standing alone, about twenty feet from me, watching two boys kick a soccer ball toward a lamp post in the park. They were Irish, I think, about ten or eleven years old, and angry because they couldn't hit their target. When one of them decided to quit, our man came up to him and asked for the ball, which he kicked into the post with his eyes closed! He then got both of the boys to do it. This I swear. Both of them hit the thing with their eyes shut, not once but several times. Then, as if to give them further inspiration—or maybe to see if he could do it—he faced away from the post and hit it with a backward kick.

How he accomplished all this I don't know. He didn't give them much instruction. It seemed that he taught them the trick through his example more than anything else. Or did he use your ten-dimensional strings? What do you think? Did I spot him? Unfortunately, he disappeared when my back was turned.

Will write from Berkeley,

Saul-Paul Sirag

One question, though. You said he was tall. This man was shorter than me, which would make him less than five foot nine.

For me, this report didn't carry much weight. Irons was six foot three, and it was hard to imagine that Hannigan's friend could have thought he was half a foot shorter. But Hannigan disagreed. "In a trial," he said, "witnesses rarely agree about *everything* they saw, even if they were standing side by side. Maybe the park had a slope he didn't notice."

After reviewing Hannigan's discoveries and my own experiences of Shivas Irons, we talked into the night about their complexities and implications. In the afternoon, a storm came up, with occasional thunderclaps and lightning we could see through the studio windows. The gloomy sky over Edinburgh contributed to our dark imaginings, as we tried to find patterns in the many scraps of evidence we now possessed. But a coherent picture wouldn't emerge from the jigsaw puzzle. I was uncertain whether Shivas Irons still lived, and wondered, as I had for thirty-one years, what he and Seamus MacDuff were ultimately trying to achieve. Much about the two men was still hidden in mist, like the figure we'd seen in the necromanteion.

CHAPTER EIGHT

A TOWERING THUNDERHEAD rose from the platform of cumulus clouds advancing across Loch Awe. The steel grey column stretched more than forty thousand feet, I guessed, above the storm moving in from the west. From my vantage point above the abandoned distillery, it seemed to reach all the way to God.

Lightning flashed in the approaching clouds, momentarily illuminating the distant ridges of Ben Cruachan. This was a different vista than the one I'd experienced three days before. Though there was blue sky to the east, darkness was spreading through the morning light. The long bank of clouds was laced with black. The thunderhead was growing in size and majesty. As if to announce its approach, a sheet of lightning lit up the loch, and there was a gigantic thunderclap.

Sensing that rain would soon arrive, I drove down the hill, parked my car, and found refuge with my golf clubs under the overhanging roof of the abandoned distillery. From here I could watch the advancing storm and the enormous mushroom-shaped cloud above it. The thunderhead's eastward edge was brilliantly lit by the morning sun. Its dark grey cap was streaked with lavender, and its westward edge was black. More and more it reminded me of an atomic explosion.

"August 6 again, but 1950." Had MacDuff inscribed his mysterious photograph on a day like this? Maybe the reference to Hiroshima was inspired by this kind of weather, rather than things occult. The thought was reinforced by the storm's aliveness. The best things to come from my search for Shivas Irons were moments like this, rather than metaphysical speculations. The freedom that Irons and MacDuff represented was more present now, in this wild beauty of the elements, than it was in talk about materializations from hyperspace and disembodied spirits. Lightning broke loose beneath the clouds, lighting the peak of Ben Cruachan, then came distant rumbling. Zipping my windbreaker, I found a place to stay dry at the back of the overhang, and watched the rain grow heavier. There was little visibility now. Suddenly the fields below the hill disappeared in a wind-gusting downpour.

Protected by the building, I watched the rain slant past me. It was filled with dancing shades of grey, indigo, and violet, changing color like curtains of silver lamé. Something above and behind me was banging, maybe a shutter on MacDuff's old house or the limb of a tree hitting the abandoned distillery. In the wind's whistling I heard distant bagpipes, yearning, wild, and sad by turns, accompanied by muffled drums.

At irregular intervals the rain diminished, sometimes revealing a bright blue sky, sometimes the distant peaks of Ben Lui and Ben Cruachan. During one such respite, a window of sky was bordered with golden mist. During another, the clouds above me filled with rainbows. I watched these sometimes-subtle, sometimes-dramatic shifts of the elements with increasing wonder. A summer day in Scotland, Shivas Irons had told me, could have "tropical storms in the morning, a California afternoon, and an arctic night." He often enjoyed such weather in solitude, sometimes for twenty-four hours or more, discovering subtleties of land and sky that few people ever noticed. He'd given me a taste of this while crossing the Burningbush links at first light.

"Have ye ever counted shades of grey?" he'd asked. "Ye can see dozens, or hundreds, or thousands of 'em." Beyond the silver-sheened fairways, the hills of the town stood in silhouette against the dark grey sky. "Let's watch the land wake up," he'd said as we reached his car. "Every moment it's different. Every minute ye can see somethin' new." A bird was scampering on the silvery grass. Light appeared in a distant window. Beyond the golf course, the dark sea was rolling toward us.

"It's never the same," he whispered. "The light, the sound, the smells, the taste. They always can surprise ye." In the distance, a church bell sounded. It was tolling the hour, now three o'clock. As if in response, a car engine started on a distant part of the links. Were two lovers headed back to town?

"Ye know why the landscape changes?" he asked. "Do ye know the physics of it? It's because the light o' the sky comes at different angles every instant, through different air, to meet the earth's changing spectrum of color. Every hour of the day, if ye look close enough, the grass has all sorts o' browns and greens and yellows in it. And the bare ground, too, and the trees and the sea and the heather. When the lights of the sky meet the lights of the earth, they never make the same combination. The fairways are silver now, but they'll be violet soon, then shades o' green and blue and brown before the sun goes down. To a fresh eye, it's always surprisin'—*always,* even on a cloudy day, even in the dark like this. Do ye ever watch the land wake up?"

Lights were appearing on the hills of the town, each with its own unique luminosity. "We fix our sight," he said, "like we fix our thinking and our bones. We put ourselves in prisons. Our senses, our feelings, our bodies could have more freedom than we think."

An hour before, swinging Seamus's club by firelight in the ravine by the thirteenth hole, I had felt my "inner body" contract to an hourglass shape in which my waist seemed as small as a fist. Recalling the experience, I leaned for balance against the car. My boundaries weren't normal yet. There were hints of nausea in this newfound freedom.

"Ye look seasick," he said with amused concern. "Just do what I told ye before. Feel yer tummy. Take a breath. Let the woozy feelin's go."

Lowering my center of gravity, as he had suggested during our midnight lesson, I felt the nausea pass. In spite of my fatigue and light-headedness, there were first hints of a pleasurable equanimity.

"Ye see." He touched my chest. *"Ye can always come back.* No matter how seasick ye get when yer boundaries shift, no matter how strange yer mind is actin', ye can find a home in this empty space, this silence behind yer thoughts. It's always there. It's who ye are. Waitin' to be rediscovered. The truest center o' gravity is not the center of the Earth. It's at the center of the soul. And because it's everywhere, Michael, it gives us our deepest stability."

From his suggestive power perhaps, or the cumulative effects of our all-night vigil, my light-headedness gave way to the liberating emptiness I'd experienced at the end of our golf round. There was surprising stabilty in this vanishing state, a sense that nothing could limit, disturb, or attach itself to me.

"There's nothin' to knock off balance," he'd said. "This is our best center because it's everywhere—and because it's no single thing at all."

First streaks of violet appeared in the hills, and the fairways were rainbows of grey and silver. A breeze had come up, laced with the taste of salt, and seabirds were circling above us. A vow had risen in me then to spend more time at first light, watching the land awaken.

A nd a similar vow was rising now. If this storm lasted all day, I would sit here and enjoy it. It had more shades of grey and silver, more iridescence, more music than I could ever perceive. No one could count its colors and textures, or anticipate all of its surprises. And this was true of any day, or any weather. Each had a richness beyond calculation.

In all directions, the rain had turned to silken drizzle. To the northwest, through the curtain of falling dew, the peak of Ben Cruachan reappeared. Sunlight was bleaching the clouds above me, while the thunderhead, atop its platform of cumulus clouds, pulled away to the north like a gigantic battle station. Again I could see the entire column and its mushroom cap. As if to cover its retreat, it fired a few bolts of lightning, and thunder shook the roof above me.

I t was almost ten o'clock, and the rolling hills glistened in the morning light. Stepping out from under the overhang, I was surprised how warm it was. Plumes of steam rose from MacDuff's old house, giving it a golden halo. In the breeze that followed the storm, there was a fragrance of sycamore, wet grass, and oak, and a faint whistling in the roof above me. The entire property seemed reborn.

With my clubs and practice balls, I found the stretch of ground from which I'd hit drives during my previous visit. After removing my windbreaker and slipping a golf glove on my left hand, I smoothed a patch of stubble and grass and surveyed the field between me and the abandoned first green. It didn't matter that the rain-soaked ground wouldn't afford much roll. I would not begin by hitting for distance. Instead, I intended to make as complete a surrender as possible to the presence I'd felt here before. Everything else, such as hitting balls four hundred yards, would have to give way to the comprehensive intelligence that seemed to inhabit this place. There were sounds of distant thunder. To the north, the thunderhead's cap was disappearing beyond the peak of Ben Cruachan. Just a few scattered clouds trailed in the wake of the storm.

After a series of gentle stretches, I started to swing my driver. I could do this with leisure now. For this day and another week, I had no obligations. My publisher and friends had agreed that I needed to get away from my book, on which I'd worked for three years without a vacation. There were no schedules to meet, no bets to be won, no hecklers or advisors. There was nothing to keep me from the simple pleasure of hitting golf shots. When wayward impulses and voices rose, I would let them pass. If lost in fantasies, I would return to the silence behind them. By practicing in this way, I could yield more fully to the presence that was gathered here, following its guidance through the challenges, charms, and illusions of MacDuff's mysterious golf course. If I could hold such a focus for the rest of the day, there was no telling what the place might teach me.

Again I looked down the abandoned fairway. High wet grass stretched for some 250 yards. Any balls I hit from here were likely to be swallowed in it. Then came a first hint of guidance. I would wait before starting around the course. The silence that pervaded the place was settling more deeply into my muscles and bones. I could experience it more fully now, and open to the subtleties it contained, in the simple movements required by hitting chip shots.

After choosing a target some thirty feet away, I stood back to note the images, feelings, sensations, and thoughts that formed a steady stream within me. It is a practice of certain martial arts and many contemplative schools. From it can come new sensitivities to one's environment, openings to inspired guidance, and a spontaneous pleasure.

When I'd hit about thirty balls, I realized that they were clustered in three rings around the target. Had a subconscious guidance done this? Three rings, three orbits: Maybe they signified that my practice was aimed toward the Earth, the third planet from the sun, or that this simple exercise was showing me separate spheres of consciousness. But such speculations seemed too far-fetched. With a sense of relief, I gave up my questions about the pattern. If there was any meaning in it, that would eventually become apparent. I took some practice swings with my driver. There was new elasticity in my arms and legs, something beyond my ordinary range of movement. After adjusting my cap to screen out the sun, I hit a drive toward the abandoned first green that sailed beyond the tall wet grass.

For the next six hours, with just one break to eat a sandwich, I played shots on six of the seven holes. Here are some highlights of my experience:

- Nearly every hole presented illusions that caused me to make frequent readjustments of my alignment and swing. Recognizing them one by one caused the entire place to have a provisional, shifting, even transparent quality that has carried over into my perception of other golf courses.

- Each hole produced peculiar frustrations that forced me back to that choiceless awareness, emptiness, or "mindfulness" I'd practiced while hitting chip shots. Again and again I remembered the words of Shivas Irons. "It's always waitin'," he'd said. "Aye one field afore ye e'er swung. It's our best center because it's everywhere." In letting go of feelings and thoughts, of images and particular sensations, I discovered new freedom and energy, as well as a self-renewing pleasure. The practice reminded me of Gregorian chants and similar religious music. There was regenerative power in its plain repetitions, a movement toward something timeless. "Perfect music contains the maximum amount of monotony that is bearable," wrote Simone Weil. Her sentence made more and more sense to me as the day unfolded.

• Every hole provided opportunities for shots that were specially shaped, including fades and draws, slices and punch hooks, and airplane shots that fly low before rising to clear an obstacle. Practicing these hour by hour, my connection with the ball in flight grew steadier, closer, and stronger, stretching the mysterious envelope that passes beyond our flesh. My round with Shivas Irons had shown me the power of this extrasomatic reach, and letters from readers had confirmed it. Drawing on Native American lore, the parapsychologist William Roll had called it an aspect of the "long body."*

With each curving journey of the ball, this "inner body," "long body," or "subtle flesh" came into higher definition. Toward the end of the day, as it became more dense and elastic at once, I remembered Shivas Irons saying that when it "locked in," one could hit ball after ball not twenty feet from the pin, as ordinary shot-mastery would dictate, but "three feet, one foot, two inches away on hole after hole beyond all probabilities, beyond the ordinary powers o' the brain and the ordinary laws o' physics. Someday ye'll see it on television, and the whole world will recognize it." Now I felt what he meant. More than ever before, I learned that golf is an exercise of "imagination with hands."

• And with this stretching of the "inner" or "long body," there was a subtler process still. At first it resembled a bubble

---

* See appendices.

bath in something like ginger ale; but by the time I finished the round, it seemed more than anything else as if some invisible substance was forming inside me. In certain schools of Taoism, Sufism, and other sacred traditions, it is said that humans can give birth to a body of "spirit-matter." At certain moments, especially when my focus held for every part of my swing, it seemed that the process was starting in me.

Each of these realizations developed as the day went on. For example, when I returned to the practice of relinquishing thoughts after my attention wandered, I felt a tiny wave of pleasure. Gradually these redemptive surges increased, growing closer to that condition Eastern philosophers have called "nonreferential joy" or "self-existent delight." It became increasingly evident that this simple restorative attention develops with practice, growing stronger with repetition.

And it occurred to me that when we practice such awareness as we practice golf, or as we practice any skill, we store something away for times when our thoughts and feelings wander. This centered exercise, which aligns body and mind with the restorative silence from which they come, makes that silence more accessible, more available when we fall from its grace. But these recognitions were not always pleasurable. My day of practice brought unexpected difficulties as well as illumination, starting almost as soon as I cleared the wet grass with my drive.

In my light canvas bag there were a driver, three-wood and four-wood, eight irons, a pitching wedge, sand wedge, and putter. Since I lay about 140 yards from the rise upon which the first green had stood, I decided to use a seven-iron. Addressing the ball, I visualized a line to the center of the rise, but hit the ball to the right. The ground had a springy, claylike texture that gave good feel to the shot. This was a good place to practice.

I hit a second shot; but like my first, it flew to the right. Again I visualized a line to the target, searching kinesthetically for the flaw in my swing. Was it the tendency I sometimes had to drop my right shoulder and block my pivot? I took more practice swings, picturing an even, flowing turn, and hit a third shot. But like the others it flew right. "God damn it!" I swore. I was filled with a sudden, inexplicable anger, made more acute by my resolution to relinquish such feelings.

After placing a ball on a patch of stubble, I surveyed the field again. The burst of anger had surprised me. In letting go of wayward thoughts, did one risk letting go of useful defenses? I addressed another ball, pictured its line to the target—but topped it. "God damn it!" I said loudly, shaking the sting from my hands. Was this a signal to stop? Maybe I needed a longer break before I swung again.

At that moment, I remembered Mortimer Crail's book. "We are a collection of cells that behaves like a thundering buffalo herd," the learned professor had written. "Our chief exemplar is always the person we were just a moment before." That was certainly apparent now. Something in me wanted to throw the club, or break it, or use it to hit a tree. Though no one was watching, and I was here to discover the secret graces of golf, the herd of impulsions that called itself Michael Murphy was thundering through this empty space kicking up psychic debris. Dropping my seven-iron, I looked at the fields around me. To the north, about a half-mile distant, on a hill above the abandoned third fairway, a man stood facing in my direction. Was he watching? I felt a twinge of embarrassment. Retrieving my club, I swung it back and forth, and vowed to relinquish the images clustering around my frustration. When at last my anger passed, I hit another ball. This pattern would hold for the rest of the day. When my mental discipline lapsed, I eventually recovered it. When I let go of the thing that disturbed me, a regenerative silence was waiting.

Physiologists have shown that each mental activity is connected with particular bodily tensions, and this was confirmed again and again before the day was done. Muscular inhibitions I hadn't noticed were more and more evident now, and with each relinquishment of a disturbing thought a tightness somewhere lessened. For example, a band of tension ran from my neck to my jaws, causing me to clench my teeth whenever I felt frustrated, and I tended to tighten my shoulders each time I got ready to swing my driver. These unconscious armorings relaxed as they came to awareness, giving me a firmer sense of control.

But the increasing buoyancy I felt came from something more than muscular relaxation. The silence revealed when tensions diminish contains a self-existent pleasure. The emptiness in which every impulse rises is itself regeneration. Let go of ordinary feeling and thought, and you are at once more self-sufficient. It seemed incongruous that golf could reveal this.

To my surprise, it was eleven-thirty. I'd spent more than half an hour hitting these twenty shots. After picking up my clubs and remaining practice balls, I started toward the rise. The sky was almost cloudless now. A breeze was blowing from the west. The man on the distant hill had vanished.

For the next half-hour, I hit shots to the second green. But this oddly sloping hole, which still seemed 50 yards long though I knew it was 120, didn't reveal all the secrets of its deceptiveness. Playing the right club required a willingness to override my instinctive caution, a faith that transcended first impressions, and a surrender to unfamiliar guidance. It took me more than twenty shots to swing with the conviction I needed.

Half an hour later, I sat atop the rise. Hannigan guessed that MacDuff had used esoteric geometry to design this strange little course, and I was now inclined to agree. Certainly, there was such an art. In a desert between Tashkent and Samarkand, I'd been led by a Russian-Uzbek friend to an underground mosque with cavernous vaults designed according to principles of Islamic sacred architecture. Like this innocent-seeming stretch of land, it had a presence that was hard to account for. Our group had prayed and meditated there, with an aged Sufi master who'd preserved certain mystical secrets of Islam through decades of Communist rule. Both body and soul, he'd told us, are influenced inescapably by our surroundings. We can't help looking up at Reims or Chartres, following the thrust of spires and nave toward God on high. Again and again on every side, Gothic cathedrals lead us toward the Transcendent. But in a Zen Buddhist temple, the walls might open to gardens all around, guiding our attention to the immanence of the world's secret splendor, and in these dark and resonant vaults, listening to chants older than the Prophet, we were led into depths of consciousness inaccessible by the light of day. If MacDuff had learned such things from his mother, who'd been raised among African Sufis, there could be resonances between this Scottish estate and that mosque near Samarkand. Though one was built beneath the ground for religious worship, and the other on rolling hills as a field of sport, in both it was evident that the contours of a physical environment exert mysterious influences upon one's cells and consciousness. Conceivably, such influences might extend to any spirit-body in which our flesh is situated.

A cloud was passing overhead, giving relief from the sun. I wondered what lines of force connected MacDuff's old house to me. There must have been days like this when Shivas Irons sat here, on this very spot, absorbing his teacher's mystic geometry. As if in prayer, I asked for clues to his whereabouts. What was he doing now? Did he ever play golf, or had his practice taken him to other activities? But no hint of an answer came. After a moment of expectant but unanswered waiting, I decided to continue around the course.

D uring the next hour I played perhaps fifty shots on the long, curving field which had served as MacDuff's third fairway. This part of the day comprised a learning plateau, during which I persisted with no dramatic result in the practice of golfing nonattachment. Anger was not a problem now. No insight mesmerized me. Boredom was only an occasional enemy. It was good that a gentle breeze was blowing. It gave relief from the sun. And wonderful to smell the summer grass and breathe the heather's fragrance. Again and again the questions rose: Why don't more people do this? How have we learned so well to avoid these simple pleasures? Why do so few of us appreciate the joys of thoughtless silence?

A round one o'clock I climbed from the abandoned third green up the hill to MacDuff's tall house, and found a relatively sheltered spot where, for a leisurely twenty minutes, I enjoyed the lettuce-and-prosciutto sandwich I'd brought from Edinburgh. To this day, I remember the taste and smell of its thinly sliced, freshly baked rye bread, and its mayonnaise, parsley, pepper, and dill. My thought-free condition seemed to facilitate this vivid and lasting memory. Maybe the practice of relinquishing thoughts allows the brain to register olfactory and gustatory impressions with supernormal fidelity. I've often wondered if that prosciutto sandwich was as delicious as I now remember it. Maybe its afterglow is imprinted, and thus enhanced, in the taste buds of my spirit-body.

A fter this brief but memorable lunch, I stood on the narrow ledge which had served as MacDuff's fourth tee. The narrow canyon below seemed more threatening than it had three days before. The hole's narrow, bush-enclosed target beckoned and challenged at once. It would be interesting to see what lessons about it had registered in my golfing unconscious.

Placing my clubs at the back of the ledge, I looked for good turf to hit from. Then I paused. After the storm, the crevasse would be soaked, and any balls that landed there might be buried. As I studied the dark declivity, it seemed to wink. This was more than a passing illusion. The entire almond-shaped opening had appeared to close, then open, then close again. Though I'd blinked away the impression, the canyon stared up at me now with taunting innocence. Suddenly embarrassed, I turned to look around me. About half a mile away, on the hill from which a man had watched me, there stood a woman. I looked at the canyon again. Its eye still gazed in sly repose, beguiling, teasing, laughing at me. It was urging me to meet its playful challenge.

Both golf and contemplative exercise make us naked to the eye of the soul. Now it seemed that they worked in concert to undress me. Since adolescence, the twin attractions of sex and asceticism had crisscrossed my heart, struggling to achieve hormonal dominance. That their tug-of-war would surface now was further evidence that this was a day of initiation. How had Mortimer Crail put it? That a golf hole with a female aspect could threaten annihilation? I looked to the distant rise again. Yes, the solitary figure was a woman. She looked directly at me now, her hair and a gossamer cape flowing in the wind behind her.

"You're an idiot, Murphy!" I exclaimed, picking up my seven-iron. "To hell with it!" With a carefree swing, I hit a ball to the left of the glen and watched it curve right for several seconds then drop into the dark declivity. This time it didn't wink.

I stood back from the tee. The ball had split the crevasse precisely, after a delicious, curving ride, and would be played in my memory again and again, perhaps for the rest of my life. With exhilaration, I looked toward the hidden target. The shot brought an uncanny sense of release, and feeling of culmination. Why deface it with further efforts?

With my bag on my shoulder, I started toward the fifth tee. It was liberating to leave my ball there. Perhaps like a seed, it was buried in the canyon's little spring, and would be found one day by another pilgrim to Irons and MacDuff. Then I stopped. It wasn't a woman on the rise. The person standing there was a man, and the thing I'd taken to be a cape was a kite that was trailing behind him. Golden and mandorla-shaped, it rose higher and higher in the gusting wind, swooping playfully every few seconds. When I reached the fifth tee, it was still visible though its owner had vanished. A few seconds later, it dropped beneath the rim of the hill.

Looking down the fifth fairway, I felt a streaming effervescence. It had occasionally come to awareness during the last three hours, but my shot on the previous hole had increased it. Shielding my eyes against the sun, I studied the field that confronted me. It was covered with high grass all the way to what remained of the green nearly four hundred yards away. To my right, the hill on which MacDuff's house stood rose steeply for some thirty or forty feet.

The effervescence was stronger now, streaming as if from invisible springs. Distance runners had talked about such experience. Several readers of *Golf in the Kingdom* had described it. One golfer had told me that it felt as if she were sitting in a tub of champagne, and another had said it reminded her of Schweppes tonic. I decided not to play this hole. It was better to sit here for a while, and let the state develop. What seemed to be tiny points of light were rising, as if from some invisible world, from my head to the soles of my feet.

I thought about Nadia's "spirit-matter." Was this the thing she'd tried to picture with her drawings the day before? She and I had talked about such a phenomenon reported in the sacred traditions. The Roman Catholics' "mystical luminosity," the Sufis' "man of light," the Tibetan Buddhists' "diamond body," the Taoists' "spirit child": Each in its own way represents a set of experiences that suggest we can radically alter our flesh, and prominent among these is the perception of particles, "sparks," or scintillae that revitalize mind and body.* Everything now seemed charged with the radiance that rose in my cells. The clouds, the grass, the trees were filled with the same aliveness. This effervescence, in which the whole world sat, was available to everyone. For a few moments I sat quietly to enjoy it.

Then, on a sudden impulse, I picked up my clubs and carried them to the long rolling field that once had comprised MacDuff's sixth fairway. For another hour I continued to practice, clearing my mind again and again while hitting irons to various targets. Though my legs were sore and my hands were blistering, something in me knew that the embracing awareness I experienced now had existed before I'd ever hit a golf shot.

It occurred to me that this was one of the game's greatest secrets, and a reason so many people continue to play though their score does not improve. In its journey around the course, golf is a place to let go of misfortune, to start again, to return to this ever-present delight. I thought of my friend Glen Albaugh teaching his University of the Pacific golfers to clear their minds before each shot, to learn from each failure and success, to bring kinesthetic imagination to their swings, and to constantly reclaim the purity of the moment. He and other sport psychologists have been agents of

---

* These have been called *"opintheres"* or scintillae in alchemical texts, "world-pervading soul-sparks" in Cabalistic writings, "atoms of light" by various Gnostics of antiquity, "sparks of stellar essence" by the Greek philosophers Heraclitus and Democritus, "orgone" by Wilhelm Reich, and elements of the "biofield" by Russian parapsychologists. Carl Jung studied such phenomena for many years. See: Carl Jung, *Collected Works*, volume 12, p. 301, n. 26.

an approach to the game not unlike the one I learned from Shivas
Irons.

A t about four o'clock, I walked along the seventh hole, absorbing its contours for future reference, then climbed the
hill where the buildings stood. There I surveyed the course as a
whole, imagining various shot-making experiments Shivas Irons
might have tried. Conceivably, he'd hit MacDuff's house more
than once. Did he ever break a window? Did his formidable mentor ever reprimand him?

Shadows were lengthening now on the easterly side of the
abandoned distillery. In spite of the afterglow produced by this
day of contemplative golf, I felt a tinge of sadness. What a privilege to have seen Shivas Irons hit shots here. What amazement to
hear his conversations with Seamus MacDuff. I walked around the
house for a while and pictured the two men talking. More of the
property's physical and spiritual contours than I could estimate
were imprinted in my muscles and subliminal mind. It would take
weeks and months, perhaps years, to assimilate what the place
could teach me.

But part of that teaching crystallized sooner than I expected. As
I put my clubs into the car, experiences from different parts of the
day cohered into a pattern. However tenuous some of these had
been, all had arisen from a common ground of secret capacity. For
periods ranging from a few minutes to several hours, my vision,
hearing, taste, and smell, as well as extrasensory perception, had
grown more acute; my kinesthetic awareness, balance, and dexter-
ity had improved; volition had grown more efficient; new powers
of mind over matter had appeared; and my vitality had increased.
Through most of the day these separate awakenings had been
supported by the unitive awareness Shivas Irons had celebrated,
that sense of "one field before ye e'er swung," and by a self-

renewing pleasure that seemed to rise from something primordial. Again and again, both my body's structures and sense of self had shifted to accommodate these enhancements of functioning. Perhaps the best way to say it is that I seemed more body and soul at once.

The pattern was evident now. Every human capacity is rooted in a greater life waiting to be born in us. This day of golf, this mysterious place, had briefly evoked that simultaneity of extraordinary attributes Shivas Irons was cultivating, providing a premonition of what he and his mentor called "the life to come."

CHAPTER NINE

DRIVING SOUTH ON the B840, I could see Loch Awe to my right through stands of conifers and silver birch. The green hills beyond its slate grey waters, and the dense stands of fir trees to my left, were sharply outlined now in what Scots like to call "the gloaming." Each view that appeared on the winding road had an element of surprise. The expansive, thought-free silence produced by six hours of contemplative golf made each vista a separate enchantment.

It would take another hour to reach the hotel on the coast near Melfort, where I would spend the night, but the drive gave me a chance to enjoy my new sensory acuity. The condition seemed completely natural now. On the far shore of the loch, half a mile away, in the shadows of hills that rose steeply behind it, a large white house had windows with latticework. There could be no doubt about it. Both windows had fine diagonal struts that were plainly visible to me. And to my left, violet and pink and magenta rhododendrons were etched in a cool recess of trees, magnified it seemed by some invisible lens between us. Twice I stopped to enjoy the view and absorb the evening stillness. My day at Mac-

Duff's abandoned estate had produced a quiet, lasting intoxication.

During my second stop, to test my newfound perceptual abilities, I got out of the car and looked for distant objects. Such an exercise is made easier by relaxing your gaze before refocusing. "Make the world an Impressionist painting," I seemed to remember Shivas saying. "Then turn yer eyes to a telescope." But more than oculomotor nerves are involved in such a practice. The sustained relinquishment of thought, whether in golf or religious discipline, seems to mobilize clairvoyance as well as sensory acuity. "Ye can marry eyesight to second sight," Shivas had put it picturesquely. Though the fact is not widely appreciated, the two powers can operate with marvelous coherence.

Half a mile away across the loch, in the cool shadows of fir and pine, a stone house stood beside the water, and in front of it a couple were embracing. Could I see if they were kissing? Could I tell how old they were? Softening my focus, I let the loch turn into a picture by Monet, a gently shimmering waterscape suffused with the lingering sunlight of this quiet summer evening. Then, without strain, I brought the scene closer until it seemed painted by Vermeer. The man wore jeans and a loose white shirt, the woman a wide-brimmed hat, long yellow skirt, and flowing neck scarf. This was not my imagination. She was naked above her waist, his left arm fell around her shoulder, and with his right hand he caressed her breasts sensually.

For a moment I stood transfixed. This was a new kind of voyeurism, another grace of contemplative golf, a further sign that the disciplines of Shivas Irons could deliver unexpected pleasures. As he playfully bit her neck, she took off her wide-brimmed hat and sailed it across a grassy slope that ran from the house to the water. They were in their thirties and English, I guessed—don't ask me why—and their excitement was contagious. Caught between the perceptual mode of Vermeer and Monet's soft focus, I watched with arousal and growing embarrassment. As she untied her scarf, he turned her around and kissed the back of her neck and shoulders. As she looked toward the sky, he stroked her breasts and stomach. This continued for a minute or more while she dropped her scarf and unbuttoned her yellow skirt. But a car was coming down the road, and it honked as it drew near me. Did its driver sense what I was doing? With disappointment and a hint of relief, I watched as the couple went into the house.

Driving along the loch, I felt residues of vicarious erotic pleasure, which reinforced the continuing afterglow of my day at Mac-Duff's estate. This mood was enhanced by the surprising vistas my new visual acuity revealed in all directions. But a half hour later, as the sun disappeared behind hills to the west and shadows lengthened, my feelings were colored with a faint melancholy. I already missed the mysterious property and its reminders of Shivas Irons. Would the joy and new capacities I found there last? As I reached the end of the loch, its slate-colored waters were filling with shades of indigo, dark blue, and purple. My emotions began to reflect their dark mood.

The hotel's dining room stood about fifty yards from the edge of a little bay, with a sweeping view of coastal inlets framed by mountainous islands. Shuna rose steeply above a mainland promontory to my right, Scarba reached toward the south beyond it, and the darkening ridges of Jura were barely visible on the horizon. Under the overcast sky, the three islands seemed harsh and lonely. The stillness outside had entered the room. Conversation was hushed at the tables around me.

Near the water's edge, a high-masted sailboat rocked gently on long glassy swells. Like me, it was moored at some invisible depth but moved by unpredictable currents. Anchored in the silence I'd practiced all day, I felt unexpected swells of emotion that seemed to come from distant places. Unbidden, an image of Seamus Mac-Duff, as if in a fine-grained photograph, with green deeply set eyes, bristling white eyebrows and beard, broad tawny forehead creased by three horizontal lines, and a strong aristocratic nose that gave evidence of both Scottish and African genes. And his mother: with majestic carriage, her mouth exquisitely formed in the Fulani way, her dark eyes looking toward a distant horizon. Both images were vividly etched. Had they entered deep channels of my mind as I'd hit golf shots at MacDuff's estate?

Now the bay was darker than the coastal inlets beyond it. What further impressions did the depths of my memory harbor? Another surprising image came: of Shivas Irons hitting shots across the hill on which MacDuff's house stood to the declivity that held the fourth green. Secretly, I'd known it all along. Each shot left a mark in the air, a lasting trace, a girder of spirit-matter. His graceful, upright, powerful swing, with its fluid turn of hips and shoulders, was as vividly present to me as it had been at Burning-bush. With each shot he was building something. I could see that clearly now. Something made of stuff that links the soul to living flesh.

"Would you like a drink," the young waitress said with an Australian or cockney accent.

"A glass of red wine," I answered. "Do you have Chianti by the glass?"

"Is that French?"

"No, Italian."

"Well, I'll see." She paused. "Does it matter how much it costs?"

I said that it didn't, and she turned to cross the room.

A middle-aged American couple and their son had taken seats at the table next to me. They had driven for most of the day from Loch Ness, I could hear the father complaining, and there were *no* monsters in the loch.

"But, Daddy," the boy protested. "The man said one was there."

"It's a myth," said the father, a professorial-looking man about fifty with closely cropped hair and horn-rimmed glasses. "It's like the Easter bunny."

"But they have photographs!"

"They're fake," the man said firmly, gesturing to suggest that the boy keep his voice down. "They're waves, or logs."

"But there *could* be a monster. The lake's so deep!"

"Do you believe in Santa Claus?" The father signaled to the waitress.

The boy had red hair and a freckled face, and was nine or ten years old. "Of course!" he said. "I saw him at Christmas. You gave him a glass of whiskey!"

The father didn't dispute this. Trading glances with his wife, he agreed that Santa was real. But not the Loch Ness monster! Fatigue, perhaps, and the accumulated frustrations of a daylong drive on roads narrower than he was used to, had caused him to make a stand. Santa was real, but not some underwater dinosaur conceived to lure more tourists to the loch.

Sensing that I had overheard him, the man gave me a weary shrug. "Do you believe in the Loch Ness monster?" he asked. "This has been a long debate."

"Well . . ." I hesitated. "You never know. Maybe."

"You see!" the boy broke in. "Daddy, you never know."

"Thanks," his father said with good-natured irony, and I turned to look out the window.

Then I had a troubling thought. Was I concocting my own Loch Ness monster? Was part of my experience the result of wish fulfillment? Hannigan could be right. Maybe some of the things I'd experienced this day were nothing but illusions. Had I really seen that latticework in windows across the loch, or the breasts of the woman in the yellow skirt?

The waitress placed a glass of red wine on the opposite side of the table. Did she secretly object to my having it? They had no Chianti, she said with a shrug, but this was from somewhere in the south of France not far from Italy. I ought to like it. Was I ready to eat? The dining room was about to close.

Suppressing my irritation, I ordered a salad and bowl of soup and readjusted my chair to face away from the other tables. At the foot of the incline that ran from the dining room to the water, swells broke gently on a rocky beach. A light came on in the sailboat's cabin, and another at the top of its swaying mast. On a promontory to the south, house lights were sparkling near the water. The distant islands seemed less lonely now, and my mood began to lift. In the immediate elevation the wine produced, my doubts were starting to fade. Yes, I'd seen that couple embrace, seen him stroke her naked breasts, seen her toss that wide-brimmed hat across the sloping lawn. I saw them just as clearly now as I had beside the loch. And these images of Seamus Mac-Duff, his mother, and Shivas Irons were more than fantasy. They were telling me something real, something I'd missed, something subject to laws of the strangeness curve.

The two men had built an invisible structure on the hills above Loch Awe, and many who'd been there secretly knew it. But you had to have the right kind of eyes to see, and ears to hear its hidden music, and a body that could feel its touch. Otherwise you'd think it was only neurosis or daydreams or ghosts or leprechauns. Suddenly, the entire place was present. It had layers I hadn't seen, from its dirt to its secret streamers of light, and something was using it like a bridge to move between this world and another.

As I finished the soup and drank a second glass of wine, I tried to recall the things I knew about sacred architecture. There was a growing literature about Feng Sui, the Chinese art of geomancy, and the mysteries of Stonehenge, and the mystical symbolism at

Chartres, and lore in virtually every culture about the occult relationships of buildings, soul, and special pieces of ground. No one
had made me more alive to all this than the aged Muslim we'd
met at the mosque between Tashkent and Samarkand. . . .

"L isten!" he'd admonished our group in Uzbek through a Russian interpreter. "Listen to the holy names. You can hear
them if you are quiet enough."

And then we heard the sacred chant, coming it seemed from
caves even deeper than the one in which we stood. "Allah. Al-aha.
Allah. Al-aha." The names of God rose from caverns below, sung
not by humans but the place itself. This holy space, the old man
said, was bearing witness to God day and night though the world
above was distracted. It was singing His names for eternity
whether or not we joined in.

Misha, our Russian interpreter, began to chant, blending his
bass voice with the sound arising from the vault, while the rest of
us scanned the high rock walls with flashlights and Coleman
lamps. But the old man ordered us to stop. Seating us around a
shallow pit carved in the cavern floor, he said that the mosque had
things to tell us that our noisy minds and voices blocked.

And then, as the silence grew, something altered the way we
sat, slowed our breathing patterns, attenuated our impulse to
move. All of us talked about it later. The cavernous mosque had
reformed our bodies to some degree and thus our consciousness.
The old man would tell us later that its subterranean vaults had
affected countless pilgrims in similar ways since the early Stone
Age. But shamans, Zoroastrians, and Muslim mystics had found
ways to increase the caves' power. New vaults had been opened.
People who knew about relations between the heart, the soul, and
physical spaces had added their own inspired touch to the caverns'
transformative contours.

In bed that night, looking through a window into the starlit sky, I remembered the aged Muslim's talk about the body's architecture. Like the underground mosque, he'd said, our muscles and bones can be configured to induce particular states of mind. We did that by bowing toward Mecca, or kneeling in prayer in a Christian church, or sitting cross-legged like Indian yogis. Every posture induces a characteristic set of mental attitudes, and unique condition of the heart. Each of our physical acts—even those of which we're unaware—has distinctive effects upon our body, our soul, and every person we meet. Somatic patterning is a social act. It helps determine our ethics, our philosophy, our beliefs about God, and all our relationships. And because it can be cultivated, it can enhance every part of our life.

I thought about Nadia Kirova and her praise for the bodily configurations of love. Had she learned something about them in the Sufi group to which our Muslim guide belonged? Her rapturous postures in the necromanteion suggested that her convictions were based upon more than theory. The light in her eyes and music in her voice as she celebrated the sexual play of angels gave evidence of her deep delight in the body's erotic structures.

My mind was drifting now, and I fell into a half-sleep filled with images of the mosque near Samarkand, of Shivas Irons hitting shots with highly improbable swings, and of MacDuff's abandoned golf course. The property had different faces; beguiling, ugly, and surreal by turns, sometimes attractive and threatening at once. On a dark night under heavy rains, a stalwart bearded man—probably Seamus himself—stood beside the house exulting; and on a cloudless winter day, the fairways were covered with glistening snow like the distant white peaks of Ben Cruachan; and at first light, Shivas was hitting long shots toward the evanescent first green. Day by day, season by season, the place was still unfolding, giving birth to something just out of my reach.

But sleep, too, is influenced by somatic architecture. Turning onto my right side, I tried to find a better posture with which to summon dreams that would bring me closer to Shivas Irons. I moved toward an image just an eyelash away. There was a solitary light on the island of Shuna, a fragrance of conifers and the sea. The deep black sky, the starlit bay, the sounds of waves on this quiet night, seemed to rise within me. There was no separation now between me and the fields of MacDuff's estate.

The golden brown fairway pointed west, gently rolling in the noonday sun, and halfway to the distant green there was a beckoning light. "Walk toward it," I heard Shivas Irons saying. "Go toward it like ye're going home."

It was larger and brighter than it had seemed from the hill. If I came closer, it would swallow me up. . . .

I woke with a start, banging against the headboard. Clouds were moving across the stars, and wind was banging tree limbs against the roof. Then a shadow crossed the window. Had someone glanced inside? Rising quickly, I opened the sliding glass door. But no one was standing on the little porch, nor were there any trees or bushes behind which someone might hide. Deciding I'd imagined the thing in the window, I pulled curtains across the door. The dream that awakened me was vivid still, and gave rise to this series of thoughts:

The man named Haig knew things he hadn't told Hannigan.

There was a passage in Crail's book with clues to MacDuff's mysterious inscription, "Sunrise at noon. August 6 again, but 1950."

I should read the letters Hannigan had gotten with reports of possible Shivas sightings. There were connections between them that we had missed.

The dream—and my reaction to it—made sleep impossible now. Listening to rain against the windows, I decided to leave the hotel at dawn and drive back to the village near the Ramsay Distillery. People there could tell me how to find the property's former caretaker, the man named Haig who claimed that his body had somehow been altered by forces that lived in the place.

CHAPTER TEN

NEAR PORTINNISHERRICH, A village south of Mac-Duff's former property, there is a narrow unpaved road that runs east from Loch Awe and the B840. It winds through stands of conifers, some of which had been brutally clear-cut in 1987, past fields bordered with low rock walls toward higher elevations. On this rainy afternoon, its rutted surface forced me to drive with care until I reached Haig's little house on a slope of Beinn Bhreac, more than a thousand feet above the loch.

The stone cottage was enclosed by a dry-rock wall. Behind it, on a field that rose toward Beinn Bhreac's summit, sheep and milk cows grazed. I got out of the car and looked around me. To the west and far below, Loch Awe was barely visible through silken drizzle, framed on its western shore by the wooded ridges of Inverinan Forest. Again I was struck by the majesty of the Scottish Highlands. Vistas such as these caused thoughts to stop. For several minutes I watched mist-shrouded peaks appear as the rain receded.

Then I turned and walked past an empty cowshed and a battered Land Rover. Though the sky was darkly overcast, there was no light in the house or smoke coming from its chimney. On each side of a rough wooden door, like baleful eyes, deeply recessed windows faced me. "Mr. Haig?" I called. "Mr. Haig, are you there?"

There was no answer. "Haig!" I called more loudly. "Mr. Lauder, the innkeeper, knows me. He said I should see you!" This wasn't exactly true, but was warranted, I told myself, by the importance of what the man might tell me. My search for the truth of Shivas Irons was as legitimate as Haig's passion for privacy.

There were no sounds inside the house, nor movement in the cowshed. Maybe Haig had gone to tend his animals in the hills nearby. After leaving a note that I wanted to ask him about the distillery, I walked back to my car and put on my running shoes. Something told me not to leave. Perhaps I could see him from higher ground.

I started up a narrow path through the field behind the house, stopping occasionally to enjoy the view. Sheep scattered as I approached, and two calves ran away down the hill. Then I hesitated. Near the path about twenty yards from me, a cow faced in my direction. Or was it a bull? No udder was visible through the knee-high grass in which it stood, its neck was formidable, and it seemed to be glowering at me. Certainly Haig wouldn't keep a bull here. This wasn't a breeding farm. But if it charged, was there a place to hide? Glancing back at my car I saw that a man stood near the house, watching me intently. Neither he, nor I, nor the animal moved.

"Hello!" I shouted. "Is that a bull?"

He didn't respond, but the animal lowered its head and aimed its horns like a pair of guns.

Alarmed, I backed away. I seemed to remember that bulls didn't like to charge downhill. Could I outrun it to the house? The man stood motionless, some fifty yards from me. How long would it take to reach him? The animal stood perfectly still, its nose pointed toward the ground, its eyes rolled back as if to fix me in its sights. Disconcertingly, I thought of England's Princess Diana. She sometimes had this very look, her head bowed slightly with eyes looking up in earnest engagement. But there wasn't time for such thoughts. The creature snorted, took a few steps, and charged.

I turned and sprinted down the hill. Behind me there was a clatter of hooves, in front of me a tricky slope covered with stubble and animal droppings. As I hurdled the rock wall near the house, the man threw up his arms. "Eeyah!" he shouted, commanding the animal to stop. "Eeyah! Go back!"

It stopped when it got to the wall, mooed in a plaintive way, and looked at me with soulful eyes. Between its legs there was an udder, and its horns were shorter than I'd thought. The man was cursing, in Gaelic or thick Scots English. "Ye scared the bejesus out o' it," he snarled. "Go awa' now, lassie. Git bach!"

The man had a gnarled elfin face, was five feet seven or eight inches tall, and wore a grey shirt and black pants held up by purple suspenders. "It's a wonder ye didna' break yer neck." He looked me up and down. "If ye're lookin' for strays from the distillery, ye've come to the wrong place. I read yer note. I've nothin' to do wi' the Ramsays or their whiskey noo'. They're bastards, all of 'em, and I wouldna' work in tha' hellhole again if ye promised me a thousand pounds."

"This has nothing to do with the Ramsays." I decided that niceties would get me nowhere. "I'm here to find out about the hauntings. I know Buck Hannigan."

"Ye're a journalist? If so, ye'll have to excuse me. Eeyah!" He waved his arms at the cow, which still was standing by the wall. "Go bach, lassie. The man'll not disturb yer calves. Now git!" Limping and slightly bent from the waist, Haig walked swiftly to the front of the house. At the front door he stepped on a flagstone that brought him up to my height. "I've nothin' to tell ye," he said with a hard, penetrating voice. "I've not been back to the Ramsay Distillery for ower two yeers. Talk to their new caretakers."

"I'm sorry to bother you." I pretended apology. "I know this is an imposition. But if you don't mind, I brought something for you. Lauder said you liked the whiskey from Oban. I brought you a couple of bottles."

We faced each other in silence, our faces no more than three feet apart. "Ye brought me whiskey?" he asked after a moment's pause. "And wha' is it ye want to talk about?"

"Wait just a minute!" I said. "Let me get it." Before he could respond, I turned and walked to the car for the box with three bottles of whiskey I'd bought at an inn near Portinnisherrich. Haig looked confused when he took it from me. He seemed to be caught between desire for the whiskey and a growing suspicion of me. He lifted the box as if judging its weight. "There's moor than two bottles heer." He scowled. "What else is in it?"

"It has three bottles, not two."

Straightening his back, he looked down from his flagstone perch with a hint of embarrassment. "What's yer name?" he asked.

"Murphy. Michael Murphy."

"Well, that explains it. Ye're lookin' for leprechauns." A tiny smile appeared. "And ye probably want a drink."

"It's a little early for that." I smiled back. "But yes, I'm looking for leprechauns."

"Well, I suppose it'll be the only way to get rid o' ye." Placing a hand on the door, he paused, as if undecided whether to ask me inside. "Let me put it this away," he said. "It'll be better to talk outside." A moment later, he reappeared with a walking stick and led me swiftly up the hill. Though he looked to be in his late sixties, he moved like someone younger. "There's a good place to sit up there." He pointed to a high grey cliff on the incline above us. "We can talk there while I watch the animals."

Five minutes later, we sat on a ledge beneath the cliff with a view of Haig's sheep and cows. "Ye want to talk about Ramsay's distillery," he said, hardly winded. "Well, ye can see part o' it down there, three ridges past my house." Following the line of his pointing finger, I recognized MacDuff's two-story house, nestled several miles away between a wooded rise and grass-covered hills beyond it. The rain had stopped, and we could see what seemed to be the entire length of Loch Awe, winding through mist-shrouded ridges toward the distant peaks of Ben Cruachan.

"That's where I want to keep it," said Haig, nodding toward the abandoned distillery. "Far away from me. It might look nice from heer, but it's a hellhole, I tell ye. A godforsaken place. But not because it's haunted. That's a story the locals made up. There was an owner there before the Ramsays, a crazy old bugger named Seamus MacDuff, who had atomic waste dumped on a golf course he built around the house. That's what the Ramsays won't admit. None of 'em! Atomic waste! Spread all ower the place for reasons just the old bugger knew." He shook his head disgustedly. "They don't want to pay for cleanin' it up. Nor me for my injuries there. Nor the workers who were poisoned by it."

"Atomic waste?" I said. "How do you know that?"

"From surveyors in Cladich and Inveraray, and other locals who know." He pointed to his neck and the small of his back. "The place gave me arthritis, headaches, the gout. And more. It did somethin' to my dreams, my sleep, my digestion. To my mental state. It's a creepy place, I tell ye. Sometimes at night ye can see it glowin'. Radiation all ower the stinkin' little course he built, producin' God knows what kind o' monsters. 'Tis said by some that old MacDuff was tryin' to mutate himself! To grow a new head or eyeballs or fingers or somethin'."

"What do your doctors say?"

"Doctors. Aagh!" He spit the words out. "Wha' do they know? No doctor 'round heer knows how to deal with somethin' like this, and I canna' afford the ones in Glasgow."

He sat about four feet from me, avoiding eye contact as he glowered at the abandoned distillery. I asked how long he had worked there.

"Nine months, in '83 and '84, after the place was closed. Worked until I could barely move! Toward the end, the pain nearly killed me. I've not been able to walk right since. Or sleep a full night without wakin' up."

"But you almost ran up this mountain," I protested. "I could hardly keep up!"

"Aye, but it hurt like hell. *Hurt like hell.* I *should* be able to walk here. I've done it most of my life, and I'm not fifty yet." I was stunned. He looked to be twenty years older. "So, Murphy," he said, still looking away from me, "what's yer question? What is it ye want to know?"

Having interviewed people for many years about their experiences at the edge of the strangeness curve, I was aware of the difficulties involved. Usually it's best to let interviewees reveal themselves at their own pace, as they come to trust you, especially when they are deeply defended against the things they have perceived. A conversation about such matters can drift away, or end abruptly, if it becomes too threatening. Whatever it was that happened to Haig had created defenses in him that bordered on paranoia. It would take patience and luck to get past them.

"It's not for a story, in case that's what you're thinking. And I won't tell anyone what you say if you tell me it's off the record."

"Off the record?" he exclaimed. "You a government man?"

"No! No!" I exclaimed. "I've never worked for the government."

"Wha' do ye do for a livin'?"

I hesitated, then decided to take a plunge. "I'm writing a book about things that are hard to explain. That's what led me here. Hannigan and Lauder said you had some experiences that fit what I'm writing about. It's a kind of scientific research." The ploy had worked before. For the sake of science, certain people not given to self-disclosure are willing to open up.

But not Haig. "Scientific research?" he said. "I'll not submit to that! Ye're tellin' me ye want to put me in a book?"

"Not without your permission."

"What's yer background, Murphy?" His eyes narrowed suspiciously. "What kind o' writer are ye?"

"Psychology. Philosophy. Religion. Sports . . ." I was fumbling for words. "I still have a problem telling my publisher what the book's about."

He cocked his head to one side, as if to appraise me from another angle. Then the hint of a smile—just the smallest hint—appeared in his eyes. "Wha' does he *think* it's about?" he asked.

"He has faith. Great faith. At times he's almost saintly."

It was my first stroke of luck. "Aye, Murphy!" he said with a twinkle. *"Faith.* Perhaps 'cause he has no other course!" Though it seemed to strain his facial muscles and was lined with broken yellow teeth, his smile had a charm that surprised me. But it didn't last long. Shaking his fist at MacDuff's estate, he started to talk about his strange experiences, interrupting his story two or three times to shout at his animals with a snarling, resonant, and penetrating voice that cut the air like a whip. I said little, for I knew that much can be learned nonverbally during confessional narratives of this kind. Experience at the limits of the strangeness curve is revealed as much by unintended hints, innuendos, and things not said as it is by explicit verbal report.

He had leased the Ramsay place to run his sheep in 1983, a few months after the distillery was closed, until the summer of 1984. For the entire nine months, he had used the house to cook his meals, but after two weeks he couldn't sleep there. "It's not built right," he said. "Seems to lean when it gets cold, and howls at times like a family o' banshees. MacDuff was an engineer, but he didna' know how to build a place fit to live in. It's a wonder it doesna' collapse. Forget the rumors about its ghosts. The whinin', the bangin', the howlin', they come from the wind, and loose joints when thunder hits. I know. For two weeks, I spent every night there. 'Twas then that my troubles started." He pointed to his neck and the small of his back. "On the second night. That's when the pains began and I got my first hints about the old bugger's experiments. Aye, Murphy, the house—ye've heard some o' the stories— all o' it started to glow. The walls, the floors, the roof. Even the windowpanes! All o' it! Tha' was the first clue I got that MacDuff had dumped atomic waste around the place. Got it, some people suspect, after the war from people he knew through his work with missiles."

Masking my disbelief, I asked if it glowed every night.

"No. It takes certain kinds o' weather. But I could *feel* it every night. I could feel it, Murphy. A kind o' radiation, comin' from all around, from the ground and the buildings and the air itself, above and below and inside me. That was the clue. It was comin' from both inside and outside me. That's the way it works, all right. Makes ye buzzy and jumpy all ower. Sometimes with little points o' light, ye can see 'em everywhere. I've read books about it. Radioactive elements spread like manoor all ower the property. Ye can bet that some o' it is buried still in cellars under the house. 'Tis amazin' that no one's found it.

"Aye, on that second night. That's when the pain began." He pointed to the base of his spine. "It started heer. In this very spot. Like a fire. Like a knife. And then, at the moment I saw the place glowin', it went up with a rush to my skull. Every day after that it spread, tightenin' me here, tightenin' me there, until I was sufferin' all ower. Then I had nightmares. Dreamt one night that I was walkin' back 'n forth through the walls lookin' for a way to escape, until I rose up through the ceilin' into MacDuff's old study on the second floor. And woke to find myself in the room, up there wanderin' in my sleep! After that I slept in the distillery and felt a little better, but my ailments have never gone away."

"Haig," I said, "let me ask you a strange-sounding question. Was there any point where this stuff, these points of light, whatever it is, made you feel *good?*"

"Good?" he exclaimed. "Now, that's what I call a stupid question. A really dumb one. Why'n hell d'ye ask me that?"

"Because some people exposed to radioactivity say that for a while, they have new energy."

"Murphy," he said caustically, "I think ye made that up. I've never heard o' it. Never heard o' it. Don't try to tell me that atomic waste gives people energy."

"But some people *feel* that way." I persisted in the fabrication. "Did you?"

"Not for a minute. I never felt good in the place, not once. None o' my parts have worked right since. I'm just forty-seven, but look at me! See what the radiation's done? It's an old man ye're lookin' at. An old man!" He seemed to be growing more defensive. Had my fabrication triggered the beginnings of a self-recognition?

"But you can walk faster than me, and look, you don't have a sweater. We're almost the same age, but you're stronger and more energetic."

"That's a crock! A real crock." He was visibly angry now. "It's been hell since '83. Hell, I tell ye. MacDuff and the Ramsays, they've poisoned me. Every cell in my body is filled with the stuff." He paused. "So ye might as well know this, Murphy. Sometimes at night I see the glowin' *heer*. That's right. The same glowin' heer, the same as it is in MacDuff's old house! On some nights it's spread all 'round me, all ower my arms and legs, from the plutonium in my cells." Sadness came into his gnarled face. "I don't know wha' to do about it. Don't know wha' to do. I suppose it's just a matter of time before the cancer comes."

Suddenly he seemed completely vulnerable. For a moment we didn't speak. Finally I broke the silence. "In writing this book, I've come across cases like yours that don't have anything to do with radioactivity."

"That's news to me," he said. "I never heard o' it, and dinna' believe it. But go ahead and tell me."

There are moments when crucial recognitions can either come to fuller life or be swallowed by one's usual defenses. Was Haig approaching such a juncture? "It's past five," I ventured. "Any chance we could have some of that Oban whiskey. I could use a shot."

"Finish what ye were sayin'."

"It'll take a few minutes. It's getting cold. When there's no sunshine, a little whiskey helps."

He eyed me suspiciously, paused for a moment to survey his animals, then stood with startling agility. "Aye, ye're right," he said. "A shot o' whiskey'll do us good. But ye'll have to put up with a drafty place."

The cottage's single room reflected its occupant's ascetic and unforgiving nature. Walled with stone and dimly lit, it had a peaked smoke-blackened ceiling made of roughly hewn boards, a small rock fireplace and wood-burning stove, a cot tucked into a tiny alcove, and a heavy wooden table with two stiff-backed chairs. Haig lit a kerosene lamp and put it on the table, then went to a set of shelves bolted to the wall near a metal sink, and found a half-finished bottle of whiskey. The box I'd brought stood in a corner, next to a rifle, saw, and axe.

It was colder than it was outside, but he made no move to light a fire. Sitting across from me at the table, he filled each glass, shoved one toward me, and took a swallow. The whiskey had a peaty smell, and I held it near my nose. Then I took a sip.

"It's strong," I said.

A tiny smile appeared on his elfin face. "Wait," he said. "Just give it a minute."

The whiskey's burn went deeper, into my sinuses and past my heart.

"Wait some more," he insisted. "Just wait."

The burn went deeper still, into my stomach and down my spine. It was the most powerful whiskey I'd ever tasted.

"Have another taste," he said proudly. "Ye willna' get this in the States."

I followed his instruction. This time the burn spread into my arms and shoulders. The bottle had no label. "Is this from the Ramsay Distillery?" I asked.

Facing me from across the table, his features softened by the light of the kerosene lamp, he was a gentler presence than before. "It's not Ramsay's," he said. "That stuff, if there's any left, isna' really whiskey. It's rocket fuel. All o' it, I suspect, has traces o' radioactivity." There was no anger in this remark, nor any sense of recrimination. His features had relaxed, and for the first time he seemed undefensive. This might be the moment to offer him another view of his troubles and the happenings at MacDuff's estate. Still, there was a serenity about him now, a softness that I didn't want to disturb. It was better to nurture the trust between us. I sensed that without much leading from me he would make more self-disclosures.

And there was another reason for waiting. The drink had produced a state in me too wonderful to interrupt. My curiosity about him had lost its urgency. The winds off Beinn Bhreac, the views of the loch, and the whiskey had produced a marvelous elevation.

"It's good medicine." I nodded toward my glass. "Who makes it?"

My remark didn't prompt a response. He sat erect, elbows on the table, holding eye contact for the first time since we'd met. His features seemed less pointed now, his posture more relaxed. It was almost as if I were facing another person.

"It's a good one all right," he said at last. "Got it from a cousin who's got a distillery. It takes away most of the pain." He rose and, without a limp, went to the fireplace, placed two logs on a pile of sticks, and started a fire. "Let's sit where it's warm," he said, carrying his chair, the bottle, and his glass to the hearth. I joined him, and we sat looking into the flames. "Aye, it's good medicine." He poured himself a second glass. "Heer, have another."

"Carrying the chair over here, you didn't limp," I ventured. "Has your stiffness gone away?"

"Not all o' it. But this helps." He nodded toward his glass. "Especially with those feelin's I told ye about. A shot o' whiskey changes that. Like right now. Instead o' the buzzin', it feels like I'm floatin' in a mineral spring. In soda water or somethin' like tha'. It's a relief, I tell ye."

"Like soda water?" I pretended innocence. "And it feels good?"

"Aye, it does," he said matter-of-factly. "I feel like a new man now. But it won't last long. The feelin's'll pass as soon as the whiskey's worn off."

"And what about your other pains?"

He flexed his neck and shoulders, and lifted his left arm over his head. "Well, they're gone, to tell ye the truth. All gone. But they'll be back." He poked the fire with a stick. "So Murphy! Finish wha' ye were tellin' me. Those things ye're puttin' in yer book."

"How much do you want to hear?" I asked.

"Take yer time." He stretched his feet toward the fire. "I've got another bottle before we break into yers."

For the next fifteen minutes or so, I told stories about luminous phenomena that accompany exalted states of mind. Without any reference to him, I described auras, halos, and other radiances attributed to shamans, yogis, Roman Catholic monks, Zen Buddhist roshis, Hasidic masters, Sufis, and modern Protestant saints; and similar lights reported by mountain climbers, golfers, and other sportspeople. He followed most of this with what seemed to be genuine interest, finishing the whiskey bottle, then opening a second from his cousin's distillery. But not once did he give the slightest hint that he connected such things with his own experience. When I said that as a result of athletic or religious discipline, some people experience a life-giving effervescence, like "bubbly mineral springs," as well as luminous phenomena, he gave no sign that he equated such feelings with the odd sensations he attributed to his radioactive poisoning. Toward the end of my recitation, he started to nod. When I finished, he was snoring. "'Haig?" I said, fearing he might drop his glass. "Haig? What do you think?"

He woke abruptly. "Think? Sorry, Murphy, I didn't hear ye. Think about what?"

"About these lights that yogis and athletes see around the body."

"Aye." He sat up to revive himself. "I believe ye. It's an old tradition in the Church. My mother was Catholic. Talked about the 'little Teresa' and the halos that people saw around her."

Finally my patience was waning. "Haig?" I asked. "Do any of these things resemble what you experience? The glowing? The burning? The buzzing? The tingling?"

"Noo, it's not the same at all. Atomic poisonin' isna' the same as wha' yer talkin' about. It has nothin' to do with that at all. For one thing, yer saintly activities wouldna' account for the glowin' around the house."

"But no," I said firmly. "There are stories about places that glow. The caves of Tibetan yogis. Monastic cells. I spent some time in a room where Sri Aurobindo, the Indian mystic, lived, and I swear to God, it had a light you couldn't account for."

"But not MacDuff's!" he said with finality. "There's been no saint nor mystic there. The place is just an atomic dump." He gazed reflectively into the fire, then stood to stir it. "But ye know, Murphy, a strange thing. What ye're sayin' reminds me o' somethin'. There was a man come round the place from time to time when I was sleepin' in the distillery. Tall. Red-haired. Talked to me once about these things, and caused the damnedest thing to happen. *The damnedest thing.* It was the last time I saw him, one day after sundown. He was walkin' across the hill where I was watchin' the sheep, about a hundred yards from the house I'd say, when the place begins its glowin'. About the time he reaches me, I jump up shakin' my fist and yellin' how the place has ruined me, and he says—cool as ice—that he can stop it. And with that he comes right to my side, shakes my shoulders, slaps my back, and there's no more light at a'! Just like that! Nothin' to it. The house was back to normal. Then he squeezes my shoulder, gives me a great big smile, and says he couldn't've done it without me. Now, wha' do ye make o' that?"

"How old was he?"

"About forty, I'd say. What's that got to do with it?"

"Just curious." I held back my excitement. "Was he a Scot?"

"From Fife, I'd say. First time he showed up, he talked about buyin' whiskey from the distillery, and how he didn't like comin' so far to get it. Lived at a distance, he said, but felt like the land heer was a second home. Said he missed it whenever he left, missed it so much he was thinkin' o' 'bringin' his entire body heer to live.' "

"Bringing his *entire* body here? That's an odd expression."

"That's the way he put it, 'bringin' his entire body' to live heer. But wha' d'ye make o' wha' he did, makin' the glowin' stop? Have ye come across anything like that?"

"Yes, as a matter of fact. Indian yogis say you can learn how to see auras at will, or not see them. They have Sanskrit names for it, all sorts of names, and say you can turn the ability on or off with practice. Muslim mystics talk about the 'inner eye,' which they can open whenever they want. Martial artists teach people how to see 'ki,' the energy that's supposed to surround us. He might've done something like that to you."

"Is tha' right?" Haig stood motionless in front of the fire, then turned to face me. "Ye know, Murphy, sometimes I can do it! Every now and then, in the right mood, I can turn the glowin' off. Around the house, around my body, ever since the stranger did it."

"Which could mean you don't have radioactive poisoning."

"Nooo . . ." He stretched the word for emphasis. "Noo. I can turn the glowin' off sometimes, but not the stuff that causes it. Not the poisonin'. Not the iodine or plutonium. Some people with cancer canna' feel it, but tha' doesna' mean it isn't there." His resignation was a palpable force. It seemed futile now to argue with him. "Murphy, I've got to get the cows for milkin'. It'll take an hour or moor. I suppose ye'll need to be movin' on."

He was coming to the end of his tolerance for company, but I wasn't going to leave without learning more about the man with red hair. "I'd like to go with you," I said. "Do you mind?"

"The cows'll not like it," he said, carrying our glasses to the sink. "As ye've seen, they're jumpy with strangers."

"Well, this has been good." I stood to leave. "But let me ask you two more questions."

"What are they?" He moved toward the door. "There's not much time for the milkin'."

"That man, the one who stopped the glowing—did he give you any indication that he'd been to the property when MacDuff was alive? Any hint of that at all?"

"Not that I can think of. But he looked to be forty, and as far as I know MacDuff died more than thirty years ago. If the man had been there then, he would've been a little boy."

"Did he tell you what he did for a living? He wasn't a golf professional, was he?"

"He gave no hint o' that. But judgin' by his energy, and his stature, and his sense o' command, he might've been a sea captain. It seemed he traveled in different parts o' the world."

"How did you get that idea?"

Haig opened the door and stepped outside. "Oh, I don't know." He gazed across the loch. "It's just my feelin'. The way he spoke. The way he looked. There was somethin' big about 'im. Not just his physical size, but somethin'—I don't know—somethin' full o' the wide world. Like he'd been to distant places."

Far below, the loch had turned to steel grey, and the lowering hills were growing dark on this overcast summer evening. "It's been a good talk, Murphy." Haig offered me his callused hand. "Thanks for the whiskey, and good luck with yer book." Then he limped away, and disappeared in the fields behind his house.

CHAPTER ELEVEN

*G*OLF: *ITS ROOTS* in *God and Nature,* with Appendices, Supplements, Index, and Notes. Professor Crail's well-worn but handsome tome, all 733 pages of it, was a reassuring presence. I laid it on the desk of my hotel room and admired its embossed leather cover. It was good to know that as early as 1893 a learned professor of Greek philosophy had entertained the possibilities represented by such chapter titles as "Clairvoyance on the Links of East Lothian" and "The Unmasking of Atheists in Golf." Hannigan and I were not alone in our openness to golf's spiritual anomalies. Turning to the appendix describing the apparent demonic possession at Muirfield, I read:

> After the infamous match, upon the entreaty of several friends, the unfortunate Garrick, with Mrs. Garrick, turned for help to the Society for Psychical Research, and were interviewed by Frederic Myers himself as well as his colleague Frank Podmore. Besides providing evidence of golf's ability to evoke supernormal events, these conversations comprised a form of "metatherapy," to use a term now favored by certain clergy associated with the Society. By all accounts, the Myers-Podmore ministration was successful, re-

lieving both husband and wife of various psychic afflictions, including their murderous impulses toward one another. It also led to notable improvements of Mr. Garrick's golf. The eminent gentleman, it seems, has since been able to play the game without a curious disability he had suffered for several years, namely, the illusory perception of a loathsome toad squatting obscenely upon each hole into which he would putt.

But most important for my general thesis here, the material uncovered by Podmore and Myers prompted the Society chapter in Edinburgh, of which I am a member, in collaboration with the American Society for Psychical Research and its Boston chapter, to collect other incidents in sport involving phantom figures and related phenomena. During activities as diverse as mountain climbing, long sea voyages, and ballooning, disembodied figures have appeared, either to console, terrify, guide, or inspire the persons involved. This is especially true for golf. As of this writing, several dozen firsthand reports have been drawn from reputable witnesses of apparitions on golf courses in Scotland, England, Ireland, and America, and these have been supplemented by several dozen more in the general literature of adventure and sport. These incidents have usually involved a single witness, but on several occasions, as in the Muirfield case, a fairly large group has witnessed the ghostly entity.

The material we have collected comprises a "census of phantom figures in golf" analogous to the much larger "Census of Hallucinations" lately conducted by the Society under the leadership of Mrs. Henry Sidgwick. From this material, it is possible to draw the following conclusions:

• Most of the percipients involved have been brought to a state of hypervigilance, either by strenuous physical exertion, extreme danger, or, as in golf played by its truest devotees, unremitting mental frustration and continuous psychic trauma. Such vigilance resembles the condition sought by Hindoo yogis, whirling dervishes of the Middle East, and tower-dwelling Christian ascetics such as St. Simeon Stylites.

• This condition is often accompanied in golf by a subtle sensory deprivation resulting from a compulsive attention to the ball that gives freer play to latent telepathic, clairvoyant, ectoplasmic, and other powers that are normally inhibited by visual and auditory stimulation. That golf has been called by various wits "a form of penitential prayer," a "dark night of the soul in broad daylight," "hypnotic somnambulism" and "a good walk spoiled" shows that this is the case.

• The phantom figures in these cases frequently appear in two or more places at once, or in a second or third location after an interval so extremely brief that they could not have traveled there by any ordinary means of locomotion.

• Such apparitions are sometimes accompanied by music, voices, or fragrances for which there is no apparent cause; increases or decreases of temperature; inexplicable luminosities; or sensations of supraphysical touch.

• In several cases, the phantom involved tried to communicate with the percipient (or percipients), either telepathically or by means of gesture and movement, to warn, admonish, uplift, or otherwise instruct them. Sometimes, however, such communications have no readily discernible purpose. In the Garrick case, for example, a few of the onlookers claimed that the apparition merely mimicked the behavior of the four cursing men, flailing about "with an ectoplasmic stick."

Hannigan had been right in thinking that the book might help to restore my confidence. Since my return to Edinburgh two days before, the phenomena surrounding Shivas Irons had grown more and more distant, and almost to the vanishing point after our rousing arguments the previous night with Hannigan's fellow professors. Every story about Haig and the abandoned distillery that I'd summoned the courage to tell had been dissected wittily, sliced thoroughly, and ground to conceptual powder. I opened Crail's book again, and turned to the chapter titled "Ochema: the Subtle Body in Golf," in which I found this:

> Terms such as *astroeides* or *augoeides,* the "star-like" or "silver" body—which was distinguished by certain Platonists from the *soma pneumatikon,* or soul vehicle in its inferior aspects, and from the *eidolon, imago, simulacrum, skia,* or *umbra,* different forms of the soul after bodily death—represent states of luminous embodiment intuited or directly experienced by ancient initiates. They stand for something real. They are not merely philosophical abstractions. They point us toward that greater condition terrestrial evolution might one day produce.
>
> *Astroeides, or augoeides,* I propose, has a certain resonance with the condition and character of Angus Pattersone, the former golf champion of Fife, and are just as apt as any other noun or adjective with which writers of the day described him. No one could adequately portray or explain the man's extraordinary brightness of body and soul, or the uplifting effects of his ebullience on others. These terms of Platonic mysticism, perhaps, are better suited to the task than ordinary English.

Following some half-conscious instinct, I turned the page to discover this passage, marked with a star on its margin and underlined with ink:

> These richly suggestive terms associated with Pythagorean, Platonic, and Neoplatonic doctrines of the subtle body can, when

joined with contemporary studies of supernormal experience, give us hints about the life to come, in both senses of the phrase as I use it here, namely life after death and the higher earthly existence that our world is struggling to realize. By assembling the different kinds of experience that such terms represent, we might better envision the next great stage of human evolution.

Given the "S" on the back of its cover, it was conceivable that Crail's book had been owned by Shivas Irons. Had he underlined these sentences? Seamus MacDuff had talked about "the life to come" in much the same way as Crail. For both men it had a double meaning, referring at once to the afterlife and a greater, more luminous existence on earth. Had MacDuff met Crail or read his book? *Golf: Its Roots in God and Nature* had more leads than I'd thought to the thinking and work of Shivas Irons. It might have been a map of sorts for him and his teacher and, if so, would help us track their course.

A reading lamp was the only source of light in the dark high-ceilinged studio. Sitting beside Hannigan at his desk I could barely see Nadia, who sat on a couch some thirty feet away watching us as we studied MacDuff's faded photograph. " 'August 6 again, but 1950,' " Hannigan read from its inscription. "It must be their way of saying that somehow they've found a better way than atom bombs to release the energy contained in matter. The question, of course, is 'How?' What in hell is this light, and how in hell did it get there?"

Both of us looked at the picture in silence. "So what have we got?" Hannigan said finally. "Let's separate certainties from conjectures. First, we know that Irons and MacDuff believed that both human consciousness and the flesh are capable of radical transformations into a higher condition. This is obvious from your conversations with Irons, from notes in his journals and books, and from things we've learned about MacDuff. Second, we know that both of them *practiced* higher states, as well as supernormal powers, and that both of them were led to this early in life, Irons in his teens, MacDuff by his mother, probably from the time he was born. Third, we know that their practice had a purely contemplative side but also involved what they took to be some sort of materialization—of 'spirit-matter' or 'soul-stuff,' they gave it different names—that somehow brings the flesh to new levels of embodiment. This goes back to MacDuff's old lady and her African shamanism, and to MacDuff's early interest in the 'fourth dimension.' All of this we know for sure."

He paused to look at the lists he'd made in his artist's sketchbook. "Then there are things we suspect but aren't quite sure of. First, four possible Irons sightings—three described in reports to me, one from Haig's story about the man who stopped the glowing. We can't be sure about any of these, but they are certainly suggestive. Second, Crail might've influenced them. His vision of human evolution, and his use of the term 'the life to come,' are just about the same as theirs. Through his book, he could've been Irons's second mentor. If that's the case, we've got another set of leads to what they were doing. Third, it's conceivable that MacDuff, with Irons's help, established a presence on his property, by some kind of spiritual and occult means, that still reflects what they were doing. It gets into workers at Ramsay's Distillery—they think it's brownies or ghosts. It gets into Haig—he thinks it's atomic poisoning. It gets into you, ye hit a drive 420 yards, and begin to have mystical experiences. And fourth, our visitor in the necromanteion. It's not too far-fetched, we agree, to think that the thing was connected to either Irons or MacDuff—or to them both. Nadia, don't ye agree?"

"Oh, Baahch," she said, filling his name with a long and affectionate sigh. "It was trying to tell Mackel something. But I don't know if it was your golf man. Maybe Mackel should go to Moscow, and meet Boris. Mackel, would you like to go? Maybe Boris can call our visitor again through his tower in Peredelkino."

Pretending not to hear her, Hannigan examined his lists. Written in his small, elegant hand, they looked as beautiful as his hyperspace equations. It occurred to me that he could sell them as visual art. "And then," he said, "there are items that are *mainly* conjecture, but too suggestive to dismiss. The things we channeled after our night in the necromanteion. The burn marks at Mac-Duff's house. Your vision with Irons on the eighteenth green. The different *responses* to whatever it was that happened there. Your glimpse of a phantom on the thirteenth hole, and Irons's different responses to it. The inscription, 'Sunrise at noon.' Irons in North Africa during the war, and his vision there. And MacDuff's trip to Africa in '45. . . ."

"Baahch. Baahch!" Nadia interrupted, rising energetically from the couch. "This is not the way. Not with all those lists! Not with all those lines connected to the other lines, and those other ones *not* connected to the ones over there, and this one on top of that one. It is not mathematics, Bach." She threw her hands up in a Russian gesture of solicitous reproval. "You cannot analyze it, Bach. Maybe, *maybe,* it will be like those little dot diagrams where finally you see a face or a cow or a map or saahmthing. Maybe when you have enough dots, you will see it. See who they really were, what they were really doing, or whether Mr. Irons is still alive. Or maybe, Bach, maybe Mr. Irons will suddenly appear. Maybe he will hear about you or Mackel, or read Mackel's book. Or maybe Mr. MacDuff will come, like the stranger in my necromanteion. But you cannot find them with those little lists!"

Hannigan sighed. "Murphy," he said, "will you please explain what we're doin'. Tell her that's what we're tryin' to do. We're trying to connect the dots."

She stood with a hand on a hip and the other on Hannigan's

couch, her striking figure accentuated by tight-fitting white slacks and brown sweater. I felt no impulse to argue with her. "Mackel," she said imploringly, "don't you agree with me? Tell Bach."

"Baa . . aahch." Hannigan mimicked her inflection. "Baa . . . ahch. She uses it like a weapon."

"Mackel," she said. "Tell Bach."

"That's what he's trying to do. His lists are a pattern-recognition diagram. That's what you mean, Nadia, don't you? A pattern-recognition diagram?"

"Whatever you call it, Mackel. But you don't have enough dots." She tossed her head impatiently. "Or maybe you have the answer already, somewhere deep, deep down in your soul."

I looked to Hannigan, who was studying the work of art he'd made with his beautifully constructed lists. "All right," he said. "Maybe we need another consciousness to see what we have here. That's what she's driving at. Let's break out a bottle of Ramsay's whiskey."

Neither Nadia nor I objected. A moment later, we stood waiting for the whiskey to work, looking down at Hannigan's sketch pad. She put an arm around his waist, winked at me mischievously, then started to laugh. "What is this?" she asked, pointing to one of his notes. "What does this mean, 'improving the cell's MI5'? That is funny!"

"It's from a note in one of his books," said Hannigan. "Irons thought that our cells can improve their ability to find things, like master spies, to the extent that we become more spiritually alive and clairvoyant. Information, proteins, minerals, oxygen—or spirit-matter! Theoretically, each cell has all of these at its disposal, but can get better at finding them, like an intelligence agency. Body and soul mirror one another. What's so funny about it?"

"A billion little KGBs! Oh, it's funny, Bach. Just funny. A Raahshian writer would not use that example!"

"What's this?" I pointed to another of Hannigan's notes. "A loathsome toad squatting on every cell!"

"It is," said Hannigan, "another Irons comment, and further proof that he was influenced by Professor Mortimer Crail. There's a passage in Crail's book about a gentleman who saw a loathsome toad squatting on every hole into which he was about to putt. Apparently, Irons thought that each of our cells, like the gentleman's golf holes, can be squatted upon—yes, squatted upon—by particular images. In other words, our body is like a golf course."

"And maybe Irons was cracked." I laughed. "For him, everything was a golf course. Sometimes I think the game did him in."

"The whiskey's workin'." Hannigan's burr was more pronounced than ever. "Nadia, here's yer altered state, but it's producin' only protests and giggles."

"Is this the bottle we had the other night?" I asked. "Christ, it's psychedelic!"

"It's a different bottle," he said. "And stronger than the last one. Stronger by far! Wha' d'ye see in my lovely lists now?"

"I see that Mackel should go to Moscow," said Nadia. "And meet Big Boris there. And look into the big, tall glass in his dark and terrible necromanteion."

"And you, Murphy. Wha' d'ye see in *yer* new consciousness?"

"That maybe Haig was right about Ramsay's whiskey. It could be radioactive."

Large or small, each group of people has its own inexorable chemistry. The Kirova-Hannigan-Murphy group, at least in 1987, tended toward the Dionysian and subsequent erasure of memory. For the second time in a week, I could not precisely remember all the heights we had reached when I woke the next day. Perhaps this failure of recall came in part from an instinctive emotional economy. By rising above our erotic impulses into a self-forgetful, mystically charged hilarity, the three of us could avoid complications we didn't want.

But two images seemed indelible. The materials that Hannigan and I had collected were indeed like a pattern-recognition diagram, which if added to would become more and more recognizable. And something in me also knew that the adventure of a lifetime waited in Russia, along with part of the greater mysteries represented by Shivas Irons.

CHAPTER TWELVE

PARTLY TO SATISFY my lingering nostalgia, but also to further my research, I played golf at Burningbush on the day before my return to America. Though I had wondered if the round might evoke signs of Shivas Irons, I didn't expect the symmetries it produced. The first of these was evident when I reached the first tee a little before twelve o'clock.

Thirty-one years before, I'd been paired with Irons and a dour, methodical little Scotsman named MacIver. Now my playing partners would be a tall, red-haired west Texas professional named Sam Magee and a middle-aged Japanese gentleman about five feet six inches tall who referred to himself only as "Mitsubishi." A threesome then, a threesome now, with members who had roughly the same height, build, and level of skill as their counterparts in 1956.

But this wasn't all there was to it. Magee was instructing Mitsubishi with a booming Texas drawl, using phrases as mysterious to me as Irons's admonitions to MacIver. Mitsubishi listened to these attentively, just as MacIver had done, accepting them with quick little bows and applying them with an obedience which at first was painful to behold. After teeing his ball, he pointed with a ramrod-straight left arm down his intended line of flight, flexed his knees three or four times, and drove with a backswing no longer than one he would use for a pitch shot. His ball went straight, for perhaps 150 yards, whereupon he bowed to Magee again with a look of embarrassment combined with tightly controlled satisfaction.

Then the professional turned to me. "Have at it, Murph," he boomed, as if addressing a stadium filled with spectators. "Let it rip!"

Caught between a desire to be sociable and my hopes of playing with the concentration I'd experienced at MacDuff's estate, I took a few practice swings, teed my ball, and hit my drive straight down the fairway. "We've got a ringer here!" Magee said loudly. "Look out for him, Mitsu. He's dangerous. Don't make any bets." Then he hit a prodigious drive that almost reached the green.

Walking down the fairway, I decided to keep enough separation from Magee for the revelations this round might produce. Though it was tempting to think that he might have resemblances to Shivas Irons beyond his red hair, height, and build, it was clear that if I got too close, there would be a whirlwind of challenges, wagers, and jibes that would last for eighteen holes. This intuition was confirmed after we both got birdies, and he asked if I wanted to bet. How about a hundred a side, ten for the longest off each tee, ten for the closest to each pin, ten for each birdie, and five hundred for the eighteen? When I didn't respond at once, he proposed cutting the wagers in half. When I said that I wasn't in a betting mood, his interest in me faded. For the rest of the round, he gave Mitsubishi most of his attention.

On the slightly elevated second tee, I took my first long look at the course. The fairways were browner than they'd been two weeks before, but framed more lavishly by yellow gorse and first streaks of violet in the heather. A few cumulus clouds, their easterly edges trimmed in gold, were moving across the high blue sky, and the sea that was visible beyond the links, like a harlequin's suit, was dramatically striped with lavender, blue, and grey. It occurred to me that these ever-changing vistas, like a hallucinogenic drug, amplified the slightest alterations of mood. This magical terrain, this soulscape, opened one's consciousness to a greater freedom as well as an awareness of self-imposed sufferings.

"After you, Murph," Magee said in his Texas drawl. "Birdies first!"

My contemplative moment broken, I hit a drive down the left-hand side of the fairway, then watched as Magee and Mitsubishi hit theirs down the middle. I was grateful that they were absorbed in their lesson. Memories of my round with Shivas Irons were pressing in upon me.

At first it seemed I could hear his voice, repeating advice he'd given me, describing features of the course, or shouting encouragement to MacIver. But after two or three holes, kinesthetic images reinforced these auditory memories. This wasn't a deliberate exercise. His carriage and gestures were suddenly there in my muscle memory, causing me to lengthen and loosen my stride, find a lower center of gravity, and add elasticity to my swing. By the ninth green, Magee had noticed this. "You're swinging slower, *and bigger,*" he said, and then, to my astonishment, asked, "What's come into you, Murph? It's like someone's whisperin' in your ear." Such are the ways we read one another telepathically.

This phantom presence continued through the first twelve holes. At times it seemed he was standing near me, suggesting, perhaps by a subtle gesture, some readjustment of my swing, or sharing the enjoyment of a good shot, or appraising my mental state with his sympathetic and contagious good humor. This invisible companionship varied in intensity, but when we reached the thirteenth tee was suddenly magnified. This was more than muscle memory, or familiar visual imagery. Shivas Irons seemed about to precipitate into living flesh. As I looked across Lucifer's Rug to the treacherous green on the hill above, I felt him aligning my stance, distributing my weight, and helping me grip my two-iron so that I would hit a low fade against the wind that was blowing from right to left. All of this was accomplished, as if by telepathy, while Mitsubishi and Magee watched with apparent fascination.

My ball sailed low up the clotted gorse, white against yellow as it curved toward the pin, then white against blue as it hovered above it. "Fuck it, Murph!" Magee exulted. "You might have a shit-faced hole in one!" After teeing his ball, he focused more intently than he had all day, and hit a shot on the same trajectory. We had painted two parallel streaks on the golf sky.

Walking up the narrow path along the ravine that borders the hole, I thought of the shot I'd hit in 1956. It, too, had been guided by something beyond my normal reflexes. Then I pictured the unflappable Bailie MacIver, dressed from head to foot in white and black.

Neither of us had spoken as we walked up the path, and I guessed that like me he'd been emptied of thought by Shivas's extraordinary rituals. He walked briskly, head down, his stride measured, intent to find his ball in Lucifer's Rug. His expensive white pants and black cardigan sweater contrasted sharply with his unsmiling demeanor.

Shivas had gone ahead, and stood near the green, looking down at the crevasse. For two or three minutes, as MacIver hit his ball from the gorse, he stood completely motionless. Was he looking for someone, or simply lost in thought? After marking my ball, which sat just a foot from his on the putting surface, I waited for him to move. There were tremendous views in all directions from this vantage point.

The rolling fairways below were filling with the shadows that grace Scottish links when there's sun in the late afternoon, while beyond the course, a mile and a half away, reflected light flashed from a clubhouse window. The land and sky seemed to be pure consciousness, a diaphanous soulscape. Then into it came a man in black who had something important to tell me. Standing at the edge of the green, he spoke without moving his lips. "Remember your name. Remember who you are."

Then he vanished. Just like that. Leaving no trace behind him.

Shivas, it seemed, hadn't seen him, and sank his putt for a birdie. Stunned, I placed my ball where I'd marked it, and rolled it into the cup. Each of us had scored a two, but Shivas said nothing about it. As we walked to the fourteenth tee, he gave no hint of his thoughts or feelings.

N ow Magee sank his putt for a birdie, just as Shivas had done, and I sank mine as well. But as I lifted my ball from the cup, I remembered that the man in black had said something more before he vanished. "Ye'll not remember," he'd said with a Scottish burr that I now seemed to hear with perfect clarity. "You and Shivas are brothers. Ye'll never be completely separated. Part o' ye will travel with him wherever he goes, even to the ends of the Earth."

Astonished by this small reverberating voice, which was conveyed with the peculiar resonance and force of an auditory hallucination, I turned away from my playing partners. Shivas and I would never be separated completely. Secretly, I'd known it all along. Which meant that my search for him reflected, however imperfectly, his movements, activities, and whereabouts.

Sensing that something had disturbed me, but not knowing

what it was, Magee and Mitsubishi hit their drives in silence. Their unspoken sympathy, and Magee's restraint, filled me with gratitude. "I'm sorry," I said as I stepped to the tee. "This place calls up the damnedest memories." As both of them nodded in agreement, I felt a sudden unexpected affection for them. Magee's attitude especially, which seemed strikingly at odds with his manner when we'd met, reminded me again that golf has a genius for bringing out what is best in us.

As we played the next few holes keeping a respectful distance, my encounter with the figure in black continued to unfold. Like a slowly sprouting seed, my memory of it had emerged for thirty-one years in response to different stimuli, whether conversation with Shivas and his friends in 1956, reports of golfing epiphanies from readers of *Golf in the Kingdom,* or my walk two weeks before around the thirteenth green. Our exchange seemed more real now than it had when I first remembered it. The stranger's voice conveyed an urgency and impulsion from somewhere beyond my ordinary thoughts, and had an immediate physical impact. Part of me would go with Shivas wherever he went, I could hear the voice condensing still into words that were perfectly articulated with a Scottish inflection.

It was difficult now to focus on golf. Every hole of the inward nine brought reminders of my round with Shivas Irons. Shot by shot, my game deteriorated, partly because of my excitement, partly because of a gratitude I couldn't explain, but also because I was struggling with doubts. It was possible that the voice I'd heard came from subconscious · confabulation. Like certain dreams, the man in black might have been my own production, an ingenious wish fulfillment, another attempt to find what I'd lost when I walked away from Shivas Irons. If part of me would follow him wherever he went, parts of me would not. On the eighteenth green, remembering the shining presence that opened at his side, I felt an instinctive resistance. If it made another appearance, my contraction would be just as immediate as it had been in 1956.

"A pleasure, Murphy," said Magee as we walked to the starter's shack. "That was one fucking shot on the three-par. And Mitsu? What a round you played! What did ya shoot?"

Mitsubishi was putting last touches on his scorecard. "Ah, Magee!" he exclaimed. "You have 67. I shoot 84. And Murphy, you shoot 86! Thirty-four on the front side, 52 on the back. Not bad!"

In 1956 I'd shot the same score, but with 34 on the back side and 52 on the front. Then I remembered that Shivas had shot 67, and MacIver an 84. Certain fateful coincidences are not confabulated, and they cannot be produced through wish fulfillment.

After changing shoes at the starter's shack, I stood by the clubhouse, divided. An American member had gotten me access to its storied meeting room, but the rules and sociability I was likely to find there might make it hard to assimilate what I'd experienced during this remarkable golf round. Still, the place might give me further clues to the activities and whereabouts of Shivas Irons.

With its high paneled walls and ceiling, and its mementos of a treasured past, the spacious room impressed me again with its warmth and rich sense of tradition. I had been here twice before: the first time in 1956, accompanied by Shivas Irons; the second time in 1970, with an introduction from a friend who was a member. It was not an easy place to visit. Women were not allowed. I was here as a friend of Grant Spaeth, soon to be president of the United States Golf Association.

None of the men in the room were familiar to me. Sonny Liston, the affable presence who'd served me on my previous visits, had left Burningbush a few years before, and none of the members I'd seen were in evidence. The handsome young barman

hadn't heard of Shivas Irons, Seamus MacDuff, or the other people I'd met in 1956. When I realized that he had no leads worth
following, I took the beer he gave me to a window that faced the
eighteenth green. It was a good place to recapture the hour I'd
spent in this room with Shivas Irons. He'd been a magnetic presence that night, from the moment we walked through the door.

"What ye' doin' to the lad?" a man named Burns had
shouted when we entered. "Takin' his money, Mr. Irons?
Or his mind? *Or his soul!*"

Shivas had only nodded in response, while telling me loudly to
disregard him. Then Burns had shouted something back. By the
time we reached the bar, it seemed that everyone in the place had
turned to see us.

Waiting for drinks at the bar, I turned to survey the room. The
paneled wall above us was adorned with a tartan kilt and crossed
swords hung in a great gold frame, and photographs of Old Tom
Morris, young Tom Morris, Harry Vardon, Bobby Jones, and
other renowned golfers. On the other walls there were paintings
of club captains, local aristocrats, a former Prince of Wales, and
two or three British prime ministers. Some of these imposing figures wore costumes of the eighteenth century.

After Sonny Liston poured us each a glass of whiskey, I asked
if they'd spoken in Gaelic. "It's English," said Shivas. "Not the
King's kind, but the language as spoken by Robert Burns." Then
he turned in the direction of the man named Burns and, with a
resonant voice, recited these lines by the great Scottish poet:

> *Let other poets raise a fracas*
> *'Bout vines, an' wines, an' drucken Bacchus,*
> *An' crabbit names an' stories wrack us,*
> > *An' grate our lug;*

I sing the juice Scotch bear can mak us,
In glass or jug.

Several men turned as his voice rose, and some responded with other lines celebrating Scotch drink. A group near the fireplace lifted their glasses toward us. The recitations had triggered a show of friendship that stretched across the entire room. As if to confirm this sense of community, Shivas declaimed another stanza from Burns:

An' now, Auld Cloots, I ken ye're thinkin,
A certain Bardie's rantin, drinkin,
Some luckless hour will send him linkin,
To your black Pit;
But, faith! he'll turn a corner jinkin,
An' cheat you yet.

"The devil doesn't have us yet, my friend." Shivas lifted his glass toward Burns. "Yer ancestor, if he was indeed yer ancestor, would've agreed!"

"You're too confident, Mr. Irons." The man nodded toward me. "I hate to think what trouble you're visitin' upon that handsome young man."

Burns shouldered his way between us and demanded that Liston serve us more drinks. He was a burly man, about an inch shorter than Shivas's six foot three, and over his dark brown jacket and tie, he wore a matching cape. "When ye recite tha' poem," he said, "we know ye're up to somethin'. But let me warn ye. Ye must let the young man have a mind of his own."

Shivas placed a hand on his shoulder. "Burns," he said, "have faith. The man can hold his own." He introduced us, and Burns shook my hand with a powerful grip. He had strong features reddened by drink and the elements.

"So what's he tellin' ye?" Burns leaned back to appraise me with an eyebrow cocked. "About his hole-in-one on the *moon?* Or his match with Old Tom Morris? Or how he beat Ben Hogan!"

Another member approached, then a third and a fourth. Soon Shivas stood in a spirited group, trading mock insults, toasts, and challenges. Watching this ebullient exchange, I took the glass of whiskey that Liston gave me and moved away without anyone's seeming to notice

Grateful for a chance to be alone, I sat by the fireplace. Though there was light of the gloaming outside, the fire cast shadows on the paneled walls, and gave rich textures to the portraits above me. One in particular caught my eye. It depicted a fierce-looking, bearded man who'd been a colonel in Queen Victoria's Indian regiments. Later Shivas would tell me that a Himalayan yogi had taught him to walk as if he were levitating.

The men at the bar were singing now, and the high, dark walls began to glow as the light outside grew dimmer. The wind, the sea, the summer grass had left their traces in me. Looking across the darkening links, listening to cheers from the eighteenth green, I sensed that everything was happening inside the greater body we secretly inhabit.

But as the hour passed, my mind and senses began to fall from this state of grace. Perhaps it was the dulling that follows the immediate liberations of whiskey, or simply my nerves' inability to sustain this encompassing joy, but questions began to trouble me. In the philosophy department at Stanford University, where philosophic and linguistic analysis were in their ascendancy, there had been general agreement among my teachers that spiritual illuminations don't give us knowledge of things outside the self. As one professor had told me, a mystic's asserting he'd seen angels or God simply meant that he felt good. For all I knew, my elevations on the inward nine had come from hypoglycemia.

Warmed by the friendship that filled the room, and resonating still with the magic of our golf round, I realized that I was closer than ever to the illuminations I would seek in India. And yet I was starting to doubt them.

A nd now, thirty-one years later, sitting in the same convivial place, I felt a similar conflict. If part of me would go with Shivas Irons, as the stranger had said, parts of me would not. My resistance to him seemed as strong as it had been in 1956. But somehow that wasn't disturbing. There were leads to him everywhere, some hidden in the depths of my memory, some appearing from the world at large in response to the search I shared with Hannigan. It was more evident than ever before that there were several ways to find him.

And, for the first time, I was beginning to sense that, in some mysterious way, he was reaching out to me.

PART TWO

. . .

FALL,

1994

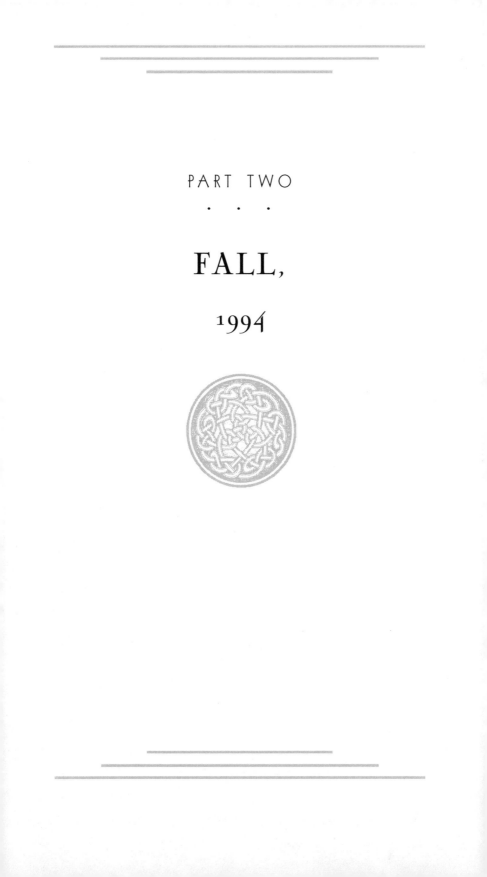

CHAPTER THIRTEEN

THE FIRST RUSSIAN Open Golf Championship was held in early September 1994, at the Moscow Country Club, on a golf course designed by Robert Trent Jones, Jr., Don Knott, and other members of Jones's architectural firm. Steve Schroeder, the firm's business manager, won this historic event, which was scheduled for three rounds but stopped by rain after forty-five holes. Schroeder shot a 186 to defeat some fifty-five players from thirteen countries, among them Michael Bonallack, Secretary of the Royal and Ancient Golf Club of St. Andrew's and a former British Amateur champion. To my lasting regret, I didn't compete in the tournament, but did play the course two weeks later with Horace Ziparelli, the colorful Italian amateur known in the golf community as "Horace Zipper."

More than any other person living or dead, Ziparelli has tried to become that ball-striking paragon Homer Kelley called "The Golfing Machine." Perhaps you have read Kelley's book, and studied his Star System of Geometrically Oriented Linear Force (or G. O. L. F.). If so, you know that the golf stroke has twenty-four basic components, among them grip, plane line, plane angle, address, hinge action, pivot, shoulder turn, hip turn, hip action, knee action, foot action, left wrist action, lag loading, power package assembly point, power package loading action, power package delivery path, and power package release, each of which has from three to fifteen variations. And you know, too, that the golf stroke has twelve sections through which every one of its twenty-four components must be tracked to be given its "full recognition, application and continuity," and that it also has three zones of action "occuring throughout the twelve sections." When I met him in 1994, Ziparelli had memorized much of Kelley's book, *The Golfing Machine, its Construction, Operation, and Adjustment,* and frequently quoted from it at length. Here is a passage he recited to me in Moscow, with references to diagrams in Kelley's book without which one cannot possibly understand the Star System:

> The hand relationship is invariably established at impact fix (7-8) with
>
> 1. the left arm and clubshaft in-line (4-D, 6-B-3-0-1)
> 2. the right forearm "on plane" (7-3, 6-B-3-0-1)
> 3. the back of the flat left wrist and the lag pressure point (6-C-2-0) both facing down the angle of approach (2-J-3). Otherwise, per 7-3, both must face down the right forearm impact fix Alignment (alternate target line) regardless of the true angle of approach (2-J-3, 7-5).

Ziparelli also quoted the following passage, which seemed especially important to him:

> Because of the dominant role of accumulator 3, golf strokes are very dependent on the right elbow activity deriving from its locations and the nature of the subsequent right arm participation. The elbow must always be someplace and as there are only three

definable locations, there are three major basic strokes—punch, pitch and push.

And this:

> The proportion of the separation rate to the approach rate expresses the elasticity involved, and is called the coefficient of restitution which is 80% for the better golf balls—but drops below 70% at high speeds. Of course, this is assuming there is no Compression Leakage (2-C-0).

When Ziparelli recited from Kelley's book, he left each disjointed sentence intact, almost as if it were holy scripture. For it was his life's project to master every principle of the Star System, and thus realize an immaculate execution of the golf swing, an unprecedented perfection of golf mechanics, and a consolidation of vectors of force that would set new standards for amateurs and professionals alike.

He was nearly six feet tall, with a plump but elastic physique and round olive-complexioned face with large dark eyes that often had a look of astonishment. During our time together in Moscow, he was stylishly unshaven, and his thick dark hair fell over his ears, giving him a bohemian look that contrasted with his expensive, high-style, all-white wardrobe. But there were contradictions in Ziparelli beyond those suggested by his grooming and dress, most notably that through his mechanical mastery of the golf swing he aspired to "unzip" three-dimensional space (hence his nickname), and thus turn himself into a hypercube. He had been led to this by a confluence of Kelley's principles with Salvadore Dalí's painting, *Christus Hypercubus,* which shows Christ crucified on a tesseract, or unraveled hypercube, to suggest his ascension to hyperdimensional life and its immeasurable splendors. It didn't matter to Ziparelli that a hypercube, which has four spatial dimensions, is a mathematical abstraction. He believed that a perfectly executed golf swing can, through the guidance of Kelley and by its synchronization of thousands of vectors of force, open up—or "unzip"—the world as we usually know it, and propel us into regions beyond. Our configuration in this superordinary state would be, precisely, a hypercube. When he announced this to me over beers at the Moscow Country Club, I thought for a moment that he was joking. But I should have known better. His behavior during our golf round that day had dramatically reflected his beliefs about golf and the fourth dimension.

Russia's first championship course, which is seven thousand yards long from the blue tees, is set in a forest of pine, maple, and silver birch, with bent grass fairways and greens, manmade ponds, and wetlands nourished by natural streams either beside or cutting across the third, fourth, fifth, and eighth holes. In 1994, given the broken-down condition of most Russian parks, it seemed a miracle of design and maintenance. Indeed, it seemed a miracle that it existed at all in the heart of the former Soviet state, and a wonder that in its first year it was already frequented by players from Western Europe, Australia, Japan, and America. If its maintenance held, it promised a long and storied future. Given Russia's epic flair for the unexpected, there was no telling what prodigies of body and soul it would produce in the years ahead. But as I waited on the first tee for the partner the starter had promised me, I didn't anticipate the surprises that would come in the next few minutes.

Then I saw Ziparelli. As if on oiled ball bearings, he was gliding through the pine trees with his caddie. From the beginning, there were hints of the golfing machine.

His back was straight, his stride was fluid, and his arms swung in uniform arcs as if he were marching to a metronome. But the most startling thing about his movement was the way he held his head. It moved as if on a laser beam above his long and rolling gait, without the slightest rise or fall. As he approached, he raised his left arm in greeting, with what looked very much like a Roman salute, and shouted a hearty *buon giorno.*

"Murphy!" he said expansively. "I am Ziparelli. This is my caddie, Signor Georgi. He knows this course, all of it, every hazard, every green, every fairway, every swamp, as if he built it himself. Is that true, Georgi?"

The caddie, a short, dark, unshaven Georgian dressed in a ragged red shirt and faded blue jeans, nodded in my direction. He spoke no English, but a little Italian, and—I would soon discover—had a pistol in Ziparelli's golf bag in case we were accosted by members of the Uzbek, Chechen, Georgian, Armenian, Sicilian, or other Mafias.

I was struck immediately by Ziparelli's loose white shirt and elegantly pleated white pants, obviously the product of Italian high fashion, and his expensive white leather golf shoes. Given his dress, his bodyguard, his unshaven face, and expansive manner, I guessed that he was either an actor or a businessman on the little-policed frontiers of post-Soviet capitalism. Or could he be a mafioso?

But my speculations about Ziparelli's employment were soon overwhelmed by my wonderment at his approach to golf. "I hope you will forgive me, my friend," he said a few seconds after we'd met. "But I must now prepare! Play when you are ready." As I examined the scorecard and took some practice swings, he started the ritual he would often repeat to reinforce what Homer Kelley called "machine feel." In *The Golfing Machine,* Kelley gave the following instructions for achieving this golfing beatitude:

> View the left shoulder as a hinge arrangement, not as a shoulder at all. The right arm becomes a piston—with steam or air

hoses and the whole bit. The hands become adjustable clamps with two-way power actuators—for vertical and rotational manipulation. The left wrist is merely a hinge-pin allowing wristcock but no wristbend. The more of this translation a player can accomplish, the more understandable the procedures become.

Following this instruction, Ziparelli swung his driver with his left arm, held ramrod straight, while making uppercuts with his right fist and hissings that were meant to simulate the action and sounds of a piston. He had learned to synchronize these separate movements with remarkable grace; but not knowing Kelley's system, I was at first disconcerted and then astonished by them.

Meanwhile, Georgi patroled the tee, watching for figures that might be lurking in the trees that bordered the fairway. He seemed unfazed by his employer's ritual, which now comprised an elaborate review of the golf swing's twenty-four basic components. Ziparelli carefully rehearsed his grip, plane line, plane angle, address, left-wrist hinge action, shoulder turn, hip turn, foot action, power-package loading action, power-package delivery path, and other parts of his swing as if each were a clearly separable act, apparently to anchor them in that interface of mind and body he called his "fourth-dimensional muscles." At no point during this elaborate exercise did he appear the least self-conscious. Only later would I realize that he was already inducing the hypnotic state that would bring him to a full actualization of the golf machine and thus to the splendors of hyperspace.

Three or four minutes had passed, but his ritual wasn't finished. As if they were parts of a steam engine, his right fist pumped methodically while his left arm swung in perfect arcs, up and down, up and down. Now I was swinging with him, holding my driver with my left hand, pumping my right arm and fist hypnotically to his relentless beat. "So now we begin," he said at last. "But please, after you, Signor Murphy!"

A little dizzy but strangely energized, I teed up my ball and looked down the tree-lined fairway. According to the scorecard, the hole was a 300-meter four-par with a slight dogleg right, but it seemed longer than that. Ziparelli's ritual had filled me with images of my swing's many parts, and a vivid apprehension of its immense complexity. Standing back, I surveyed the fairway again. It had to be longer than 330 yards. Maybe the Russians who managed the place only gave distance approximations. As I addressed the ball, my golf stroke seemed impossibly complicated. Ziparelli's ritual had dismembered my sense of its unity.

When I swung, my elbow jabbed my side, my wrists at the top of my backswing flapped, and my power-package delivery path burrowed into the ground. A divot flew farther than the ball, which rolled about twenty feet, and I thought for a moment that one of my ribs was broken.

Ziparelli said nothing as he came to the tee. Holding his driver with his right hand, he let his left arm dangle; then, with great care, gripped the club and took a swing which I still find hard to describe. One could call it "cubistically fluid," or an "act of dismembered unity," or simply a triumph of self-interruption. For, between address and finish, it had five barely perceptible pauses, the first immediately after takeaway, the second halfway through the backswing, the third at the top of the backswing, the fourth after impact when the club was extended, and the fifth near the finish of the follow-through. Calling it to memory reminds me of golf books with long rows of photographs depicting the phases of famous swings. Ziparelli's golf stroke was, as much as anything else, like a series of freeze-frames, and I can still disassemble it in my mind as he did while warming up.

At that moment, however, I was stunned. I'd seen eccentric swings before, but never one like this. Was it ugly, beautiful, swift, or slow? I couldn't tell because it was so unfamiliar and powerful. The ball split the fairway on a low climbing path, then faded with the dogleg right until it bounced and rolled to the green. Tossing back his long hair, Ziparelli picked up his tee, handed Georgi his club with a lordly air, and extended an arm to suggest that I play my ball from where it lay. Taken aback by this strict adherence to the rules, I picked up my golf bag and walked to the white tees. "Is your pistol loaded?" I asked the caddie with sudden irritation.

When he didn't respond, I turned to Ziparelli.

They exchanged words in Italian, then he nodded to say that it was. "With armor-piercing bullets," he said, his round eyes narrowing to a menacing squint. "It is not completely safe here, Murphy. No more KGB. No more militia. But play." My irritation gave way to alarm. If there was danger lurking, he might indeed be a mafioso.

It took me two more shots to reach his ball, where I was forced to wait while he again rehearsed the swing's twenty-four basic components. But this ritual was different from the one on the tee. Instead of his drive, he rehearsed his chip shot, segment by segment, frame by frame, anchoring each movement in his fourth-dimensional muscles. When he finally hit the ball, it ended six inches from the cup.

He turned to me with a dashing smile, dropped his club, and threw his arms in the air exultantly. "You like it, Papa?" he shouted, looking to the sky. "It is for you. *For you!*" It was hard to tell whether he was joking or expressing genuine religious sentiment. Was he talking to himself, to God, to the Pope, or to his deceased father?

On the green, there were more surprises. Standing a few feet from his ball while staring intently at the hole, he swung his arms and wrists like a pendulum or metronome. Again he seemed not the least self-conscious, and was completely oblivious of me. After sinking his six-inch putt, he gave me another stylish smile but no acknowledgment of my patience. I wondered what gave him such a sense of entitlement.

Leaving the green, I decided not to watch any more of his rituals. Already they'd affected my swing adversely, and they promised to hurt it badly. But to my surprise, as we left the next tee I found myself walking as he did. In spite of the golf bag on my back, I felt myself gliding with little effort, my head on a perfectly level plane, such is the power of unconscious mimicry. Georgi was also gliding along, as if on a laser beam. This clone-like behavior reinforced my intention to distance myself from them both.

During the nine-and-a-half holes we played, our exchanges were—with a few exceptions—limited to polite smiles, occasional compliments, and gestures to indicate who should hit next. No mafiosi appeared in the woods, though for a moment we thought so. After the second hole, I didn't keep score. And after shooting 32 on the front nine, the golf machine broke down.

Because in defending myself from Ziparelli I screened my perceptions of him, but also perhaps because his rituals somehow put me into semitrance, recalling our golf round is never an easy exercise. We seem located at a distance, like figures in a movie, and I never quite seem to be myself. For example, I see:

. . . him on the second tee shouting at Georgi, causing Murphy to fall on the ground because he thinks that someone is about to shoot them.

And Georgi firing his pistol accidentally, making Murphy hit the ground again while Ziparelli continues his ritual unfazed, swinging his putter back and forth while hissing like a piston.

And Georgi chasing a man and woman through wetlands beside the fifth fairway before he realizes that they are searching for mushrooms. As he wades after them through the swamp, waving his pistol above his head, they scramble into the woods beyond.

And Murphy's drive on the seventh hole—fading, then hooking, then rising at the end as if propelled by psychokinetic forces caused by his growing dismay and frustration.

And Ziparelli addressing his tee shot on the three-par eighth hole, but having difficulty starting his swing. After hitting the ball, he turns to Murphy, as if for help.

And finally, Ziparelli on the tenth fairway unable to stop his review of the swing's twenty-four basic components. When he finally manages to address the ball, he seems paralyzed. Standing immobile, he looks at Murphy with a helpless expression, and invites him to the clubhouse for drinks.

Z iparelli's seizure brought me out of my partial trance, so it is easier to remember what happened next. We went directly to the newly constructed clubroom, ordered beers at its polished hardwood bar, and stood in silence to collect ourselves. It is never easy to watch compulsive rituals implode. I was as shaken as he was. But Georgi seemed oblivious. He sat at a table nearby, watching the room intently, his pistol protruding from a pocket of his jeans. It was best, I thought, to let the beer relax Ziparelli. The room was a spacious and airy place, with yellow pine walls and handsome French doors through which we could see the forest of pine and silver birch. A few men were sitting at tables, but no one else stood near the bar.

Ziparelli looked away from me now, his lips moving silently. Was he reciting a prayer or a passage from Kelley's book? I wondered whether his golf machine had ever locked up like this. "Well, Murphy!" he said at last, pulling his shoulders back and standing up straight as he turned to face me. "That was a round! You hit some big shots. Some big ones! I like your golf game."

Though his expansive air had returned, there were suggestions of fear in his big dark eyes. But I didn't know how to help him. Certain obsessions are risky to probe, especially when they are supported by disciplines as intense and elaborate as his. Still, I could reach out in small ways. "You worked hard today," I ventured. "You must play a lot of golf."

"I am not a professional, but I practice more than anyone since Ben Hogan." He tossed his hair back, took a long draft of beer, and wiped his lips with gusto. "And I have studied the golf swing for many years. I have theories about it!" He looked at me expectantly, as if he wanted me to ask what they were.

"What are your theories?" I asked.

"They are based on the work of Homer Kelley. Do you know his great book, *The Golfing Machine*?"

I said that I didn't.

"It is a work of genius. Kelley is the Isaac Newton of golf. But no one understands this game completely. No one has a perfect swing. Don't you agree?"

"Yes." I replied, grateful that his confidence and high spirits were back. "The older I get, the more I see that. There's no such thing as a perfect swing."

He seemed troubled by my remark. "Well, Murphy," he said after taking another draft of beer, "there is not a perfect swing *yet,* but one day there might be. If one uses Kelley's *instant-simplification* and stroke-pattern concept. You've never heard of them?"

I said that I hadn't.

"Well," he said grandly. "It is my lifework to advance these principles."

Again there was silence. Then his eyes widened. "But Vladimir!" he exclaimed. "You have it!" He spread his arms toward a tall, broad-shouldered, long-jawed man dressed in a brown ill-fitting suit.

The man's smile revealed several gold-capped teeth, and conveyed a vague sense of menace. "It is everything you expect, Horaahss," he rumbled, handing Ziparelli a cardboard tube. "Everything and more."

"Have a vodka, Vladimir." Ziparelli placed the tube on the bar. "This is Signor Murphy, from the United States. Murphy, this is Bondarenko. The great Bondarenko. Bondarenko of the Russian Space Command!"

"Not Space Command! And not vodka!" Bondarenko protested in a voice that seemed to come from his solar plexus. "Strategic materials, Horahss. The 'Center for Strategic Materials.' It is private enterprise now. And give me a double Scotch."

While Bondarenko got his drink, Ziparelli removed a golf club from the tube. It had a silver shaft and oversized gold triangular head. Evidently, it was a driver. Whistling with admiration, Ziparelli waggled it with arms extended. "Titanium?" He nodded toward its shaft. "And the head, Vladimir. Is it real gold?"

"Not titanium," Bondarenko whispered, glancing around the room. "Something new. A secret. It is only here in Raahsha." He looked at me, as if deciding what he could reveal. "Only here," he whispered. "For the Z-bomb. Call it what you like, Horahss. Siberian steel. Virtual diamond. Metatitanium." He drained his Scotch, and ordered another. "You will hit the ball further than ever, Horahss." An evil smile appeared on his face. "It has been tested in wind tunnels and on the firing range. It is a weapon. You like its warhead?"

"It is so big!" exclaimed Ziparelli. "But so light! Is it gold-plated?"

"For you, Horahss. It is favor for you from the Director."

"But why is it shaped like this?" Ziparelli examined its head with distaste. "Except for the gold, it is ugly. It is very ugly, Vladimir. I want a *beautiful* driver."

"It is new aerodynamic design." Bondarenko looked around

the room again to make sure that no one could hear us. "It is like a missile during the backswing. You see its conical shape. But in your downswing, Horahss, in your downswing, it is a missile flying backward. It reverses wind flow and acceleration. It both speeds up the warhead and slows it down, compresses it and expands it at once. It is hyperspace weapon, Horahss. It was designed for ballistic missiles aimed into wormholes!"

They traded knowing looks, but I couldn't tell if Bondarenko was serious. Did Ziparelli believe him? "There is only one way to test this!" he exclaimed. "We must hit balls! Real balls! Talk to the starter, Georgi. Get the first fairway *now."*

A moment later we stood on the first tee, with permission to use it as a driving range. Seemingly forgetful of his seizure, Ziparelli used the club to examine his swing components. Plane line, plane angle, pivot, hinge action, shoulder turn, hip turn, hip action, knee action, foot action, lag loading, power-package loading action, and power-package delivery path were quickly reviewed, as the golden warhead zipped back and forth with an eerie whistle. Meanwhile Georgi patrolled the tee, his pistol sticking from a pocket, and Bondarenko watched with sinister self-satisfaction.

Two or three minutes passed, but the ritual went on and on. "With this warhead, you will not need so much practice, Horahss," Bondarenko rumbled. "Now hit the ball. Please hit it!"

But the swing analysis wouldn't stop. Now Ziparelli was making right uppercuts and hissing to simulate a piston. "The ball!" Bondarenko said loudly. "Hit the ball, Horahss!"

Finally, Ziparelli swung. *"Ave Maria!"* he shouted as the ball disappeared down the fairway. "Bondarenko, you are a genius! Tell your director I love him!"

The big Russian's jaw seemed enormous as he followed the

flight of the ball. "It is over the green, Horahss," he said. "You make the hole a three-par."

"And myself a hypercube!" said the golf machine. "You do not believe me, Vladimir. I will unzip the world!"

The remark eluded me, but Bondarenko seemed to understand. "You are crazy guy, Horahss," he said. "Forget hyperspace. Three dimensions are enough. Hit another over the green!"

Ziparelli hit a second ball, which sailed farther than the first. But it curved in two directions. "Is that Raahshan ball?" Bondarenko rumbled. "Horahss, are you hitting Raahshan balls? They are not round! They will not show what the warhead can do."

"You gave them to me," Ziparelli protested. "So I use them!"

"You are crazy," said Bondarenko. "Use American balls. Then you see real Raahshan science!"

"Let me see one," I asked. "I didn't know Russians made golf balls."

"We make balls, we make clubs, we make courses," said Bondarenko. "We are capitalist nation now." He gave me an ugly smile. "Khrushchev was right—but backward. We will bury you, but as capitalist nation!"

I examined the ball Ziparelli threw me. Its dimples were oddly spaced, and the single word "golf" was painted above a row of Cyrillic letters. Had I hit one like it on the seventh hole? My drive had curved in two directions.

Ziparelli's next shot sailed even farther than the others, high into the autumn sky, past the distant pin on the fly. It had sailed for more than 300 yards, perhaps for 350. "Hurray for Russia!" he shouted. "You are a genius, Bondarenko. A genius for all time!"

Bondarenko's menacing look was replaced by a childlike expression of pride. He smiled broadly, causing sunlight to glance from his golden teeth. "Launch another," he rumbled. "It will go even farther. It will be intercontinental!" Suddenly he reminded me of the steel-toothed giant "Jaws," who appears in some of the James Bond movies.

Ziparelli's excitement had overcome his need to review the swing's basic components. He teed another American ball, but during his takeaway the club produced an eerie whistle, and at impact two objects flew from the tee. Behind the ball the club head sailed, spinning like a golden discus, until it hovered high above us. Then, slowly and ominously, it turned its pointed side to earth and headed in our direction. We all ran toward the club-house for cover.

Georgi pulled out his pistol. Ziparelli turned to Bondarenko. But the big Russian waved them both away. "It was good missile launch," he said proudly. "Did you see how high it flew, Horahss? And how it turned? Now you see it is aerodynamic. No other club head would go that far, or come to earth with such perfect balance. It is beautiful!" He glowered at Georgi, and the caddie ran to retrieve the lost part.

A few minutes later, we sat at a table in the clubhouse. "We need superepoxy, Horahss," Bondarenko said gravely, inserting the metatitanium shaft into its golden warhead. "And special screws made of strategic materials. This warhead is too strong for normal means of attachment."

"How many can you make?" His client got down to business. "When can you start deliveries?"

"When the money is in Moscow," said the Russian in his lowest register. "Two hundred American dollars a club. You can sell it for a thousand."

"You said one hundred." Ziparelli narrowed his big dark eyes. "That was not our agreement, Vladimir. We make a deal, we stick with it."

"The Director says two hundred." Straightening his back, Bondarenko looked at Ziparelli with menace. "It is that or nothing, Horahss."

"What would *you* pay for it, Murphy?" Ziparelli turned to me. "What would you pay in America?"

Glancing at Georgi, who watched gravely from an adjoining table, I said that I'd pay five hundred. Then I glanced at the glowering Bondarenko. But a thousand, I added, if its head was really plated with gold!

No one responded, and I asked what they would call it. A good name might help to raise the price. "It is good question, Murphy." Bondarenko glanced around the room. "I have studied this. We could call it 'The *Big* Warhead' or just 'The Big One.'" He gave me a sinister look. "Also 'Fat Boy,' like the bomb you dropped on Hiroshima."

"Fat Boy?" I asked. "That might not be good for sales in Japan."

Bondarenko pondered this. "Da," he said grudgingly. "Da. Horaahs, we should leave its name to the Americans. They are marketing geniuses."

As they argued about the price and other details of the transaction, Georgi circled the spacious room, then ordered another drink. It was about five o'clock, and several men had come to the bar, all of them Italian or German. Georgi, it seemed, was accentuating the fact that besides the barman, Bondarenko was the only Russian in the place. At the bar he caught Bondarenko's attention, then touched the bulge in his pants caused by his loaded pistol. Increasingly dismayed by this ritual of intimidation, I said that I needed to make a phone call.

When I returned ten minutes later, Bondarenko was gone, Ziparelli sat alone at the table, and Georgi still stood by the bar. "Ah, my friend," said Ziparelli. "Will you join me for dinner?"

Though Georgi made me uncomfortable, my fascination with Ziparelli and curiosity about business in post-Soviet Russia prompted me to accept the invitation. After moving to a secluded part of the dining room, we spent two hours eating, drinking, and talking. At first Georgi sat at the bar. Then he moved to a table beside the French doors from which he could protect us.

Our meal began in a Russian way, with vodka, black caviar, and dark rye bread, then moved through roasted potatoes, lamb chops that were better than any I'd had in Moscow during my previous visits, a mediocre Italian red wine, a salad of cucumbers and sliced tomatoes, espresso, and a powerful Armenian brandy that I was content to breathe rather than swallow. As the meal progressed, Ziparelli trusted me with more revelations about his experience as a golfing machine. He had learned about Kelley's book from an American he'd met in 1982, and with the six-piece swing it inspired, had begun to win amateur championships in Ireland, Great Britain, and Europe. For twelve years, he'd tried to perfect the "machine feel" that Kelley celebrated, but never with complete success. Over the lamb chops, he confided that despite his complete dedication to his master's principles, he couldn't hold all of the swing's components in his mind at once. "My feeling of the swing is partial," he said with a sad expression. "I have not achieved instant simplification. Therefore, I am still hypercuboidal."

"Hypercuboidal?"

"*Almost* a hypercube. A pitifully three-dimensional hypercube. Murphy, I am only a tesseract." He leaned toward me, and lowered his voice to a whisper. "If we can hold something as complex and dynamic as a golf swing in perfect awareness, in all its parts, inch by inch from start to finish, we come closer to the fourth dimension." He paused for emphasis. *"And then we might go across.* For a microsecond, perhaps, or a millisecond, or maybe for one hundreth of a second. That is the way it will happen."

Golf has a genius for evoking such passions, but I thought he might be putting me on. "What will it feel like?" I wondered.

"It will feel good!" he said, with a smile that enlisted his entire face. "You will never be the same after that. After one glimpse, your body will know it. Have you studied Salvador Dalí's *Christus Hypercubus*? Dalí is my teacher, too."

After vodka and several glasses of wine, and this evening of spirited conversation, I felt empowered to ask how he was able to spend so much time doing research on the fourth dimension. "My glorious papa," he answered without hesitation. "He has given me a fine endowment."

"But you're a businessman, too. Aren't you importing golf clubs from Russia?"

"You mean Bondarenko? That is not business! I will buy his warheads for my friends and use them for tax deductions. You know how that works. Playing golf here, you must be familiar with tax codes."

"I don't have offshore accounts, if that's what you mean. But I do have a trust fund."

"So, my friend, what is *your* occupation?"

I told him about the book I was writing and asked if he'd heard of *Golf in the Kingdom*. When he said that he hadn't, I told him about Shivas Irons. He was certain at once that Irons was almost hypercuboidal and began to quiz me about him.

But our talk was interrupted constantly by his need to demonstrate Kelley's system. Once he stood without warning, hissing and pumping his fist like a piston, and wouldn't sit down until I pulled at his shirt. When our waiter had cleared the table, he rose again without embarrassment to reveal secrets of knee action, backswing, and pivot. And over brandy he insisted twice on showing me Kelley's "power-package loading action," each time standing to cock his wrists, turn his hips, and swing his arms in vigorous arcs. Though a group of Germans objected to these demonstrations, sometimes reproaching him loudly, the Russian barmen and waiters seemed not to mind. On this evening, the

Moscow Country Club displayed a typical Russian tolerance for exuberance at evening meals.

"Look!" Ziparelli scribbled this equation on a napkin:

$$v = U \times \frac{1 + e}{1 + (m/M)}$$

"It gives the velocity of a ball hit with a driver. What will it be with Bondarenko's warhead?"

"Where did you get that equation?" I asked.

"From another great book. Ah, Murphy! *The Search for the Perfect Swing.* A book as great as Kelley's. It shows that a golfer is a double pendulum. Do you know a golf shaft's rate of vibration?"

When I said that I didn't, he drew this equation beside the one for ball velocity:

$$f = \frac{L}{2\pi} \sqrt{\frac{3EI}{(M+0.24m)L^3}} *$$

"Golf," he sighed. "There is no end to it."

Never had I witnessed such a joining of obsessional behavior with unembarrassed flamboyance. Ziparelli's elastic personality reflected his elastic physique. Both had enough stretch to accommodate compulsivities that would cripple most of us. I asked who raised him. "A glorious aunt and tutors in Roma, all of them supervised by the best father in this world," he replied with gusto. And where did he live? "Roma in the winter, or on the Amalfi

---

* For the first equation: v=velocity of the ball immediately after impact; U= velocity of the clubhead immediately before impact; m=mass of the ball; M= mass of the clubhead; e=the coefficient of restitution. For the second equation: f=times per second; M=the mass of the clubhead; m=the mass of the shaft; L= the length of the shaft from the point of clamping to the head; E=an elastic property of the material of the shaft; I=a quantity which depends on the precise cross-section of the shaft, and which represents its ability to resist bending. From Alastair Cochran and John Stobbs, *The Search for the Perfect Swing.* (Philadelphia: Lippincott, 1968), Appendix I.

coast. Near Marbella in the spring, and Lake Constance in the summer. And now Septembers in Moscow! It is a good life. There is enough freedom to pursue my theories. Enough money to perfect my swing. Enough time to reach the fourth dimension."

"Who were your tutors?" I asked.

"Swiss. Like my aunt. They were very strict, but loved me very much. They made me fluent in four languages and taught me calculus and the history of science. They were disciples of Rudolf Steiner."

"Ah, Steiner! That's how you came to the fourth dimension?"

"Absolutely not!" He was adamant. "I came to it twenty years ago, before Kelley, when I was eighteen, through Salvador Dalí himself. He was a friend of Papa's. He told me to meditate on his *Christus Hypercubus*. If I could visualize the tesseract—the three dimensional-cross upon which Christ is crucified—as a true hypercube, I would then be in hyperspace. This he told me. This I believe. This I will do." He slapped the table, then added, almost as an afterthought, "With the help of Homer Kelley, and his Star System of Geometrically Oriented Linear Force."

I didn't want to tell him that I'd met a stunning young woman in London to whom Dalí had given similar advice as he was making amorous advances. Dalí was famous for such remarks, and she'd taken it to be a joke.

The room was almost empty, and Georgi approached the table. Like Ziparelli, he had what seemed a two- or three-days' growth of beard. They talked for a moment in Italian. Then Ziparelli said apologetically that they had a meeting in Moscow, a meeting he couldn't miss. "But will you meet me tomorrow?" he asked. "We will play again!"

"How can we get in touch? Tomorrow I have a meeting with someone I've been trying to see for years. It's impossible to postpone it."

"Well perhaps the day after," he said with disappointment. "You can reach me at the Metropole for the next three days." He stood abruptly, signaled the waiter to cover our bill, and walked away with his long, rolling stride. Georgi followed him closely, glancing in all directions to ensure that no danger was lurking.

CHAPTER FOURTEEN

BORIS RYZHKOV LIVED in a secluded stretch of birch forest near the village of Peredelkino, about an hour's drive from the middle of Moscow. His two-story log house, which he shared with a few of his students, had been his family's dacha since the nineteenth century and his home for more than twenty years. Like other dachas of the Russian intelligentsia which had survived the revolution and Stalin's purges, it had architectural touches from different decades. Among these were paneled doors from the 1890s, a faded 1920s art deco tableau in its kitchen, a tiled oven from the 1960s, and (according to Nadia) Finnish bathroom fixtures of the 1980s. It was Ryzhkov's ancestral home, monastery, academy, and fortress. With a few exceptions, only his dearest friends, relatives, and students were allowed on its premises.

For five years, I had tried unsuccessfully to see him. Nadia's entreaties, recommendations from two other mutual friends, and my letters hadn't moved him to give me an audience. Ryzhkov was that rarity of contemporary Europe and America, an intellectual who was also a practicing mystic, and he had no aspirations for celebrity or a cult following. He was known to Russian religious scholars as an authority on Islamic, Jewish, and Russian Orthodox mysticism, and among the intelligentsia of Moscow and St. Petersburg as a leading light of hesychasm, the Russian way of contemplative prayer. His reputation had also spread to Central Asia, where his essays were read by Christians, Jews, and Muslims alike, and to the Caucasus. But strictures of the former Soviet regime, his failure to publish in English, and his desire for anonymity had kept him invisible to Westerners. He had refused to see me in 1989, and again in 1992, but had relented at last two weeks before this trip to Moscow. However, this visit might be brief. A woman with a sultry voice and heavy Russian accent had warned me on the telephone that I shouldn't expect a long conversation. Ryzhkov would have other visitors on the evening we were scheduled to meet.

Driving in my rented car along the dirt road that led from the motorway to his property, I felt a growing discomfort. Nadia had told me that he was deeply suspicious of most contemporary speculations regarding mystical experience and the occult. The gurus and healers now appearing on Russian television dismayed and sometimes disgusted him. He considered Russia's neglect of its great pre-Communist philosophers a national tragedy. And he scorned the game of golf. It was hard to know what he thought about my search for Shivas Irons.

On this late September afternoon, the slender white birch trees that bordered the road had lost more than half of their leaves, and the shadows they cast made it hard to see all the ruts and potholes. Two cows forced me to stop as they trotted into the forest. A broken-down truck lumbered past, looking as if it might collapse any minute. And I had to stop a second time as a girl with pigtails crossed the road in pursuit of a stout red-faced woman in a head scarf who might have lived in the time of the czars. This Russia seemed a century away from the modernizing streets of Moscow I'd left just an hour before.

It was five o'clock when I reached his property. A battered, dust-covered jeep and 1960s Mercedes stood in a turnaround area beside the road, and I parked my car between them. The birch trees glowed in the autumn light, and shadows were forming in blue pools around them. I got out of the car, zipped up my windbreaker, and opened a rickety wooden gate set into a picket fence. The steep wood-shingled roof of Ryzhkov's house was visible at the end of a leafy path, and just beyond it, half-hidden in a thick stand of pine trees, stood the building Nadia had described, the tall stone tower that housed Ryzhkov's necromanteion.

As if she'd been waiting, a woman walked toward me through the trees, a hand raised to her shoulder in greeting. She was Russian, I guessed, about thirty years old, and came from a different era than the babushka I'd passed on the road. "Good evening," she said in slightly accented English. "You're Murphy?"

Blond hair fell just past her ears, framing a slightly upturned aristocratic nose, suspicious blue eyes, and a mouth with an arched upper lip that suggested both toughness and refinement. Her white blouse, sandals, and faded blue jeans, as well as her stylish makeup, reflected the eye for Western style prevalent among privileged Russian youth of the 1990s. She wasn't the kind of person I'd expected to meet. I'd pictured the people near Ryzhkov to look more ascetic.

"Hello," I said. "Yes, I'm Murphy."

As she led me toward the house, she said that Ryzhkov would be occupied for another ten minutes. Pointing to a wicker armchair near the front door, she asked if I wanted a cup of tea.

"No, thanks," I said. "I'm happy to wait. It's a beautiful evening."

"You are a friend of Nadia Kirova." She framed her question as a statement. When I said that I was, she looked me up and down with what seemed to be amused curiosity, then turned and went into the house.

Though the armchair was set about twenty feet from the house, I could hear voices that were sometimes accompanied by a squeaking that sounded like rusty hinges. Perhaps Ryzhkov was giving his visitor lessons in hesychast prayer. I tried to picture the man. Nadia had told me he was about fifty-five, and well built. Growing up in Tashkent in a Russian family, he'd mastered Greco-Roman wrestling because his father, a powerful Soviet official in Uzbekistan, had deemed it necessary if young Boris was to hold his own with the Muslims. You could tell that his nose had been broken more than once, she'd said. He didn't look like a scholar or mystic, but more like a working man. From the moment I'd started hearing about him, Ryzhkov had seemed intimidating, but the impression was heightened now. I thought of the Winter Palace and other buildings in Moscow and St. Petersburg designed to humble Europeans. By keeping me out on the porch like this, he might be instinctively following the old Russian custom of putting foreigners in their lesser place.

Ten minutes passed. Shadows were lengthening in the trees, and a deeper quiet was settling over the property. The murmur of voices continued, broken occasionally by periods of silence and the slightly hypnotic squeaking I'd heard when I first sat down. Would he have much time for our meeting? Fortunately, we wouldn't need an interpreter because he was fluent in English after a year at Cambridge studying Islamic religious texts.

More time passed. The woods were darker now, and the sky that was visible through the canopy of birch was turning to deeper shades of blue. Besides the murmuring in the house, the only sounds I could hear came from the gentle rustling of leaves and an occasional distant cowbell.

Then there were footsteps inside, louder voices, and the sound of a door banging shut. I stood. The woman who'd greeted me stepped onto the porch and, with a look of quiet anticipation, said that Ryzhkov was ready to see me. I felt a wave of anxiety as I followed her through the door.

"He will be here in a moment." She pointed to a chair near a glowing floor lamp. "It was cold outside. It is almost winter. By now you must want tea." Her features were even handsomer in the muted light than they'd been a half hour earlier. When I accepted her offer, she left the room through an old paneled door through which I glimpsed a long wooden sideboard under an art deco tableau.

I removed my jacket and looked around me. Every window was shuttered, and the high, slanted ceiling was dark. The only light came from the lamp at my side, which was crowned with a tasseled shade that appeared to date from the nineteenth century. About six feet away, at the other end of a rug that could have been made in Bukhara or Samarkand, there was a rocking chair. It must have caused the squeaking I'd heard.

There were voices in the kitchen now. The woman was talking to someone who sounded like a teenage boy—in French, it seemed, though he responded in Russian. I continued to scan the room. One wall was made of the thickly calked timbers that comprised the house's exterior, two were made of yellow pine, and the fourth was covered for much of its length by a tile oven that almost reached the fifteen-foot peak of the ceiling. Near the rocking chair were two stacks of pillows that looked to be from Afghanistan, and on a round wooden table by the lamp was a green trinket box with Persian designs, a silver drinking horn from the Caucasus, a large magnifying glass, and several books. From their covers, I could see that two of the books were in Russian, two in Hebrew, two in German, and one in Arabic.

The woman returned with a tray that held a pot of tea, a tall silver-handled glass, and three bowls with condiments. Placing this elegant array on the table beside me, she suggested I drink the tea Russian-style, with blackberry, raspberry, or gooseberry jam.

She left and I filled the glass. In the next room there was another exchange, this time entirely in French, then receding footsteps. A door shut. Someone called from a distant part of the house. Then it was silent again. After flavoring the tea with jam, I sipped it carefully, held it for comfort to my chest, and rehearsed the questions I'd framed. But at that moment—without warning—Ryzhkov entered the room. "Don't stand up," he said as I put down my tea and started to rise. "I am sorry. Today there are many visitors." He settled carefully into the rocking chair. "At last we meet," he said in a rich, slightly accented baritone. "I have read your letters, and Nadia's, and Yerofeyev's, and Kapitsa's." He looked me up and down. "You have waged a good campaign to see me! But I don't know if I can help. You know, I am completely ignorant about golf."

Though I sensed by the way he sat down that he was protecting an injury to his back, he gave an immediate impression of physical vigor. His cheekbones and jaw were well defined, his closely cropped brown hair had no grey in it, and his skin had the telltale glow of regular exercise.

"You're good to see me," I said. "Nadia's been urging me for years to meet you."

He leaned back in the rocking chair, his hands holding its arm rests, with a genial squint that produced vertical creases in each cheek. "She has written me three times about you," he said. "Three times! You have made a large impression on her. Remind me now. When did you meet?"

"In '87. In Edinburgh. In her necromanteion!"

"Ah, yes. Yes." He nodded. "And you had a visitor. She told

me." An engaging smile appeared on his face, accentuating the creases in his cheeks. "How many times have you seen her since?"

"Just twice. In '89 and '92."

Though he didn't alter his posture, Ryzhkov seemed to settle more deeply into his chair. "I must apologize for having so little time." He folded his hands in his lap. "How can I help you?"

Realizing that he had knowledge of things related to my search for Shivas Irons that few people on the planet possessed, and that this visit might be brief, I had prepared my questions carefully. "Nadia wrote to you about our visitation," I began. "That was seven years ago, and still it haunts me. She says today, as she did then, that she's never experienced anything like it. Do you have any sense of what it was?"

Placing his hands on the arms of the chair, he held my gaze for a moment. "That is all? You must have other questions. Tell me something about Shivas Irons."

"Shivas Irons?" I hesitated. "As I said in my letters, I met him in '56, wrote a book about him, then started this search for him in '87. That's how I met Nadia. Her friend Buck Hannigan, the mathematician in Edinburgh, had been interested in him, too, and had begun to think that he and his teacher were doing something extraordinary. . . ." Again I hesitated, uncertain how to proceed.

A stillness deeper than the quiet in the room was beginning to gather around us. "Our language is poor," he said, almost in a whisper. "But do your best. In one of your letters, you said they were trying to realize, what? 'A new kind of embodiment?' That is abstract. Can you tell me things that suggest what Irons and his teacher were actually doing?"

"What they *are* doing." I amended his question. "Hannigan and I have heard from people who might have seen Irons during the last few years. Though every one of these reports is a little odd, they give us reason to think he's still alive. But what are Irons and MacDuff *actually* doing? That's hard to say. It's easier to guess what they've tried for. They believed St. Paul when he said, 'All flesh is not the same flesh.' I wrote you about this. In their view, human nature isn't finished yet. It's still developing, with the potential for new consciousness and—well, this is the most difficult part—a new kind of embodiment. Unlikely, or far-fetched, as it seems, there is reason to think they've tried to do it."

Ryzhkov rocked in his chair, gazing steadily into my eyes. " 'Behold, I show you a mystery.' " He quoted as I had from First Corinthians. " 'It is sown a natural body; it is raised a spiritual body. We shall not all sleep, but we shall all be changed. The second man *is* the Lord from heaven.' " The words were from the St. James version of the New Testament, rather than an Orthodox text. He had recited them to confirm our mutual acquaintance with St. Paul's language of glorification.

Stunned by this recitation, I didn't respond at once. "Did you know," he asked, "that in a letter near the end of his life, Dostoyevsky said that he and his 'young friend,' Vladimir Solovyov were no longer primarily interested in the salvation of the soul, but instead the resurrection of the body?"

"Solovyov the philosopher!"

"They were friends. They went to monasteries together. Solovyov nursed him after some of his epileptic fits, and was the model for Alyosha—and Ivan, perhaps—in *The Brothers Karamazov*."

"Dostoyevsky used that term, 'the resurrection of the body'? What did he mean?"

"Behold! I give you another mystery." Again Ryzhkov cited First Corinthians. "It is not certain what he meant. But you know the Orthodox doctrine of *theosis*, that human nature, all of it, including the body, can be lifted closer and closer to God. He must have had that in mind. He and Solovyov were not the only Russians to think that all of our parts have a spiritual future. You've heard of Fyodorov and Merezhkovsky?"

"Vaguely."

"They had seeds of the same idea. Before the Bolsheviks, our intellectual climate here was more receptive to such a vision than Western Europe's, perhaps because the Resurrection is more prominent in Orthodox faith than the Crucifixion. Following Christ, 'we all can be changed. We all can be raised a spiritual body. And this mortal must put on immortality.' " Recollecting himself, he gazed at the rug. The room was filled with an extraordinary silence.

Following his example, I looked at the beautifully woven rug. Its reds and golds were merging so that every one of its lines led me toward the intersecting triangles at its center. "But continue," he said. "You have more to say. It will help if you can tell me, item by item, what leads you to think that Irons and his teacher are doing something unusual."

So few words. So few gestures. So little time together. Yet Ryzhkov had somehow filled the room with a clarity and stillness that made it easy to list what he'd asked for. I briefly described my day in Burningbush in 1956, the mysterious presence in Mac-Duff's estate, the photograph with the strange inscription, the margin notes in Irons's books, various descriptions of MacDuff and his mother, and a few recent Shivas sightings. During the ten or fifteen minutes it took to make this recitation, Ryzhkov followed my words with care, interrupting me only to clarify golf terms with which he was unacquainted. "You could write an encyclopedia," he said when I was finished. "Your files must be bigger than the ones British intelligence has on Philby, or the KGB had on Sakharov!"

"He's more elusive," I said. "Sometimes I think we're chasing a ghost. For example, look at this." From a jacket pocket I took this letter, which Ryzhkov scanned, then read with care:

Dornoch, Scotland

July 20, 1992

Dear Mr. Hannigan,

There are rumors that you have made inquiries in Dornoch the past few years about a golf professional named Shivas Irons. A member of the Golf Club recommended I write to you in this regard about a curious encounter I had with a gentleman that in some ways fits descriptions of him.

I am a widower, recently retired here, with a home overlooking the golf links. Two weeks ago, at about half-past ten in the evening, I was standing in the garden behind my house enjoying the evening sky. As you know, we have magnificent outlooks here from the cliffs above Dornoch Firth. From my house, for example, you can see the long gorse-covered bluffs on which the first eight holes of the course are situated, as well as the fairways and dunes of the incoming nine below. There was still enough light on the evening in which my encounter occurred to see the Firth beyond the links, and its further shores on a distant promontory.

There was no wind, and the sky was colored as I have never seen it. Against a background of deep blue and violet, there was an array of gold and yellow clouds that appeared to emit its own light. This stupendous display has been much discussed in Dornoch since, and has been attributed by some to a peculiar condition of the currents offshore and by others to the jet streams of fighter-bombers which had flown maneuvers that day near the Firth. Without hesitation, I can say that it was the most striking evening sky I have ever seen. Viewing it, I was filled with gratitude that I had retired to Dornoch.

Then I noticed a man standing just a few feet beyond my garden wall. He stood motionless, seemingly as rapt with the view as I was, but his presence was a little disturbing because there is no easy access to the place where he stood. The only way he could have gotten there was either through my garden or by ascending the bluff, which can be treacherous in daylight and extremely dangerous in the half-light of a summer evening. For several minutes he didn't move. I didn't want to call out, for fear I would cause him to lose his footing, nor did I want to go inside and leave him lurking near the house.

Finally, to get his attention, I approached him, whereupon he turned to face me, as if he had known all along that I was watching, and asked if I would let him sit for a moment on my garden wall. He was a tall man, casually dressed, with a resonant musical voice of Scots inflection. Reassured by his calm demeanor, I said he could sit there, but to make sure he was up to no mischief sat on a chair about ten feet from him. He fell silent, as if he were again absorbed in the view, then started to hum a song, which I took to be Irish, with such feeling and grace that I wondered if he were a professional singer. It was a plaintive tune, filled with both sorrow and joy, that conveyed a state of mind which I still have trouble describing. The best way to characterize the mood it caused is to say, at risk of seeming excessive, that it embraced many moods at once, an entire range of feelings both happy and sad, in a joy and peace that seemed eternal.

This condition, which felt perfectly natural at the time but seems extraordinary now, lasted for several minutes, until the last traces of yellow in the sky were gone. Then he turned, and with quiet gravity, asked my name. Normally I would have been startled, or even disturbed by such directness, but the evening beauty and his song had produced such a deep serenity in me that without inhibition I introduced myself and asked who he might be. He didn't answer at once, then said with a wry Scots inflection, "On a night like this, I'm not sure. It's changing like the sky there. Do you ever feel trapped by your name?"

Surprised but disarmed by this response, I admitted to a recurrent sense that my life would have been different if I'd been born with a different name. "William Smith" sometimes makes me feel invisible.

I remember his words vividly. "Ah!" he said. "Invisible! Doesn't that bring relief?"

"Yes and no," I answered. "What is your name?"

"There's no relief there!" he said with a laugh. "It is not conducive to invisibility. It's a rare name, from Aberdeenshire. Shives. Do you know it?"

I said that I'd heard of Chivas Regal.

"It's related," he said. "But you say it *Shives,* with a long 'I,' like 'hives' or 'thrives.' "

I was about to ask if this was his Christian or family name, when he stood with a great warm smile and said it was time to leave. He hoped he hadn't disturbed me. As he said it, I heard my telephone ring, asked him to wait, and went inside to find that whoever was calling had hung up. When I returned to the garden, he had vanished. There was no sign of him on the cliff below or along the side of the house. I was left only with the mood he had conveyed, and wonderment at our encounter.

Two members of the Dornoch Golf Club have told me about your search for Shivas Irons. What do you make of this?

Sincerely,
William Smith

"The pronunciation of his name?" Ryzhkov asked. "Is that how you say it? *Shives?* Like 'hives'?"

"No, *Sheevas,* with a long 'e.' Or with a short 'i,' like 'give us.' At least that's how people in Burningbush say it."

"This is an interesting letter. By his tone, one believes this William Smith." He paused. "But I must ask you a question. Your search for Shivas Irons has lasted a long time—almost half your life, it seems. Do you think you are closer to finding him now than you were, say, a year ago?"

Surprised by the question, I hesitated. "A year ago? Probably not."

"Are you closer than five years ago?"

"Five years ago? I'm not sure. Maybe, maybe not."

"Ten years?"

"Well, yes! Certainly ten years. I hadn't met Hannigan then. I'd never heard about MacDuff's property, or the reactions people have there. I didn't know much about the personal histories of Irons or MacDuff, and nothing about these Shivas sightings."

"But are you closer to finding him?" Ryzhkov leaned forward intently. "Not just learning *about* him. Do you think you are closer to *finding* him?"

"That's hard to say. We have more clues. But I can't say for sure whether we're actually closer to finding him."

He continued to hold my gaze. "Have you ever wondered whether you might be using the wrong methods? Maybe there is another way to look."

"But we've tried every method we can think of."

"It is curious that in this letter, and many of your sightings, he seems elusive by design. A hint here, a hint there. This minute you see him, the next minute he's gone, as if he lives in the spirit world. But you and Hannigan continue to look for him as if he is an ordinary person and you work for MI5, the CIA, or the KGB. Maybe he is different than people you find through police work or intelligence gathering. Maybe you have to approach him another way."

"But we're more than detectives!" I protested. "To me, we're doing natural history, or anthropology, if you like. Hannigan has even tried mathematics. Nadia's told you I suppose about his theories. I promise you, we're coming at this from more than one angle."

"Has mathematics brought you closer?"

"Well . . . no."

"Or your natural history?"

"Not yet."

"So neither way has worked. Is it possible that all the methods you have tried are inadequate, separately or taken as a whole. They have not worked so far. Have you thought that maybe they will never work?"

"So what do you propose?"

"You say you are doing natural history. But sometimes ethologists must accommodate to the animals they study. I have a friend who works with snow leopards. To enter their habitat, he learned to move as they did, to lie in wait, to make their sounds. And I know an anthropologist who studies Siberian shamanism. He told me it is best to approach a shaman like an initiate. To know one well, you must live like him, adopt his ways, build his trust. Maybe this is what you have to do."

"But MacDuff is dead, and we don't know where Shivas Irons lives or even if he's still alive!"

He leaned toward me, a gentle smile accentuating the strength in his face. "Your 'natural history of the extraordinary' is a good thing," he said. "It might contribute to our understanding of human nature's greater possibilities. I am not questioning that. I am only talking about your search for Shivas Irons. Like my ethologist and anthropologist friends, you could learn to move and think and feel like he does. Maybe that way you will come closer to him."

"And how would I do this?"

"Take hold of what you know. Go further into your feeling for him. *Imagine* his life, his work, his location. Imagine them deeply. Then let your body follow your mind. Even intelligence officers do this with elusive people."

He stood and crossed the room. Suddenly he seemed a massive presence, both threatening and friendly. With his powerful shoulders hunched, and his muscular arms outstretched, I imagined him confronting another wrestler. "Ah!" he exclaimed, taking something from a shelf. "Here it is!" He handed me a book by Henry Corbin, the eminent student of Islamic mysticism.* "Read Chapter two, section four." He sat in the rocking chair. "It says something about imagination as I just used the term. Maybe it will suggest some ways to approach your man directly."

The book's second chapter was titled "The Mystical Earth of Hurqalya," and its fourth section contained a brief catalog of terms for various kinds of spirit-body. These sentences stood out immediately:

. . . the body of "spiritual flesh" made of the elements of the Earth of Hurqalya . . . possesses organs of perception that are seventy times more noble and more subtle than those of the body of elemental flesh in which it is hidden and invisible. It has shape, extent, and dimension, and is nevertheless imperishable.

The "grave," that is, the place where it continues to be after death is . . . the mystical Earth of Hurqalya to which it belongs, being constituted of its subtle elements; it survives there, invisible to the senses, visible only to the visionary Imagination.

"Is the visionary imagination the organ one uses in a necromanteion?" I asked.

"You can use it in a necromanteion, or not. You can use it in

---

* Henry Corbin, *Spiritual Body and Celestial Earth* (Princeton: Princeton University Press, 1977).

meditation, or not. You can use it in many activities." He paused for effect. "To find Shivas Irons, you can use it on a golf course. It seems he did that when he played. You started to do it on his teacher's property. In one of your letters, you said that the game invites imagination. Accept the invitation fully!"

He rocked slowly in his chair, making the same hypnotic sound I'd heard while sitting outside. It took me a moment to gather my thoughts. "Irons talked about 'imagination with hands,'" I said. "Is that what you're talking about?"

"Imagination with hands . . ." Ryzhkov savored the phrase. "That is one way to say it. And imagination with arms, and legs, and eyes, and ears. Imagination in this sense is the seed of our future body. It has its own ways to move, to feel, to see. It perceives *actual* things, *living* entities, *real* bodies—and worlds beyond the range of our physical senses. It has a life that embraces—but goes beyond—the ordinary self."

I looked again at Corbin's book. "'Spiritual flesh,'" I said. "Irons used that term. Corbin says it is composed of elements from the 'Earth of Hurqalya.' Is that a metaphor?"

"Not for those who have been there. For them, it is the Earth where our secret body lives, 'the Earth of Resurrection,' from which our spiritual flesh will rise to join its eternal soul." From the floor by his rocking chair, he picked up a small set of beads, and began to finger them with his left hand. "It is a radical teaching, but resembles the Orthodox *theosis,* and certain kinds of Jewish, Christian, and Islamic mysticism. Its central idea appears in new guises now, as it gathers in the world's imagination. I don't have to tell you that Sri Aurobindo, India's greatest philosopher of this century, claimed that a new kind of embodiment will appear on Earth, and give rise to the next great phase of evolution. A similar vision is growing in minds around the world like a great thought experiment. Your detective work, your natural history of extraordinary life, contributes to it. All vision today must rest on empirical fact." He fell silent for a moment. "I have learned that you visited a place near Samarkand where people bore witness to such thinking and practice."

Though I'd suspected he knew this, his announcement was unsettling. "The Well of Light." I nodded. "Yes, I was there fourteen years ago. How did you find out?"

"Few Westerners know the place existed, and even fewer Soviet officials of the day. It is one of Sufism's best-kept secrets." A look of amused curiosity came into his face. "There were speculations that you might be a spy."

"You don't believe that, I hope."

"Shouldn't I? Would you tell me?" He studied my face with even-tempered good humor. "But this does not worry my friends in Samarkand or Tashkent. The place had no military secrets. In a sense, aren't we all spies?"

"The only secrets I learned there had to do with sacred architecture. But you talk about it in the past tense."

"It is sealed up," he said without emotion. "An earthquake collapsed the entranceways into its underground vaults. There is no secret mosque now, no Well of Light, no witness to the Earth of Hurqalya. Members of the school believe that the catastrophe was foretold by the school's founder, Ali Shirazi himself. He said, in a phrase that few people have understood, that it would 'open up the Well of Light.' "

"What a tragedy!"

" 'We live between the death of the old gods and the birth of the new.' " He quoted the German poet Hölderlin. "The great esoteric schools are mutating into forms we cannot predict. That is the case with the fellowship of Ali Shirazi, with most Sufi groups of Central Asia, the Caucasus, and Iran. It is also true for nearly every school of hesychast prayer, and most Cabalists. It is hard to know what will take their place. There are a thousand new prophets now, and an avatar born every day. But just a few will last. Most mutations perish." He said all this with the same even-tempered expression he'd displayed since our talk began, giving no evidence of regret. "But unfortunately, our time is up." He rose slowly, still holding the beads he'd picked up from the floor. "It is past six o'clock. I hope I have been helpful."

Surprised, and disappointed, I didn't respond at once. As I rose, he shook my hand. "Let us walk to your car together." He ushered me into the night. "It is a beautiful evening."

Outside, the air had a fresh autumn bite, faintly laced with smoke from a distant chimney. He went ahead of me down the path, making no effort at conversation. Only our footsteps broke the stillness.

Then I slowed my steps. Someone was groaning, or chanting, or calling for help. As I turned to locate the sounds, I saw a tall, narrow light beyond the ghostly birch trees. It came from a window in the necromanteion. "What is that building?" I asked, pretending ignorance.

Ryzhkov stopped. It was evident now that the sounds came from some sort of prayer. "It is my own Well of Light," he said. "Would you like to see it?"

I was startled by his invitation. "Yes," I said. "It would be a privilege."

He led me through birch and pine trees to a clearing near the building. The chanting was louder now. It involved two, or perhaps three people. He gave a low whistle, and a second, and it stopped. There were no sounds of human movement, no rustling of leaves. Then the light in the window went out. "Wait," he whispered. "Someone is coming."

A moment later, the woman who'd met me an hour before came around the tower. Ryzhkov said something in Russian, gestured for me to follow, and led us to a wooden door. Pulling it open, he waited for her to pass, then gestured for me to go inside.

Lowering my head, I stepped into a cool black space filled with a fragrance of incense and stone. The only thing I could see was a narrow, faintly luminescent rectangle some eight or ten feet above me. It was impossible to tell where the woman had gone, or estimate the dimensions of the building. Ryzhkov touched my shoulder. "Sit here," he whispered, helping me to a bench.

There were receding footsteps, then silence. The dim rectangle hovered almost directly above me. But as my eyes adapted, a few parts of the ceiling appeared. It seemed that the tower was thirty or forty feet high.

The place was deeply silent. There was no rustling of clothes, no movement of feet, no sounds of breathing. I looked again at the luminescence. Something had appeared in its frame, just a flickering. There was a tiny point of light, blinking as if to send me a signal. "Take hold of what you know." I heard Ryzhkov's voice. "Take hold of it now!"

Startled, I looked around me. The place was still silent, and no figure was visible in the dark. Deciding I'd imagined the words, I looked again at the tall, narrow light. In the brief moment I'd glanced away, a second luminous point had appeared within it.

Had the tower moved? The thought sent a shiver through me. Something about the place was changing, and I held onto the bench for support. My body seemed lighter now, my hearing more acute, and from a distant echo chamber there whispered the voice of Shivas Irons. "Michael, the stars are all around ye. They're even heer beneath yer feet." I remembered the moment he'd said it in the ravine by the thirteenth hole. "See the stars beneath yer feet. . . ."

Then his voice came more clearly, with all the r's rolled and each nuance of his manly inflection intact. "The entire world is heer inside us." It was almost by my side. "Ye don't have to move an inch."

There could be no doubt about it now. The voice was coming from somewhere beyond my ordinary process of recollection. "Ye can find me," it said. "Keep comin'. I'm not very far away. The whole world is heer inside us."

Holding the bench to keep my balance, I noticed for the first time that it was made of stone. For reassurance, I grasped it with both hands, and felt the rock floor with my feet. Each of the words had Shivas Irons's unmistakable burr, and they were coming from somewhere near me.

And in a darkness deeper than the tower's dark, in a place beyond sleep and dreams, there was the image of a face . . . a long face with blue eyes and red hair falling across its forehead. "The Kingdom's coming, but it's already here." His voice was immediately present. "But no words, or philosophy, or state can hold it." Waves were breaking, and there was a smell of the sea. I sensed that he wanted me to go for a swim from the rocks beyond his shoulder.

"Where are you?" My question welled up as if it were always being asked. "How can I find you?"

"Keep coming." His speech shifted from Scots to King's English. *"Imagine. Practice. Start again. I'm not so far away."*

Wonder, fear, joy, and sadness, all were suddenly present in me. My feelings were changing as fast as his face. "Are you living in Scotland?" I asked.

"Yes," came his suddenly distant reply. "And other places, too. But ye can't reach me with a touring map. Ye've got to be more agile. Move more freely, see with more of yer eyes, feel with more of yer heart. There's more freedom where I'm living, to love, to know, to move, but ye never have to go from home."

There was just the darkness now, and the cold stone floor beneath my feet. The tower was deeply silent. The little lights were gone. Even the rectangle seemed to be fading. Still holding the bench for support, I wondered whether there were vaults beneath me. Did the tower rest on a cavern as deep as the Well of Light?

"Murphy," Ryzhkov whispered. "Be careful when you stand." He helped me up, and led me slowly through the dark. At the door I turned to see a taper lit on the tower wall, and a narrow ledge near the ceiling upon which two figures sat. Disoriented, I stepped outside and looked around me. Stars were shining through the trees, and two jumped through the branches toward me. They were the tiny points I'd seen. The luminescence had come from the sky that was visible through the necromanteion's window.

Ryzhkov shut the door behind us and started toward my car. Had he heard the voice of Shivas Irons? When he stopped to open the gate, I asked if he'd felt something strange.

"What happened?" he asked matter-of-factly.

I described the voice of Shivas Irons, repeated its admonitions, and asked if he had heard it.

"No," he answered. "It spoke to you."

"Is your necromanteion like the mosque near Samarkand?" Even as I asked it, the question surprised me. "Are there vaults underneath it?"

"When the old schools die, we must give them new form." Amusement came into his face. "As you could see, it is not as big as the Well of Light. But it is big enough."

"Could I build a necromanteion?"

"You already have one," he said. "The golf course on Mac-Duff's old property."

"But it's closed now. Like the mosque. An English family

bought it and tore down all the buildings. They use the place for hunting."

For a moment, he didn't respond. "But you have other places," he said. "Any golf course can be a necromanteion. Each can be a Well of Light."

CHAPTER FIFTEEN

THE HIGH BRICK Kremlin walls with their towers and parapets, and the striped onion domes of St. Basil's Cathedral, all brilliantly lit on this balmy September night, gave Red Square the same power and sense of place it had under Soviet rule. But the place was different now. Walking up the cobblestone incline from the former Marx Prospect, now given its old Russian name, Okhotny Riad, I looked around me for beggars, potential pickpockets, and Russian toughs looking for fights. As if to confirm my caution, two Japanese tourists were shouting after a man in a leather jacket who appeared to have stolen something from them.

The center of Moscow wasn't as secure as it had been, but was alive this night with good feeling and a sense of adventure. Several young Germans came striding past, shouting, flirting, and breaking into sprints across the square. Someone was singing an Italian aria as a large Uzbek family, evidently on a tour, gathered with broad smiles to let a Japanese group photograph them. Checking to see if the hip pocket that held my wallet was buttoned, I skirted a gathering of swarthy young men who looked to be from the Caucasus. With a conspiratorial look, one of them held up a silver flask, apparently to offer me a drink. When I waved him away, one of his companions held up a box of condoms. I had never experienced such vitality and latent disorder in Red Square. There were new freedoms here now, more diversity, and a sense of lurking violence. How many people in the crowd were carrying knives or guns?

Still, it seemed a good place to get my bearings. In its huge well-lit expanse, there was enough room to be alone while assimilating my experience in Ryzhkov's tower. Halfway between Lenin's tomb and the GUM department store, I found a relatively open space where I could enjoy the kaleidoscope of human activity and begin to sort out my thoughts.

For all these years, had I used the wrong ways to find Shivas Irons? Ryzhkov's proposal seemed to have been confirmed by the voice I'd heard in his necromanteion. "Keep coming. I'm not so far away." During my drive from Peredelkino, the words had run through my mind relentlessly, with every nuance of Shivas's burr intact. It was uncanny that his voice had come just a few minutes after Ryzhkov's suggestion. There had been other moments in the last seven years, at MacDuff's property, in Nadia's necromanteion, during moments of vivid and unexpected recollection, when some presence or power related to Shivas had come especially close. They were moments to build on. They gave me doors to pass through. If nothing else, my search had taught me that memory and imagination have well-guarded thresholds beyond which life-changing discoveries await us.

A few feet away, a tall, bearded man in brown denim slacks and a blue windbreaker stood looking in the direction of Lenin's tomb. "There must be a high wind blowing," he said with what sounded like a British inflection. "See those flags on the Kremlin wall? How do they keep them flapping?" It wasn't clear to whom he spoke, but no one else stood near us. Had he addressed the question to me? "What do you think?" he asked. "It's quiet here. Is there a wind above the Kremlin?"

He was about six foot three, had reddish brown hair, and his left eye was slightly crossed. But it was hard to tell how old he was. He might be thirty or sixty.

"I've heard they use a wind machine," I ventured. "It adds to the drama."

"They're good at spectacles," he said with admiration. "You've got to like their spirit. The Tatars, Napoleon, Hitler. No one has conquered them, unless you count that fellow in the tomb, and the other one who used to be there. They could fly kites on a windless day."

It was an odd string of thoughts, but triggered a sense of recognition. Had I met the man before? "I've seen Russians try it," I said. "For all they've been through, for all their sufferings, they harbor amazing hopes."

"You mean fly kites on a windless day?" He turned to face me. "You've actually seen that?"

"There was a contest here in one of the parks during the Brezhnev years. I was there. I saw it. Fifty or a hundred people with the damnedest contraptions you've ever seen, trying to get them in the air without any wind at all. It was hilarious."

"It's something to learn from." The man gave me a winsome buck-toothed smile. "You never know when a wind will come up. No one can predict it perfectly. Are you a frequent visitor?"

Now I was sure I'd met him. "Since 1980, but I came here first in '71. My wife organizes Soviet-American cultural exchanges. She's been here fifty times."

"Well, she must be willing to fly a kite on a windless day!"

"Haven't we met?" I asked. "You look familiar. Do you come here very often?"

"Perhaps we've met at Spasso House." He referred to the

American ambassador's sumptuous residence. "Did you know Matlock or the Hartmans?"

"The Hartmans. They were good to us. Yes, we could've met there. What do you do here?"

He turned to look at the Kremlin. "Trade," he said vaguely. "And a little finance."

Then I remembered. His name was Wilson Lancaster. I'd seen him at Spasso House in the 1980s, during a performance by Pearl Bailey staged by Arthur and Donna Hartman, the ambassador and his wife. Gennady Muhammadov, who had taken me to the Well of Light in the deserts near Samarkand, had pointed him out to me, claiming that he was Britain's chief of intelligence in Moscow. From the moment I'd seen him, I'd been struck—and was again now—by his resemblance to Shivas Irons. The same height, the same reddish hair, the same slightly crossed left eye, and now this metaphor. During our day together, Shivas had said more than once that we are kites in the winds of spirit. It was stunning that the man had appeared an hour after Ryzhkov's suggestion and the voice I'd heard in his necromanteion.

But there are different kinds of synchronicity—some false, some evanescent. I wouldn't force this one, or make any judgments about it. "Business must be tricky here," I said. "Are you having any luck?"

"It's like the Klondike, or the California gold rush." He turned to survey the square. "You've got to be lucky, careful, and quick on your feet."

"How's foreign investment going?"

"Slow, I think, for you Americans. A little better for the Germans. But surprisingly well for the Italians." He paused. "And speaking of Italians, hello!" He waved toward a group of young men who looked to be from the Caucasus, in the midst of which

stood Ziparelli! "Hello, Horace!" he shouted, then excused himself and strode away.

Keeping passersby between us, I followed at a distance. If this
was a meaningful set of coincidences, I wanted to see if it would
unfold without my interference.

Ziparelli introduced Lancaster to his leather-jacketed companions. "These are my friends from Georgia!" he exclaimed loudly
in English. "They are traders, international financiers, and pio-
neers of the Russian recycling business!" Apparently, they shipped
wastepaper and other garbage down the Volga through the Black
Sea to Sicily. There were five in the group, and at least two of
them carried pistols.

Lancaster asked about the Moscow Country Club and watched
a brief demonstration of the golf swing's basic components. Then
Ziparelli saw me. "Murphy!" he cried. "You are here! I cannot
believe it!" He had shaved and was dressed in a stylish grey suit.
"This is a great golfer!" he said. "Murphy, meet my friends!" He
introduced me to Lancaster and his companions, reciting a series
of Georgian names too rapidly for me to remember. "Wilson," he
said, "this man can hit the ball! We should have a threesome
tomorrow!"

"Ah, what a shame! I can't," said Lancaster. "I'm leaving tomorrow morning."

"But you are a free man. Stay." Ziparelli put a hand on his
shoulder. "I will call our friend Bondarenko. He is my partner
now. My partner, can you believe it? He no longer works in
secret."

Lancaster looked at me. "Bondarenko?" he asked, an eyebrow
arched. "How do you know him?"

"Horace introduced us," I said. "We only met yesterday."

He gave me his buck-toothed smile and turned to Ziparelli.
"Horace, I'm sorry," he said, with what seemed to be genuine
regret. "We'll have to wait until you're in London next."

One of the Georgians tapped my shoulder. He was about five foot six, had thick black eyebrows, and hadn't shaved for several days. "For you," he whispered, offering me a box of condoms. "It is cheap."

Every one of the Georgians smiled. "What kind are they?" I asked, not wanting to be a spoilsport.

"Russian." He winked at the others. "They stand up by themselves!"

"They are made from old tires," said one of his companions. "They are from Russian recycling and still have treads. Once you get in, you cannot get out."

This caused the whole group to laugh, except for Ziparelli. "Give me that." He grabbed for the box. "My friend does not need robbers!"

The Georgian raised a mocking finger. "Why not?" he asked in broken English. "You get part of the profits. Remember, we are partners."

With conspiratorial smiles, the other Georgians crowded close. "You like this?" One of them held up a brass belt buckle. "From Afghanistan," he said with a heavy accent. "From dead Russian. Cheap! Just one hundred dollars!" There was a sense of challenge in his offer. I backed away with a smile, reaching instinctively for my wallet and looking to Lancaster for support. But he had disappeared. "Where's your friend?" I asked Ziparelli. "Where the hell did he go?"

Lancaster had made an extraordinary exit. He was nowhere to be seen. "My friends!" Ziparelli cried, waving the buckle away. "Mr. Murphy and I have business. *Arrivederci!*"

Ignoring their jibes, we walked off briskly across the square, agreed to have a drink at a new restaurant he'd found, and hailed a taxi on the Okhotny Riad. But as we settled into the cab, I had an inspiration. If Ryzhkov's admonitions, the voice in his necromanteion, and Lancaster's appearance comprised a set of coincidences that signaled a turn in my search for Shivas Irons, more signs might be catalyzed by the right intersection of spiritual forces. I knew such a meeting place—the apartment of Djuna Davitashvilli. Promising Ziparelli that Djuna would understand his theories about the fourth dimension and give him tips about his golf from her unique perspective, I redirected our taxi.

Moscow's Arbat, which was a marketplace before the Revolution, was restored to much of its original charm in the 1980s. Surfaced with cobblestones and lined with lampposts reminiscent of its early history, it runs for several blocks between two- and three-story buildings with their pre-Revolutionary facades intact. Closed to motor vehicles, it had become a principal Moscow arena of glasnost and capitalist entrepreneurship, filled with small vendors of kitsch, wandering entertainers, and orators supporting various social and political causes. It was so crowded on this balmy night, that I had trouble recognizing the side street that led to Djuna's apartment. At about ten o'clock, we rang at her door.

We were greeted by a tough-looking middle-aged woman with henna-reddened hair and a cigarette hanging from her lips. I introduced myself as Djuna's writer friend from America and, after motioning Ziparelli to stand aside, whispered that he was very rich. The woman looked me up and down, drew deeply on her cigarette, and flicked its ashes onto the street. "How rich?" she whispered with a barely perceptible sneer, making sure he didn't hear us. And why was it important that Djuna meet him?

There were certain code words among Djuna's entourage. I said that for several decades Ziparelli had been a friend of Salvador Dalí.

"Hmm," she answered, taking another drag on her cigarette. "Dalí? Wait."

Leaving the door ajar, she disappeared up the flight of stairs to the main floor of the apartment. While we waited in the street, I told Ziparelli about Djuna's reported ministrations to Brezhnev in the early 1980s and to Yeltsin in recent months. Hearing this, he adjusted the cuffs of his black shirt, straightened his silver tie, and tugged at the collars of his stylish grey jacket. "The son of Yasser Arafat?" he asked as I listed some of the celebrities I'd seen here on previous visits. "You saw him in this place?"

"A friend did. But I met the ambassador from Iraq."

The lady sauntered down the stairs. "Djuna is busy," she said with affected casualness. "You will have to wait. Bring your friend up."

Inside, two men who appeared to be guards looked us over as we passed, and another inspected us at the top of the stairs. The woman ushered us into the apartment's main room and suggested we get drinks at Djuna's well-stocked bar. I poured Ziparelli a cognac, myself a glass of vodka straight, and we stood watching three men and two women gathered around the television set. They were Hungarians, I guessed, and were absorbed in a soccer game. None of them turned to see us.

"That's how people pay her." I nodded toward a wall that was covered with icons. "A few of them were made in the fifteenth century."

Ziparelli gave a low whistle. "It is good she has guards," he whispered. "That is a dangerous collection to have. It is priceless." One of the women, about forty years old and dressed in a white sheath that showed off her broad-shouldered, full-breasted figure, appraised us coolly, then turned back to the soccer game. "Zsa Zsa Gabor," said Ziparelli, rolling his eyes in mock admiration.

Then I heard a commotion, and Djuna's commanding low voice. Accompanied by one of the guards from downstairs, she stood motionless as everyone turned to greet her. A white blouse accentuated her dark complexion, tight black pants dramatized her well-formed rear end, and golden, high-heeled sandals gave her a height to match every man in the room. Her black hair was drawn back, and her dark, slightly upturned eyes shone brightly. After glancing at Ziparelli and me, she greeted the others. Every one of them seemed flattered—especially the woman in the white sheath, who seemed barely able to contain herself. But Djuna didn't turn toward us. Was she irritated by my coming without invitation, or simply intent to show us that she wasn't excited at all by Ziparelli's wealth and friendship with Salvador Dalí? With a shrug, Ziparelli led me back to the bar, and both of us refilled our glasses.

Five minutes later, she finally approached us, summoning the woman with tinted red hair. "She is glad to see you," said the woman, who would be our interpreter. "But she wants to apologize. She is too tired tonight to speak English."

I introduced Ziparelli, who took Djuna's hand with a flourish and kissed it. "And you are a painter?" asked the interpreter. "A cousin of Salvador Dalí?"

"Yes, I paint!" he said without hesitation. "I paint with my inner eye, and with my heart, especially after I meet someone so beautiful."

Djuna gave Ziparelli a seductive look. "And that is your work?" asked the interpreter.

"My *inner* work," said Ziparelli, eliciting a smile of appreciation from Djuna.

"And what is your outer work?" the interpreter asked.

"Golf!" he said, with not the least sign of discomposure. "It pays me no money, but is my art, my science, my religion."

Djuna took this to be a wonderful joke and seemed to be instantly charmed. But Ziparelli wasn't finished. "Djuna," he said exuberantly, "you are an adept of the inner life. I want to bring you to my summer home in Capri, and introduce you to the sages and mystics of Rome. I have wanted to do this from the moment I heard about you many years ago. May we talk privately about it? Michael Murphy will not mind."

As the interpreter relayed these remarks to Djuna, Ziparelli glanced my way. Startled, I shrugged and asked if he wanted me to leave the room.

"No!" he said. "Djuna and I will leave."

And indeed they would. With a smile of apology for me, Djuna led him and the interpreter into an adjoining room. Through its half-open door I could watch them.

At first they conversed in whispers, all three of them huddled close. Then Djuna gave him a chaste embrace, made several passes down his back, and watched with apparent fascination as he showed her his six-piece golf swing. This lasted for several minutes, and I sensed from the interpreter's growing frustration that he was describing the swing's basic components. Wondering what Djuna would make of "power-package delivery path" and "lag loading," I poured another vodka and sat where I could watch them. Again all three were huddled close. When they finally emerged from the room, the woman with the hennaed hair looked exhausted, but Djuna and Ziparelli had the rosy glow of a couple who'd made wonderful love.

"She is coming to Capri," he confided as she joined her other visitors. "She understands the game like an angel, and gave me some unbelievable tips. Unbelievable! Murphy, thank you! Have you heard her talk about physical movement and the aura? She works with Olympic wrestlers and gymnasts, and with horses!"

"Has she ever been on a golf course?"

"At the Moscow Club." He leaned close. "With the head of the new KGB."

"Do you believe her?"

"Did you meet the ambassador from Iraq? She says she will introduce me." He paused. "But without Georgi. The guy has his own protection. One of his bodyguards brings a machine gun and another a rocket launcher!"

"Just like Clinton," I said. "When he plays, the course is protected with ground-to-air missiles in case of airborne terrorist attack. A friend who played with him told me."

Djuna went to another room with the woman in the white sheath, and our interpreter said that she wouldn't rejoin us. Taking this as a hint that we should leave, I led Ziparelli outside. "I will go," he said. "Will you share a taxi?"

Thanking him, I said that I wanted to walk in the Arbat. But I couldn't resist asking whether he would follow through on his invitation to Djuna.

"I have to." He popped his cuffs with style. "She said she likes my bio-plasma, and wants to increase it greatly with a special massage. I think we will have a good time in Rome and on the beaches of Capri. Thank you, my friend, for the favor."

He walked away with his long, fluid stride, and I turned onto the Arbat. More people were begging than an hour before, and many more were drunk. The place looked run-down and tawdry. Passing little tables with Gorbachev, Yeltsin, and Brezhnev dolls, and babushkas selling wilted flowers, and tired artists waiting for someone to sketch, I felt far away from the power of Red Square or the well-dressed people at Djuna's or the quiet refinement of Ryzhkov's retreat. Russia's sad, dark side was vividly present now, making my search for synchronicities seem a frivolous exercise. Suddenly dejected, I headed toward Smolenskaya Square, where I could hail a taxi.

Then I stopped. On the far side of the Arbat, about forty feet away, Wilson Lancaster was walking in the same direction. He moved slowly, surveying the street as if he were looking for someone.

There is a state of mind, which is hard to convey to someone who hasn't experienced it, in which events are suddenly charged with supernatural significance. In one of his most provocative essays, Freud described the condition: "One is curious to know what this peculiar quality is which allows us to distinguish as 'uncanny' certain things within the boundaries of what is 'fearful.' . . . [it] is that class of the terrifying which leads back to something long known to us, once very familiar."*

These words capture what I felt seeing Lancaster. My skin was a gauge of this. It crawled because his appearance seemed exceedingly strange but at the same time deeply familiar. I'd expected more signs that Shivas Irons—whoever, whatever, or wherever he might be—is real in a way I knew secretly. That Lancaster might be an undercover intelligence agent lent irony to this recognition, and suggested the whimsical, even hilarious creativity involved in our rediscovery of things long known to us.

Beyond the Arbat stood the tall towers of the Foreign Ministry, built in the 1930s by Stalin as a symbol of Soviet might. My skin crawled again as I saw it, at another unexpected recognition. Something in me knew that Lancaster was headed there, knew it with a certainty as strong as my sense that his appearance was connected to the other strange turns of this night. But I would have to watch him closely. He had disappeared in Red Square like a ghost, and might use his spycraft again to shake off potential observers.

He paused to look at a shop window, and I approached to within thirty feet. As if lost in reverie, he looked through the glass for a minute or two, then casually entered the store. Keeping its

* Sigmund Freud, "The 'Uncanny.' " Volume 17, in *Complete Psychological Works: Standard Edition* (New York: W. W. Norton, 1976).

entrance in sight, I found a place where he couldn't see me. But he didn't come out. After several minutes had passed, I guessed that he'd left through another door.

Alternately walking and jogging, I left the Arbat and turned left toward the Foreign Ministry. The thirty-story tower loomed above me, a huge and forbidding but dingy presence with too many entrances to check. It would be impossible to find him now. Evidently he'd spotted me in reflections of the street he'd seen in the shop window. A taxi pulled up in front of the ministry to let off a passenger. Before it could pull away, I got its driver's attention and directed him to the Savoy Hotel, where I had a room.

Lancaster's double appearance and striking elusiveness would be noteworthy on any occasion, but partook of the uncanny now. He seemed a figure from an edge of the world, like the voice in Ryzhkov's necromanteion, like the possible sightings of Shivas Irons, reflecting something real but just out of sight. As the cab hurtled through crowded streets, I let the recognition deepen. The messages of this night cohered. They were pointing me toward a new kind of intelligence gathering, a new turn of my search. Following their lead, I would go back to MacDuff's old property. As Ryzhkov had suggested, it could be my Well of Light, and a place from which to approach Shivas Irons more directly.

CHAPTER SIXTEEN

IN RECENT MONTHS, Hannigan had been increasingly dismayed and frustrated by Nadia's chastity. When it started half a year before, he had taken it to be a temporary condition prompted by a surplus of contemplative ardor. She had a peculiar estrous cycle, he'd complained, that included a month of sexual renunciation every April or May. "It has nothing to do with you, Bach," she reassured him constantly. "You are more beautiful than ever, my best friend, the greatest lover in Scotland! But something is calling me from the dark. Something I never knew. Be patient, Bach. Still laahve me."

At first—at least in his letters and faxes to me—he'd accepted, even enjoyed, this exhibition of her mysterious "Russian soul." But as her abstinence continued for two, then three, then six months, he had gradually lost his tolerance. His affection for her unpredictable ways, and his covert admiration for her contemplative gifts, were strained more and more by his deprivation and jealousy. This had been evident in our recent phone conversations. Her estrous had reversed, he said. She was hot for spirits instead of men. In her necromanteion, she'd mated with an incubus.

So it was a surprise when he greeted me at his studio by announcing, with no sign of ambivalence at all, his excitment at the results of her six-month sequestration. In the last week, something had happened that would interest me greatly. But first, he said, I would have to read this passage from Mortimer Crail's book:

As science has discriminated universal qualities of material objects such as mass and density, it has advanced our knowledge of the physical world. In analogous fashion, we can identify the fundamental attributes of spirit-bodies by turning to different accounts of them given by mystics, seers, and shamans. By way of example, the Islamic teacher Ahmad Ahsa'i has proposed a "physiology of the Resurrection Body," or "spiritual flesh," which after the death of our physical body resides in the "Earth of Hurqalya," a world with objective existence beyond the directions and dimensions of ordinary space, from which it will rise to join its eternal individual soul.

Among the qualities and features of "spiritual flesh" explicitly noted or indirectly referred to in the Shaikh's sometimes obscure writings, there are volume, boundaries, surface, texture, density, radiance, heat, impassability, telekinetic power, auditory projectability, vitality, refractoriness, resilience, mutability, "curvature," and what for lack of better terms I will call "interdimensionality" or "psychic mobility," the capacity to move from one realm of existence to another with great agility. These are referred to, either briefly or at length, with a wide variety of words drawn from Greek, Persian, and Arabic writers, and are described with reference to a vast lore of ecstatic mysticism.

"This is curious," I said. "Ryzhkov gave me a book with references to this Shaikh, Ahmad Ahsa'i. But what's this got to do with Nadia?"

Hannigan gestured to a chair by his desk. "Sit down," he said.

"I want to hear about Ryzhkov, but first ye've got to listen. Our adventure has taken a turn, and that passage ties into it." He sat across from me, switched on his desk lamp to counter the gloom of this autumn morning, then paused as if searching for a way to start. "Something's happened to Nadia," he said. "Ye'll see when she gets here. But I don't want ye to be alarmed. She doesn't look good, but she's fine."

"What's happened!"

"It's all right." He held up a hand to reassure me. "She's lost some weight. She's gotten quieter. She doesn't want to wear makeup. But she's not sick. Ye might think so, but *she isn't,* I promise ye. She's seen a doctor, a good one at the university here, and he examined her from head to toe. There's no disease, no organic disorder."

Holding back my alarm, I watched him fiddle with a pencil. "Murphy," he said, "I used to think MacDuff's inscription on that photograph, 'August 6 again, but 1950' was simply his way to say they'd found a better way to release the energy contained in matter, but now I think he meant more than that. He was also sayin' these transformations can be dangerous. Nadia might've been close to death last Wednesday night." He paused to study my face. "What were ye doin' then, say about nine o'clock Russian time?"

"Last Wednesday? I was with Ryzhkov. He showed me his necromanteion."

"Was there anything unusual?"

"I heard a voice."

"A voice?"

"And saw a face that looked like Shivas Irons."

"Well, for Christ's sake! What did the voice say?"

"To keep looking for him, that he's not far away."

"That's all?" He leaned forward, his eyes narrowing behind his steel-rimmed glasses. "That's all it said?"

"There's more, but I'm still trying to sort it out. It was pitch-black. It didn't last long. I was disoriented. And Ryzhkov had incense burning that might've been hallucinogenic. But what's all this about? What are you driving at?"

He eyed me suspiciously, as if sensing I'd held something back. "Because Nadia's been changing since she went on this six-month chastity kick, and she went through the biggest changes of all last Wednesday night. She knew you were there at Ryzhkov's, and she thinks that there's a connection."

"Jesus!" I said. "What's going on. What kind of changes? Is she sick? Does she have stigmata?"

"You figure it out," he said coolly. "Different people see different things. Tell me when she gets here."

"And when will that be?"

He glanced at his watch. "In a few minutes. Do ye want a cup of coffee?"

Suddenly I felt a sharp anxiety. What had happened to her? Would I be shocked by her appearance? We drank our coffee in silence. Crail's book lay open in front of me, and this passage was underlined:

"Surface" as a quality of spirit-bodies is infrequently noted by religious authorities and would not occur to most of us as a descriptive term for our various supraphysical forms. But it seems important to the Shaikh Ahmad Ahsa'i and to Swedenborg, both of whom refer to the garments, skin, and other coverings of spiritual entities, which depend upon their metaetherial location and level of development.

"She's here." Hannigan stood. "I hear her car."

He left the studio and opened the apartment's squeaky front door. There was a muffled exchange punctuated by brief silences, then he ushered her into the room.

Her skin was paler than before, and was made even paler by the grey sweater and slacks she wore, but her almond-shaped blue eyes had an extraordinary light. "Hello, Mackel," she said, almost shyly, reaching to take my hand. "I want to hear about Boris and Peredelkino."

As Hannigan got her tea, she sat erect at one end of the couch, hands clasped around her knees. She'd lost ten or fifteen pounds, and was more subdued than I'd ever seen her. "Sit down." She nodded to a chair. "Don't stand in the dark like that."

I sat on the chair a few feet from her. Her quiet manner had begun to dispel my discomfort. "You look wonderful, Mackel," she said. "We have a lot to talk about. But first! I must hear about Boris. Did you have a good visit with him?"

"Yes, but not for long. We talked for half an hour, maybe, then spent a few minutes in his tower."

Hannigan brought her a mug of tea, and sat as I did on a chair some five or six feet from her. As she thanked him, I was struck by the look of her skin, which seemed to shift in texture and density each time her expression changed. Was this the feature that Hannigan had warned me about? "So, Mackel," she said. "What happened in Boris's necromanteion?"

Vaguely unsettled, I briefly described the voice of Shivas Irons. When I was finished, she held her mug to her heart, both hands cupped around it, and studied my face with serene curiosity. The only sounds came from a passing car and the radiator's gentle hissing. Hannigan stood, and carried his mug of tea to the sink.

For a minute, or longer perhaps—it was hard to tell afterward—she gazed into my eyes. "Mackel," she said at last, "I thought I was with you in Peredelkino. Being with you now, I am sure of it. But last Wednesday night I experienced more than that." She gave me an affectionate smile. "For seven years, you and Bach and I have been a little circle. I have to tell you what has happened."

She paused. "Mackel, we die again and again. How did Rumi say it? 'After each death, there is another, and we knock again at the old scarred door.' Six months ago, a big shadow came and covered the sun. There was no light for me. You know something about this, how I quit my job and was a nun." Bowing her head, she gave Hannigan a searching affectionate look. "So you know I lived like that since April. Is it too strange? Was it selfish? But Mackel, little by little, the shadow has moved away from the sun, and a new light came, and the old scarred door has opened—into a world. . . ." She paused again. "Ah, Mackel, how to tell you. Into a world so beautiful. So great. So near us. It is impossible to say it, but I must tell you some of its signs."

She put down her mug and took both of my hands into hers. "There are some things I cannot tell, Mackel. I tried with Bach, but a big hand came to my throat and almost killed me. Maybe I am superstitious, but there seem to be taboos about describing the life to come, things we cannot tell even our best friends and lovers. But there are also things we can tell, and things we *must*."

She let go of my hands, but still leaned close. "Last Wednesday in the necromanteion, I went into a place—or, better to say, a place came into me, where there is joy in every atom, and love in every touch, and forgiveness, Mackel, forgiveness in everything we do. That place opens—how to say it?—with each glance, each touch, each meeting of souls." She stopped to gather herself. "Now, this is hard to say, and maybe you will not believe it. On Wednesday, that place and this place joined." She pointed to her heart, then gestured to indicate her entire body. "It can join for everyone. It can happen on Earth. That is what I have to tell you."

She joined her hands as if in prayer. "And then in the mirror I saw it. More clearly than I see you now. Not an apparition, not a ghost. It was more beautiful and terrible than that. More alive.

More present than anything in Boris's tower or the Well of Light. It could destroy me. It could save my life. But Mackel, it was strangely familiar! It was showing what we can be, but also that it has been waiting a long, long time." She leaned toward me. "It has been waiting a very long time, *though it is reborn every instant.* This is a paradox. It is also a fact."

She took my hands again. "Now Mackel, you can believe this or not. After I looked into the glass and saw the thing I just described, there was another shock. My body—the one you see— was different. Bach can tell you."

Hannigan stood at the end of the couch, watching us both intently. "Murphy," he said. "There's no denyin' it. Something happened to her."

"But Bach and I saw different things," she whispered. "When I looked at myself in the mirror, and then moved a hand or changed my position or had a new expression, my skin changed."

"I saw it," said Hannigan.

"Like I'd eaten some mushrooms!" She smiled with a kind of innocent wickedness. "And everything I touched sent thrills everywhere. Everywhere! All through my body, down to my toes! Everything was alive. This, and that, and that, and that." She pointed to objects in the room. "They are alive for me now. This world, Mackel, is not very far from the place I lived on Wednesday night. This couch, it touches me back. Bach's voice, your eyes . . ." She sighed. "But it couldn't last. I would've died. On Thursday morning, when Bach saw me, I was changing back to normal."

"But not all the way back," said Hannigan. "I can still see a part of it now." He looked at her with an expression of wonder I'd never seen in his face before. There was no trace of his practiced dismissiveness, no hint of that little sneer. "Murphy, on Thursday I didn't know who she was. Nadia, or not Nadia . . ."

The telephone rang, but he didn't move. After five or six rings, he answered it reluctantly, and Nadia turned to face me.

In part perhaps because her revelations had been disorienting, but also because this intimacy was so charged, I have trouble remembering what happened next. She was stationed below me on the couch, bending forward with a graceful deference characteristic of many Russian women as they facilitate difficult exchanges. But her attitude arose from more than cultural conditioning. It came as well from the essential nature of her experience. The beauty and power and joy she'd known, her posture was telling me, is for all of us. No matter how threatening it seems to our fearful perception, it is gentle and gracious and ever-present.

She took my hands. "So cold!" she whispered, rubbing them gently for warmth. "Do you want a cup of coffee?"

Uncertain what had happened, I looked around the studio. Nadia had gone to the stove. Hannigan continued to talk on the phone. But everything had shifted. A moment before, his sweater's checkerboard pattern had been dominated by reds and browns, but now its golden squares stood out, and on the wall beyond him, the indigos and greens of an abstract painting had receded into a maze of vermilions I'd never noticed. Nadia brought me a cup of coffee, and sat again on the couch. Her eyes appeared to have turned to deeper shades of blue, and her skin seemed darker. Had our silent exchange altered my figure-ground perception? Or had she experienced another subtle transformation?

Hannigan left the room, and I tried to compose myself. Nadia drank tea from a mug. I sipped a cup of coffee. But I found myself attempting in various ways to normalize what was happening. The lambent light of her skin, for example, reminded me of

Ben Jipcho, the Kenyan middle-distance runner. I remembered him vividly now, two nights before a meet, downing two double gin and tonics. There was a quiet but wild light in his eyes, and blue in the ebony of his skin that constantly shifted in hue and intensity. Mike Spino, the pioneering track coach, had talked about him later that night. Jipcho's skin, he'd said, and smell, were signs of world-class physical conditioning. But they showed more than that. There was something unfamiliar, something supernormal about them. Jipcho was in better shape than anyone else on the planet! Two days later, some of us declared Spino a prophet when Jipcho posted world-class times in three events, at 880 yards, a mile, and two miles, during a one and a half hour span of the meet.* No one had done such a thing before. Jipcho was in supernormal territory, and Spino had sensed it in his eyes and skin.

Sensing my need to integrate the intensity I felt with familiar things, Nadia recalled the wonders of her own athletic conditioning. How could she forget the power and beauty and lift, or the fire she'd felt on the winter ice? Her training was cruel, but filled with graces. It was the cost, after all—and the gift!—of trying to make the Soviet team. But last Wednesday night, she had gone beyond the rewards of Olympic training. The grace-ladened capacities that world-class athletes realize at the peak of their physical conditioning are merely transitional to what she had experienced.

But the integration of unfamiliar experience can trigger the questioning mind. Coming back from the phone, Hannigan was quick to see this. "Ye're not buying it all," he said over my

---

* Jipcho finished his performance with a 54-second final lap to win the two-mile race in a time of 8:43.

protestations. "But ye weren't with her last week. And ye haven't seen this!" From his desk he took a black-and-white photograph. "Take a good look," he said. "Then tell me what ye see."

Startled, I took the picture. "She's striking," I said. "Maybe African . . . maybe Fulani. Good God! Is it the mother of Seamus MacDuff?"

"The mother of Seamus MacDuff!" He laughed. "Murphy, ye should be a writer. What an imagination! Now tell me why ye think she's African."

The picture showed just the woman's face, looking straight into the camera. Her high cheekbones, slightly upturned eyes, and generous curving lips hinted of aristocratic breeding. "She looks Fulani to me," I said with a shrug, "with maybe a little Tuareg and Arab blood."

"No," said Hannigan. "It's Nadia last Thursday morning."

Shocked, I compared the photograph with the Nadia in front of me. "There is a resemblance. But . . . Nadia, is this really you?"

"Bach says so," she said with a little shrug. "He took the picture."

"Did you look like this in the mirror?"

"No. I didn't look like that. But everything was so, how to say it? So changing. So unstable. So different every minute."

"Buck," I said. "Could you have gotten your film mixed up?"

"Oh, God!" he groaned. "It's not a mistake. And there's more." He held up another photograph. "Will ye tell me what ye see in this one."

It showed her necromanteion—there could be no doubt about that—in the middle of which a luminous oval stretched from floor to ceiling. "Shit!" I exclaimed, fighting the recognition. "It's like the picture of MacDuff's first fairway, and the thing I saw near Irons on the eighteenth green. When did you take it?"

"Maybe a minute, maybe two, after the other one. Call it

thoughtography, spirit photography, or whatever you want, but there it is." No one spoke. Hannigan and I had often talked about the long history of photographic anomalies,* and here were two highly disturbing examples.

I handed him the photographs. "Nadia," he said with hesitation, "you should finish telling him why you thought what happened last Wednesday night had something to do with his being at Ryzhkov's."

Clasping her hands on her lap, she closed her eyes to gather herself, then looked at me with a trace of the wickedness she'd exhibited so many times before. "Mackel, come here," she said. "I need to see you when I talk."

I sat on the chair by the couch. "There was a moment," she said, "after my vision in the necromanteion. For a few seconds, or a minute, or maybe ten minutes—it is hard to tell because everything was happening in another way—I saw a tall red-haired man with complicated blue eyes and a face that has enjoyed and suffered very much, sitting on the step of a little cottage looking down a slope to the sea. It was in the west of Ireland, I think, or maybe one of Scotland's Western Isles." Her voice softened almost to a whisper. "He didn't see me, but said my name out loud! Then sang me a song, a wild, mystical Irish ballad, as he watched the sun go down into the rolling grey sea. Oh, Mackel!" She lifted both hands to her mouth as if the thing she'd seen was suddenly present. "It was so beautiful! He wasn't made of flesh like this." She pointed to her cheek. "He was like the thing I'd seen just a moment before, made of spirit-fire, but human like the rest of us, sitting there on his little step watching the sun go down."

She looked at Hannigan, who stood by the couch like a senti-

---

* For a brief history of photographic anomalies attributed to paranormal influences, see: Jule Eisenbud, *Parapsychology and the Unconscious* (Berkeley: North Atlantic Books, 1983), pp. 111–29; and Michael Murphy, *The Future of the Body* (New York: Tarcher-Putnam, 1992), Appendix A.8.

nel. "When did I tell you about it?" she asked. "Was it on Thursday morning or afternoon?"

"Thursday morning. That's when you said it had something to do with Ryzhkov's tower."

"Mackel, what I just told you happened on Wednesday night, but I didn't remember until Thursday that in the little time I saw him, more happened than what I just told you. As the sun set, he went for a swim in the sea—in waves that were huge, tremendous, like giants! He swam with them and through them and under them, and came up laughing again and again, and dove from a big black rock. Then stood in seawater near the beach to watch the sunset. Mackel! It was like a different planet, with golds and pinks and violets, and colors I'd never seen. He stood there naked, and so beautiful!—enjoying it all with those unforgettable blue eyes, and then . . ." She snapped her fingers. "Then just like that, he sat in a pub with three or four friends, reciting a poem by Robert Burns—yes, Robert Burns! I could hear it, about every one of them getting away from the Devil! He said it with such a smile that two of them started to dance. There was a band. It was Irish, I think. And that was when I thought of you. He called my name again and told the others I would join them. And when he did it, he smiled. An unforgettable smile! I was certain you would be there too."

"At that very moment?"

"Right then. When he smiled and called my name."

"That was Wednesday night." I looked at Hannigan. "About the time I was hearing the voice and seeing the face of Shivas Irons. But God! Wait! For an instant—just a split second—I thought he wanted me to go for a swim!"

"Did you dream?" Hannigan asked. "Or did you and Nadia see him clairvoyantly, in Ireland or the Western Isles? Or did you both glimpse another world?" He went to his desk and held up Crail's book. "In this passage, Crail quotes an obscure Iranian

Shaikh, this Ahmad Ahsa'i, and his 'physiology of the Resurrection Body,' which has to do with life in the 'Earth of Hurqalya.' Isn't it curious that on Wednesday night Ryzhkov gave you a book with references to this? Just before you heard that voice. Just as Nadia was having that experience. How many people know about Ahmad Ahsa'i or the Earth of Hurqalya? Is that where Irons is living?"

Nadia sat on the edge of the couch, looking to shadows near the ceiling. In a voice so low I could barely hear it, she said, "In the mosque near Samarkand, it is thought that the Well of Light is a door to Hurqalya. When you go through it once, you can again, and again until you live there. That teaching led me to Wednesday night. They say that Hurqalya is coming. It is the future of our Earth. Mackel, your voice said, 'The Kingdom is coming.'"

The studio was dimly lit on this overcast day in October, and in its growing shadows her face gave the impression it might dissolve. "Mackel," she said, "you went to the mosque. You sat in the Well of Light. Did you know that its lineage goes back through Ali Shirazi to Ahmad Ahsa'i? By giving you that book, Boris was showing you a way to his teaching."

"And maybe to Shivas Irons," Hannigan said with a weariness that surprised me. "Ryzhkov said that to find Shivas Irons, you might need more than detective work. But it's not an easy path he proposed. Murphy, the question for you and me is, 'Will we take it?'"

More than two years have passed, but I can still feel the silence that followed his remark, and the pain of my recognition. Ryzhkov had given voice to what I had suspected. To find Shivas Irons, I might have to do more than collect evidence of his activities. I would have to live like him, with a practice as wholehearted and all-embracing as his and Nadia's. Otherwise I might circle indefinitely around the evanescent clues he was leaving.

Observing Nadia as the day unfolded, I felt this recognition grow. My attraction to her aliveness and joy, and my envy for her discipline, were signs of its validity.

For an outing that afternoon, we drove to Gullane, which is located on the Firth of Forth about an hour's drive east of Edinburgh. But we didn't have an easy walk after Hannigan decided we should climb to the summit of Gullane Hill by way of the second hole on the Number One Golf Course. If you've been there, you know what we faced. The fairway slants steeply upward through a saddle of the hill into which the prevailing wind is funneled at you. When we started the climb around two o'clock, the gale that was clearing the sky above us threatened to blow us all the way back to the parking lot.

"Nadia!" I shouted, suddenly concerned about her delicate state. "Let's go back. This isn't worth it!" But she only quickened her pace. "Buck!" I yelled. "All she's got is that windbreaker!"

By now he was ten feet ahead, and she was right on his shoulder. Neither of them responded to my shouts. Alarmed, I ran to catch them, but they had moved even further ahead of me. In Hannigan's studio, observing her translucent skin and listening to her sometimes-faltering voice, I couldn't have pictured the athlete ahead of me, walking faster than I could run.

At the clubhouse an hour later, people would tell us that the wind coming through the hill's funnel had reached eighty miles an hour at two o'clock. But neither of them slowed their stride, and gradually pulled away from me. When we reached the third tee, I sat down. The wind wasn't as strong as it had been, but was gusting to about fifty miles an hour.

"Mackel!" Nadia cried, the collar of her jacket flapping wildly. "Look up!"

Almost directly above us, framed against a bright blue sky

partly covered with racing clouds, an enormous flock of Siberian geese hovered in the wind. Beating their wings gracefully to stay there, they moved neither forward nor back. This lasted for thirty seconds, perhaps, and then, in nearly perfect unison, they tilted left so that most of them caught a ray of the sun. All at once, the flock turned from black to gold.

We stood transfixed. "Feel them!" Nadia shouted. "Can you feel them?"

Like a sheet of gold lamé, they shimmered against the clearing sky, then tilted right again turning to various shades of grey, and moved north like a giant armada.

"They're alive!" she cried. "Alive! And part of one another. What a victory!" The fierce exaltation in her voice brought me to my feet. Leaning against the wind, we followed their flight across the sea. Far below us, white-capped waters stretched for miles to grey hills in the Kingdom of Fife.

But we had farther to go. With the wind coming hard from our left, we marched across unmown rough to the summit of Gullane Hill. Another breathtaking sight awaited us. In nearly every direction, there were fairways and flagsticks of the three Gullane courses, and to the east we could see the green arabesques of Muirfield.

Hannigan turned me around. "That's Edinburgh." He pointed west to the sharply etched horizon. "Ye can see the castle now, and land in fourteen counties!" In the newly cleansed air, we could see the tall buildings of Edinburgh, the rolling fields of East Lothian, and across the Firth to the Kingdom of Fife. Watching the land and sea grow more distinct as the clouds' shadows were lifted from them, I became more acutely aware of Nadia. She stood motionless, not saying a word, in a state of exaltation.

Hannigan pointed across the Firth. "Look at the sunlight there!" he shouted.

Fifteen miles away, beyond the slate grey water, white houses and barns were appearing like tiny points of light. On the rolling fields below us and the distant hills of Fife, everywhere shadows were lifting.

Nadia stood silently, her head tilted back, the wind ripping at her white windbreaker. An hour before, I wouldn't have anticipated the strength that flowed from her, the high color in her skin, or the ferocity of her enjoyment. Her Olympic training showed. The fragile appearance produced by her six-month retreat was no longer evident.

My mind made a sudden leap. The thing she'd seen on Wednesday night was pressing closer to her. Could I glimpse it, feel its energy, or hear an echo of its music? As if sensing my thought, she gave me a sideward glance and smile, and a sudden thrill passed through me. Then she turned again toward the wind, and for an instant her entire body was enveloped by an imperceptible fire that stretched toward me and Hannigan.

"Bach!" she cried, brushing her windblown hair from her face. "I race you to the car!"

And down the hill she went, bounding with athletic and purposeful strides that kept her twenty yards ahead of Hannigan and eventually a hundred ahead of me. When I got to the parking lot ten minutes later, she was breathing normally but her face was aglow and her hair was hopelessly tangled. As soon as I saw her, something in me knew that she and Hannigan would end her self-imposed chastity before the night was done.

S ome of the world's older psychologies hold that certain emotions carry the wisdom of guiding spirits. Alone at my hotel that night, this principle seemed self-evident. Three feelings especially gripped me, each of them taking ascendancy as I reviewed the events of the past eight days. Before supper, still alive with the winds of Gullane Hill and the immediate afterglow of Nadia's presence, I felt an excitement that approached exaltation. In this mood, there were premonitions of the condition I'd glimpsed at Burningbush in 1956, at MacDuff's abandoned golf course in 1987, and with Nadia for much of this day. Yes, a new life could enter our world, and its basis was already here inside us.

But in that exaltation there were seeds of two other strong emotions. The more I thought about Nadia, the more I envied her discipline; and during supper, that feeling gave way to depression. Each of these moods was telling me something. Each was the messenger of a truth. There *was* a new life pressing close, but it required the one-pointed practice I envied, and its absence was reflected by this dark mood. Wine at supper deepened the pain I felt, and a beer at a pub afterward only made it worse. Shivas Irons had been born with a genius for transformation, and Nadia, too, had gifts I did not possess. If they represented a ladder to the greater life we harbor, I stood on its lower rungs. With such thoughts, my depression deepened.

But then there was a subtle shift, a turn that began with rising anger and a new resolution. Anyone could practice the life represented by Shivas Irons. Wasn't that what every great teacher said? Wasn't it what he'd told me?

A series of painted panels on the wood canopy over the bar dramatized a well-known Scottish legend about a hero's progress—perhaps it was Rob Roy's—through valleys and thickets and torture chambers of an English lord. Each frame showed one of the hero's tests. Each represented a new beginning. Scanning the episodes one by one, I thought of the voice in Ryzhkov's tower. *Imagine. Practice. Start again. I'm not so far away.*

Start again! I could hear his resonant voice, and feel the power it contained. The words held more than a suggestion, more than a simple command. There was knowledge of victory in them, a fire and irresistible force. It was my voice, reaffirming a vow I'd made before meeting Shivas Irons.

All at once my mood reversed, and I saw my search of these last seven years from a new perspective. Though I'd only circled around Shivas Irons while collecting evidence of his life, I'd come closer to him. There was more basis for practice now, more leads to the place that was calling to us, more ways to start again.

In the last panel above the bar, the hero reaches home with fellow warriors, friends, and a mysterious light. This sparked another recognition. The light resembled the one in MacDuff's strange photograph and the apparition I'd seen at Burningbush in 1956. Suddenly the vow that found voice in Ryzhkov's tower took a more definite shape. I would alter my search, and begin practice anew, with a specific act. At first light I would drive to MacDuff's old property, and make a vigil for Shivas Irons.

CHAPTER SEVENTEEN

Iɴ 1989, ʜᴀᴠɪɴɢ learned that the Ramsays were about to sell their abandoned distillery, I tried to see it before it was razed. But the property's main road had been gated, and a young Scotsman stopped me when I tried to hike in. "Nae visitors at a'. 'Tis fer huntin' noo, 'n shootin' clay pigeons," he said with a Scots burr so thick that I could barely understand him. Later, when I tried a back road, he threatened me with a rifle; and that night, when I tried again, he fired in my direction. In Edinburgh the following day, Hannigan had advised against further attempts to see the place. The caretaker had shot at several trespassers, and several years before had been convicted of involuntary manslaughter. Parking near the property now, I wondered if it was still guarded so fiercely.

The sky was darkly overcast on this early October afternoon, and to the north Ben Cruachan was a lonely presence half-covered with menacing clouds. The landscape I'd seen in the summer of 1987, that shimmering array of greens and golds, had changed to a cold and forbidding vista, a countryside to test human will and resilience. I climbed a hill from which I could see the whole property. All of its buildings were gone, some of its trees had been cut, and the first two holes of the abandoned course had been bull-dozed to the level of the fields around them. Though Hannigan had described these changes, they produced an immediate shock. More than buildings and trees were cut down. The air itself seemed scarred. The soul of the place was wounded.

In Portinnisherrich, a local had told me that it was unlikely on this dreary day that anyone would be hiking or hunting in the hills above the loch. Keeping watch nevertheless for men with rifles, I entered the property. After inspecting the trapshooting field that replaced the first and second greens, I climbed to the site of MacDuff's old house. Only stones from its hearth remained. Its cellars were filled with dirt. The hilltop was covered with bushes, weeds, and wild grass.

This was a bleak necromanteion. Nadia's chamber, Ryzhkov's tower, and the Well of Light gave protection, stillness, and a sense of focus for contacts with the beyond; but these grey horizons and wounded land scattered the mind and sapped the heart. On this barren hill there was no hint of the presence I'd felt in 1987. But I heard his words again, as I had for most of my trip from Edinburgh. *Imagine. Practice. Start again. I'm not so far away.*

Then I remembered a line he'd quoted from a Spanish mystic. Prayer when the skies of your heart are overcast, prayer in the dark night of the soul, is greater in the eyes of God than prayer with immediate graces. It is the strongest practice, and ultimately the shortest path. Through it the soul comes to itself, and knows God with a deeper embrace than it does all bathed in sunshine. I found a sheltered place to sit near the remnants of MacDuff's old hearth. This dreary property mirrored and challenged my separa-tion from Shivas Irons. It was a perfect necromanteion. I would spend the rest of the day here.

At four o'clock it was nearly dark, and a bitter wind was blowing. But the resolution which had built for the last three hours formed a wall against the cold. My only focus now was the voice I'd heard in Ryzhkov's tower. "Keep coming. The whole world's here inside us." His encouragement—and my vow—were older and stronger than the things that would suppress them. I would stay on this cold and barren hill until I couldn't see the fields below.

At five it was completely dark. There'd been no sudden visitation, no lights like the ones I'd seen in 1987, but the fire inside me had grown stronger. Though my fingers were numb and my legs were stiff, there was pleasure in holding this steady focus. After walking around the edge of the hill to restore my circulation, I resolved to wait an hour more.

At six the wind was blowing fiercely, with an eerie howl. Was its sound caused by trees turned to harps, or a mixture of air and invisible spirits? My resolution grew against the night. It was a self-sustaining presence. By subtle degrees, it was giving birth to a self-recognition, a stability and constantly rising pleasure that didn't need signs from beyond or any other external support.

At seven, I seemed to be stationed in a place barely subject to the laws of gravity. This was a new condition for me, and it gave sense to premonitions I'd had for much of my life. How had Shivas Irons put it? That there is a second stability, beyond one's usual concentration, with no need for compass sightings, no sense of ups or downs. In it, ordinary gravity becomes "true gravity."

It's our truest center, he'd said, because it's everywhere. There's more elasticity in it, more room to move. Don't you remember, Michael? We can't be limited then to particular feelings or thoughts, or any state of mind.

I left the hill after eight o'clock. Or perhaps it is more accurate to say that my body did it. As if with a mind of its own, it found its way across the abandoned golf course while I watched from another place. It went between the two long rises where MacDuff's first fairway had run, across the trapshooting field, and up a rise to the road that would take me north to the A819. In this, two centers collaborated; one in the flesh, the other with little sense of boundaries on this starless night. I got into the car and wasn't in it; and drove knowing other cars approached before I saw their lights. As a child at times, and again when I'd met Shivas Irons, I had struggled against losing my boundaries. All my life there had been premonitions of this condition, which didn't move though the car moved through it, which waited at every turn of the road, which always passed beyond me.

At 9:10, I sat near a fireplace in the restaurant of the George Hotel, enjoying the afterglow of my seven-hour vigil. The winds from Loch Awe were still a fresh presence on my skin, their bite alive in my face and hands, their smell of dry grass and conifers still lingering like an aura. I savored these traces of the long afternoon; and then, with the slightest shift of attention, surrendered to the boundaryless space in which they were suspended. This shift produced unexpected gifts. During the drive from Loch Awe, it had given intuitions of oncoming cars before I could hear or see them. As I'd approached Inveraray, it had led me to the

George Hotel. By this fire it produced an extraordinary closeness with the people around me.

While someone sang and the fire danced and the barman greeted friends and acquaintances, I felt as if there were no walls or floor or ceiling.

T wo slices of dark rye bread. A cup of broth with the flavor of sage and a warmth that passed to my legs. The young waitress smiled at my enjoyment. The elderly Scottish couple lifted their glasses toward me.

My vigil had produced no specific sign of Shivas Irons, no inexplicable presences like those I'd encountered in 1987. But it was easy to imagine him sitting in this room, taking delight in everyone, in each surprise, relishing this stupendous freedom. If he'd passed to another realm, was he sitting in cafés of the soul savoring the moments of this world? Could he be enjoying this very place?

At the far end of the low-ceilinged restaurant, to the left of the crowded bar, a man sat facing in my direction. We were like bookends, or mirror images. My will to see Shivas Irons had made MacDuff's property a necromanteion. Was the same thing about to happen now? Was the man a window for revelations? He nodded toward me. I nodded back, acknowledging our mutual enjoyment. We didn't move; we didn't want to. The room's festivity and good cheer were entertainment enough. Hoping nevertheless to invite synchronicities, I ordered him a Chivas Regal, and a moment later, making no effort to approach, he lifted the whiskey toward me. Sometimes it is overwhelmingly apparent that the best signs reside in the simplest acts. Nothing more was needed.

But something more was given.

Suddenly I realized that the man had reddish hair and an uncanny resemblance to Shivas Irons. Again he lifted his whiskey toward me, this time with a manly gesture I'd witnessed at Burningbush. Ye've made a good start, he seemed to say in his richest Scots inflection. Keep comin'. As you can see, I'm not so very far away.

Then the impression shifted, to a place between me and the end of the room. "But ye've got to come here." The voice came closer. "Not where the gentleman's sittin' there. Not back at the old estate. But heer, right heer, in the new world and body we're growin'." Then I heard Shivas Irons reciting clearly from Robert Burns:

> An' now, Auld Cloots, I ken ye're thinkin,
> A certain Bardie's rantin, drinkin,
> Some luckless hour will send him linkin,
> To your black Pit;
> But, faith! he'll turn a corner jinkin,
> An' cheat you yet.

Shaken, I knocked my water glass off the table. But the man at end of the room was gone, and my waitress approached with the bill. With apologies I helped her clean the floor, gave her a credit card, and sat back to compose myself. "Is this yours?" She picked up a scorecard from the floor. "It's from the Links of Burningbush."

Disoriented, I said that it wasn't, then quickly corrected myself. "It's mine," I said, astonished. "I must've dropped it when I sat down."

Disoriented by these events, but nevertheless steadied by my afternoon's vigil, I drove on to Edinburgh. The voice triggered by the stranger and the scorecard's strange appearance hadn't disturbed the starless space from which I watched the road. As during the drive to Inveraray, I seemed to ride both inside and outside this half-conscious frame of metal and glass. Sensing the curves ahead and slippery surfaces still out of sight, I felt the winds of Loch Fyne, the cool fields of Glen Kinglas and Glen Croe, and the rustling of conifers beyond Loch Lomond as if with organs of taste and touch and the skin of a spirit-body.

But this condition didn't last.

If you've had such a ride while lifted by some exultation, you know its dangerous possibilities. On the A82 past Arden, the part of me sitting behind the wheel forgot that this was Scotland and forced an oncoming truck to pass dangerously on my left. Shaken, I parked at a turnoff. The liberated state produced by my seven-hour vigil needed a more practiced correlation with the turns and twists of the road. It was time for new resolutions now—to redistribute attention through my body, to reinhabit my hands, to let cars pass on my right. Until I reached Edinburgh, the motorway would be a sobering necromanteion. The self that extended beyond the car would ride a vigilant shotgun for its less-experienced companion.

PART THREE

. . .

WINTER,

1995

CHAPTER EIGHTEEN

IN THE THREE months since my trip to Scotland, in my
home just north of San Francisco, I had gone back to my work
on my book about experience at the edge of the strangeness curve.
But it hadn't been easy returning to familiar routines challenged
by memories of Ryzhkov's tower and Nadia's radiant presence. I
had been able to make the transition only by spending time every
day in a vigil, however brief, that resembled the one I'd made at
MacDuff's abandoned golf course. Though I wasn't called to
Nadia's way, or have her contemplative gifts, there was new excitement in my research, a sense I'd come a few steps closer to the
life represented by Shivas Irons. But my life was still subject to
distraction, and required vows to avoid activities that would lead
me away from the immediate callings of work and transformative
practice. That is why at first I rejected an overture to play golf
with one of the world's great players.

The proposal had come from Steve Cohen, founder of the
Shivas Irons Society, a nonprofit group organized to "celebrate
golf's beauty and virtues." For reasons political and arcane, I cannot name the man with whom I was to play, and will simply call

him "John Stuart." He has won important tournaments, influenced many golfers, and sometimes criticized the "inner game" as a distraction from golf's simple pleasures. According to Cohen, if I played with him during a practice round before the upcoming '95 ATT National Pro-Am, "his appreciation of the Society's causes and sport psychology would be advanced." My heart sank when I heard the proposal. This was the kind of activity I'd vowed to avoid. Stuart would beat me by twenty or thirty strokes, and my inconsistent play would probably cause any onlookers who'd read my book to wonder why I hadn't learned more from Shivas Irons. Cohen's reassurances didn't help. I remembered the last time he'd set me up to advance the Society's causes. That had happened two years before at a reception for golf writers where I was supposed to explain an event called "The Shivas Irons Games of the Links" to be held at the Links of Spanish Bay and Pebble Beach the following summer.

The reception was at The Gallery, a restaurant next to the Pebble Beach Lodge. But instead of the small informal affair I'd been led to expect, it included most of the press gathered for the '93 National Pro-Am, several business and sport celebrities, and Bob Murphy, who would act as master of ceremonies. For several decades, Murphy had been a legendary presence at sports banquets and roasts in Northern California, and was famous for his invincible wit. No one had told me he would preside at this gathering. When I saw him, I sensed trouble.

"There's Murphy!" he announced before the meeting started. "Do you know where he got the idea for his institute? In the Fimi House, when he kissed the pig's ass!" Like me, he'd gone to Stanford, and was referring to my fraternity's initiation. Before the evening was over, he was sure to make more connections like this.

Suddenly I thought of an Irish remark which I'd never fully

appreciated. "Never let two Murphys on a podium," someone in Ireland had told me. "One or both'll regret it."

Then Tommy Smothers came to greet me, bringing Bill Murray with him. I'd met Smothers and liked him enormously, but it was surprising—and a little daunting—to see him. And meeting Murray was a bigger surprise. He'd praised *Golf in the Kingdom* on television, but why had he come to this event? When I asked, he said it was because Smothers had insisted. Both well-known comedians were playing in the tournament. They were here to offer support.

The meeting was slow to start, and I had perhaps three or four beers, though the number would be debated later. The reporters were also drinking freely, most of them in high spirits and hard to corral for what was now taking shape as a press conference.

Floodlights made it hard to see anyone from the podium, but Murphy got people's attention by remarking about the limited vocabulary of athletes from Southern California. The Stanford man who'd opened the meeting had used the word "myriad," so Murphy wanted to make sure that the USC graduates who were present realized that "myriad" was not a proper name. Then he turned to Murray, a favorite of fans and reporters at Pebble Beach, and urged him to comment on the Pro-Am. A spirited repartee followed, all of it causing applause and great laughter. It was, it seemed to me, an act impossible to complement with talk about the philosophy of Shivas Irons. Smothers gave me a look of encouragement, but it conveyed a sense he thought I might not be up to the challenge.

Then Murphy announced for the second time that I'd been inspired to my life's work by kissing the pig's ass at the Phi Gamma Delta house, and asked me with apparent sincerity about "the game's mystery." There was no levity in this. He was completely straightforward, even sympathetic. It was a question I hadn't expected.

I looked into the glaring lights, behind which the press and celebrities stood, while caustic remarks rose from the shadows. But no response came to mind. "What about golf's mysticism?" Murphy insisted. Again I couldn't find an answer.

Then Smothers came striding from the lights. "You don't know how to do this," he said to Murphy, as if he were my comrade in arms. "Let me interview him."

But Murphy protested, and they struggled for control of the podium, causing explosions in the amplification system. After a brief but vehement argument, Murphy relented.

Smothers turned to face me. With genuine sympathy and affection, he asked about the Shivas Irons Games of the Links. What could I tell the press about them? But still I couldn't find an answer. Inexplicably, my attention had passed beyond the floodlights to settle on the figure of Donald Trump. He stood by the bar, taller than everyone around him, waiting with what seemed high expectation. What could I tell him about Shivas Irons? "It's a good idea." I said at last. "It's a good idea."

Smothers waited. There were laughs. "What else?" he ventured.

"It's a good idea," I said to more laughter. But I wasn't repeating the words for effect. It was the only sentence I could think of.

"He's drunk," I heard Murphy saying somewhere in the shadows.

"No, he's shy," said Smothers, guarding my reputation.

"Aw, he's drunk," said Murphy.

"No, he's shy!" said Smothers.

"It's a good idea," I said to more laughter and Smothers's dismay. Finally someone took the microphone, and explained the Games of the Links. The incident was reported in several papers. Naturally I remembered it when Cohen proposed I play golf with John Stuart. The memory of it was vivid still, and reinforced my vow to avoid distractions. But this refusal didn't last. When Cohen called again I agreed, either from weakness or a secret inspiration, to play a round at Pebble Beach to advance the Society's causes.

U p close, John Stuart projected a presence I hadn't sensed while watching him on television, a combination of fire and composure, of aggressiveness and unflappability that would give him an advantage over opponents before he hit a shot. Nothing hurried him. Even his quickest steps seemed measured. His disregard for the starter's objection to our playing as a twosome gave the impression that he owned the course. "Go ahead," he said in a resonant voice, nodding toward the tee blocks.

My anxiety, which had grown all morning, increased as I teed a ball. Stuart had apologized that he hadn't read my book, but his courtesy couldn't mask his skepticism about our round together. It was unclear why his publicity person had arranged it, he said. Though it was only eight o'clock, hundreds of people were gathering to watch.

"Stand back!" a marshal shouted. "Everyone behind the ropes!" Waiting for the fairway to clear, I silently cursed Steve Cohen. It seemed there were two insurmountable bridges: one between Stuart and me, the other between my pride and imminent humiliation. It didn't help that my drive nearly hit an onlooker who stood in rough to the right of the fairway. As I picked up my tee, I spotted Cohen. He is nearly always a jovial presence, with a short dark beard, soulful eyes, and a stomach that waxes and wanes with the seasons. He wore a red tam-o'-shanter now, plaid knickers, and a look with at least three components. There was comradely encouragement in his face, true sympathy for my plight, and a hint of the pleasure he took in arranging these perverse challenges.

Stuart said nothing as he passed me. The look I'd seen so often on television, which enlisted his pale blue eyes in what seemed a semi-trance, was a palpable, disconcerting force. When he swung, his ball left the tee with a crack and sailed high over trees at the bend of the fairway. There were gasps. Then silence. Then shouts. "It's on!" someone yelled. "He almost holed it!" The drive had carried nearly three hundred yards, dramatically shortening the four-par hole by cutting across its dogleg. Seemingly unimpressed, Stuart walked to the back of the tee. A marshal who stood there appeared to be caught between his need to keep players moving and deference to the famous player. "What are you doing?" he summoned the nerve to ask.

"The tee blocks'll be here on Sunday," said Stuart. "I'll have to hit an iron."

The marshal, a professorial looking man about sixty, winced but nodded assent, and Stuart hit a one-iron down the fairway as he would in the tournament. Striding past me he winked, and I jogged ahead of my caddie to join him. But he didn't speak. The gallery was streaming along the ropes, its members straining to see him. Deciding against conversation, I found my ball and barely hacked it from the rough.

Stuart played his ball as it lay with a pitching wedge. Then he hit a second ball. "They're holding!" he shouted in my direction as if I were a fellow professional. The second ball sat two or three feet from the pin.

My hands shook as I addressed my mud-covered ball, and I hit it into a bunker. But no one in the gallery groaned. Hopefully, most of them thought I was one of Stuart's relatives or business partners.

Walking to the green, I silently cursed myself. How had I gotten myself into this predicament? "Pick up my ball," I told my caddie, a shambling red-faced man about forty with a constant look of solicitude. "I don't want to slow things down."

"Play it," said Stuart. "It's all right with me."

But it was more than all right with him. In the way he said it, there was a demand I play. Picking up my ball violated his code of honor.

Reluctantly, I blasted out, to about thirty feet from the cup, and took three putts for a triple bogey. Meanwhile he studied the green with care, assessing putts he might have in the tournament. He walked briskly while doing this, with quiet ferocity in his eyes, yet didn't seem to hurry. After picking up the balls he'd played from the fairway, he took two putts for a birdie with the ball he'd hit from the tee.

The second hole at Pebble Beach is a straight five par that runs over gently rolling ground to a gully about a hundred yards from the green. Surveying it now from the back tees, I wondered if my drive could carry the rough between us and the fairway. The sky was overcast, and the gallery was growing as word of Stuart's whereabouts spread. There were at least a thousand people behind the ropes to our left.

As we waited for the foursome ahead to play, Stuart turned to see me. "I've heard about your book," he said with a quizzical look. "But I don't know what it's all about. Is it a novel, or sports psychology? People say different things about it."

Taken aback by the edge in his voice, I tried to explain *Golf in the Kingdom*. "It's a story," I said. "Part fiction, but based on things that actually happened. I had to reconstruct dialogue and change some names."

He pulled up the sleeves of his yellow sweater to reveal powerful forearms covered with curly blond hair. "Is it like Zen?" he asked.

My mind made an unexpected leap. Several years before, a woman had told me she'd stood near him once in Hawaii, both of them in bathing suits, feeling naked whenever he looked her way. He wasn't making a pass, she'd said, but those eyes! They couldn't help undressing whatever they looked at. "Not Zen exactly," I said with hesitation. "But something like it."

To my surprise, a look of sympathy appeared on his face. My discomfort must have been plain to see. "Tee it up," he said. "You play first—all eighteen holes."

And thus began a stretch of golf that gives rise to memories which, depending on my mental condition, are either a source of hilarity or excruciating embarrassment. Though I recall what happened in different ways depending on my mood, I invariably remember:

Myself lying four in a bunker by the second green, in view of a crowd that groans when I shank my ball, and again when I shank it farther right without reaching the putting surface. Someone shouts encouragement, but I hear a gruff voice just behind me say, "Jesus! I hope he's not in the tournament!"

And my drive from the third tee landing in the gully that traverses the fairway, to the accompaniment of more groans and shouts of encouragement. Then I spot Stuart's publicity person arguing vehemently with Cohen, who pumps his fist in my direction as if to say, Go get 'em!

And Stuart rejecting my proposal to pick up. But it takes two shots to reach the fairway, another to reach the green, and three putts to make seven on this relatively easy four-par.

And my second shot on the fourth hole sailing to an unplayable lie in bushes beyond the green, and the shot after that landing in a bunker. My caddie's constant look of concern has turned to embarrassment. He mirrors my condition now. Indeed, he makes it worse. Then I notice for the first time that he has a Scottish inflection. "Would ye like a nip?" he asks, taking a flask from a pocket. "It can't hurt yer shots, but might help the pain." A thousand people are watching, though, so I reject the offer.

And finally my long iron shot on the narrow three-par fifth hole—a thing of beauty, my first well-hit shot of the day—bouncing high off a gallery member behind the green. My caddie whispers reassurances as we watch the man go down and says he'll give the guy some whiskey.

These events were accompanied by resentment at Cohen, anger at myself, fear and embarrassment whenever I looked at the gallery, and decisions to quit on every hole. This first hour of our round was the most painful I've spent on a golf course.

"Ye want a nip now?" asked my caddie, proffering his flask as we reached the sixth tee. "It helped the gentleman ye whacked with yer ball."

Turning down the proffered drink, I found a place to stand alone. The long cliffside fairway dropped steeply below us, then rose some three hundred yards away to a handsome promontory. To our right, beyond tall trees at the cliff edge, Stillwater Cove was bathed in light. The sky was clearing, and the fairway ahead was turning to brighter shades of green.

Then, without warning, my dream of the night before returned. "There are two ways to practice," a voice had said. "As your ego or your soul." In my sleep I'd argued against the thought, as I do in waking life. How do we ever know for certain what is ego and what is soul? The distinction is a favorite tool of moral bullies. But now the words made perfect sense. Suddenly these facts were evident:

Few members of the gallery, which stretched along the fairway for five hundred yards, knew who I was or cared. If anything, my duffer's display gave them some laughs and suggested that they could be fools in public and live to talk about it.

Here was the chance of a lifetime to watch and learn from one of the sport's great champions. Seeing him up close, it was increasingly evident that though he decried talk of the inner game, he was in many ways its secret exemplar.

By a simple shift of attitude, I could let go of embarrassment, resentment, anger, and fear, and replace them with uncomplaining surrender to whatever the next three hours brought. Call this a shift from ego to soul, or simply the exercise of good sense, it would at the very least brighten my mood, and help relieve my caddie's discomfort.

Inspiration moves at its own speed, often faster than ordinary thought. No more than a minute had passed since I'd gone to the front of the tee. "You want me to hit?" I said to Stuart. "They're out of range for me."

He looked across the five-par hole, then with a small, tight smile said, "I don't know. By the law of averages, you might nail one. Beaning a gallery member is one thing, but you don't want to hit a player."

A moment before, I might've been offended, but now I detected a hint of comradeship in his hard inflection. As I looked at the clearing sky again, my mind took another leap. There was a radiance in the air that reminded me of the light around MacDuff's old house, and I remembered my 420-yard drive. The swing that produced it was present now, waiting to be found through a state of mind like the one I'd learned from Shivas Irons. This intuition was confirmed as I stood back from my fears, and as I swung, and as we watched the ball sail far and roll on down the fairway.

"It's hard out there," said Stuart. "What a bounce!" His eyes narrowed as he approached the tee blocks as if he was focusing to meet a challenge.

Astonished, I looked at my ball again. It was resting near the fairway's rise more than three hundred yards away. Had it actually gone that far? A few minutes later, I had to check by inspecting its identification number. Stuart's ball lay three yards behind me.

Both of us now had blind shots to the green more than two hundred yards away. Stuart took a long iron with which he would try to reach the pin. But after considering the same approach, I surrendered to my new resolution. To my list of relinquished emotions, I needed to add enthusiasm. I couldn't hit irons like Stuart, but maybe I could reach the green with a three-wood.

His shot barely cleared the rise, and there were cheers from the distant gallery. From the fairway above, his caddie waved. "It's twenty feet from the pin!" he yelled.

"That's enough," Stuart shouted back. "We'll play it this way Sunday."

The steep rise looked like a fortress wall, and Stuart had barely cleared it. Could I do it with a three-wood? Gathering myself, I waited for my mind to clear as it had before my drive, and suddenly the rise seemed a friendly shoulder suggesting a more subtle approach. Instead of trying to reach the green, I would let its contours help me shape a high draw with my five-iron. A moment later, I took two putts for a par and watched Stuart sink his putt for an eagle.

It was a lesson I'd learned more times than I could count. After an improvement of attitude, even one so brief, unexpected graces are given. Instead of resenting the fact that he'd beaten me by two strokes, I felt relieved and newly buoyant. This shift of mood was further enhanced when I stopped to enjoy the view. Beyond the white sands of Carmel Beach and cliffside fairways rolling south through mist and a lingering cloud, there rose the greening slopes of the Santa Lucia Mountains and blue ridges of Point Lobos. A gentle breeze was blowing, filled with salt and smells of the sea, and the waters of Carmel Bay were filling with harlequin stripes of lavender, grey, and green. I was grateful to see all this without filters of fear and recrimination.

But as I turned toward the seventh tee, Cohen emerged from the crowd. "Murphy," he said insistently. "Come here!"

"What's happening?" I asked, guarding myself instinctively against unexpected proposals.

"You should ask me?" he said. "What's happening to *you*? Have you started to talk?"

"Talk! How did you like that drive?"

The joviality in his expressive dark eyes gave way to his irrepressible irony. "What a relief!" he said. "Everybody was complaining. I told them you're his father."

"But I'm only twenty years older!"

"That's old enough." He waved me away. "Start talking to him. Think of him as your son."

The seventh hole at Pebble Beach is only one hundred yards long, but has a small tightly bunkered green below the tee and seawater to the right and beyond that swallows wayward shots. Depending on the weather, it plays in radically different ways, and can prompt different kinds of golfing magic. I remembered Sam Snead in a near-gale putting down the hard-packed path that runs from tee to green, content to play for a bogie, and in contrast my friend Andy Nusbaum holing his tee shot the year before during the second Shivas Irons Games of the Links. What contrasts and surprises awaited us now?

"Murphy?" said Stuart as we waited for the foursome ahead to clear the green. "You know those things you said about golf becoming a martial art? I've got to tell you I don't buy it."

"You mean my speech in Kyoto?" I masked my astonishment. "Where did you read it?"

"In Japan, in the English edition of some magazine there. Do you really believe that stuff?"

Did the challenge in his voice have something to do with the drive I'd just hit? "What stuff?" I asked. "I don't know how they translated my speech."*

---

* I gave the speech at the Second International Resort Conference, which was held in Kyoto in November 1991. My talk preceded one given by Robert Trent

"Didn't you say that golf is becoming some kind of Buddhist practice, or martial art?" He fixed me with his penetrating blue eyes. "Or did they get your meaning wrong?"

For an instant he seemed to wear a shield, some sort of invisible breastplate. "What else did it say?" I asked, taking time to respond.

"That we should call the game *golfdo*. Like judo. Were you joking?"

"Calling it 'golfdo' was a joke." I hesitated, searching for a way to avoid an argument. "They used to call martial arts 'jutsus,' but changed that to 'do' from 'tao' when they became ways of self-cultivation instead of killing methods.† Instead of ju-jutsu, ju *do*. Instead of aikijutsu, aiki *do*. But I was only making analogies."

"Just analogies?" His look had the same composed aggressiveness that it did when he stood to a shot. "Just analogies? You sounded serious."

Taken aback by the charge in his words, I didn't answer at once, then remembered that we were here to have this kind of conversation. "Golf isn't Zen," I said. "But with all the sport psychology now, and course management, and attention to practice rituals, and emphasis on the inner game, it's changing like the martial arts did. For a lot of people, it's becoming a more conscious exercise."

"But Murphy, it's only a game."

"Well!" I exclaimed. "There are different ways to play a game. A philosopher once said, 'There's nothing more serious than a child at play!'"

Jones, Jr. on golf-course design. Zbigniew Brzezinski and the eminent psychologist Richard Farson also addressed the conference.

† In Japanese, *do* (with a long "o"), or *michi,* means road, path, way; journey; course; duty, morality; teaching; specialty. *Jodo* (with two long "o's") means attaining the way, or Buddhahood.

He shrugged, paused, then gestured toward the tee. "Swing away!" he said. "Show us the inner game."

His challenge reverberating, and blood rushing to my stomach now, I took a pitching wedge, teed a ball, and visualized my shot. In books and articles, Stuart had described ways to do this. Bring your image to your hands, he'd written, to your kinesthetic sense of the swing. Following his advice, I mentally shaped the ball's trajectory, felt a rhythm to produce it, and swung with perverse pleasure. As my ball landed on the green, I enjoyed the irony of using the mental strategies of a great and famous player who'd helped me appreciate—and yet dismissed—possibilities of the inner game.

And my enjoyment grew as Stuart unselfconsciously demonstrated the same approach, lining up his shot with fierce but quiet concentration, drawing some invisible line in the sky, and nailing his ball to a piece of earth six inches from the cup.

But was it possible? Was he competing with me?

Trailing him down the slope to the green, I was startled by my caddie's wink. "No nips from the flask," he whispered. "He's takin' ye on." In other circumstances the thought would alarm me, but something in me relished this unexpected possibility. I sank my putt for a birdie to match his tap-in.

We didn't speak on the eighth tee, and I remembered my new resolution. Was a contest with Stuart, which was certainly high comedy, a function of ego or soul? I decided to leave it an open question and accept the challenge as a grace. Maybe the mysterious guidance which had led me to Shivas Irons and through the occult dimensions of golf would reveal itself if I played without worrying about the reasons why or eventual consequences.

"Swing away!" said Stuart.

One's drive on the eighth hole at Pebble Beach must clear a rise and sail straight. Otherwise an approach to the green is impossible. Addressing my ball, I felt a strangely detached excitement. Playing a match without handicap against John Stuart was absurd, but I would accept the challenge gladly. My drive sailed down the middle.

If you've played the Pebble Beach Golf Links, you know that its eighth fairway curves around a diminutive inlet of Carmel Bay to a green you can reach with your second shot by hitting across seawater far below. Stuart nodded for me to play first. Given his far-greater length with irons, he would use a five-iron while I used my seven-wood.

On the sixth hole, I'd felt a conservative guidance playing my second shot, but now came a bolder inspiration. The pin was two hundred yards away, in the far left corner of the multitiered green, while running from it to me, superimposed on the cliffs and grass between, there streamed an unmistakable airway in which the ball could fly. I heard the voice of Shivas Irons. "Imagination with hands," he said, his Scottish burr intact. "Paint yer shot on the golf sky so tha' no one'll e'er forget it!"

I felt the cadence of the words, addressed the ball, and hit it.

And watched it sail over the cove.

And stretched with some tenuous part of myself as it fell on the green's lowest tier, bounced once, and rolled to the hole. I was in position now to make another birdie.

Stuart didn't speak as he walked off the distance from his ball to the cliff's edge. Our developing contest wouldn't interfere with his preparations for the tournament. But my caddie had a few words to say. "He'll play a couple o' shots," he whispered, the smell of whiskey in his breath. "But this is the one for yer match. He's not sayin' it, but he's takin' ye on." He nodded toward the other caddie. "Me and Pete started bettin' on the seventh. Match play. I'm takin' ye for five a hole."

"You're betting on me?" I said with astonishment. "I'm old enough to be his father!"

He snorted. "Or his gran'father the way ye looked startin' out. That's wha' makes it interestin'." He looked at me with a sly fierce look, filled with happy anticipation, his former solicitude and embarrassment gone. "MacDonald's ma nemme." He extended his hand. "Celts all 'round. Go get 'im!"

And so began another series of holes that calls up different responses in me. But instead of winces or groans, it evokes a range of questioning thoughts. To this day, I'm not completely sure about what was secretly happening.

As my caddie predicted, Stuart played his first shot with special care, hitting it to twenty feet of the hole, then took two more from different spots from which he might have to play in the tournament. I sank my four-foot putt for a birdie, and with his first ball he took two putts for a par.

If our secret match had begun on the seventh hole, I was now one up. On the ninth tee, coincidentally or not, Stuart again questioned my proposal that golf was acquiring elements of a martial art. Though they tried not to show it, our caddies listened with enormous interest. Both seemed to take our verbal exchanges to be part of the contest on which they were betting.

"It's not happening with everyone," I said in response to his challenge, "but with enough players to command a sport historian's interest." During the past seven years, I'd counted more than twenty articles in leading golf magazines and at least twenty books that emphasized the inner game. Then I reminded him that he was the author of one such book, and at least two of the articles. He only smiled in response, as if he enjoyed my taking him on, and ushered me to the tee blocks.

A moment later, he drove his ball 100 yards closer to the green than mine, and ten minutes after that, his par beat my bogie. We didn't speak while this went on, and I had time to center myself in a remarkable calm that was descending around me. It intensified on the green and again on the tenth tee to give my swing greater arc and my drive extraordinary carry. This kinesthetic epiphany seemed related to the first of three curious synergies between me and Stuart.

Giving no visible sign that he sensed what was happening in me, he exchanged his three-wood for a driver. In the tournament, he would use the safer club to avoid the cliffs to our right; but my shot, or my state, or both, had changed his present strategy. There was a cooling of attitude, a recession of his usual fire, as he took two practice swings. But I could tell by the speed of his hip turn and the sound of his club head unzipping the grass that his adrenaline was running freely. He stood to the ball with a newly focused serenity, a winsome but deadly force, that stretched like an aura around him. I'd sensed this in Hogan once, on this very hole. When he swung, none of us could follow his shot.

"I lost it!" his caddie yelled.

"I've got it," Stuart said calmly.

And then the rest of us saw it, rolling to a point more than 350 yards from the tee. He wagged his head, with no smile, word, or other acknowledgment, and handed the driver to his caddie. Had he appropriated something of the presence I felt, or simply been charged by our competition? Ten minutes later, both of us sank short putts for birdies.

Our second telepathic confluence occurred on the thirteenth hole, the only one I dislike at Pebble Beach. As on the tenth tee, after I'd felt an inexplicable elasticity and driven for extra distance, he exchanged his three-wood for his driver. This seemed more than coincidence. On the eleventh and twelfth holes, I hadn't swung with such command and he'd stayed with his first club selection. Again he hit a towering drive that the caddies and I couldn't see until it hit the fairway. He got a birdie to beat my par and didn't change his first club selection again until the seventeenth hole. Meanwhile, returning more times than I can count to the resolution I'd summoned on the sixth tee, I went two holes ahead in our match by hitting both the fifteenth and the sixteenth greens with five-iron shots and sinking twenty-foot putts for birdies. But instead of the excitement I might've felt, an unfamiliar quiet held me.

L ooking at the seventeenth green, which was framed by bunkers and Stillwater Cove more than two hundred yards away, I remembered the last round of the 1972 U.S. Open. From the beach club, which stands near the tee, I'd watched on television as Jack Nicklaus hit a one-iron into a difficult wind, and had then looked through a window to see his ball hit the pin. There was an analogy between the two occasions. Both times I had multifocal vision—then by way of television and the beach club's large bay window, now through my complex state of mind. It was apparent to me now, for example, that golf is simultaneously a venue of absurdity and revelation, a frequent source of embarrassment and relentless teacher, and a game which to play as well as you can demands the best of your practical skills and surrender to unexpected inspirations. In the surreal arrangement of mist and clouds that arched toward Point Lobos, there were columns of light that joined the sky and water. In this dazzling array, what seemed a human figure was forming.

"Look!" I exclaimed. "In the sky above the green!"

But no one responded. Stuart asked his caddie for a three-iron and ushered me toward the tee blocks.

With difficulty I looked away from the light, took my four-wood, and addressed the ball. Then, like the bright strands you see when squinting at a flame, streamers came out of clouds. Our caddies would talk about it later. Filaments broke in showers of gold all across the golf course, and as they did I hit my ball through them. Above the streamers the sun broke through, blinding me for a moment.

"Where is it?" I yelled.

"Damn!" said my caddie, turning away. "It's bright as Hiroshima!"

But there were shouts from the gallery by the green, and Stuart announced calmly that my ball had hit the pin. When I finally saw it, it was lying just a few feet from the cup.

Without emotion, Stuart put his three-iron in his bag, studied the hole again, and took out his four-iron. It was the third time he'd changed clubs after I'd hit an inspired shot. The sun went back behind the clouds, leaving the bridge of mist and light that arched toward Point Lobos. But still something that looked like a human figure hovered in the sky ahead of us.

"Christ!" my caddie muttered. "Look at that!"

Stuart's ball left the tee on a high trajectory and was burning brightly. Were my eyes traumatized by the sun? Now it floated over the green, alive with the light of the figure beyond, and landed a few feet from the hole.

"Did you see it?" he asked.

When his caddie said it was next to the cup, he looked with astonishment at the green. "I thought I hit it short," he said, then turned and looked at me quizzically.

But much of the gallery was cheering now. "You're the man!" someone yelled. "This is your tournament!"

And there was even a cheer for me. "Way to go, Daddy!" someone shouted, reminding me where I stood on golf's ladder of merit.

But my caddie ranked me higher. "Pete's pissed," he said as we walked toward the green. "I've got 'im fer ten. Ye've got the big guy where ye want 'im!"

Stuart was two down in our secret match. Our scores went to three and five under par respectively for holes seven through seventeen, and the secret contest was done, when we sank our putts for birdies. As we left the green, the dazzling array of clouds broke up and the luminous figure vanished.

W
e stood on the eighteenth tee in silence. About 540 yards away, beyond the leftward-curving seawall, the green was shrouded in spray from Stillwater Cove. It seemed set apart, as if in some enchanted world that challenged and beckoned to us. As we waited to play, I turned away from Stuart. The vistas south of us contained the whole spectrum of light, from violets in the distant hills to blues and greens in the harlequin sea to shades of red in the rocks below. The air's fragrance—part pine, part grass, part rolling surf—evoked a quick succession of moods. My complex emotions were matched by this revelation of the senses.

It was a lesson I'd learned again and again. If a part of us opens up, the rest begins to follow. Different moods and states of mind, and an extraordinary range of sensations, were simultaneously present now. This condition seemed to reflect my search for Shivas Irons. I remembered his voice in Ryzhkov's tower. The kingdom is coming, and already here, but no word, or system, or state can hold it. Joy and wonder, puzzlement about the synchronicities of our round, sadness that all of us fall from such grace, and gratitude were present at once, each revealing some part of my past, my present and future. Each was connected, for better or worse, with lasting patterns in my life. All of them served to reveal a part of the world's richness.

I turned again to see the hole. The gallery stretched from tee to green to the right of the curving fairway, its members pressing for better views of their champion. Our secret match was over now, my caddie had collected his bet, and members of the press were questioning Stuart about his prospects for winning the tournament. In contrast, my gallery consisted of a single person—the ever hopeful and now-vindicated Cohen. Standing near the tee, he held up two fingers in a V for victory.

But a moment later, as if to reestablish the natural order, Stuart outdrove me by a hundred yards. And a few moments after that, he hit his second shot with a rise at the end so that it hovered above the pin as if deciding whether to remain in this dimension or another. When it fell to the green, a tremendous roar came down the fairway. He'd fired a double eagle. "Did you see it?" he asked with irony, wonder and, yes, revenge all present in his look.

I was too astonished to answer.

The Tap Room at the Pebble Beach Lodge has a bar at one end, and walls that are either paneled with hardwood or covered with dark green felt. Clustered at various points are pictures of participants in U. S. Open Championships, Crosby Pro-Am's, and other tournaments played on the Monterey peninsula. Stuart and I sat at a table trying to finish the exchange we'd started on the course, but people kept interrupting. After we'd ordered beers, I sat back to watch him hold court. Word of his presence had spread through the room, elevating people's excitement and making a private conversation impossible.

But this was a welcome respite. Besides the afterglow of wind and sea and astonishing golf shots, there was an elevation that came from less-definable places. To the physical graces of our round, another exhilaration was added. As Stuart signed his name on caps and golf cards, I lifted my tall glass of beer, enjoyed its amber light, and savored its sharp effervescence. There were vistas beyond this room which anyone could experience with practice, and a joy that arises from challenges met with an attitude of soul instead of ego.

"You turned it around," said Stuart when we finally had a moment alone. "After the sixth hole, you were, what?—five under par?"

My caddie had gotten it right. Without saying so, Stuart had been comparing our scores. "It's your influence," I said. "I've never played Pebble so well."

"What did you have on the first five holes?" He seemed genuinely curious.

"I was 15 over. I shot an 82."

"Well"—he feigned modesty—"on the last twelve holes, playing my first ball, I was only one shot better than you." Perhaps modesty kept him from telling me that with his first ball he'd shot a 62, but it didn't compel him to say that from the seventh hole on, he'd lost our secret match.

He paused as if searching for words, and I felt a sudden gratitude that on the first holes he hadn't let me quit. "There was something happening out there," he said at last. "The game'll do that. Get out toward the edge—you know what I mean? Like something else is going on." He smiled with a warmth I hadn't suspected, then eyed me steadily as he sipped his beer. Something unspoken was passing between us, a feeling of comradeship, a genuine liking, and a recognition of something we secretly shared.

But word had spread about his shot to the eighteenth green. Someone loudly announced the double eagle and predicted that Stuart would win the tournament. "It's been too long," another shouted. "John, it's your turn now!"

Afterword

WHEN PEOPLE ASK me now if I know how to find Shivas Irons, I warn them about useless meanderings around the Links of Burningbush, or in the hills above Loch Awe, or across Scotland's Western Isles. Those are among the most beautiful places on Earth, but not his likely refuge. All the evidence we have of his nature and whereabouts points in a different direction.

Nor would I advise you to look in Moscow. If you think he resembles Wilson Lancaster, the intelligence man I saw in Red Square, you are greatly mistaken. I met Lancaster in London last year, and after a remarkably frank conversation about his Russian activities, can tell you for sure that he isn't Shivas Irons.

And don't look at Pebble Beach. All my research indicates that if he sometimes makes a visit there he doesn't stay for long. It's better to start looking for him in the way Boris Ryzhkov suggested, by imagining him as well as you can, by practicing the awarenesses and virtues he practiced, and by opening to the leadings such practice brings. In such an effort, you can build on those "premonitions of the life to come" he celebrated. A sample of these can be found in the pages that follow. If Ryzhkov is right, by imagining the transformations of my extraordinary mentor and living as he recommended, we join one of the world's most promising thought experiments and adventures of embodied spirit.

And how might we characterize that adventure? One way to start is with something he told me as we parted in 1956. "Michael," he said, his disappointment plain to see, "ye'll forget a good part o' what happened here. I think some of it's gone already. But remember this. Ye can always recollect yerself, and start again. There's a fire in yer secret heart, and in all the world we see, that's stronger than the sun. It's been burnin' since the world began." As soon as he said them, I knew the words would haunt me. "Science is showin' us that our universe has come a mighty journey, from hydrogen and stone to livin' creatures and this human brain. Think of it, Michael, think of its prodigious course. From atoms at the world's birth to heather on these fragrant hills to Beethoven, Burns, and the love o' God." He leaned close. "But I've got a secret for ye. The *journey's only gettin' started!* Ye had glimpses o' that last night, glimpses of where it could take ye. The fire, the joy, the glory's waitin', always there to lift ye up, to be yer companion on the road, to show ye who ye really are. Remember it. Practice it. Live it with yer body, heart and soul!" He shook my shoulder. "And when ye forget . . . start again. With all its meanderin's, that's what the world does. It always starts again! The fire in yer secret heart will always find an answerin' grace, and take ye further than ye dreamed."

Forty years have passed, but the power and truth of his words still grow. He had it right. Science increasingly reveals the terrible beauty of our world's advance and human nature's capacities to drag it down or take it further. And he correctly saw I'd forget the way he showed me. But I've always been able to start again, and claim something more of the secret fire that burns in the world around us. I finished my book about metanormal experience, am exploring practices not unlike those he showed me, and enjoy vigils that bring me closer to the presence I felt in Ryzhkov's tower and again at Pebble Beach.

And all the while Shivas Irons goes ahead—of that I grow more certain—to a place beyond life and death as we know them. If he is at one remove, he is freer to enter, enjoy, and inform the Earth's remotest places. If he seems to have passed away, he dies and rises more quickly. If he is more spirit there, I suspect he is more body, too.

And Nadia Kirova follows: I know because she stays in touch like a pathfinding angel. Though I hear from her only once a month, and haven't met Shivas in the flesh, they draw me in their wake. Even without their transformative gifts, we can find ways to go in their direction. We can open our hearts as they have done, turn to our secret source, and bring from it gifts for our families and friends and people who will never meet us. With each act of this kind, we move the world a little closer to that place which, in the spirit of this book, we might call the Kingdom of Shivas Irons.

Appendices

PREMONITIONS OF THE LIFE TO COME

For Shivas Irons, the phrase "premonitions of the life to come" referred to both life after death and the more luminous embodiment he and his teacher envisioned for humans on Earth. Such premonitions come from earliest infancy until we die. In one of his journals, he had listed more than a hundred of them. Here are a few from that list, with my brief commentaries. His words are in italics.

- *clarities and clairts, on golf courses, in the mind's eye, in a divided heart, at Loch Awe.* According to *The Scots Dictionary* compiled by Alexander Warrack (1911), "clairt" is a Scots word meaning "any dirty or defiling substance" or "any large, awkward, dirty thing." Irons sometimes used it in marginalia and journal notes in conjunction with the word "clarities" in referring to extraordinary moments of perceptual, emotional, or volitional lucidity that are subsequently obscured by inhibitions or densities of our habit-ridden nature. These moments occur, often when we do not expect them, as sensory events (for example on golf courses), in the mind's eye (perhaps while reading a book), during illuminations of the heart (as when a friendship is magically restored), or at places with numinous power such as MacDuff's property on the hills of Loch Awe. Since the publication of *Golf in the Kingdom,* I have received many reports of such clarities in golf. A woman leaving her course at sunset saw the light of the setting sun "replaced by another light." A man on the tee of a four-hundred-yard hole saw a ball marker on the green. Think of such moments in your life, when some dimension of the inner or outer world opened up. Shivas Irons believed they are expressions of metanormal perceptual capacities pressing for birth in us. Once acknowledged, they can be cultivated.

• *elevations and levitations, beginning with our mother's and father's arms.* These begin in the very first moments of life as we are held in the nurturing arms of our parents, or doctor, or nurse—and even sooner as we float in our mother's womb. They are reflected in phrases such as "I was walking a foot off the ground" or "I rose above myself" or "my heart was lifted up" (sometimes just a part of us is elevated). Though typically such elevations come when we don't expect them, they can be deliberately evoked, for example by skipping across a schoolyard (children instinctively know this), or in dance, or floating on a summer day in a lake or quiet sea. In golf they can happen when our mind sails high with a monster drive, which is why most of us love big hitters.

• *self-existent joy, in good times and suffering, sometimes when we least expect it.* Shivas Irons had a remarkable eye for joys that go unnamed in English, some of which he gave Sanskrit or Gaelic names. In one of his margin notes, for example, he called a shank an opportunity for *raudrananda,* which in Sanskrit means the conversion of pain to pleasure.

"Ananda" is an important word in the Irons lexicon. As used in Indian philosophy, it generally refers to the self-existent delight revealed by contemplative practice, but it can also blossom within a familiar pleasure, or on a dreary day, or as we suffer with a friend, lifting us beyond the contingencies of our internal and external environments. During our midnight talk in 1956, Shivas Irons predicted that medical science would never pin down its mediations. "They're finding the molecules of certain pleasures," he said, "but not the ultimate joy they come from. It'll outjink 'em, because it came first and is inside and outside and way, way bigger than any arrangement o' physical elements."

• *music, voices, and rhythms of the inner ear.* In his monumental *Phantasms of the Living,* Edmund Gurney, a founder of modern psychical research, cited several cases in which a person, couple, or group heard music with no apparent cause. Similar auditions have been reported by Catholic and Orthodox saints, Sufis, shamans, and Taoist sages. Hindu contemplatives have celebrated *nad,* the supraphysical music that secretly informs us all, which can be heard by means of yogic practice. Shivas Irons told me that Bobby Jones was using his "inner ear" when he grooved his swing to the melodies and rhythms that rose spontaneously in him. Such hearing gives us a foretaste of auditory powers we will have in the life to come.

• *disappearances—in a mirror, looking into the eyes of a friend, falling into deep sleep, or alone in the gloaming after 54 holes.* With this one I identified immediately, for as a child I had sometimes been threatened by a sense that I was more than the big brown eyes and freckled face staring back from the mirror. Who am I? The question would arise with the beginnings of panic. I wasn't the thing in the glass. I wasn't my body. I wasn't my name. There was nothing left to tell me. Only when I learned about the observing self of contemplative meditation, and how it can relinquish any thought or image or sensation, did I realize that my childhood recognition was a premonition of that liberated condition in which our deepest identity resides. Perhaps something like this has happened to you, looking into the eyes of a friend or lover, or falling into a clear deep sleep, or after a long day of golf that left you empty as the sky.

Seamus MacDuff and Shivas Irons believed that these five kinds of "premonition," and many more, arise from our latent supernature. They are first signs of greater attributes pressing for birth in us, the budding limbs and organs of our life to come, and primary pointers for a comprehensive transformative discipline. By cultivating them, we can find where we secretly and most deeply want to go.

In tantric disciplines of the East, natural impulses are used as pathways to enlightenment. Hasidic mystics have taught us that the *zohar,* God's splendor, can emerge in our everyday acts. "Ye can turn an impulse into an exercise," Shivas Irons told me. "Every premonition of the life to come shows us a way to practice. It gives us a way to grow. Every part of us harbors a greater possibility."

THE LONG BODY

Ben Hogan and other great players have wondered whether something beyond their usual skills supervenes during certain rounds of golf. Having made practice an art, Hogan was acquainted with the further reaches of shot mastery, but there are times, he said, when balls end closer to the cup than seems possible for merely physical abilities. When this happens on hole after hole, the phenomenon is usually attributed to luck.

But there is reason to think that during such streaks of wondrous play something more than luck and physical skill is involved. Parapsychologist William Roll has cited Native American lore in regard to the "long body," an extrasomatic relationship among members of a group, or between two persons, or between a person and an object, that brings the parties involved into supernormal coherence. Such rapport is evident in musical ensembles, sports teams, and lovers when their creativity reaches new heights, and in golf when shot after shot ends not twenty, but three feet, one foot, or a few inches from the pin. Hogan said that "the more you practice the luckier you get," but we can develop the "long body" as well as our swing. By exercising the awarenesses and energies that reach beyond our flesh, as it were by "becoming the target," we increase our chances of playing self-transcending, odds-defying golf.

PARANORMAL PHOTOGRAPHY

Since the 1860s, many people have attributed certain images that appear inexplicably on light-sensitized surfaces to disembodied spirits or telepathic transmissions from living persons. Many examples of this phenomenon have been produced by Ted Serios, an American who for many years made images on unexposed film, apparently by mental influence alone, in the presence of skeptical witnesses; and reports of similar anomalies have been noted in English, French, German, and Japanese journals of photography and psychical research.* In the fall of 1994, I turned to the literature on the subject after Hannigan received this letter with a photograph that showed a partly transparent human figure:

Dear Mr. Hannigan,

At Archie Baird's museum at Gullane I was told of your interest in golfing anomalies, and for that reason enclose this photograph. It was taken by a friend on Gullane Hill this June, at about seven o'clock in the evening, as he, I, and another friend were

---

* See Jule Eisenbud, *The World of Ted Serios* (New York: William Morrow, 1967), and Michael Murphy, *The Future of the Body* (New York: Tarcher-Putnam, 1992), Appendix A.8. According to Eisenbud, ". . . more than two dozen persons in a half-dozen countries have claimed to do spirit photography, including *scotography* (images caught directly on nonexposed film, without the mediation of a camera), and *psychography* (film messages allegedly in the handwriting of deceased persons).

". . . Thirty-five references to spirit photography can be found in the *British Journal of Photography,* mostly in the 1870s. Numerous articles and notes [on the subject] appear in the journals and proceedings of the British and American Societies for Psychical Research."

about to play the seventh hole. He had taken the picture to capture the hill's incomparable view. There is no possibility whatsoever that it is a double exposure.

The ghostly figure is strange enough, but is made stranger by the experience our threesome shared shortly after the picture was taken. Have you read Henry James's *The Turn of the Screw?* We felt something like the uncanny presence featured in that story. It was so intense that we joked about having a foursome.

Over drinks at Greywalls later, not knowing what the photograph would reveal, we wondered if a deceased golfer had tried to join us, or whether he might be enjoying the view. As you know, it is one of golf's very finest, and on this evening was surpassingly beautiful. Curiously, none of us felt that the mysterious presence was a woman, and indeed, the thing in the photograph looks like a man. In any case, I am glad to send it along. Make of it what you will.

> In the spirit of inquiry,
> Anthony Hamilton

Hamilton's picture resembles other paranormal photographs in its half-congealed look. The figure's torso is solid through the waist, with an open-necked stiff-collared shirt, but the rest of it is transparent. Through the ghostly outline of its trousers, one can see the Firth of Forth, and through its face the hills of Fife.

OTHER DISCOVERIES OF
PARAPSYCHOLOGY RELATED TO
SHIVAS IRONS

In the early 1970s, the American parapsychologist Helmut Schmidt developed a "random-event generator" to study psychokinesis, the power to influence objects by mental influence alone. His device comes in different versions, but typically has a patterned display of moving lights triggered by random events caused by electronic noise. A subject can alter the lights, presumably by introducing order into their random triggers, simply by "willing" such change, or holding an image of it, or in some other way affecting the machine without physical manipulations. In many hundreds of experiments, all sorts of people have gotten statistically significant results with Schmidt's generator, to such an extent that some researchers of paranormal phenomena regard them to be the best experimental evidence for the power of mind over matter.

I have been a subject of Schmidt's research, have read his reports for more than twenty years, and have experienced the unmistakable rapport reported by many of his subjects with different versions of his little black box. During a party at my house, for example, in high spirits with my friend George Leonard, I felt a powerful connection with a machine that Schmidt had sent us. Inspired by a sudden affection for this inorganic yet lively friend, I watched its circling lights reverse—not once or twice or three times, but in a continuous revolution. To the astonishment and delight of those who watched, this went on and on and on, producing results significant to a level beyond calculation. If you've ever been the subject of a parapsychology experiment, you might know what I mean by "certainty." There could be no doubt that the flashing display was responding with vigor to me. If you will forgive me, the best, most exact way to say it is that for a moment we seemed madly in love.

Other results of parapsychology experiments have a bearing upon phenomena related to Shivas Irons. For example:

- Several researchers have found that subjects placed in the same locations as previous targets of spiritual healing experiments frequently exhibit more paranormal influence than subjects in other places. This phenomenon has been called the "linger effect," and has been attributed to haunted houses, sacred grounds, and "power spots" in which people encounter a special presence. If it is possible to influence machines or particular locations by mental influence alone, it is plausible that such influence can linger in a house after its owner dies, or in a monastic cell where a saint has prayed for many years, or in a cave where shamans have conducted ecstatic rituals. This surmise is supported by the lore of contemplative life and sport. There are legends in every land about places where holy persons lived that uplift visitors for decades or centuries afterward, and many writers have described the uncanny influence of certain sports arenas. Even implements have been said to exhibit the linger effect. In *Zen and the Art of Archery,* Eugen Herrigel claimed that his teacher's bow helped transfer secrets of inspired action.

  Shivas Irons gave credence to such reports. His armchair, he told me, was "meditating for him," and Seamus MacDuff's baffing spoon could "swing by itself." The principle was certainly evident at MacDuff's estate and the Links of Burningbush. Have you felt such a presence in golf—on a particular course or hole, in a treasured wedge or driver, or near a great champion?

• In virtually every culture it is held that psychic influence can be transfered telepathically from one person to another, for better or worse, through loving or hateful thoughts, prayer, or the "evil eye." Breaking with many of his colleagues in 1925, Sigmund Freud concluded that telepathy is a fact, and suggested that it operates in largely unconscious ways, often in the service of destructive impulses, and that it is mediated by the same defense mechanisms that condition sensory cues.* Several researchers have tested extra-sensory influence, sometimes with startling results. I have been particularly impressed with a group of thirteen such experiments conducted by psychologist William Braud and anthropologist Marilyn Schlitz, in which different "influencers" were presented with polygraph records of their distant subjects' electrical skin activity, which they tried to quiet or excite by mental imagery and intention alone. These experiments, conducted over a period of several years with 62 influencers and 271 subjects, yielded extraordinary evidence of telepathic influence, and have stood up to critical scrutiny.† Knowing and trusting the experimenters, and having acquainted myself with the results of related studies, I am convinced that any reasonable person must conclude, as Freud did, that we influence one another in extra-sensory ways, often at a distance. And it is then conceivable that if there is a spirit realm, we might be telepathically influenced by its members.

* See Ernest Jones, *The Life and Work of Sigmund Freud* (New York: Basic Books, 1957), Volume Three, Chapter Fourteen.
† William Braud and Marilyn Schlitz. 1989. A methodology for the objective study of transpersonal imagery. *Journal of Scientific Exploration,* 3:51.

• Again and again, contemporary parapsychology confirms the discoveries of older cultures. This is evident in studies during which people subjected to sensory deprivation enjoy special success in telepathy experiments. Both contemplative teaching and modern research indicate that our attention can turn more easily to extra-sensory impressions when freed from sensory inputs. This is a primary reason perhaps why golf courses can, if we play as the Scots once did looking at no more ground in front of us "than will cover our grave," become theaters of the uncanny and sublime.

BIBLIOGRAPHY

Coover, John Edgar. *Experiments in Psychical Research*. Stanford: Stanford University Press, 1917. With a foreword by David Starr Jordan, Chancellor Emeritus of the University. This volume contains reports of experiments conducted by the Division of Psychical Research of Stanford's Psychology Department. See especially Appendix E, "Catalogue of Literature in the Library of Leland Stanford Junior University Relating Directly or Indirectly to Psychical Research."

Corbin, Henry. *Spiritual Body and Celestial Earth*. Princeton: Princeton University Press, 1977.

Crail, Mortimer. *Golf: Its Roots in God and Nature*. Edinburgh: The Crail Press, 1893.

Darwin, Bernard. "The Links of Eiderdown." In *Mostly Golf,* an anthology of Darwin pieces edited by Peter Ryde. London: A & C Black Ltd., 1976.

Dodson, James. *Final Rounds*. New York: Bantam Books, 1996.

Eisenbud, Jule. "Psychic Photography and Thoughtography." In *Parapsychology and the Unconscious*. Berkeley: North Atlantic Books, 1983.

Hogan, Ben, with Herbert Warren Wind. *Five Lessons. The Modern Fundamentals of Golf.* New York: Golf Digest Classics, 1985.

Jones, Robert T. *Down the Fairway.* Norwalk, Connecticut: Series of Golf Classics, 1984.

Leonard, George. *Mastery.* New York: Dutton, 1991.

Leonard, George and Michael Murphy. *The Life We Are Given.* New York: Tarcher-Putnam, 1995.

Moody, Raymond. Reunions. New York: Ballantine Books, 1993.

Murphy, Michael. *The Future of the Body.* New York: Tarcher-Putnam, 1992.

Saltmarsh, H. F. *Evidence of Personal Survival from Cross Correspondences.* New York: Arno Press, 1975.

Updike, John. "Farrell's Caddie." In *Golf Dreams.* New York: Knopf, 1996.

Von Schrenck Notzing, Albert. *Phenomena of Materialization.* New York: Arno Press, 1975.

Wilber, Ken. *A Brief History of Everything.* Boston: Shambhala, 1996.

ACKNOWLEDGMENTS

My special thanks to George Leonard for constant guidance; to William Shinker for extraordinary support and making this project enormous fun; to Fred Hill for long-standing encouragement and for introducing me to Shinker; to Sylvia Timbers, Richard Baker-roshi, Steve Cohen, Andy Nusbaum, Michael Miller, Dulce Murphy, and Anya Kucharev for important suggestions; to Barbara Kasten for countless labors; and to Charles Conrad for these wonderful finishing touches.

THE SHIVAS IRONS SOCIETY

T he SHIVAS IRONS SOCIETY is a non-profit corpora-
tion organized to further the pleasure of golf and
explore its many mysteries. It is a network, open to all, of
individuals who share a common love for the game and an
admiration for those inseparable qualities of mind, body,
and spirit exemplified by the character for which it is
named.

A mong the purposes of the SOCIETY are the fostering
of education through golf and the furthering of the
personal and social transformations the game can bring. We
celebrate golf as a game of great beauty and virtue and we
honor its history and Scottish roots.

B y bringing together the many admirers of Shivas and
promoting the values and principles he represents, the
SOCIETY will create synergy leading to as yet unknown
pleasures to be gained from this indecently alluring game.

For membership or other information:

The Shivas Irons Society
Post Office Box 222339
Carmel, CA 93922-2339

Internet: *http://www.golfweb.com/shivaslives*

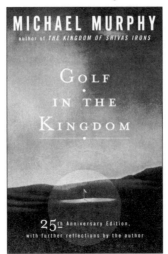